W9-AVR-385

Petty Business

Judaic Traditions in Literature, Music, and Art

Harold Bloom *and* Ken Frieden, *Series Editors*

FEB   2021

PETTY BUSINESS

Yirmi Pinkus

Translated from the Hebrew by
Evan Fallenberg & **Yardenne Greenspan**

Syracuse University Press

The author gratefully acknowledges the support of this translation by the Israel Institute.

Copyright © 2017 by Yirmi Pinkus

Syracuse University Press
Syracuse, New York 13244-5290

All Rights Reserved

First Edition 2017
17 18 19 20 21 22   6 5 4 3 2 1

Originally published in Hebrew as *Bi'zer Anpin* (Tel Aviv: Am Oved Publishing, 2012).

∞ The paper used in this publication meets the minimum requirements of the American National Standard for Information Sciences—Permanence of Paper for Printed Library Materials, ANSI Z39.48-1992.

For a listing of books published and distributed by Syracuse University Press, visit www.SyracuseUniversityPress.syr.edu.

ISBN: 978-0-8156-3551-2 (hardcover)   978-0-8156-1091-5 (paperback)
978-0-8156-5417-9 (e-book)

Library of Congress Cataloging-in-Publication Data
Names: Pinkus, Yirmi, 1966– author. | Fallenberg, Evan, translator. | Greenspan, Yardenne, translator.
Title: Petty business / Yirmi Pinkus ; translated from the Hebrew by Evan Fallenberg and Yardenne Greenspan.
Other titles: Bi'zer anpin. English
Description: First edition. | Syracuse, NY : Syracuse University Press, [2017] | Series: Judaic traditions in literature, music, and art
Identifiers: LCCN 2017038936 (print) | LCCN 2017040529 (ebook) | ISBN 9780815654179 (e-book) | ISBN 9780815635512 (hardcover : alk. paper) | ISBN 9780815610915 (pbk. : alk. paper)
Subjects: LCSH: Pinkus, Yirmi, 1966—Translations into English.
Classification: LCC PJ5055.37.I55 (ebook) | LCC PJ5055.37.I55 B5213 2017 (print) | DDC 892.43/7—dc23
LC record available at https://lccn.loc.gov/2017038936

Manufactured in the United States of America

For Rutu

The eyes of the world are upon the municipal elections.
—Prime Minister Yitzhak Shamir, February 1989

Contents

Reality—a tailor's dummy;
The author sews the suit.
He'll find a way to custom make it,
His needlework astute.

He adds some fringe in one place,
Some sequins in another;
And even though he lies a lot,
It's all the truth, no other.

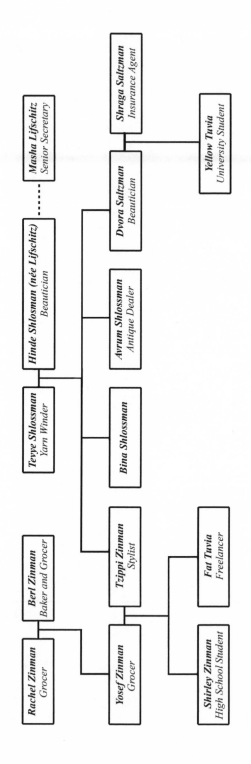

PART ONE

Two Businesses

1

Two Sisters

A.

"Seven in the morning. You're probably thinking: what's so special about seven in the morning? And that's where you'd be wrong, Mrs. Gitlis, because *their* seven in the morning is not *our* seven in the morning. Over there it's still half dark, and sometimes rainy. Who'd be crazy enough to want to get out of bed? But me, I'd get up real quiet so as not to wake Tzippi. I'd put on a sweater and go out on the balcony. What can I tell you, Mrs. Gitlis, it takes your breath away! Now you and I have known each other for more than a little while, haven't we Mrs. Gitlis, and you know I'm not a person that gets worked up over nothing. So if I say it takes your breath away—I mean, AWAAAAAY!—here's you, and there in front of you, the whole of Austria. Just like that. The forests, the mountains, the snow. Not another soul around, maybe a cow or two. But otherwise—*gornisht*! Nothing! And the smell of green, and the flowers. What flowers! And those little houses, and you can hear bells from far away . . . two hundred grams?"

"Make it three hundred, but sliced thin."

"People say, Yosef Zinman is a millionaire, Yosef Zinman can afford it. Let's say that thank God I'm wanting for nothing. So that means I'm supposed to go to London? Sit in the Hilton, against my will? I'm very sorry but I'm not interested in hobnobbing with the who's who. Here comes Dvora, you can ask her."

"It's true. In our family there are no snobs," said Dvora Saltzman.

3

"Give me an easy chair in a little inn and I'm in heaven. Anyone who understands what Seefeld is knows what I'm talking about. There's this one inn we've been going to for years now. Exactly ten minutes from the center of town. Cozy place. Eight rooms, tops. The owners, they took a shine to us. Nice people, both him and her. You should see the smiles they give us. Not once did we get to our room and there wasn't some chocolates waiting for us, on the house. They really know how to treat people. And you know the funniest thing of all? We've never paid more than forty or fifty dollars a night! . . . You want a little more?"

"No, that's enough. It's already too much for me. What about these? Are they fresh from this week?"

"Came in two days ago. Look how pink. You want?"

"Let me see . . . you know what? Go ahead, give me four halves. But wash your hands first."

"Where were we? Seven in the morning. So anyway, a person's got to eat, right? And what do they give you for breakfast, you ask? Well, I'll tell you. The lady of the house sure knows how to work up a person's appetite. Take the hard-boiled eggs, for example. Now who isn't familiar with hard-boiled eggs? So just to make them look nice she puts them in a kind of wicker basket shaped like a chicken. And never once are those eggs cold, there is always a little warmth left in them from the boiling. And the yolk—you've never seen a color like that. Bright orange. Not like our eggs."

"You don't say . . ."

"I only hope, Mrs. Gitlis, that one day you'll have the chance to eat such an egg. And the cheeses, and the rolls . . . I happen to be crazy about homemade jams. So every morning I find two jars of jam next to my plate. Sometimes it's raspberry, sometimes it's apricot. Depends on the season. And everything is served with *also bitte, also bitte*. She hands you a cup of coffee: *also bitte*. Pours some milk for you: *also bitte*. I wouldn't be surprised if she says *also bitte* when she farts."

He paused to allow the two women to chuckle.

"We finish eating and take a walk down the pedestrian mall. The shops sell all kinds of tchotchkes, you know, like animal figurines made of crystal. For your information, that's an Austrian specialty. Not interested? Across the street there's a bakery that makes your eyes pop out of your head. How can I describe it? It's impossible! The strudels, the tortes, the little plum tarts with *krishkelakh* sprinkled on top." He sighed and nostalgically patted his bloated paunch with its protruding navel. "What can I do? I'm only human. But don't think that Seefeld is just sitting around and stuffing your face all day long. There is what to do, and how! Take us, for example: we love a nice excursion. So we get in the car and drive. Ever heard of the Zugspitze?"

Mrs. Gitlis was forced to admit, shamefacedly, that word of such a place had never reached her ears, which prompted Yosef Zinman to tell her about this mighty mountain and about the wide balcony at its summit where tourists in sunglasses and parkas sit drinking beer and sunning themselves in the snow. "Now ask me what there is to do in the evening."

"*Nu?* What?"

"Oh ho! You should know that I'm a person who likes to raise a little hell. In Seefeld, you go out every evening, without exception. After all, why go there if not to have some fun? There's this one place we really like, a sort of restaurant-nightclub all in one. There's a floor show during dinner, usually sixties music. Before dessert is served we're already up on the dance floor, pulling everyone along after us: young people, old people, Italians, French. You don't get the riffraff there, only the right kind: the lawyers, the doctors, the professors. It's often the same people over again, year after year. Two years ago we went with Danny and Dolly Shem-Tov, from the dry cleaners; we happen to be friends with them. One evening I ordered screwdrivers for the whole table, on me. On trips, I like to be generous. Danny Shem-Tov drank a little too fast and decided some Dutch guy was hitting on his wife. 'Danny,' I told him, 'don't get such ideas in your head. This is Seefeld! I dance with this chick and she dances with that guy and it's no big deal. Take it as a compliment that your wife attracts attention.' But he got all puffed up and turned as red as a monkey's ass and stood up all at once from the table right in the middle of them dancing the paso doble."

"And what happened?" asked Mrs. Gitlis, taken aback.

"Nothing. Up close he could see that the Dutch guy was three sizes bigger than him. Dolly Shem-Tov was so embarrassed she looked like she wanted to dive under a table. Will that be all, Mrs. Gitlis?"

"I don't know. What else do I usually take?"

"You got enough low-cal yogurt at home? Prunes? The gummy candy you like . . . ?"

"Do me a favor, Yosske," his sister-in-law Dvora butted in, "I've got to get home. Just give me two poppy-seed challahs, not the burnt ones. Add a carton of skim milk to my account, too. I'll call in later with the rest of my order."

"You don't scare me."

"Tell me, are the kids coming with you tomorrow?"

"Tuvia for sure will, he wouldn't miss your *cholent*, especially in this weather. But Shirley? I couldn't say," Yosef Zinman said with a sigh as he wiped his hands on his trousers. "Depends on her mood."

"I've got to run, we'll talk later. Shabbat Shalom, Mrs. Gitlis. Sorry for butting in."

"Toss in a kilo of Osem flour, what the heck," Mrs. Gitlis said, coming out of her reverie.

Thus, with a bag dangling from one hand and a bag dangling from the other, Dvora Saltzman crossed Judah the Maccabee Street and went up the stairs to her apartment. It was already eight-thirty in the morning and once again it was starting to rain. She entered the kitchen out of breath, tossed her bundles onto the countertop, and turned to her husband, Shraga Saltzman, who was sitting in a tracksuit drinking a cup of coffee without even a single, insignificant thought floating through his head. "Shraga," she said—these are the exact words she uttered—"I'm sick of it. Just once I want to go to this Seefeld everyone's always visiting."

B.

Family by family was the world created, each with its own core, its own essence—a motif, a desire, a talent—around which all the family members circle, each in his own way, never tiring of discussing it over and over again. We have heard, for example, of literary families: the grandfather was a bookseller, one granddaughter edits a journal and flits about wildly with poets while another, whose name precedes her in translation circles, gets starry-eyed each time she thinks of the name Fyodor Mikhailovich Dostoyevsky. We know, too, of musical families: at every family gathering someone will pull out an accordion and a *darbuka* drum; the head of the family will burst into song, the grandmother will astonish everyone with a cadenza that is especially hers and all the others will join in for the chorus. And let us not forget the historical families that never grow weary of recounting the glory of past generations, or, on the contrary, families that adhere to the principle of suspicion, whereby at Friday night dinners they will recount a litany of intrigues plotted against them and will try to reveal the schemes hiding behind the smiles of neighbors, clerks, local politicians, and even one another, incessantly suspecting that their children are freeloaders, their siblings, deceitful, and even they themselves cannot be trusted.

The Zinmans, and their relatives the Saltzmans, preferred to focus on their intestines and the functions therein. They took an interest in knowing what was excreted from people's bodies and under what set of circumstances, and whether suffering was involved or perhaps pleasure. They always listened cheerfully to one another, encouraging the speaker to report on everything taking place within his bowels. Their advice was plentiful: your movements are sluggish—try this, do that; your movements are too swift, irritable—take this or that. Their bag of tricks was stuffed full of incidents—a hair-raising treasure trove!—that had befallen them in the past. Upon leaving the lavatory they would issue comparatives and superlatives, and if some special episode had occurred they did not hesitate to pick up the phone to the others. No texture was foreign to them: a volcanic stomach was thought to be a sign of virility in a man and an expression of joie de vivre in a woman. Flatulence was so pleasant to them that they created and bestowed upon it its own special language, each term representative of a different embodiment of the phenomenon, from minor releases, the traces of which evaporate in a flash, to Napoleonic displays that make a formidable impression on others. And if their luck held out and someone among them passed wind in a manner heard by all, their laughter could bring them to tears. Thus, the reader can imagine that slow-cooking stews were the apotheosis of their family life.

In the early days of 1989, a frost took hold of the country. Storms lashed out for an entire week without mercy. Pine trees fell, streams overflowed; in Safed, water froze in the pipes; in Jerusalem, boilers were lit day and night; and in Tel Aviv the traffic lights broke down again and again, wreaking havoc on traffic. For a whole week, residents of Tel Aviv walked about in soaking wet socks and helplessly chased after the skeletons of umbrellas snatched from their hands by the winds. Finally, on Saturday afternoon, the storm abated. The water that had flooded the streets receded at last into the drainage system. The sidewalks glistened. A fine scent of wet earth arose from all the gardens and yards. The streets were nearly completely tranquil, except for here and there a barking dog or a passing car whose wet tires raised a thin whisper. Windows were hidden behind shuttered blinds. Apartment stairwells steamed up with the smell of cooking foods, and anyone who cocked an ear would hear the joyous sound of cutlery clinking in the apartments. At a little before two o'clock on Judah the Maccabee Street in north Tel Aviv, the entire family gathered at the home of Dvora Saltzman for *cholent*.

"Who even wanted to get out from under the covers?" grumbled Aunt Masha Lifschitz, a tiny, dignified crone shrouded in a cloying scent as she wiped the soles of her shoes on the straw welcome mat. "As far as I'm concerned you could have saved yourselves all the trouble of this luncheon."

"Greetings!" bellowed the shopkeeper Yosef Zinman as he walked in, his potbelly leading the way. "What a smell, Dvoraleh. Great job— you can smell the *cholent* all the way down to Café Alexander. We are going to have a gooooood time!"

"Maybe *you're* going to have a good time," said the old woman, turning her head to him, "but I feel sorry for your poor wife. What a concert she's going to get afterwards."

"Shraga, hang Ciotka Masha's coat up for her," the hostess instructed her husband as she kissed Aunt Masha's soft, powdered cheeks, two virgin plots of land in a field of wrinkles. "And where's Tzippi? Didn't she come with you?"

In place of an answer came the family whistle announcing that the stylist Tzippi Zinman was on her way up the stairs. Her magnificent head appeared first, then her shoulders and her body ensconced in a red coat with frizzy lining. She was carrying an enormous jar containing homemade pickles.

"Shabbat Shalom to one and all!" she proclaimed. "I'm starving, I haven't put a bit of food in my mouth all day."

"Where are the kids?" her sister asked, gazing toward the stairwell.

"Tuvia is parking the car," Tzippi Zinman said. "And Shirley—who knows? Yesterday she went to sleep at a friend's house and we haven't heard from her since."

Although the two sisters do not, strictly speaking, look alike, you would not doubt for a moment that they are blood relations. Both are quite tall—identically so, in fact—and have the same ample family breasts and rounded figures. The similarity between them, however, does not stem from any of these but, rather, from an accrual of details: gestures, expressions, intonation, and other small but decisive factors inside which is folded an entire lifetime. The four decades they have spent living side by side have distilled themselves into a pronounced family look that is unmistakable: the pursing of lips that accompanies the end of questions; scratching the tip of the nose in moments of embarrassment; the preference for wide tunics that fall nearly to the knee; and the huge plastic-frame glasses that both wore. Dvora had always been considered the more beautiful of the two, and even now, at forty-eight, she still turned heads. She wore her hair short and cut like Princess Diana's, with soft highlights that blended well with her delicate skin and green eyes and hesitant, captivating smile. And yet her sister overshadowed her; the wife of the prosperous shopkeeper had a weakness for plunging necklines and swirling skirts and leather bags adorned with huge metal bangles. Her honey-colored hair burst forth like a lion's mane, although on closer inspection one would find her scalp to be slightly denuded thanks to her habit of incessantly curling, straightening, dyeing, and washing her hair. Her gestures oozed theatricality, and whenever she waved her arms—which happened regularly—all her bracelets would jangle. On Judah the Maccabee Street she was considered a bohemian.

"What's new with your people, Shraga?" Tzippi asked, her blue eyes shining and her smile full of teeth as she handed her coat to her brother-in-law.

"Your sister is sucking the will to live right out of me, but other than that, everything's fine," he joked. Shraga Saltzman was lean and haggard, not tall, and his thinning hair was an unnatural shade of red. "What do you say about all this rain?"

"Shraga, move. You're blocking the way in. Yosske, Ciotka Masha, do me a favor and go sit at the table."

"Need help with the pot?"

"No, I can manage with Tzippi. Sit, sit."

They all moved to the dining room and sat in their regular seats. The two brothers-in-law sat at the head and foot of the table, while the seats closest to the kitchen were reserved for the two sisters. Just as they were about to serve the *cholent,* their older brother, one Avrum Shlossman, a retired antiques dealer—now twenty minutes late, as usual, knocked at the door, carrying—also as usual, a gift for the hostess: a Rosenthal china sugar bowl.

■ ■ ■

The Saltzmans' apartment was divided by a long wall that separated the public rooms from the three bedrooms. While the living room was narrow, the furniture was capacious. The couch and armchairs, bought on a greedy spree in one of the more expensive stores in Tel Aviv, were now worn and seedy, and the nickel plating on the legs of the table was peeling here and there. In one corner stood a television set; in another, a hazelnut china cabinet. Even though the time had already come to "freshen up the living room" as Tzippi Zinman had pointed out on numerous occasions, Dvora had managed to enhance the charm of the room with the help of all sorts of trifles: a lace curtain, potted plants, vases, a large Dutch plate hanging on the wall, and other such touches. It was stuffed, crowded, overflowing; everywhere there were signs of a desperate effort to grow and spread beyond what was physically possible. Once, the living room had been smaller and opened onto a balcony, but that had been annexed some fifteen years earlier. The enormous dining table, glowing with furniture polish, was nearly always in a dim corner at the opposite end of the room. At mealtimes, and especially on such a gloomy Saturday, it was necessary to turn on the lights.

"What a day I had yesterday," Yosef Zinman began as he poured salt energetically over the mountain of food on his plate. "What can I tell you? The place was like a loony bin. Peretz must have made fifteen deliveries, the poor schlump. Three to the Bavli area, one to Hamedinah Square, and then all the usuals. Rebecca, the American, placed her regular monthly order. What a pain in the *tuches*, I'm telling you. How many times have I told her, 'Rebecca, not on Friday!' I mean, we both know it's not urgent for her, so what does she care if I send Peretz around on Wednesday, when it's peaceful, no pressure. She likes to be annoying on purpose. And she's on the third floor, no elevator, and those people drink a lot, *kein eyna hora*. All those bottles of soda alone take him four trips up and down. How did it go by you?"

"Not bad," muttered Shraga Saltzman.

"You don't have to tell Yosef any *meises*," Dvora scolded him as she stirred the cabbage salad. "We barely had a soul in the place all day."

"Gitlis didn't come in? She said she'd stop by after the vegetables."

"Yeah, yeah, she came by. Big deal. She did us a big favor and bought local-made hairspray. That's not the way a perfumery makes any money."

"I've never liked her," said Avrum Shlossman as he blew on his fork. "She's a miser. Even back in Mother's time she'd drive you crazy over every shekel."

"A completely insufferable woman," proclaimed Shopkeeper Zinman. "May her ass clog up."

"I saw her last week at Dr. Etziony's," announced Tzippi Zinman. "You should all know that she is not a healthy woman. Have you noticed how jaundiced she looks lately?"

"You'd better remember to bring me with you to her funeral," Aunt Masha warned her nieces and nephews, arching her penciled eyebrows (which in her opinion brought out her eyes, but which in fact gave her a permanent look of doubt). She drew her mouth toward a hollow marrow bone drenched in fat and noisily sucked out all the bits of barley that had taken refuge inside. Her large, intelligent eyes, with their puffy eyelids above and pale, drooping bags of skin below, glared at the people seated around her. As she chewed, her broad lips moved as if of their own accord. The tip of her impressive nose quivered with concentration. If you add to all these the tuft of short, dyed brown hair you find yourself with a portrait of an aged hatchling. The matron Lifschitz had one shortcoming she was unable to overcome, even though it embarrassed her: her astonishing gluttony coupled with the lazy desire of a spinster or old bachelor to dine at the tables of others. Although she was certain she kept this hidden, it did not go unnoticed by her relatives, but because they treated her dignity with care, as is proper with the lone, grand remnant of her generation who would one day leave behind a handsome inheritance, she was invited to all family functions.

"There goes another client down the drain," lamented Dvora. "A person could go crazy from it. The old ladies expire, the young ones don't even come in, and if they do, they buy the knock-offs made in some Arab village that sell for five shekels. There's almost no one left who understands handmade products. Carmela Nakash, now there's a serious client, the poor thing; what she pays a month for that awful skin of hers . . . if it weren't for her and four or five others like her we'd have had to close up shop ages ago."

"Where's Bina?" asked Fat Tuvia, raising his eyes from his plate of cholent and wiping his meaty lips. "Why isn't she sitting with us?"

"She isn't feeling well again. Something she ate."

"She could at least say hi. I'll go call her."

"Let her be, the poor thing. It took her so long to fall asleep . . ." Dvora Saltzman said.

"Shraga, you old gonif! Making off with the entire plate of kishke, huh?" This was Yosef Zinman ribbing his brother-in-law. "Pass some over here!"

"What for, Yosef?" Aunt Masha said, her lower lip protruding. "Believe me, you sure don't need it."

"Let every man look at his own plate," said the object of her concern. "Dvora, I'll tell you what your problem is. You people don't keep your business up-to-date. Worse than that: you haven't updated anything for years. Years! When's the last time you remodeled? When your mother was still alive."

"And just where are we supposed to get the money for that? Excuse me for saying so, Yosef, but it's easy to give advice when the cash register in your place never stops ringing. You and Tzippi can replace a refrigerator any time you want. What do you think? That I don't want to remodel? That I wouldn't like to finally have a proper window display, a new counter . . . I'm embarrassed to tell you what condition the floor's in."

"You kill me, Dvoraleh," Tzippi said. "It's not like in Mother's day. You don't have to do everything in real wood these days, just the veneer. And how much would that cost?"

"I don't even have the money for wood veneer. The little I manage to scrape together I'd rather set aside for my Tuvia in America, so he'll study and make out a little better than his mother and father."

All the while her husband, Shraga Saltzman, sat at the head of the table with his red-dyed thinning hair, hunched over the stew on his plate and eating contentedly, as though it were not he being discussed, as though his in-laws had not, long ago, pinned such high hopes on his insurance business. Even he himself could not for the life of him recall the last policy he had sold, and although he had never officially closed his agency he spent most of his time doing nothing at all behind the counter of the perfumery that his wife had inherited from her parents.

"You know what, Dvora?" said Tzippi. "I have a fashion show this Tuesday evening and no one to help me. Why don't you come? You can help with the folding and dressing the models and I'll pay you 120 shekels. Why not? Yoss, leave the pot alone already. Come on, enough! You're going to gas me up all night!"

"Now you remind me?" Yosef Zinman said with glee, his face contorted. "Let me enjoy life a little!"

"Is there dessert?" asked Tuvia as he extended his plate to receive a little more of the beans. The shopkeeper's son was his spitting image. Although he was not yet twenty-three years old he sported a potbelly not much smaller than that of his progenitor.

"Look at yourself," said Aunt Masha. "Such a handsome boy, and so fat."

"I don't know," Dvora said with hesitation. "You'll probably need me from the afternoon . . . how can I leave Shraga alone in the store?"

"You yourself said the place is empty," Tzippi retorted. "So what does it matter?"

"And what if some client *does* come in? There needs to be a woman there."

"You two are disgusting!" shouted Aunt Masha. "You just keep shoveling it in and shoveling it in, especially you, Yosef, with that ulcer of yours . . . what kind of example are you for the boy? Shame on you!"

In a tizzy, the old woman stood up and pushed her chair back with a flourish, bent down to pick up the pocketbook sitting on the floor next to her, and marched off to the bathroom. Even before she had reached the wall that divided the apartment in two, a grin rose on Yosef Zinman's face and he bit his lip, stretched his chin, and glanced at Tuvia, who was making a futile effort to stifle a snicker. The snicker became a chortle and the chortle, a guffaw, and when at last it seemed they had managed to control themselves a loud snort of joy burst from the shopkeeper's nose, causing his son to howl with laughter.

"What is with you guys?" asked Tzippi Zinman as she looked at her son and then her husband.

"And *she* tells *us*," Fat Tuvia chirped in a shaky falsetto, smacking his forehead, "*she* tells *us*, we're disgusting!"

"Your aunt!" Yosef cackled, spraying saliva. "Your Aunt Masha!"

"What about her?" said Tzippi with a confused smile.

"She sent regards with a song!" said her brother.

"She lit the burners!" explained her son.

"She's a real trumpeter!" said Yosef Zinman, laughing hysterically, his enormous belly jiggling. "Toot, toot!"

"Nice work!" screeched Shraga from the opposite end of the table, beating his sunken chest.

"Pffffffff!" Yosef Zinman fired a round through his lips, his face aglow.

"Pffffffff!" Fat Tuvia fired in return, his eyes tearing. He said, "A tuba player!"

It turned out that when Aunt Masha had bent down to retrieve her pocketbook, there occurred one of those involuntary incidents, those mishaps that increase quite naturally with age. Whether Aunt Masha hadn't noticed what happened or purposely chose to ignore it, we'll never know, but it was her misfortune that the moment of her bending down was accompanied by a very short but unmistakable blast that caught the attentive ears of the Zinman men. By the time she returned to the table the father and son had composed an entire prelude based on that musical phrase of hers and sang it in harmony to the delight of all the others as they now choked with laughter, their heads rolling and their arms flailing and their lungs gasping for air.

"What are you so happy about?" The old lady pouted as she took her seat.

"Avrum told a joke," Tzippi said, coming to their rescue. "Just something stupid, really."

"Since when did he become such a comedian?" Masha Lifschitz wondered.

"Everything's fine, Auntie," said Shraga from the other end of the table, laughing and burping and quivering with pleasure. "Do you like the *cholent* today? Nice work, nice work!"

"Oy, it's gotten really hot in here," said Fat Tuvia, spluttering with laughter.

Dvora Saltzman, taking pity on her aunt, rose from her place at the table, gathered the plates and the cutlery with excessive clanging and banging, and asked who was interested in plum compote and who was not. In the kitchen with her sister—one ladling the compote into small bowls, the other placing them on a tray—Dvora Saltzman told

Tzippi Zinman that she would indeed be available to help her out at the fashion show on Tuesday. For 120 shekels, she thought, why not?

C.

Tel Aviv is a cinch-waisted lady. The northern suburbs are her blowzy hairdo—the south, her weighty thighs—and in the middle she is pressed upon and narrowed by adjacent cities. Were it not for the Aya-lon stream that guards her eastern flank, her neighborhoods would long ago have sliced her in two and blazed their own trails to the sea. In the area of the Arlozorov Street train station she is so thin that it seems she can be encircled by the length of an arm. Whether by mistaken planning or by some stroke of genius as yet unrevealed, the city's nobility established near that train station a triangular park imprisoned between three major traffic arteries. Thanks to its special shape, the park does not boast a single quiet spot where one might escape from the din of the city; from every angle one can glimpse speeding cars and one can hear the choking coughs of passing buses. Every few years some efforts are made at its rehabilitation—statues are erected, oleander is planted, colorful rubbish bins are brought in, and in the end a decorative lump of concrete inscribed with the names of big donors from Chicago or Johannesburg is ceremoniously planted— but in spite of all the effort the park remains naked in its wretchedness and returns to serving its lone purpose—that of providing a shortcut for pedestrians wishing to reach the train station. The grass is always filthy, the battered trees grow at odd angles, the benches are ruined then replaced, only to be ruined and replaced again. The western side of the park, which faces the city itself, is known as Haifa Road, whereas the side that faces the suburban wasteland did not even merit that, and it is hard to believe that any Tel Aviv resident could actually name the street along which it runs. All sorts of urban leftovers, desired by no one, have gathered there: a gas station, a tin-roofed building used as a garage, a wedding hall whose day has passed, a workshop with metal poles poking through its exposed walls, a meager office building hous-ing electronics importers and notaries who cannot afford an office closer to the courthouse. It was to this building, and, more specifically to the Last Chance nightclub on the ground floor—that our acquaintances, the sisters Tzippi Zinman and Dvora Saltzman—were headed on Tuesday. It was early evening but the parking lot in front of the building was still empty.

"Come, give me a hand."

Tzippi Zinman opened the trunk, which was lined with a wool blanket. With great care she extracted several plastic-wrapped evening gowns she had borrowed from the manufacturer on Kalisher Street that morning and piled them into the waiting arms of Dvora.

"Don't crush the sequins, the dresses are all on consignment."

"I can't help wondering who buys these things," Dvora said.

"No one. They're not even for sale. I just bring them for the show. Oh, here's Paloma Bianca's car, they're always the first to arrive. But where's Estee Creations? I hate the ones who show up at the last minute. Never mind, let's go up. Can you carry any more?"

"Yes."

The atmosphere the sisters were met with at the entrance to the nightclub was feverish. In just one hour the first guests would be arriving and everyone was busy: bartenders were sticking toothpicks into sugared cherries; waiters were spreading tablecloths; the duty manager—dissatisfied with the lighting—was scolding the technician; Ronny Amrussi, the singer with a thousand styles, was tapping the microphone; the kitchen help were running back and forth; the cooks were greasing the pans; the cleaner was polishing, once again, the bathroom sink. Dvora traipsed after her sister to the far side of the club where, in a cordoned area, wide stands had already been set up. To one side she saw a squat little man of about fifty with a high forehead and wild curls, none other than Mr. Nachliel Zarfaty, the main personality behind the Paloma Bianca fashion house. He was busy refolding colorful sweaters and shawls in order to make them look as attractive as possible. Sitting on a white plastic chair tucked into a niche was a very tall, dark-skinned young woman of about twenty wearing heavy pancake makeup and jiggling her crossed feet incessantly. When she saw Tzippi Zinman she rose from her chair and greeted her with a kiss on each cheek.

"Gali, meet Dvora, my sister. Dvora, this is Gali."

"Nice to meet you."

"You're the first one here, I see."

"Dana just called and asked me to tell you that there's a traffic jam just outside Netanya."

"What is this—updates from the traffic helicopter?" Tzippi fumed as she looked at her watch. "What do I care about traffic jams? If she's not here on time then I'm through with her, end of story. She'd better learn not to take advantage of my good heart. I'd like to see her pull that on Anita Shagrir, ha! She wouldn't last with her for a minute!" She patted Gali's cheek affectionately, expressed her regret that not all models were as responsible and organized as she, and predicted a great future for her. Tzippi opened a side door and the three women entered a hidden storeroom that served as an improvised changing room. In the middle stood a tall, metal clothing rack upon which Dvora hung the evening gowns and peeled back the protective wrapping. In the meantime, another model arrived; after some screeching and hugging the two models went off to the side to chat in private. More vendors appeared as well: a jeweler with a nose so short she looked like a Pekinese dog; an elderly Russian couple peddling knock-off plastic fashion watches; a manufacturer of velvet dinner jackets; a woman vendor who sold knitwear. Not all of them had shops, and in fact for most, such events were their main source of income. Although they greeted one another with smiles and small talk, they eyed each other's tables with suspicion in case they had somehow been cheated of their rights. They appraised the location of their tables vis-à-vis the others' and checked to make sure their colleagues were displaying only those goods they had received permission to sell and were not, heaven forfend, expanding to their own market share. Each vendor displayed their wares according to his or her own principles and business instincts: while one tossed items into a cheerful mess in order to create an impression of low-cost sales, another preferred to set out few samples so as to appear exclusive, and a third organized his stock in a businesslike manner.

It was nearly eight o'clock. The lights in the main hall were dimmed and soft music was playing in the background. The first guests, who had paid eighty-five shekels a couple for dinner, entertainment, and the fashion show, began occupying seats at the tables. The men ordered vodka for themselves and piña coladas for their wives. A few women approached the stands, perfunctorily fingered some of the merchandise, and returned to their seats.

"What a letdown," Nachliel Zarfaty complained to the eager ears of the Pekinese jeweler. "Had any nibbles yet?"

The Pekinese grimaced. "About a dollar's worth," she said.

"Listen to me, and listen good," said Zarfaty, a conspiratorial look on his face. "I'm no newcomer to this business and you can rely on my instincts. I'm telling you, this is going to be a fucked-up evening. These aren't the buying types. Zinman'll have to bring down the price she's charging us. One thing's for sure: there's no way *I'm* going to pay a hundred bucks."

"Calm down, honey buns," said the Pekinese as she patted her chest with an open hand. "We've got Estee for that. We're not paying a cent if there's no sales."

"Believe me, I'd pay double without batting an eye if Anita Shagrir would have me. I used to ring up *very fine sales* indeed with her Hadassah events."

"Don't even talk to me about that puffed-up frog."

"Who's a frog?" asked old Papa Frumkin as he paced back and forth, his hands clasped behind his back. He worked his jaw incessantly, genially appraising the merchandise all the while.

"Papuchka, Papuchka!" cried his wife. "Not to talk now, now is time for clients, please." She was a rustic old woman with thick ankles and a cataract muddying one eye. At her watch stand, several bored men had gathered, an overpowering scent of cologne rising from them. One of them—a man who most definitely did not appear to be the adventuresome type—was asking about a diving watch and was requesting technical information. While Papa Frumkin detailed at length all the virtues of the watch in question, the man sent worried glances in the direction of the adjacent stand, where his wife was already signing with a flourish a check made out to Paloma Bianca.

To the dismay of the vendors, things continued to move sluggishly for quite a while. Dvora's ear picked up more and more of their grumbling, and as this troubled her she decided to inform her sister. Tzippi, who sat smoking in a corner, grinned dismissively; but although she was accustomed to the vendors' chatter, their disputatiousness, she nonetheless foreshortened the lifespan of her cigarette and returned to them simply in order to show her face. In the meantime, the bustle increased, and by nine o'clock the club was full to capacity. The waitstaff ran back and forth from the kitchen window to the hall carrying platters filled with bonito with orange slices, blintzes stuffed with chicken liver, and many other delicacies, most of which were topped with a sprig or two of parsley. In those days, the chefs of our city sought to lend a touch of the French to their cooking, but since most of them had never set foot outside Israel, nor had they ever tasted a properly seasoned stock, for example, for them "a touch of the French" meant a sort of whimsical mixture of ingredients swimming in a whitish stew. And while the crowd ate voraciously, Ronny Amrussi crooned: Italian romances during the hors d'oeuvres, local favorites during the main course, army ballads as the waitstaff cleared the tables. His accompanist, a phlegmatic type with thick glasses, sat indifferently at his electric piano as he squeezed an entire orchestra from it. The merry revelers, who by now were stuffed with food and brimming with drink, joined the musicians with gusto until everyone was singing and clapping; a few people even stood to dance a bit. In order to ratchet up the merrymaking, the bartenders were sent around to distribute maracas. Four or five potbellied guests drew near the singer, gyrating to the music and shouting "Olé!" and "Bravo!" and "Groovy!" while stuffing twenty-shekel notes into the pockets of Amrussi's suit jacket with great fanfare. He repaid them with two encores. The duty manager glanced at his watch. It was time for the fashion show.

D.

"Ladies and gentlemen, ladies and gentlemen, please take your seats for the next part of our fannnntastic evening!" intoned Amrussi in a near whisper. On his crude face—the wide nose, the oversize chin, the brows crowded together in a single, wide furrow—was plastered the unflagging, seductive smile that gave him the look of a panderer. Further, he had taken to narrowing his eyelids, which he believed made him enthralling, like someone who had already seen it all and was now observing the world with resigned indulgence even though—truth be told—he was not yet thirty-five years old.

The lights were dimmed further, then, at a sign from Tzippi Zinman, the spotlights were lit at once to illuminate a long carpet that ran through the sea of tables. The amplifiers came alive with the hits of a famous Swedish singing group.

"Ladies and gentlemen," whispered Amrussi, "let's hear it for our team of terrrrrific models with all the hottest styles of spring 1989. First up is Dana Avital in a track suit from Paloma Bianca with earth-tone appliqué work, a lovely ensemble that's just as good for a casual evening out as it is for home wear . . ."

The celebrated model—Tzippi Zinman liked to broadcast the bigger names right from the opening—entered with flair, her mouth in a forced pout and her back stretched to its limits in an attempt at endowing Nachliel Zarfaty's *shmattes* with some semblance of elegance. She marched to the end of the carpet, froze in place for a moment, then flung her head backward as if surprised at hearing someone calling her name. On her way back, she passed the next model, the newly minted Gali Habousha, whose sparkling black eyes and hair pulled into a tight bun caused people to say she reminded them of *the* Tami Ben Ami! To the sound of applause she presented in a pink cotton waistcoat with large appliquéd lilies, a white shirt and loose-fitting fisherman pants, also in pink and held up with an elastic waistband. Amrussi, pleasantly surprised by the flow of praise spewing from his own mouth, got carried away and ended with a recommendation for wearing this ensemble at bar mitzvah celebrations, weddings, and receptions at the president's residence. All the while, Nachliel Zarfaty stood behind his merchandise, tormented as usual. He shot endless worried glances in every direction trying to gauge the mood of the women in the crowd. To his consternation, he was not granted admission to the dressing room and could not observe the models up close; now he was cursing himself for failing to instruct them to wear his knitwear. After all, not every woman wished to try on a pantsuit after downing half a chicken with fried potatoes, but no woman would be adverse—even at such moments—to wrapping an interesting scarf around her neck.

Had the hapless clothier glimpsed the behind-the-scenes madness going on at that very moment he might have expressed his gratitude that he had been prevented from entering the dressing room. Who knows if his nerves could have withstood the sight of pantyhose, shoes, shirts, bolero jackets, gauzy skirts—in short, everything the models wore and then cast off—tossed to the floor and trampled on. Dvora's hands were kept busy as she bent down to pick up and fold and roll and stretch and button and zip and clip and unclip and reverse inside to out and vice versa and rehang and take care not to unravel a seam. In other words, she had been charged with carrying out all those dozens of tiny actions that could be summed up as "woman changing clothes." In the meantime, her sister was occupied on a different front as she adorned the girls with beads and chains and earrings, and sent them out at the right intervals of time, and took care to keep the collections separate, and made sure that no curious onlookers found their way into the dressing room. The models entered and left, entered and left, at a dizzying pace. The vortex grew wilder and wilder. The crowd's excitement grew, too, culminating at the sight of the models marching in a line wearing evening gowns adorned with shiny metallic scales. What happened next was that in the entire nightclub not a single purse remained shut; before Ronny Amrussi had finishing rolling a string of thanks and acknowledgments off his tongue the guests had stormed the stands, pushing and shoving and purchasing everything in sight. Zarfaty's plastic portable credit card swiper could not keep up with the pace and fell apart. Two hefty women from Petah Tikva nearly slapped one another over a pale blue knit tunic, the last in their size. The men—weren't they human beings as well?—gathered around the Frumkins' table; in the ensuing tumult one even managed to slip a watch with hands the shape of lightning bolts into his pocket.

While everyone ran amok, Dvora, who had finished restoring the evening gowns to their plastic wrapping and had received no further instructions, sat taking in the scene from the side. Her eyes widened at the sight of the wad of bills that Zarfaty stuffed into his bursting pockets, noting that in the perfumery she did not see such proceeds in an entire week. She watched as the old woman with the rheumy eye hid her wad in her sock. The Pekinese jewelry saleswoman, the knitwear designer, the man who sold sheets—each had their own way of squirreling away the earnings (and it would be superfluous to add that no one bothered with receipts; no one, that is, but amiable Papa Frumkin, who made out a single receipt for seven and a half shekels simply to ward off the evil eye). Suddenly, she caught sight of a man the looks of whom she did not like. He was about sixty, with a pock-marked face and small eyes that peered out from under heavy brows. He made his way around, glancing at this and that; at one point he took interest in a man's gold ring, but more than the merchandise he was interested in the bills that were passing from one side of the tables to the other. All at once he turned toward her, sneered, and started making his way directly toward her. Dvora Saltzman was startled; her suspicious mind was already imagining a tax sting. But her fears were proven wrong quite quickly: it turned out that the man, who introduced himself only as Albert, had thought she was Tzippi Zinman's personal secretary. He did not wish, at that time, to bother the organizer of the event, but since he wanted to discuss a business matter with her he would be happy if she would pass along his business card. The card itself contained no information beyond his name and two telephone numbers and Dvora, who figured he was another one of these ready-made clothing manufacturers, promised to give the card to her sister at the earliest opportunity. The man, who thanked her with a smile that revealed rotten teeth, bowed his head and disappeared with the same suddenness with which he had appeared.

In the meantime, the storm had slowly abated. The indifferent keyboardist was playing a tango medley, the shoppers were returning to their seats, and while they ate their desserts they displayed for one another the goods they had purchased. Estee Creations, who had promised the Frumkins a ride home, was already returning her jewelry to its boxes. The duty manager came up to Tzippi Zinman to thank her and to give her her fee—$150 under the table, as agreed upon in advance. After paying the models their due, she lit a Kent and approached the vendors to collect what they owed her.

"Well, Zarfaty?" she said, turning to the sweating manager of Paloma Bianca fashions. "Aren't you sick and tired of counting all that cash? And after driving us all nuts with your constant complaining. One thing's for sure: you never would have made such a killing with Anita Shagrir."

One after another the vendors left, all but Nachliel Zarfaty, who decided to take full advantage of the exceptional attention his *shmattes* had garnered, and he stayed on a while longer. The time came to leave. Tzippi Zinman, who was suddenly ravenous, suggested to her sister that they go get a bite to eat on Yirmiyahu Street; Dvora, who was unaccustomed to such nighttime adventures, jumped at the opportunity and announced that she was certainly not opposed. Secretly, she hoped her sister would offer to pay.

E.

On the south bank of Judah the Maccabee Street, exactly opposite the Zinman's grocery store, stands an obsolete business that has not changed its appearance since the day it was founded in the fifties. The portrait of a woman with long eyelashes and a bouffant hairdo is etched in black on its window, behind which stand two shelves covered in flowered paper that hold an assortment of dusty objects: imported soaps wrapped in crêpe paper, linen handkerchiefs in a faded box, a set of nail files in a case made of artificial leather, a variety of tubes. And if all these are not enough to signal to passersby the purpose of this establishment, the words *Hinde's Perfumery* are stenciled halfway up the window in enormous letters.

Sunlight penetrates this elongated niche only sparingly, crammed to the brim as it is with jars, bottles, and other unidentifiable objects. A scratched wooden counter runs its entire length, and beneath the plate of glass that canopies it lie drawers lined with red velvet and filled with the ritual tools: hair curlers, mascara, plastic rings, crystal bottles. The lights are lit even during the day; the chandelier casts a musty yellow light of bygone days.

The whiff of a scent—whether of incense or medication, it is hard to tell—always wafts from the depths of the shop. Here, behind a screen of ivory beads rattling dully, is hidden the atelier. This is where various creams and oils are concocted according to recipes kept secret for two generations. And since the founding priestess of this godforsaken altar, Hinde Shlossman, brought several of the heroes of our story into the world, it is only fitting that we should tell a little of her story.

Several months before the outbreak of the Second World War, Hinde Shlossman took her husband, Tevye, and their tiny son, Avrum, and escaped from Lodz. With the help of a foreign passport retained by the family since the days of the Empire, they managed to get to Constanța on the Black Sea; from there they wandered from place to place until they reached Tel Aviv, where they settled in to one of the wretched streets in the southern part of the city. In the early years, no job was too lowly for them. They worked hand to mouth and thanked God for their good fortune. Hinde, in the meantime, raised her family—two girls, Dvora and Tzippi, were born two years apart—and in her spare time concocted all kinds of cosmetics that she sold to her neighbors. Tevye wound yarn at a spinning mill, delivered ice, and, after the establishment of the State of Israel, found his way into a modest position with the postal service thanks to a friend's connections.

Fifteen years of hard work and tight fists yielded savings that enabled the couple to move to the north side of the city and open the perfumery. Success was not long in coming; Hinde, who was fast approaching middle age, discovered that while ageing was hard on the soul it was good for business. Her pale skin, the powdered sugar of the Polish language sprinkled heavily on her words, the fingers that had thickened, and the enormous turquoise ring she wore all rendered the advice she gave her disciples the status of ancient wisdom. Her name preceded her and was passed by word of mouth among the women of Old North Tel Aviv. There were even those who compared her to the great Helena Rubinstein at the start of her career, when she was still creating cosmetics with her own two hands. To Hinde's credit it must be stated that this praise never went to her head, not even for a moment. She never pretended she could reverse time, never gave her clients false hope. And yet, her cosmetics were known to have an ameliorating effect. Most of her fame rested upon a neck-moisturizing cream; the proceeds from this preparation alone had enabled the couple, in their very first year, to purchase a brand new cherry-wood dining room set. The lights in the perfumery were sometimes lit until ten o'clock at night. Tevye left his job with the postal service and invested his energies in running the till and keeping the books. The girls grew up nicely and on occasion lent a hand in the business. Hinde and Tevye had high hopes for Avrum, too, their firstborn, but just when it seemed that at last their efforts were bearing fruit and they entertained cautious optimism about retiring one day soon, the disaster that turned their world upside down and spoiled all their beautiful plans befell them.

This calamity was not the sudden, cruel sort of disaster that comes out of nowhere with a clap of thunder and mercilessly casts ships onto treacherous rocks. No one embezzled money and ran off with it one sunny day; no one collapsed in the street. Neither by fire nor by plague did this occur; this is not a case of betrayal or a miscarriage of justice. On the contrary, during the early months, with none of the usual external signs, it was nearly impossible to discern. As time passed, however, it became clear that something was wrong. Concern sprouted slowly, then took root. For several years, in the beginning, the neighbors spoke only in whispers about it, then later, openly. The Shlossmans' affliction became a sort of adjective that was used each time their name was mentioned. There were even those who felt the blame lay with them, for it was common knowledge that at their age one had to take precaution. With time, additional woes amassed, and although the couple found more than the occasional moment of joy, any elation was accompanied by a shadow, a pall, that never disappeared, not for a second. And if they did not suffer enough during their days, the thought of what would happen after their deaths plagued their nights. In less than nine years Tevye died of a broken heart. The whole of Judah the Maccabee Street took part in the funeral procession.

After the headstone was in place, the family gathered around the dining table for a family council meeting. Although the widow Hinde was sound and stable, misgivings were voiced with regard to the double mission on her shoulders: from now she would be responsible not only for mixing her preparations and providing daily care for the problem but also for managing the accounts. The family council went on and on and its members riffled through papers, jotted columns of numbers, reminisced, argued a little, cried, made up, and in the end, found a solution.

Was it true that Dvora had willingly chosen to "bury herself alive" as Mrs. Gitlis would later claim? Perhaps it was her brother Avrum who first floated the idea when he felt they were expecting something of him that was not his intention to offer, and he therefore turned the spotlight onto her? And what was the role of her brother-in-law, Yosef Zinman the grocer, who did not wish to see his Tzippi living out her days behind the counter with her terrible mother? And what influence did her husband, Shraga the indolent insurance salesman, have upon recognizing an opportunity for an income that would not require any effort on his part? We shall never know who first raised the idea, but in any event, the idea was raised, and once it was, to the entire family it seemed there was no more practical and fitting solution than this. Thus it was that Dvora, at twenty-three, went into partnership in the perfumery with her mother, and since this was a rent-controlled business and it would be a pity to lose the rights, the agreement extended to the very last day of the veteran cosmetician's life, which occurred sometime during the fall of 1974. The inheritress changed almost nothing in the perfumery; whether out of respect or superstition or because it seemed a shame to spend the money on making a new sign, the perfumery continued to be called by the name of its founder even as it passed into the hands of the Saltzmans. And not only that, but the late Hinde's apartment, situated above the shop, also became Dvora's, and the other inheritors hastened to sell her their portions at an exceedingly fair price, for reasons which will soon be made clear.

And so it was that the two sisters, Dvora Saltzman and Tzippi Zinman, settled on opposite banks of Judah the Maccabee Street: business facing business, life facing life.

F.

At the very last moment, just as she was about to slam the car door shut, Dvora remembered the business card that the man with the rotten teeth had slipped into her hand. It was drizzling, and as she searched through her pockets she got suitably wet. "Never mind," said Tzippi Zinman, who had driven her sister home and was now quite ready to get into bed. "What's the rush? You can always leave it at the grocery for me tomorrow." But when the missing card turned up, the show manager lost her cool and rebuked her sister for failing to hand it over earlier—sure, it might have been a bit busy at the nightclub and it is natural to forget things, but in the end they had sat for more than an hour together at a diner on Yirmiyahu Street, so she had had plenty of opportunity to remember. But how was she to know that this was so crucial, Dvora rebutted, growing angry. And who was this Albert Ben Arroya anyway? Now there was clearly some feigned innocence in Dvora's response, for at that moment she recalled where she had heard that name (and who in Tel Aviv at that time had *not* heard the name Albert Ben Arroya?). Naturally, her sister was not willing to have the wool pulled over her eyes, and from that point onward matters deteriorated rapidly: Tzippi said something to Dvora, Dvora said something to Tzippi, and by the time they had finished accusing and offending one another, the pleasant feeling that had passed between them all evening at the Last Chance nightclub had completely evaporated. They parted—not for the first time—after each secretly promised herself not to speak to the other, at least until the start of summer.

Five days after these things transpired, a blue Ibiza parked on Professor Schorr Street in North Tel Aviv and from it emerged Tzippi Zinman, coiffed and perfumed. After looking this way and that she turned into a pathway that led her to the back of one of the buildings. In spite of the precise directions she walked right past the object of her search and only when she reached a dead end turned around and found the stairs leading down into the basement. The door was opened by a wide-bottomed secretary with the face of a rat wearing an expression of utter loathing. With a quick gesture that seemed more like a dismissal than an invitation, she instructed Tzippi to take a seat. The guest was surprised at the derelict appearance of the office: tiny windows with glass crisscrossed by iron strips, a do-it-yourself bookshelf, ratty armchairs, a philodendron crying out for a little light—this was not the way she had imagined the office of the famous producer and entertainer. Shoved into the corner was a stack of boxed toasters, a picnic table, four shrink-wrapped folding chairs, and a host of other prizes of the type desired by the winners of game shows. Colorful brochures lay spread out on a coffee table and Tzippi picked one up as she lit a cigarette.

A buzzer sounded. "You can go in!" the secretary barked without bothering to look up.

"Hello, hello," said Albert Ben Arroya as he rose to shake Tzippi's hand. His face wore a cordial smile meant to freeze the blood of more fragile creatures than Tzippi. "What an honor! Please, would you like a cup of coffee?"

"I wouldn't refuse," said Tzippi Zinman. "Turkish, with two Sweet'N Lows."

"Tzilla!" the host roared, summoning his secretary without altering the smile on his face. "Turkish coffee with two Sweet'N Lows for our guest. The usual for me."

A faint murmur came from the outer office in response, though it was unclear whether this was a growl or a clearing of Tzilla's throat.

"She's a bitch," Ben Arroya explained cheerfully.

Tzilla appeared quickly with a tray containing two large ceramic mugs and a plate of cheap jelly-filled boxed cookies. As she turned to leave, her boss was overcome by an enormous yawn. He stretched his arms with great purpose and accidentally passed his hand over her buttocks.

"So," he asked as he took a noisy sip from his boiling hot coffee, "how's it going?"

"Fabulous."

"Obviously. You should know that I wasn't at the Last Chance on Tuesday by . . . chance."

"I figured."

"I was very impressed. Very impressed. The show was tops, no two ways about it. I've been in the business for a long time and I know how to spot talent. How come I never heard of you? Where've you been hiding?"

"Nowhere," Tzippi Zinman said. Hiding out was not a concept in her personal experience. "Up till a year and a half ago I worked as Anita Shagrir's assistant."

Ben Arroya's face darkened. "Listen, *meydeleh*," he said in his burnt-out voice, "if you want us to be friends, don't mention that name in my presence. I've had it up to here with that woman." He signaled an invisible line above his head. In spite of this he told her how he had worked with Anita Shagrir back in the day and had plucked her from the wretched fashion shows she had organized for Hadassah charity functions, how he had taken her under his wing and let her organize the most prestigious shows of them all, at the Plaza Hotel, the Diplomat, the Hammam—everywhere! And how he had shared all the connections he had made over many years without giving it a second thought; it was hard for him to believe he could have been so guileless. And how, in exchange for all that, she had stolen—yes, that was the word, and he had no problem repeating it, and she was welcome to sue him for libel if she wanted—right from under his nose the country club, and the Atmosphere nightclub, and how she had taken over several hotels in Tiberias and had brought in a third-class entertainer whose name was better left unmentioned in his presence, and how that she-devil, that crook, had caused him this damage and that, even to his spirit, his soul, why deny it? After all, he, too, was just a human being. He was willing to tell Tzippi Zinman about all those things but he did not want to wear himself out.

"Now listen, my friend Tzippi, I'm going to tell you something very top secret," he said, leaning forward far enough so that his guest could feel his breath, "but if this leaks—you're through. Finished."

Ben Arroya's entire façade was scabrous and seared, as if he had been raked with an iron comb: the scarred red skin of his face attested as much to the pimples he had had as a youth as to the many hours he had devoted since then to fairs and exhibitions. The wattle under his chin was reminiscent of that of a turkey's. His resplendent mane of hair was still black, but his thick eyebrows were threaded with silver. The nostrils of his pug nose—a disaster on any man—sprouted a curly thicket. His voice was smoky, his jeans worn, his leather safari vest was coming apart at the seams. In a certain sense he made one think of the dregs from the bottom of a burnt pan. And yes, despite all these merits, the veteran producer looked far younger than his fifty-nine years; in the presence of such ugliness, the ravages of time are relatively unnoticeable.

"You know how to count?" he asked.

Tzippi Zinman sat up straight.

"I want to get that straight from the start," he said, "because soon you're going to be counting wads of shekel notes. Sweetheart, the cash register's gonna be ringing away like you've never dreamed it could. Listen to me, and listen good: I'm gonna offer you something big. Huge. Not just another rinky-dink nightclub or some convalescent home in Netanya. My dear lady, Albert Ben Arroya is going to bring you up to the premier league. It isn't going to be easy, so don't say I didn't warn you. You're not gonna have time to breathe. Forget about your family, forget about your friends. You'll get home so worn out that you won't even have the strength to heat up a plate of leftovers. Naturally, you'll have to bring things up to snuff, make some changes—I want you to blast the crowd with collections, I want big names, I want top-tier models. Sexy, sexy, sexy. Tzippi Zinman—Anita Shagrir is gonna be history when you and I are through with her."

"What exactly are you talking about?"

"*Bubbeleh*, when you get to know me a little better—and I hope that'll happen—you'll understand I don't mess around. Minor events don't interest me. I'm talking about the chance of a lifetime, your lifetime . . . I'm talking show business, I'm talking . . . *Kibbutz Shefayim*."

Shefayim. The moment that Ben Arroya planted that bomb, Tzippi Zinman's body reacted in the usual family manner; in other words, our friend Tzippi suddenly felt, in the depths of her body, a tiny, restless bubble making its way along in search of an exit route. Accordingly, she was afraid to utter a single word and sat holding herself in tightly, all the while concentrating on a single spot until the danger passed.

"You're in shock, eh?" asked Ben Arroya as he relaxed into his chair.

Tzippi nodded tepidly, which came as a slight surprise to Ben Arroya.

"I'm currently negotiating with the administration of the water-park at Shefayim," he explained, "and until I have a signed document I can't promise a thing. I'm going to present you as my new show manager, and I'll need a few names from you. Who're you working with these days?"

"Dana Avital, Gali Habousha—she's a young talent I discovered on my own."

"No, no, no, my dear lady," Ben Arroya said, his flushed wattle swinging back and forth. "You're not on the right track at all. At this stage, no 'young talents' or any such nonsense. I want you to prepare a list for me in, say, two or three days, that includes at least two beauty pageant winners. Junior Miss is okay, too. Someone of the caliber of Natalie Peper, for example . . ."

"No problem, she's crazy about me!" Tzippi chimed in, then tightened her stomach; the bubble was threatening to burst into the open air.

"I also need a list of the fashion houses you work with, and a few ideas for special events. Don't give me bingo or Brazilian drummers, I've already got those. We're talking about summer vacation, two full months, July 1st to August 31st. Four fun days a week on the average. I'm working on an exclusivity contract with them. Without boasting, there isn't another producer in Israel with as many connections as Albert Ben Arroya. I've got the military industry employees' committee, the policemen's union, the X-ray technicians, the Dan Bus Company drivers—all the most important workers' committees are in my pocket. It's no problem for me to fill the park with four to five thousand people a day, and I want to give them a good time. You get it?"

In the meantime, her internal storm had abated and Tzippi was finally able to lean back in her chair and fix him with a scrutinizing gaze. "I get it," she said, "of course I do. But you haven't said anything about what sort of terms you're offering me."

Ben Arroya, who, until that moment, was aflame, grew suddenly sullen. "I can't offer you more than $150 a day," he said.

"For that kind of money you won't get first-rate models, period, exclamation mark," Tzippi said, slightly miffed at his offer. "I'll level with you: models like those take $120 each at the very least, and sometimes you have to pay their taxi fare, too."

"There's nothing I can do, you'll have to work it out."

"Well I can't provide beauty queens for that kind of money. Maybe Anita Shagrir has some sort of method . . ."

The value of a well-timed quip is priceless; in the case before us, it was worth $90/day. At the sound of his nemesis' name, Ben Arroya consented to paying $240 for every fashion show and allowed Tzippi to rent out ten stalls (!) to vendors on her own accord. They agreed that in the beginning at least two first-rate models would be part of the team but that after a few days—here, Ben Arroya winked—the kibbutz administration would trust them and would stop checking up, so that only one first-rate model would be necessary. Since both parties were satisfied, their meeting was concluded with a handshake, and the respected producer rose to escort his new partner to the door.

Finally, after two very chilly weeks, the clouds dispersed and a wonderful sun appeared. Swallows jumped about merrily on sidewalks. Three children on their way home from school tied their jackets around their waists and were busy licking candy bars. From the kiosk at the corner of Ibn Gvirol Street came a few energetic notes that signaled the start of some radio program. And if you had happened by at that golden moment you might have noticed Tzippi Zinman standing at the nearby payphone and calling her sister, Dvora, to inform her, before everyone else, of the news.

2

The Concert

A.

Berl Zinman the baker, an old-school Jew, lived in the Florentine section of Tel Aviv with his wife and his only son, Yosef. One day a rumor reached his ears about a street that was being paved in the northern part of the city, right along the Yarkon River. He begged money from a rich relative, borrowed a little from here and a little from there, and bought, with key money, a shop that was neither large nor small. He affixed shelves to the walls, as many as they would hold, and in the gloomy backroom he installed a large refrigeration unit with three heavy metal doors; then he made agreements with wholesalers and filled the shelves with all the best merchandise that money could buy. He placed his beloved Rachel at the cash register and hung a sign on which was drawn a large bar of margarine and, in even larger print: B. ZINMAN, CONSUMER GOODS AND BEVERAGES. And that was how Judah the Maccabee Street came to have its very own grocery.

It is well known, however, that death does not bother to knock politely at one's door. In 1958, before he had even completed his fifty-second year, the wick of Berl Zinman's life was prematurely snuffed out by a bus that deviated from its lane. His son, Yosef—a young bachelor with his life ahead of him—suddenly fatherless, thus jettisoned his plans to study at university and instead threw his full support into helping his mother. Under their joint management the shop flourished and became a magnet for the entire neighborhood. This was the place where you could buy on credit, where you could ask for a certain item to be set aside for you, where you could return items that had spoiled. This was the place where they knew what you purchased each time and what you would never purchase. This was where you could buy eggs and oil even during times of scarcity and rising prices. This was where children were sometimes given lollipops free of charge, and where the regular clientele were even invited to sample olives taken from cans only just opened. From the very beginning of the enterprise it became customary on Thursday evenings for Rachel Zinman, the mother-shopkeeper, to pour the water remaining in the cheese barrel into a large jar and to collect the broken eggs from the egg cartons. From these she would make a golden, succulent, dense cheesecake that was neither too sweet nor overbaked. On Friday mornings she would cut small squares of it and serve them to whoever visited her shop: the Tnuva cooperative milkmen, the early rising elderly, the housewives with long shopping lists, the bachelors who bought little and never checked their bills, the Smuts Street synagogue beadle who bought Kiddush wine—there was miraculously enough for each and every person to receive a slice.

The years passed. Yosef Zinman, in his time considered one of the more handsome young bachelors of the neighborhood, took—as is already known to the reader—as his wife Tzippi Shlossman, daughter of the perfumery owners across the street. Rachel Zinman was quite anxious about the match—after all, the entire neighborhood knew about the Shlossmans' family problem, and it was often expressed that this might be hereditary. In the end, the couple had healthy offspring.

Still, Rachel the shopkeeper never drew pleasure from her daughter-in-law, whom she considered to be an ostentatious spendthrift. She watched in shock as Tzippi sat from morning to evening in cafés with the glittering wives of importers and lawyers while she, after a lifetime of saving every penny, allowed herself nothing—not even a proper wool coat! In her later years she, like Tzippi's mother, Hinde, was consoled by her grandchildren: Tuvia, a plump and good-hearted boy with wheeler-dealer tendencies who looked just like his father, and Shirley, his sister, a pale girl with a serious face.

From the day that Rachel departed from this world the family grocery prospered even more; as long as she stood behind the counter slicing pastrami her son dared not suggest innovations. But when he became boss he sold the small apartment she left him and used the proceeds to renovate the shop. At the time, shades of yellow and orange were all the rage, so Yosef Zinman made a sign in yellow and orange stripes emblazoned with a large salami and the inscription SELF-SERVICE, Y. ZINMAN & SONS. The old refrigeration cabinet was replaced with a modern doorless unit and on the orange aluminum shelves was displayed an impressive assortment of products, just like in a supermarket: yogurts and puddings with illustrated labels for children to collect; pickles sold by weight; cubes of feta cheese; slivers of herring. The low-fat, low-profit cheeses in ugly packaging were shoved into an obscure corner, hiding as well the prized Philadelphia cream cheese that was prohibited at the time as a way of protecting the local dairy market. In the front of the shop the ambitious shopkeeper installed a metal counter they called the "hot spot," where you could find fried patties, vegetable pancakes, pierogis, and other such ready-to-eat delicacies popular among the clerks who worked in the area. For a while there was even a large rotisserie in the front window with six impaled chickens spinning and tempting passersby. But several local shopkeepers, envious of Yosef Zinman's success, bribed an old lady into complaining to the municipality over headaches she allegedly had from the scent rising from the grill. One morning a letter arrived from the Sanitation Department, grounding his chicken business once and for all.

There were long-term ramifications to this conspiracy; the prohibition against roasting chickens proved a huge disappointment to Yosef Zinman and from that moment on he no longer wished to make so much effort, as he liked to announce regularly to his acquaintances, since all he had really meant to do was offer good service to his clients. And what came of it? Snitches emerged to trip him up. Truth be told, he was more worried about his business being shut down than the humiliation involved. An ongoing threat always hovered over him: without a proper kitchen he did not have a permit for selling prepared foods and now that they had their eye on him he wished to let sleeping dogs—in the form of inspectors—lie. Quickly, the hot spot disappeared like the rotisserie, and with it the vegetable pancakes, the stuffed peppers, the pans with gummy mushroom dishes. But even without all these, the business flourished. Shopkeeper Zinman earned enough to allow him two cars and two trips abroad each year with his Tzippi. The bulk of his business was not the chance shopper but actually the older customers, and in order to compete with other small groceries like his he maintained a delivery service. For that purpose he took on Peretz, a seedy bachelor of forty who had, until then, made a living through all manner of random jobs and spent his free time watching videos of action films over and over again.

Peretz cost him next to nothing, a few hundred dollars a month excluding tips, which could reach as much as two hundred shekels a week, and the right to purchase whatever he wanted at cost. This was enough to provide for his desires. Peretz was a neighborhood-guy type, loyal as a dog to his master, and had no wish to deal with matters beyond his reach. When given authorization to pick up a registered letter at the post office he got so excited that it was necessary to repeat the instructions as to how the procedure worked each time. At the outskirts of his kingdom the shopkeeper was kind enough to carve out a small domain over which Peretz could lord, a back room whose main assets were the refrigeration unit for the milk products and the desk on which the cold cuts were sliced and the olives weighed. The trusted employee spent the majority of his day there. And even during the deadest hours he did not rest for a moment, always polishing the refrigerator, wiping up the milk-water that dripped onto the floor, sharpening the knives, removing the grease from the counter—and all this, miracle of miracles, with a single rag. Since he was very interested in the news he was always quick to turn on his tinkling radio at six-thirty each morning; one ear was open to Zinman's instructions, the other to public radio programming, one program after another all day until two o'clock. He knew the entire schedule by heart, including which broadcaster was on at what hour, and the names of all the technicians as well. When in the mood he would hum the jingle of the midday program and when an important personality was being interviewed he raised the volume. He shouted the important news items from his corner to the other side of the shop in order to update his boss. So it will come as no surprise that he was the first to hear about the terrifying drama that took place in the afternoon of the Purim holiday of 1989, a drama that marred the merry proceedings of the holiday and sowed panic in the heart of Dvora Zinman as well.

B.

"Tuvia's right here next to me eating a pita. Where's Shirley?"

"She's not with you?"

"If she were here would I be asking you where she is? Maybe she's at Mutzafi's?"

"I already called over there. She's not there and neither is Mutzafi."

"I think she told me yesterday that they were planning to go to Sheinkin after school," Fat Tuvia recalled as he leaned against the refrigerator with a bottle of juice in one hand and salami on pita in the other, chewing leisurely.

"Tuvia says she's on Sheinkin Street. What about Aunt Masha? Have you gotten through to her yet? I mean, she lives right there!"

"I just spoke with her, you have no idea what luck . . . she got home ten minutes before the whole thing started. Sheinkin? Is he sure?"

"Are you sure?" Yosef Zinman asked his son.

"No," Tuvia admitted, sucking juice through a straw. The relaxed expression never left his face. No worry troubled his broad brow, as though everything that was happening at that moment only streets away from their shop was actually happening in Australia.

"He's not sure. Maybe you should phone your sister. Maybe she knows something?"

But before he could even hear the answer, Dvora Saltzman in the flesh rushed in like the wind, her eyes startled and her breathing ragged. "Where's Bina?" she shouted. "Have you seen her?"

"How should I know where Bina is—? Yes, it's your sister . . . no, not Bina—Dvora . . . how could I if she walked in this second? Who?

Probably Shraga. Hang on—Dvora, Tzippi's on the line. She's asking what happened."

"What happened? You can tell her that Bina's disappeared, if that makes any difference to her. This morning she was with Shraga at home watching television, then later she came down to the store and sat with me a little in the atelier. She wanted to play Monopoly but I had an order for neck cream so I didn't have any time for her. About an hour ago she said she was tired so I figured she went upstairs to lie down. I didn't hear a word about what happened until Shraga phoned a few minutes ago and said maybe I should close the shop because who knows if there aren't a few more of them running around the neighborhood. I locked up and walked up to the apartment, and just as I'm sitting down in the kitchen to listen to the radio Shraga walks in and says, 'Isn't Bina with you?' And I said, 'No, isn't she in her room?' So we ran to her room and she's not there! It's as if the earth opened and swallowed her up!"

"Do you happen to know where Shirley is?"

"Isn't she at her boyfriend's house?"

"Three people have been stabbed!" Peretz shouted from his perch, never leaving his radio.

"Men or women?!" Dvora shouted in return.

"They didn't say."

"Peretz, come here!" Yosef commanded.

The radio monitor obeyed with obvious displeasure.

"Have you seen Bina today?"

"Yes."

"When?"

"Before."

"Before when, you idiot?"

"I don't remember when exactly. Before. When I went out to the storeroom."

"Did she talk to you?"

"Yes."

"And what did she say?"

"She said, 'Hello, Peretz. Look, I'm a cat.'"

"What?"

"That's what she said, exactly those words. 'Hello, Peretz. Look, I'm a cat.'"

"Did she say anything else?"

"She asked me for a cigarette but I didn't have one."

"Was she alone?"

"No. She was with Shirley."

"With Shirley?!" Dvora yelled. "That girl is completely out of line. Who gave her permission to take Bina out?"

"Don't get so upset, Ciotka Dvora. Your blood pressure's gonna go up," advised Fat Tuvia as he peeled apart the layers of a chocolate-covered wafer.

"She was with Shirley!" the shopkeeper bellowed into the phone. "Peretz saw her before, when he was on his way to the storeroom."

"And did Shirley say anything?" Dvora cried.

"She said, 'Hello, Peretz, how are you?' just like Bina did."

"And that's all?" The vein on Yosef Zinman's forehead swelled. "Maybe she also said she was a cat?"

"No, she didn't say that. Can I get back to the radio, boss? Maybe there's something new."

Dvora suggested phoning the police and reporting a woman with such and such problems—who knew where she might end up on her perambulations. After all, Mount Nevo Street was only ten minutes away on foot. Her brother-in-law dismissed the idea; he said there was no reason to bother the police since at that moment the safest place in all of Tel Aviv was Mount Nevo Street thanks to all the units dispatched there. And anyway, chances were that Bina was at the nearby Yarkon River where she liked to sit and watch the fishermen. In the meantime, Peretz reported that an old man had been killed and two others were injured.

"I'm willing to bet you all there'll be more injured," Fat Tuvia announced.

"Why do you think that?" Dvora asked, alarmed.

"Quiet so we can hear!" Zinman said. "Peretz, turn up the volume a little."

Everyone fell silent. From the old radio, the ecstatic, almost celebratory chatter of the broadcasters hummed and crackled as they repeated every scrap of information over and over in order somehow to bridge the terrible gap between rushed reporting and the slow unfolding of events. Indeed, the events had their own rhythm.

Where could a man go who has just this moment stabbed to death—to death!—another human being? Imagine that you happen to be at a party overcrowded with people and then suddenly, without any prior warning, one of the guests, a person like every other whom until now you haven't even noticed, grabs a tray filled with glasses and smashes it to the floor in hateful rage. After the crash there will be silence; even he himself will be gripped with hushed astonishment. Something irreparable has been torn. Everyone gazes at him, expectant—what will happen next? And lo, only brief moments pass before reality resumes itself, as always: someone will turn down the music, someone else will bring a broom, someone will stand scratching his ear. However, for the outcast—a status difficult beyond measure—there is but a single recourse: to sabotage the world even more. To destroy the buffet table, to shatter the pitchers, to tear the shelves from the walls, to rip, to rupture, to ruin.

On March 21 an anonymous young man appeared on Mount Nevo Street with a knife in his hand. After stabbing to death an elderly passerby and injuring two others—all the while, it was said, shouting *Allahu Akbar!*—the assassin turned into Joshua Son of Nun Street, burst into one of the buildings there, and ran up flight after flight of stairs knocking at the doors. At one of those doors two girls screamed but did not open it. Since he encountered no other people on his way he continued to the roof of the building, desperate and drunk with fury, and hurled whatever he could find at the street below: potted plants that stood on the railing, gas cylinders, junk. In the end, the police shot him. It was reported that they fired at his lower body and left him paralyzed.

C.

It was nearly five o'clock, the sky was darkening. The search party, comprised of Peretz and Fat Tuvia, returned from the banks of the Yarkon without luck. Dvora Saltzman sent her husband, Shraga, to the Dizengoff police station and, just to be sure, phoned Ichilov Hospital. Since it was impossible in her present condition to open the perfumery—or, for that matter, to remain at home by the phone—she went downstairs to her brother-in-law's grocery; at least they could wait together. A few customers were gathered around the cash register to listen to Zinman's take on the events of the day. Peretz, who had been released for the remainder of the day, chose to stay, knowing that no one would phone *him* to pass along any news. Dvora had no patience for chitchat at that moment and stood in the doorway of the shop, a thick sweater thrown over her shoulders, keeping an eye out.

Suddenly, from behind the number twenty-four bus station on the opposite side of the street, two familiar silhouettes appeared, those of a tall young woman with long hair and a backpack slung over one shoulder, and next to her, that of a tall, awkward woman with a strange gait that made it seem as though with every step forward she was falling back.

"Here they are!" screeched Dvora as she ran to the curb and flailed her arms at them. "Bina, Shirley, I'm over here!"

The two held hands and crossed the street.

"What were you thinking, taking her without telling me?!" Dvora shouted at Shirley. "Do you have any idea how worried we all were? All the phone calls we've made? Are you two all right? Do you know that your Uncle Shraga went to the police? How could you not have phoned your mother so she wouldn't worry? And where have you been?!"

"I came by this afternoon and found Bina looking in the window of Shoshana's chocolate shop," Shirley said. "She looked bored so I thought it would be nice for her to walk around Sheinkin Street with me a little."

"Look, Dvoraleh, I'm a cat!" Bina said, giggling.

"You think I don't know that you took her to Sheinkin so people would say how special you are? And what are these markings on her face? As if people don't stare at her enough already!"

. . .

Even though you "can't really tell"—as acquaintances repeated over and over in order to make it easier on the family—you could actually see something from the very first glance, the strange, little signs: the slight dipping of the head, the movements that didn't quite suit their purpose (too sharp, too sluggish), the eyes filled with only the present moment and nothing of what came before or what would come after. The signs were not always so clear; the child of Tevye and Hinde Shlossman's old age, the younger sister of Avrum and Dvora and Tzippi, came into the world like all newborns, nursed like all newborns, bleated like all newborns. But just months after her first birthday it began to sink in. She was taken to experts. The tests showed not what was there but what was not. The word they had not dared utter was spoken aloud, at first under the breath, then later, routinely. When it became clear what could be hoped for and what could not, the father of the household cloaked himself in sorrow. The mother needed assistance. She did not dare ask it of Avrum, her firstborn, for the veneration in which she held him was essential for her belief in his greatness. Tzippi was too selfish—even in her youth, whenever she was asked to do something she would threaten to drop out of school. But the old beautician knew it was Dvora she could blindly trust. This daughter had been blessed with the ability to feel and give compassion—a rare trait, it must be said, at an age when the heart is full of boys and dresses. At first this compassion depended upon the innocent belief—deep, groundless—that something could still be done, but in the face of the difficulties that grew and grew and as hope evaporated and nothing was left but pain, compassion never ceased to flow in Dvora's heart.

Each morning the Shlossmans would awaken to new sorrows that the tragedy rolled to their doorstep, heaps of them amassing and demanding classification and treatment. It was not always possible to make all the necessary arrangements in advance, and there were periods when they simply enlisted whoever was in the vicinity. By the time Dvora became a partner in her parents' business, matters were already set in motion, and routines were eventually determined without anyone ever expressing an opinion or questioning them. In short, everyone grew accustomed to "Dvora has taken upon herself to . . ." And so, when the time came and she inherited the perfumery, her relatives made sure she inherited Bina, too.

▪ ▪ ▪

"But it was her idea to paint her face!" Shirley retorted.

"And what did you give her to eat? What did you let her have? She'll probably keep me up all night with diarrhea."

"I only let her have what she's allowed. I bought her popcorn and then some chocolate—she ate almost the whole bar so I think she isn't hungry."

"Pussy cat, pussy cat, where have you been . . . ?"

"Yes, sweetie, I see. Good for you."

"We were planning to walk to Sheinkin but we got stopped at Basel Street," Shirley explained. "There were ambulances and a lot of police and they wouldn't let us through. When it was all over we caught the bus to Sheinkin anyway because Bina said I'd promised and I didn't want to disappoint her. Ask her yourself. It was really cool, wasn't it, Bina?"

"Groovy, groovy, groovy!" Bina affirmed. "There were clowns and we went to see Shirley's friends and Shirley played music."

"It's not bad enough that you hang around with those beatniks, now you have dragged her there, too?!"

"They're not beatniks—they're punkers. And anyway, she had a really good time."

"Look! Shirley bought me a present. A ring!" Bina spread her chubby fingers in front of them with great pride.

"Again you wasted money on her?" said Yosef Zinman who had just popped out of his store. "*Nu*, never mind. The important thing is that you two are fine. Now do me a favor and go in and call your mother, she deserves at least that, don't you think?"

"Oh ho, oh ho, look who's here!" Peretz's scraggly head appeared from behind Yosef Zinman. "So? Did you see something? Did you hear the shots?"

"No, nothing," Shirley said.

"We saw a man dressed up like Alexis Carrington," Bina reported, "but he didn't have a cap gun."

"So you don't know about the slaughter that went on there?" Peretz asked, his eyes bright; at last he had found someone to update.

"Do me a favor, Yosef," said Dvora angrily, "and send this genius home already, will you? How can he talk like that with Bina around? She'll keep me up all night!"

Despite Bina's protests that she loved to "talk politics" and her hope that her brother-in-law would let her have a sweet from his shop, Dvora announced that she had had quite enough for one day and took her sister by the hand, dragging her to her home on the other side of Judah the Maccabee Street. Shirley informed her father that she was going to Oren Mutzafi's house and would be home late and that they should not hold dinner for her. Thus it was that the little gang on the street split up and Peretz, unsatiated, leeched onto an elderly customer who had come in to buy eggs and recounted to her, for the umpteenth time, how, that very day, at around two o'clock in the afternoon, one Dr. Kurt Shalinger—it had been reported that he was a divorced agronomist—went out to purchase food for the Purim feast he was preparing to make for himself and his bachelor son, and how, that very day, at 3:10, as he returned home with his shopping baskets and parked his car and stood with his back to the street as he locked it, a young Arab man suddenly stabbed him and stabbed him and stabbed him until he fell at his feet and his soul departed his body. Peretz also told of the blood that pooled on the sidewalk and how the victim was seventy-three years of age at his death, and how he had come to Israel as a refugee just before the Second World War. It had also been reported that he was a cousin of Austrian Chancellor Bruno Kreisky, and the customer, for whom Kreisky was odious and abominable, an apostate and an Arab-lover, sighed and said it was the irony of fate. But even Peretz the worker, who missed no news be it large or small, could not tell why it was that the deceased agronomist had planned such a tiny feast, or which foods he had bought for the purpose of gladdening his heart and that of his son, and why he had only invited that son, and what meaning could be attached to the disaster that had befallen him. And thus it was that although they threw so much light on every stage and every detail of the affair, it was still shrouded in an incomprehensibly sad fog.

D.

In spite of the flattery, the tears, the pouting, the threatened hunger strike—a groundless threat, it should be noted, from a creature lovingly referred to as a human vacuum cleaner—Dvora Saltzman did not agree to bring her sister Bina with her to Shirley's concert. Dvora said that after all the trouble she had caused over the past week—walking off like that with Shirley without asking permission in a country like Israel, where anything can happen, and indeed did happen and could have happened to her, God forbid—it was impossible to trust her and thus she did not deserve to be invited, and perhaps this punishment would teach her a lesson for next time. It must be mentioned that behind the curtain of grand pedagogy one can glimpse the big toes of absolute self-interest sticking out: Dvora wanted to go out for once to a family party without having to keep an eye on Bina; to be free, for a single evening, from the ongoing anxiety over potential mishaps. Truth be told, even before she spoke with her ward there were offers from several interested parties with their own reasons to stay behind to watch over Bina. And so, since the matter was decided in advance, Bina had not even the slightest chance of appealing the severe verdict and was left to console herself with thoughts of the chocolate promised to her as compensation.

Avrum Shlossman, who for a long time wished to host a salon "like in Europe," was the one who came up with the idea one afternoon during a visit with Tzippi at Aunt Masha's house. There is no secret in the fact that his proposal was not free of a certain provocative and uncontrollable impulse that assailed him from time to time, causing him to concoct a family porridge, stir it well, feed the flames covertly until it boiled, and then stand to the side to watch with great pleasure as the fruits of his handiwork bubbled and spewed themselves in every direction. It was well known that Tzippi Zinman, along with her husband, Yosef, took a dim view of their daughter's unique instrument of choice for expressing her musical ambitions. Nor were they pleased with her dark wardrobe or her army boots. "One morning she's going to wake up and kill us all, like in those stories you hear about in America," said the worried mother more than once. But that afternoon at Aunt Masha's house, while they were drinking coffee and nibbling lemon biscuits, Avrum asked matter-of-factly how Shirley was and how she was getting along with her playing and mentioned that he had not heard her in quite some time, and suddenly he smacked his thigh and announced that he had a wonderful idea and offered to host, at his home, two or three weeks hence, a small concert; not something grandiose, just family and perhaps a few close friends. The old lady—who loved gatherings and events, especially those with a potential for controversy—immediately sensed that there was an opportunity for some enjoyable family mayhem and expressed her strong support at once. After all, she said, she loved that charming girl so much, and there was nothing she would like better than to hear how she's progressed. Tzippi figured that this was another of her brother's cockamamie ideas; Avrum had a tendency to spin grand plans then lose interest in bringing them to fruition just as quickly. She figured by the following morning this idea, like its predecessors, would disappear, and so as not to attach any unwarranted importance to it she muttered a noncommittal response. Two days later, when she was out of the city for one of her fashion shows, Avrum phoned Shirley and worked out the details for the family get-together. From that moment on it was impossible to stop.

The preparations for the little family party awakened in Avrum Shlossman a joy that was comparable in its potency to the reluctance of his brother-in-law, the father of the young musician. When the grocer learned of the concert that was materializing before his very eyes, he complained to his wife and informed her that she was going to have to eat her brother's porridge herself this time. He found a thousand

and one reasons not to attend: Avrum's party was on a Wednesday, the busiest day for home deliveries; Tuvia, who helped him, would also be extremely tired. Moving the party to Thursday was no good since that was when Maccabi Tel Aviv held its games; everyone knew that in spite of his corpulence Yosef Zinman was an avid sports fan. Friday was out, too, since Zinman would not give up on Sabbath dinner with the family; Tuvia could do with a little tradition, couldn't he? In the end the concert was set for a Saturday night and when Yosef saw that none of the earlier excuses was succeeding he decided to feign illness. However, no flu or sudden attack of sciatica could stave off his true worry—not for himself but for his son, Tuvia. He gathered—not incorrectly—what type of people would be among the invited guests, and although he had never broached the subject with Avrum about his lifestyle or the people in his circle, he certainly did express his opinion to Tzippi alone in their bedroom, resorting, even, to obscenities. In short, Yosef Zinman had gotten it into his head that his naïve son might fall into the hands of those dubious types. And so, when all other escape routes he had planned for Fat Tuvia were exhausted, Yosef crossed Judah the Maccabee Street one morning, entered the perfumery, and asked his sister-in-law, just between the two of them, whether she was planning on "dragging" Bina with her to the concert. The hidden intention did not escape Dvora, who recognized the advantages at once. In an instant it was decided that Bina would stay home under the supervision of Zinman and son. There was nothing left for Dvora to do but use the opportunity to teach her younger sister a lesson and to prepare refreshments for the pair of babysitters.

E.

After entering and leaving several different departments at the university without remaining in any one of them longer than two consecutive semesters, Avrum Shlossman, in his mid-twenties, picked himself up and left Israel. When the small bankroll his mother had handed him shriveled, he ended up in Frankfurt, where an old army buddy had made good in certain business dealings. It was 1963 and these were the days of the economic miracle; the recovering city seemed to Avrum like a bath of cream, and for four or five years he splashed about in it with enormous pleasure. In the photographs he appended to his letters—which arrived far too infrequently—he is in the center, tall, elegant, a broad smile on his face. In the winter the photographs showed parties, balls—here he was wearing a fez, or there, embracing all sorts of exotic people. In the summer the photos came from vacation spots, leaning over a railing wearing a narrow-brimmed hat in the style of Jean-Paul Belmondo. Once he even sent a Polaroid snapshot.

All throughout that period no one in his family knew how he was supporting himself, what he was doing, who he palled about with—in short, what his life was like. Frankfurt was shrouded in a fog that Avrum himself did his best to preserve. Still, even his tendency to conceal and keep secrets was a sort of exhibitionism; he enjoyed imbuing his life with a kind of shady glory, albeit while rolling his eyes and grinning perversely. Incidentally, mostly these were quite mundane matters, and in any case far less sensational than what his family was imagining. The general consensus was that he dealt in antiquities, though there were those who believed he dealt in furs, and, in fact, in 1968 he sent his mother a rabbit stole with a matching beret. Even when he returned to Israel, Frankfurt continued to cast its long shadow over Judah the Maccabee Street. For several months each year Avrum Shlossman would stay in Germany "on business" (as Hinde would explain importantly to her clients at the perfumery without ever having a clue what she was talking about), and he always returned with bursting pockets. After every such visit—at some point it was no longer clear if he lived in Israel and visited Germany or vice versa—he would shower his family with gifts. Just as he knew how to enjoy life and spend money on luxuries, so too did he wish this upon others, and was lavishly generous with them. When he turned fifty he traveled to Frankfurt one last time, disposed of his business and property there, and returned to Israel with a large enough sum of money to enable him to stop working and live off the interest.

Although he did not regret his decision to settle down in Tel Aviv, he was nonetheless nostalgic for other lands. He decorated his flat on Spinoza Street in a style that can be called General European. On the wallpaper-covered walls he hung copies of the Rococo portraits of Sir Joshua Reynolds in gilded frames. Because he detested typical Tel Aviv floor tiles he carpeted every square centimeter with two layers of rugs. The apartment overflowed with an abundance of items he called abat-jour and fauteuil. Ugly but essential appliances like the television set were concealed behind the polished doors of a mahogany sideboard.

The curtains were fringed, the armchairs antique, heavy, uphol-stered in wine-colored satin, the tables were covered in Italian inter-locking wood. A plethora of lamps—one of which was in the shape of a black servant holding a torch—gave off a soft light. But the pride and joy of the apartment's lord and master was the huge tapestry, a valuable item he had brought from Germany that took up half the wall and portrayed a pastoral scene of shepherds. In a niche there was a Victorian desk that held bottles of choice liquor. The tiny drawers that once housed inks and stamps now contained small pipes, scissors, roll-ing paper—in short, everything one needed for smoking a little hash. There was no doubt about it: Avrum Shlossman loved to host, and he knew how to do it. His salon, a palace in miniature for its owner and hell on earth for his cleaning lady, served as the headquarters for a group of hedonistic sworn bachelors, and, over time, it became a true "salon"; even if no great philosophical or literary pronouncements were ever made there it still had a certain air about it. Social eve-nings were conducted according to a pleasant, if rigid, protocol that included, for example, the pouring of cognac only after ten o'clock and never before the Campari. The sticks of incense were lit one after another. Provocative magazines were placed hither and thither about the room. The tiny drawers were opened around midnight, just as the Turkish delight was being served. Even the music tinkled inces-santly—at first Vivaldi, then, toward the end, Marlene Dietrich.

This, then, was the backdrop to the productions staged in Avrum Shlossman's salon twice weekly, and with great success. Only one scene was missing from this tableau: the home concert. Thus, from the time that his niece Shirley had begun to play it was only a matter of time. And so, after negotiations with the young talent's parents were completed and details were ironed out with the soloist herself,

Avrum announced to everyone that they should keep the last Saturday evening of March free and he threw himself into preparations, as though this were a piano or violin concert.

F.

"Where should I put the cake?"

"What did you bring that for? I specifically said don't bring a thing! I swear, people make work for themselves . . ."

"Shraga, do me a favor and go to the living room instead of getting underfoot in here like a bump on a log."

Tzippi Zinman entered the kitchen singing a traditional end-of-Sabbath song in their father's voice and intonation. Her hair was pouffy and she glittered from head to toe.

"*A gut Wokh*, a good week!" Avrum joined heartily in response.

Tzippi grabbed the end of the dish towel he was holding, opened her blue eyes wide, and spun in front of him like a bride under the wedding canopy.

"Oh, I'm such a dummy," cried Dvora. "I forgot the cupcake liners! Do you happen to have any?"

"*Oy yoy yoy*, the cupcake liners," Avrum intoned, drawing his other sister into the dancing circle.

She laughed. "You and your nonsense. Let go of me and get me the liners and a knife already. And where's Aunt Masha?"

"*Ikh bin do!*" the aged hatchling chirped from the hallway. Dvora could smell her familiar cloying scent.

"There she is!" Tzippi Zinman proclaimed with joy.

"I came by *taxi*," Aunt Masha added with a reprimanding gaze.

Everyone exchanged kisses. The old lady surveyed the heavily laden table with satisfaction then wet her finger to gather several crumbs from the tin that held the *bourekas*.

Way back from the time of her youth, Aunt Masha was known as an enthusiastic partygoer whose mere presence could fan the flames. True, she was never considered a beauty, but her style was noticed favorably. Right to the end of middle age she continued to haunt the ballroom dancing clubs and run around with men. Behind her back, members of her family wrinkled their noses with a sanctimoniousness meant to conceal the fact that they were concerned about the future of her assets. Still, not one of those men who passed like a cloud in the skies of the inheritors' hopes succeeded in endangering their rights. Truth be told, Aunt Masha had long since decided to bequeath everything she had to her nieces and nephew and thusly saw herself as entitled to all sorts of privileges where they were concerned.

The doorbell rang once again.

"That must be Zifrony!" cried the host, wiping his hands on the towel and moving to the door.

"Good evening. Abby, meet Igor."

"*Bonsoir, bonsoir,* nice to meet you. *Entrez s'il vous plait!*"

Tzippi had finally gotten the most out of her grand entrance and was ready to help. Dvora was organizing squares of chocolate cake onto a tray. Avrum, who had not stopped his humming, was ferrying platters and saucers from the kitchen to the salon. In the meantime, Shraga Saltzman diluted white wine with soda water and took a handful of peanuts, then sat down to stare into space for a while. Suddenly he noticed that behind the curtain that separated the living room from the balcony someone was standing and smoking: a bald midget of about fifty who brought to mind an uncooked bean. His small, greenish eyes twinkled with alertness above a splendidly hooked nose. His trousers, which were pulled up unnaturally high, were tightened with a belt to hide a small belly. The man stubbed out his cigarette and proffered his hand in greeting.

"And whose honor do I have the pleasure of meeting?" he asked sweetly.

"Shraga Saltzman."

"I'm Sammy. But you can call me Susu." The words were sprinkled with the shards of a foreign accent. He stepped into the living room redolent with the scent of aftershave and selected an armchair into which he sprawled. His short legs barely reached the floor.

"So, Shraga, what is your connection to this evening?" he asked, leaning his chin on his hand and smiling.

"My wife is Dvora, Avrum's sister."

"I see," Sammy said with a certain disappointment. "So you're the talent's father?"

"The talent?" Shraga asked, momentarily confused. "Oh, you mean Shirley. No, no, I'm her uncle."

His co-conversationalist stared at him.

Shraga chuckled uncomfortably. "I'm not part of this—I'm just here for the concert, just like you."

"Just like me," the stocky little man said, perking up. "I see. What are you drinking, Shraga?"

"A spritzer. Want me to make you one?"

"You know what?" Sammy said, giggling. "Yes. Make me a spritzer, absolutely." He made a gurgling sound, like a pigeon, then lit another cigarette and pulled close a heavy Murano glass ashtray. Shraga had never met anyone who enjoyed a cigarette so effusively. When he leaned down to present him with his drink the man suddenly thrust his hand into Shraga's stringy hair.

"Do you dye it?"

Shraga was stunned into silence.

"We Argentines are a very informal people," Susu explained. "Allow me to offer you a compliment: the color suits you. Do you use Wella?"

Shraga smiled wanly.

"What are you embarrassed about? I wish I had something to dye!" the stocky little man purred, patting his shiny pate. "So what do you do, my friend?"

Saltzman took a sip of wine. "Insurance," he said.

"Nice, nice. For your information, I'm a travel agent," Sammy chuckled.

"You don't say."

"I have a small office on Ben Yehuda Street. Top Tours. Here's my card—you're welcome to visit if you need something from me." The little travel agent tended to pronounce his words in a way that imbued even the most trivial matters with a sort of double entendre.

Shraga, who had never excelled at small talk, was tired of peanuts and began cracking pistachios.

"Oh, look who's here!" cried Sammy suddenly as he rose to his feet to shake hands warmly with Zifrony, an awkward man of forty wearing a yarmulke. "And who might this be?"

"This is, um, Igor—he arrived not long ago from Russia," said Zifrony.

"Good for you!" Susu said with a wink. "You're doing a fine job of immigrant absorption." Once again he was giving Shraga the dull feeling that there was some other, hidden, meaning to his words.

"I want Cola," said Igor, a young and impressively built blond whose face projected animosity toward everyone within range.

"Those Russians, they're crazy about Coca-Cola," Sammy told Shraga, lowering his voice as if sharing a secret with an old friend. "Couldn't get it back home all these years."

"Susu, leave the kid alone," Avrum commanded as he paraded into the room carrying *bourekas*, followed by his two sisters—one bearing a large salver with crudités and crackers—the other, a cutting board laid with slivers of cheese and a yellowish dip. The host made introductions among the guests and busied himself with aperitifs. Meanwhile, other guests arrived: a weedy fop in blue plastic glasses, a sinewy woman in a low-cut Lycra shirt who was presented to the family as an aerobics instructor, and a mustachioed thug in a jean shirt who poured himself half a glass of whiskey at once. Antonio Vivaldi was replaced with Shirley Bassey. The room grew steamy, cheeks reddened, the salon was teeming with life. Avrum's friends crowded around Tzippi Zinman, who entertained them with behind-the-scenes stories of the fashion world. Dvora, who was slightly taken aback by this flock of preeners, seated herself in a corner and recounted her litany of woes to Aunt Masha, who nodded supportively while downing hardboiled egg after hardboiled egg. In a different corner, Shraga was enjoying the company of his newfound friend. Even the Russian boy—it seemed that this time Zifrony had truly come up with one hell of a hunk—was deep in animated conversation with the aerobics instructor. The dimming stage arrived: lights, music. Without anyone taking notice, Avrum lit the candles that had been placed in their holders earlier. The hour had arrived. He stood in the middle of the salon and struck a teaspoon against his glass, and it responded with a crystal chime.

"Ladies and gentlemen!" he intoned. "Susu, quiet please. Aunt Masha. Anyone not sitting, please take a seat. We'd like to begin."

G.

Silence prevails. Enter Shirley Zinman, a thin high school student whose scowling face sports three or four dark beauty spots and whose wide-set eyes are slightly unfocused. Her black clothing—polo shirt, striped men's suit vest, tight jeans, military boots—highlight her very pale skin. She carries a large case in the shape of a hunting rifle. The living room is crowded and the case bumps the shoulder of the man in the blue plastic glasses, who lets out a shriek. Susu stifles a giggle. Shirley seats herself on a bar stool and from the case removes a dull saw of about seventy centimeters in length and then something else—a rounded wooden handle that was once part of a cheese-slicing appliance of her father's. She screws the handle into the narrow side of the blade, in the hole where one would hang the saw. The stocky travel agent, who is already red in the face from trying not to laugh, lets out a snort. Avrum Shlossman hushes him with a light slap to the shoulder. Shirley positions the saw, its base between her thighs, the wooden handle in her fists, and brandishes a bow—a real one, that of a violin—lining it up to the edge of the blade and pulling it very slowly with outstretched fingers, as if she were playing with a yo-yo. A grimace, borne of effort or perhaps suffering, is etched on her face. Suddenly, with a stunning movement, she twists the upper half of her body and leans sideways. The blade peals and lets out a sound of infinite wailing, of terrible, meaningless sadness that metamorphoses into something tangible, familiar, that stands on the tip of one's tongue: Saint-Saëns's *The Swan*. The saw writhes, whistles, its sound alternatively dies and comes to life. The tune shines from within with a mesmerizing, pallid light that freezes and warms the heart all at once. A strange smile spreads across the girl's face. She convulses, she stretches, bends over, all the while quivering her hand tremulously, creating as one with the blade a dance the likes of which none among the guests has ever witnessed.

Throughout the concert, the expression of joy splashed across Aunt Masha's face is that of a person who has just sampled nectar and ambrosia. Her eyes remain closed (except for a slit that enables her to keep tabs on Tzippi's torment), her fingers thrum her belly, and anyone listening attentively would hear her humming along faithfully. In the opposite corner, the sinewy aerobics teacher's head bobs like a pecking chicken gone mad. Sammy Greenberg, desperate to mend his ways, breaks into uproarious applause the moment the music ends. Everyone joins in. Aunt Masha, who finally snaps out of her lofty reveries, approaches the young musician with Napoleonic pomp and kisses her twice on each cheek, leaving behind pink stamps. Then she turns to the mother of the young talent. "What a special girl," she says with great import. "Tzippinka, I bless you!" And Tzippi—caught between a rock and a hard place—is forced to respond with a jaundiced smile.

Everyone thinks *the great Tzippi Zinman, the popular Tzippi Zinman*, but who among them sees the worm gnawing at her heart from within? No matter how hard she pushes her brain she is incapable of comprehending how this has happened to her, how her little girl has come to this insanity. She has already made her peace with so many things—the ear pierced with four holes, the constant complaints from school, the boy who has been sleeping with her for half a year already who doesn't even bother to put on a T-shirt when he makes his way from her bedroom to the bathroom. But even *her* patience—and you certainly couldn't say she is old-fashioned!—has its limitations. Take for example her sister, Dvora. She has only one son but he is a genius who went to Boston to study in a department with two names. But she? She has *this*. Surely there is no one who actually enjoys this sort of mewling-cat music; now they are all flowing with compliments but she knows only too well that inside they are laughing at her daughter, and worse—feeling sorry for her, for both of them, in fact. Aunt Masha heaps on the praise, Avrum fans the flames with talk of Carnegie Hall, and the more the two of them foretell the glorious future awaiting Shirley, the more Shirley's mother closes into herself. The host asks for more music and Shirley slides a piece of resin down the bow and continues playing several more gloomy lamentations that turn inward rather than outward. In spite of the conviviality of the partygoers, they are wrapped inside an eternal loneliness in which they are condemned to wandering about in what feels like an Arctic tundra. Most would have been content to end with what they heard thus far, but the host insists on encores. "Something happy!" he demands, ignoring the mute pleas his sister is sending his way. Shirley responds with sounds that surprise her audience. The mustachioed thug leans his head on his arm and his face relaxes. The bean-like travel agent is brought to tears and withdraws from his pocket a cotton handkerchief he uses to wipe his eyes gently. A certain brightness can even be detected on Dvora Saltzman's face. After all, who could remain indifferent to *Over the Rainbow*?

The applause reaches the high heavens. Some clap with excitement and some with relief. A bottle of Polish vodka is opened. Everyone speaks excitedly: Igor claims that in Russia, this would not be considered music. A debate ensues: what is music? Rare musical instruments are mentioned and someone tells of a childhood friend who strums bicycle wheels. Shraga recalls that he once saw on television an old Jew from America playing *Jerusalem of Gold* on a collection of jars. Gypsy music plays on the stereo and the volume is raised. Spirits soar. Lights are dimmed. (Under cover of darkness, Shirley takes her hunting-gun case and departs.) A large bowl of piping hot punch is brought from the kitchen, glorious scents trailing, and poured into cups. You only live once—even Dvora succumbs to temptation and drinks a whole glass. The mustachioed thug sits at the Victorian desk, clearly in the know and accustomed, opening drawers and getting to work. In no time, four handmade joints are lined up on the desk, with pieces of rolled cardboard serving as filters. The smell is pungent, cloying. A joint is passed from hand to hand, eventually reaching Tzippi Zinman, who hesitates for a moment; in her circle of friends, there has never been such a thing. She glances around and at once makes her decision: she will not give these people the pleasure; they have made her enough of a laughing stock for one evening already. She inhales once or twice. Ladies and gentlemen, presenting Tzippi Zinman, who can smoke dope no worse than any of you.

It is true that the smoke chokes her but she holds it in bravely, even longer than Stocky Sammy before her. She does not need to turn her head to know exactly the expression on her sister's face—equal portions of rebuke and admiration. At first she feels nothing, no change. She hears the sounds of laughter all around her. Although it is a cool March evening they all begin to sweat. The aerobics teacher takes off her shoes and crosses her legs. Stocky Sammy confesses certain hidden talents to Shraga; it turns out he apprenticed to a palm reader in Buenos Aires as a young man and is now intently gazing at the palm of his new friend, trailing his small, sharp pinky finger the length of the lines he finds there. Dvora tries to fish out with her tongue the small chunks of apple floating in her third glass of punch. Aunt Masha sits in her corner consuming everything within reach: olives, almond cookies, Turkish delight. An invisible hand raises the volume on the music. Sticks of incense spread a scent of orange. The thug sends out another joint; this time Tzippi does not hesitate. She wants to shut her eyes and open them wide at the same time. A pendulum sways to and fro in her bowels, her eyes burn, she tingles from head to toe. She sits up straight and in all her blooming glory tells several of the bathroom jokes for which she is famous. Avrum's friends gather around her cheering her on, growing bawdier, competing hoarsely to see who can tell the bolder tale. Tzippi chokes with laughter, sprays drops from her nose, screams that if they didn't stop she will pee in her pants. In the loudest of voices she insists to Avrum that he put on some Bill Haley for the soul, then grabs her sister's hand and drags her to the middle of the living room. In general, Dvora deplores such unharnessed behavior, but that evening the silly mood has infected even her, and she goes along with it. Everyone stands in a circle, gazing on in wonder. No one remains indifferent. Sammy-Susu, his pants drawn as high as possible, jiggles from side to side, his lips in a pout, tapping out the rhythm with his middle finger. The guitars electrify even the fellow in the blue plastic glasses, who flaps his gaunt wings. *One-two-three o'clock four o'clock rock*—they are seething and roiling, and in the middle of them all are the two Shlossman sisters, spinning round and round in perfectly synchronized movements, their feet drumming on hinged heels. No power in the world can wipe the smiles bursting from their lips. *Five-six-seven o'clock eight o'clock rock—* the saxophone moans, the bass agitates the heart, the soul is aflame. The volume is turned up yet again. Tzippi breathes in, breathes out, wets her lips avidly; Dvora puckers her lips into a kiss, raises her arm high and wiggles her finger in time to the music. Their shoulders rise and fall, they push and pull one another, drawing close and pulling away, acting out like two savages, though never trespassing the boundaries of the invisible box inside which they are sealed. Their hair sticks to their foreheads, fire scorches their cheeks, their extra pounds no longer exist, as if thirty years have not passed since the little room above the perfumery, the pumps, the 45s.

H.

Although she always claimed that her heart was sworn to each of her offspring in equal measure, the cosmetician Hinde Shlossman nurtured the fear in each of her daughters' hearts that perhaps she was less beloved to her mother than the other. She would praise Dvora's obedience, willingness to lend a hand, and lack of pampering to Tzippi's face; she hinted, as early as when Tzippi was only seven years old, about the bitter end of girls who skipped school. To older sister Dvora's ears she would extol Tzippi's verve and popularity and told her that with no spice to her personality and an excess of timidity she would never get anywhere in life.

On most days, Madame Shlossman's face looked as though she had been wronged in some way, so her family had no way of escaping the feeling that it was upon them to make it up to her. When Tevye fell ill, for example, he dared not even request a glass of water from her, since it took only one brief gaze at her suffering face to understand that his widow-to-be was close to being crushed under the weight of the burden. When Avrum, the firstborn, received a low grade in history class on the Hasmonean Period, Hinde walked about for a week so insulted that it was as though she were Johanan Horcanus, the high priest himself. When the girls saved their pennies with great industriousness and bought her a blue chiffon scarf for Mother's Day, Hinde smiled sourly (once again they've forgotten that *green* is her favorite color!) and never once wore the gift around her neck.

Nor did Avrum spare the girls. He played with them as though they were two wind-up toys: he fed them strange mixtures he concocted from margarine and powdered eggs, trained them to tie his shoes, and, when the spirit moved him, he would march them round and round the children's room to the sounds of his recorder.

And so it was that the years of the girls' childhood were spent under the aegis of the pact they made—or, perhaps more accurately, the pact that was made for them: that of two mares harnessed side by side to the same wagon, straining to pull at the same pace. Then, just as they stood at the start of their youth, already peering with curiosity at the wide expanse beyond their doorway, the family was plagued with its great sorrow. Dvora, as has been mentioned, took the yoke upon her neck and the bit in her mouth, while Tzippi, the younger by two years and the feistier, kicked and brayed with all her strength. Since she could not shoulder her family's burden she sought a way out in the form of a husband. Tzippi had never lacked for suitors, and in fact there were rumors to the effect that she had been quite freehanded with them. This was in the days of "soirees"; the two sisters—juicy, glowing—practiced rock-n-roll diligently in their bedroom and went to "have a good time" every weekend. Hinde was already preparing herself for an additional woe, and since she was not prone to suppressing what she saw, she took into account the possibility that, heaven forbid, they could find themselves with an extramarital pregnancy.

But then, to everyone's surprise, Tzippi chose the son of the Zinmans, owners of the neighborhood grocery that faced the perfumery. Hinde was overjoyed. She had never dared hope that her wild daughter would settle down so ideally. As sole inheritor of the family business, Yosef Zinman's future was secure. Surely it was true, thought the mother of the bride, that bread and milk would always be needed, so a grocery was a thriving business under any circumstances. Furthermore, the groom was good-looking and agile (for who could imagine that one day he would sprout a belly as large as a pumpkin?). So, a wedding took place, and everyone was of one mind: from the day of its founding, Tel Aviv had never seen such a beautiful couple. As naturally joyful people the young couple quickly became a cornerstone of a certain segment of society, which they referred to simply as "the gang." The gang went on treks around the country, the gang went yearly to the sanatorium on Mount Canaan, the gang danced the twist at the most "in" nightclubs, and the gang spent every Saturday evening at one of the Dizengoff Street cafés. And while the core of the group numbered only four or five couples, the gang sometimes swelled to include bachelors and bachelorettes—among them, Tzippi's older sister, Dvora. One Shraga Saltzman, a Jerusalemite newly replanted in Tel Aviv and working in the tax office of the National Health Fund, attended one of those parties. Tzippi Zinman's shy, beautiful sister did not escape Shraga's eye. Thus it was that within a single year Hinde succeeded in marrying off both daughters. The second wedding was more modest, held in the basement of Jabotinsky House. But whereas her first son-in-law gave her boundless joy, the second caused her only displeasure: he was lazy, boastful, full of self-satisfaction—unlike the rest of the family, Hinde refused to consider the solving of matchstick puzzles to be a sign of genius—so that together, these traits led her to crown him, behind his back, Mr. Good for Nothing. After he was fired from the health fund—for years he continued to claim that his position had been coveted by some relative of a person in power—Shraga tumbled from one temporary job to another until finally he landed in a small insurance company owned by a cousin who made big promises and paid a small salary. From the day Dvora entered into partnership with her mother, his insurance deals grew fewer and fewer until finally, to the open displeasure of his mother-in-law, he planted himself on the chair behind the counter of the perfumery and appointed himself cashier.

After the hardships and vicissitudes the old tyrant endured, Hinde at last reached an easier period. The Shlossman sisters gave birth without trouble, one year apart, to two male heirs. Without needing to be told, each daughter in turn gave in to her mother's will and named her son Tuvia after their late father. The old lady's joy knew no bounds, and she gave herself over to the two infants with all her heart. She spoiled her grandsons and fulfilled their wishes with the same determined devotion she had used to limit and obstruct her daughters during their girlhood. Since Dvora's son—nicknamed Yellow Tuvia for his blond hair—was a little man with a big imagination, his grandmother went and bought him illustrated storybooks every Friday. His cousin, on the other hand, who tended toward gluttony and was nicknamed Fat Tuvia, she liked to spoil with puddings and biscuits. And before she made her departure from this world, Hinde Shlossman managed to bounce her last grandchild, a girl—Shirley, Fat Tuvia's little sister—on her knees. This tiny child was her favorite of all. With crooked fingers she sewed her ornamented smocks and with her hoarse voice sang her old songs she remembered from her own childhood in Lodz. And yet, while she pampered her grandchildren she never stopped tyrannizing her daughters; to her dying day she never spared them a plenitude of remarks and rebukes.

I.

"Do me a favor, sweetie, don't make such a racket with the dishes," Tzippi Zinman said to her sister. "My head is splitting."

"Well that's no surprise," proclaimed Aunt Masha, who stood drying the clean dishes, "when you're a drug addict."

Dvora turned down the flow of the water and suggested Tzippi take another aspirin, but Avrum explained that in such situations nothing helped. Only water did any good—as much water as possible—but in any event the feeling would pass by itself in half an hour. He himself was all hustle and bustle—he shook out the tablecloths on the kitchen balcony, arranged the leftovers in plastic containers, put two garbage bags out in the stairwell and even managed to vacuum the carpet.

"It was a successful evening, huh?" he half-asked, half-declared.

"Very," said Dvora, her reddened fingers frosted with soap suds. "Did you see how my chocolate cake got eaten down to the very last crumb?!"

"The girl played very nicely," said Masha Lifschitz. "Too bad her father didn't bother to come to the concert. *Nu*, what can you expect?

His mother was a grocer, his father was a grocer, and he himself always was and still is a grocer. Shirley certainly got her talent from our side of the family. You know that my aunt Lidia Lifschitz, may she rest in peace, was a very famous actress in Lithuania before the war and even after. She was still onstage in Moscow at eighty."

"She sure didn't play the saw."

"It's the fashion now," the old lady pronounced.

Dvora removed the last dregs from the sink and wiped it down with a rag. "I don't understand anything about that, I'm not a musical person. What's important is that everyone enjoyed themselves. All in all you have some very nice friends, Avrum. Who's that Zifrony guy?"

"Oh, I've known him for years. He's a bookkeeper for an import firm."

"A really nice guy, no doubt about it. And that new immigrant who came with him, he's his gentleman friend, right? I didn't know there was such a thing with religious people."

"Oy, Dvora, sometimes you kill me how behind the times you are," said Aunt Masha, shaking her head. "You get that kind everywhere, even in the government. I read they recently discovered where that disease of theirs comes from. It all started with some Swedish flight attendant who ate monkey brain."

"Norwegian," said Avrum.

"Why did he eat monkey brain?" asked Dvora, perplexed.

"Do I know? Apparently he was hungry!"

"The Argentinian dwarf is one of them, too," said Tzippi, "I could tell at once. In my line of work you see things like that all the time."

"So maybe it's not such a good thing that he drove Shraga home," Dvora worried. "Do you think something could happen to him?"

"Worst thing is they could play doctor a little," Avrum said with a wink and a rakish smile.

"My stomach's killing me," Tzippi announced. "I'm going to go try and—excuse me—take a crap."

"We hope to hear good news from you very soon!" proclaimed Aunt Masha.

Dvora took off the apron she was wearing, sat at the kitchen table, and with a hesitant, even childlike movement removed a Kent from her sister's packet. It was clear she was unaccustomed—Shraga did not like the smell, and she only allowed herself to smoke on occasion. She looked about the kitchen with satisfaction—the wine glasses were drying upside down on a towel, the rag was folded on the lip of the sink, there was a refreshing scent of soap in the air. Avrum offered to make coffee and wash it down with something sweet, and while waiting for the water to boil she took one of the weekend supplements of the newspaper and began to read. Suddenly from the hallway came heartrending moans.

"Maybe someone should go see what's happening there," said Aunt Masha, clearly agitated.

"Don't worry, it's completely natural in her state," said the host. "Weed clogs your pipes."

"'The mattress for people with big dreams,'" Dvora read from the paper. "Aminach?"

"No. Sealy Posturepedic," said Avrum as he leaned over his sister to read. "This Passover in five installments."

"Wait, wait, not so fast. Bring me a pen."

They could hear the sound of a flushing toilet and then the slamming of a door.

"Oh!" said the old lady, her eyes bright.

Tzippi Zinman had returned to the kitchen looking like a weeping willow after a typhoon. She dropped into one of the chairs and announced that the way she felt at that moment made her wonder if she would ever have another bowel movement in her life.

"No results?"

"*Gornisht!*"

"Give her prunes," Aunt Masha said. "The more, the better."

"In such situations, only cognac will do!" announced the host as he rose to pour himself a glass.

"'I work all week and live for the weekend,'" read Dvora.

"Me too!" said sick Tzippi.

"That would be the hot springs at Tiberias," said Avrum. "Or maybe the Jerusalem Hilton."

Tzippi sat, limbs splayed, and opened a button to free her very white belly. "What are you people talking about?"

"It's a slogan quiz. Ten free tickets to London for the people who guess them all right. Want to try?"

"No thanks. If I feel like flying to London I'll buy a ticket with my own money and on my own terms."

"So which should I write? The hot springs or the Hilton?"

"You know something, Dvora, it doesn't take a genius to figure it out. Just flip through the paper till you find their ad."

"Okay, okay, you could have phrased that a little nicer, couldn't you?" Dvora was hurt. She closed the supplement and tossed it angrily onto the pile of papers.

"Are you and Yosef going anywhere during Passover?" Avrum asked Tzippi. "I've heard rumors that pretty soon they're going to lower the travel tax."

Tzippi had heard the rumors, too, and declared that that should have happened a long time ago, and that it was scandalous. "What kind of country is it," she asked, "where a person—excuse the expression—busts his ass and then has to pay a fine for wanting to spend a little time abroad?"

"Well," said Dvora, "you should know that when Shraga and I sailed to Marseilles—"

"With all due respect," Tzippi said, cutting her off, "a lot of water has flowed through the Yarkon since then. That was your honeymoon! The laws have changed since then."

"How should I know?" said Dvora, turning her head. "The farthest I ever travel is Judah the Maccabee Street to Dizengoff."

To everyone's surprise, Tzippi informed them that this year she and Yosef would be traveling north to Nahariya during Passover but that after the High Holidays in the fall they would spend a week or so in Austria. Seefeld again? Yes, Seefeld again. Yosef was crazy about the place and the truth was that she also enjoyed herself there very much.

There was nobody like those Austrians, damn them. Suddenly, her intestinal woes disappeared as Tzippi burst into a lyrical recounting of greening fields and dumplings fried in butter and horse carriages driven by men in Tyrolean hats. She spiced her tale, as was her wont, with anecdotes from their many travels: timetable errors, an unfamiliar local custom, an undecipherable menu—ordinary mishaps that led to complications and usually a big laugh. In no time, everyone was swept away by her stories and even Dvora, who was miffed at first, allowed herself to light up another cigarette. Tzippi was excited to be telling these tales again, and no less excited was her sister to be hearing them; sometimes she even filled in the punch line herself. The two got each other going, tossing each other code words much in the manner of a rebbe and his prize student: a question inside an answer and an answer inside a question. The stories came one after another, the spiciest of them saved for last, of course—a prank played by Yosef Zinman when they visited an ancient chapel. Tzippi gave in to her brother's request and told the story already familiar to them all and referred to as "the Portofino Fart." As always, they were laughing rivers of tears in an instant.

"Ha!" chortled Aunt Masha, red enough in the face to cause concern. "That Yosef of yours is really something special. When I think about the look on the face of that poor nun . . ."

"Oy, I could die!" Dvora roared.

They were all wild with laughter. In order to draw out the pleasure a little more, Tzippi repeated the last line of her story and brought about a fresh outburst of shouts, shrieks, and snorts. Each time it seemed they were about to quiet down, one of them would toss out a key word or simply gaze at the others and off they went again. It was only when Aunt Masha moaned that her ribs were hurting and that maybe they had made enough of a little wind passed seven years earlier, causing another round of merriment, that at last they calmed down.

"Too funny!" said Avrum Shlossman, wiping his eyes. "We've really all got to go away together someday."

How is it that until that very moment no one had thought of that?

"After the High Holidays we're all going to Seefeld together! All the siblings!"

The words had existed previously, they had simply been waiting—albeit for many years—for the right opportunity. The blood pumped, the heart flooded, the soul soared. The hues that had colored the years were suddenly peeled away to reveal three children with twinkling eyes about to lift off in a hot-air balloon. From the moment of the first spark, matters took their own course. All the obstacles that would stand in their way seemed trivial. The sky was clear, the world was large, life was as light as a feather. They would fly through Munich and perhaps lodge there for a night or two before decamping to Seefeld. Naturally, they would stay in a guest house with a tall roof and a chimney, and they would reserve rooms with adjoining balconies. Yosef would plan their route since he knew the area like the back of his hand. They would rent a large vehicle, Tzippi would make her excellent sandwiches for them all, and they would drive up to see snow in the mountains. They would stroll down cobblestone lanes, they would listen to Fire Department bands, they would eat crunchy wurst with potato salad, they would enjoy themselves to the wee hours of the morning, night after night. And why shouldn't they bring along their younger sister, Bina? In Seefeld they would set up a rotation schedule for minding her. And Dvora should not worry where the money would come from, it would all work out. They would have Peretz keep an eye on all their apartments and they would bring him back a fine bonbonnière. And last but not least—Aunt Masha! True, she did not like straying too far from her family doctor, but they pleaded with her nonetheless—in fact, they forced her to agree—to join them. Her presence was essential; after all, without an old, strict aunt there could be no young, naughty nieces and nephews. Thus it was that every bit of burdensome baggage was tossed away one after the next. Fur hats were donned, galoshes were slipped on, they all found their places in the huge straw basket as they floated breathlessly in the splendid balloon hovering over their heads.

3

A New Business Is Born

A.

Leaving Tel Aviv and heading east, one meets within twenty minutes of one's departure a myriad of structures—a depressing clutter of decrepit workshops, abandoned factories, the walls of which no one ever bothered to spackle, all sorts of deteriorating warehouses that inspire desperation. This no-man's-land's acidic dirt grows nothing but plastic wrappers and scraps of cardboard. All is stained, all is dusty, rusty; the sky appears yellow even when it is blue. The farther away you wander from the main road, the more miserable the buildings become. The side roads are eaten up by potholes, the gigantic trash containers scattered in the parking lots are overflowing. On one end of these empty lots, just when you think you've finally reached a dead end, an opening tears through the fence; from this opening stretches a long dirt road that circles the industrial zone and reaches all the way to the wild fields flanking it. Surprisingly, more small paths branch out of this dirt road, narrower and paltrier.

Not for nothing has the reader bothered to make this journey: at the edge of one of these paths settled Mendel Cohen, a large-bodied middle-aged Jew, after finding—God knows when—a deserted structure and turning it into a sewing workshop. The production floor takes up the majority of the space, and in the back is a crowded space called "the office," meaning a room overflowing with shelves, a coffeemaker, and a chipped sink. From here, Mendel Cohen reigns over his complex business endeavors; in fact, it is one company with many names, sporadically changing, as a way to ward off the evil eye or for reasons that purely benefit the business. "Mendel Shirts" became "MC Fashion," which morphed into "Manitex," and was eventually abandoned for the sake of "Mandy Line." Each time the phoenix rose from the ashes, old books were sealed and new were christened; sometimes a debt payment plan was announced. Later, after the appropriate licenses had been issued, receipt booklets were printed, adorned with the new logo and beginning with the serial number 001. Tax agents occasionally visiting the workshop could not make sense of the mess; the only one who was able to guide the lost was the owner himself, who did his best to confuse them even further.

Mendel Cohen was a disgruntled man usually able to exhaust anyone who took him on: his bumpy face reddened, his meaty, capillary-webbed nose vibrated and sweated, and at especially rough moments he even hyperventilated and wheezed. This terrifying vision was famous for its crucial financial significance—one time after another he used it to break off negotiations just when he had the upper hand. His clientele was very diverse—from small provincial retailers to soldiers completing basic training who ordered company T-shirts as mementos. Though he didn't pay careful attention to detail—a seam opened here, a loose thread peeked out there—he acquired a loyal clientele, having made sure to follow the most important rule of all: never miss a supply deadline. Throughout the years, his office accumulated a fine collection of patterns (half of them stolen from other manufacturers) that served his factory well: button-down shirts, long- and short-sleeved undershirts, tracksuits, and other garments that are always in demand. Each season, Mendel Cohen's workshop sold countless items, which, through agents of sorts, reached every corner, from the shelves of Tel Aviv department stores to the last of the haberdasheries in Safed. Thousands around the country warmed up in his flannel underwear in winter and sweated through his T-shirts in summer; indeed, people like Mendel Cohen, hidden from public view, are the stable foundation on which the fashion industry is built. They set its rules and they direct its course.

And just how did Tzippi Zinman encounter this hidden prodigy of confection production? Who knows? He never participated in fairs, neither with her nor with her competition. Perhaps he bought a ticket to one of her Purim balls? Perhaps they sat at the same table at some forgotten wedding? Maybe he happened upon the family shop and had a conversation with her husband? At any rate, in early May, searching for something in her address book, she came across his number, next to the words "manufacturer/men (cheap)." She instantly knew she'd found the solution to a problem that had bothered her ever since she returned from her Passover vacation in Nahariya, which, successful though it had been, had done nothing to abate her passion for Seefeld, this time with the entire family. She pictured the yearned-for trip: born, as we know, on Avrum's intoxicated breath—over and over again, from the first strudel on the balcony overlooking the mountains to the accolades, overflowing with gratitude for the planner—those words, worth more than their weight in gold, which they'd say to her at baggage claim upon their return. In her mind, she had decided they would go during the Sukkot holiday—Yosef works half-days during that time anyway, and it wouldn't be hard to convince him to close shop through the holiday. The only obstacle left was the Saltzmans' empty pockets. Ever since the recession began, the perfumery's business had fallen onto harder times, and it was clear no salvation would come from Shraga's theoretical insurance business. There was no point discussing a loan—Dvora wouldn't hear of it; the only remaining recourse was to make sure she had additional income. Not a temporary fix like that night at the Last Chance club—for which she paid her a hundred and something shekels—but a side business in addition to the perfumery that could sustain her permanently. Something, let's say, like a simple clothing stall—printed T-shirts, *shmattes* for children, cheap goods that required no expertise and would be snatched up in employees' committees fairs.

At first Dvora was shocked at the idea—what did she know about clothing, she wondered, and how would she find the time and what did she need the hassle for; even if she might be able to let Shraga tend the store on his own once or twice a week—how would she move around without a car? And even if, theoretically, they'd find an arrangement—because it was true she could fold and arrange clothes in a way that made even the ugliest *shmatte* look appetizing, and Tzippi was right, there was a chance to get ahead—she still had to admit the truth: she had no talent for the market. And besides, go figure who the clients were and what kind of people she'd have to deal with, they'd eat her up! What can you do, there were certain situations when a woman needed a man at her side. And yet, on the other hand—Seefeld.

Seefeld! The name alone was enough to balance the stakes, and it didn't take much. If she could only find someone to work with . . . someone she could trust, who also wanted to make a few bucks on the side . . . and thus, one hot morning in early May, Dvora Saltzman found herself bouncing in the Zinman's Ibiza with her new partner, none other than her nephew, Fat Tuvia, on the dirt road leading to the Mandy Line workshop.

B.

"I'll tell you the truth, kind sir: I don't want to lower your underwear. On the contrary. Allow me to speak frankly—I *want* you to make a profit off me, it's in *my* best interest—I want you to have dollar signs ringing in your eyes, like in those Mickey Mouse cartoons, if you've seen them. You'll ask—why? Good question. So here's my answer: my philosophy is that if my wholesaler is happy, I'm happy. It's well known that a satisfied wholesaler doesn't pull any dirty tricks, and I certainly don't have to tell you, or my aunt here—a business owner herself—that there's nothing more important than trust. If we make a deal—and I hope we can find an arrangement that works for all of us—we won't check up on you every other day. We work together, not against each other. Hand in hand."

Mendel fixed Tuvia with a look of amazement. How old was this goddamn chubby calf, teaching him a chapter in commerce laws? Twenty-three? Twenty-four? And already he had a wheeler-dealer air about him, like some old kibitzer. . . . A few days ago he got a call from this Tzippi Zinman—the name sounded familiar, God knows where from—who said she was sending over her son with an interesting offer. And now this guy was stuck in the middle of his office with his aunt, a handsome woman, actually, the kind of ass that put you in the mood, trying to convince him—Mendel Cohen, who wasn't new to the textile business, as we know—to sell him surfing pants for four shekels a piece!

"Let me explain to you why you should sell it to us for four. Look, Mendel—can I call you Mendel?—look at us: we're serious people, not some trash off the street. We're not playing with shit—we have a concession for the stalls at the water park starting in late June. You know what that means? It means you'd better start counting that money now, because you'll be too busy later. Five thousand people every day, at least three days a week; families, women, children—we're talking about a gold mine here, and you're making a big deal about one shekel more or less? Listen, Mendele, if not for my mother's recommendation, I'd have gone to another manufacturer. Why do we need to drag ourselves all the way to Kiryat Arye? We don't have enough sewing workshops in Florentin? Is Herzl Street all out of tricot? Kind sir, manufacturers are like flies, no offense, God forbid. Right, aunty?"

"Right, right," Dvora quickly confirmed.

"But—I have a theory that people matter too, not only merchandise. And I prefer to work with someone who comes with recommendations. Long story short, you heard our offer—now the ball's in your court. I say a person has to think big—never do petty bookkeeping," the young philosopher theorized. "Got any cookies?"

Mendel pulled a nondescript aluminum package from the small cabinet below the sink and tossed it on the table. Fat Tuvia took a wafer, dipped it in the black coffee and chewed slowly. "Great wafers," he announced, and devoured another one before wiping his mouth with his fingers. "So, what do you say, boss?" Tuvia asked, lowering his eyes to his chest and brushing off the crumbs.

"Eight shekels, not an agora less."

"Eight shekels?" Tuvia chuckled. "Aunt Dvora, get your purse, we're going to Beit Romano." And to underscore the severity of the situation he sucked the remains of the coffee loudly and banged the cup to the table.

"You're skinning me!" Mendel Cohen growled. "Take it for seven! Nothing less, no discussion."

"Four."

"Lady, instead of driving honest people crazy, why don't you take him to the ear doctor? Can't you hear me? I said seven."

"Four for a shirt, five for pants."

"Get out of here right now, or I'll call the police! This is private property!"

"Say, Mendel," asked Fat Tuvia. "Where do you buy these wafers?"

"I said six fifty!" the owner fumed, banging his fist against the table; spit sprayed from his mouth, his nose reddened and dripped with sweat—but it was no good; the guy didn't lose his cool. Dvora, on the other hand, was quite embarrassed. She was used to affable cosmetics agents who never came to shouts or threats. If this is what the fashion world had in store for her, she thought, perhaps she was better off quitting now, while she still could, going back to her perfumery and settling for what she had. On the other hand—Seefeld. Even if they bought the items for six fifty, they'd still make a huge profit: they could sell each shirt for twenty, twenty-five, and the pants for as much as thirty. The truth was, she had to admit to herself, you don't do business with professors. If not this Mendel, they'd have to find another Mendel, and no one was promising her the other one would be any kinder. She needed to be patient. There were plenty of ways to a salesman's heart; his rage attested that an ember of greed was still smoking within him and might ignite. But suddenly that fear popped up: what if they wouldn't be able to get rid of the merchandise?

The dull rattle of the sewing machine that had suddenly grown sharp pulled her out of her reveries—one of the workmen opened the door and said they were about to finish printing the Shazar School uniform set and asked what to do next. How many times did he tell them to fold the shirts and pack them up in tens! Mendel roared; his workers were a group of degenerates who couldn't get anything into their thick skulls, Mendel explained with a bark, and for dessert he expelled the worker. Now that he'd released some of his bitterness, he was relieved.

"Sir, Madam, I wish I had the privilege of sitting with you here till nighttime. But this is a business, as you can see—I'll have you know the only reason I haven't sent you away until now is because you seem like decent people. After all, we're all Jews—we sit down, we haggle, we turn up the pressure—why not? We do what we can, which is just what we should. But let's be real. I'm going to explain something, Tuvia: I'm not blaming you, God forbid—you're young, you think life is a game; for you, what's four shekels, five shekels—just words. But you, Miss Dvora, you look like a girl who has some experience. You must know that every manufacturer has his bottom line. I can't go any lower than six. Understand where I'm coming from—I have to finance my workers, buy materials, pay taxes . . ."

He rolled the last two words on his tongue slowly, regretting to part with them. The insinuation did not escape the cosmetician's ears.

She lowered her voice. "And if we pay under the table?"

"I'm an honest man and a tax-paying citizen, if you don't mind. But some buyers *prefer* to pay cash . . ."

"Excellent," said Fat Tuvia. "I happen to be one of those buyers. I don't ask you and I don't care what you do with the money. You can use it to make decorations for your sukkah for all I care. I have a motto: I pay it, I forget it. Five a piece?"

"Done," Mendel acceded. "One payment, no returns."

"Sure." Tuvia nodded with greatness of spirit.

In good time the parties had reached their agreement, and to celebrate Mendel Cohen opened a chilled bottle of Coca-Cola. Dvora was very pleased: thanks to her, the crisis had been averted! As it turned out, she had a few tricks up her sleeve too, and she could definitely teach Fat Tuvia a thing or two about commerce conduct. They chatted about the recession, about the rise in prices and about Margaret Thatcher, who had just celebrated a decade in office. In short, suspicion was replaced with good will, and Mendel Cohen invited his new customers to come onto the production floor and take a look at the samples.

It was nearing noon. The large windows of the production floor were wide open. The sunlight that streamed through them drew glowing squares on the concrete floor. Two ceiling fans, cobwebs trembling between their wings, screeched cyclically in their futile attempt to fight off the heavy heat. On the way to the warehouse, they passed several Arab workers who were sewing sleeves by a large machine. Further on was another worker—the one who had entered the office earlier, it seemed—sorting T-shirts. The large, empty hall stood deserted. Here and there were a few time-swept items: a giant iron desk, a crooked chair, some printing meshes leaning against the wall. Mendel Cohen led them into a stuffy room smelling of acidic chemicals, in which large sacks were piled. He pulled out some shirts and urged his guests to feel the merchandise.

The cheeriness that had awoken earlier in Dvora's heart was marred at once: the seams were unraveling, the fabric cheap and itchy, the prints tasteless. She had been standing on the doorstep of a glorious world that was now guffawing at her from a toothless mouth. She was gripped by an intense desire to return to her familiar grindstone, the perfumery, and to hell with Seefeld. Fat Tuvia, on the other hand, expressed immense satisfaction—he praised Mandy Line's products with enthusiasm and asked to see samples of the famous surfing pants. At this stage, he said, they'd take thirty items of each kind for a trial run. When they were smarter, they'd return to make a larger order. The kid still knew a thing or two, Dvora thought. No doubt he'd inherited the Zinmans' commercial sense. Why not trust him? Now, when they'd reached such a good deal—what would it look like if she got up and called it all off? What would Tzippi think? You try to help her, and she throws it all to hell like some nut case. It was time to face reality: the world was changing. One by one, the old stores on Judah the Maccabee Street were closing down, and in their place sprung up all those glitzy stores charging outrageous prices. Everyone around her was buying and selling, buying and selling. And where was she? When she was little, they'd give her a task each night: to stack the coins in the cash register in columns of ten. She was sure if she got a round sum, it meant the next day would be a lucky one for the perfumery, but now, who knows. . . . Maybe she had to take a chance, to break out, like Tzippi. And maybe . . .

Who knows where our friend would have arrived in her reveries had Fat Tuvia not patted her shoulder gently: "We have to pay."

She apologized and removed a stack of notes bound with a rubber band from her purse. Under the watchful eyes of her nephew, she counted three hundred shekels. To make sure, she flipped through the notes and counted them again, and then passed the stack over to Mendel Cohen, who in turn counted them himself. They shook on it. The owner called one of the workers over, and once the sacks of merchandize were loaded into the car, his two new partners said goodbye and went on their way.

Again the dirt paths, again the potholed road, this time in the opposite direction—from the forgotten nowhere to the multilane avenue, from the poor cheap stock warehouses to the store windows of the metropolis. They hardly said a word during the ride. On Jabotinsky Street, by the Elite chocolate factory, they got caught in a traffic jam. Fat Tuvia opened a bag of pretzels and placed it between them. The heat wave painted everything yellow. The air conditioning vents spewed puffs of air that heated the car more than they cooled it. When they opened the windows they were stifled by the stench of motors mixed with the steaming asphalt. Tuvia took a handful of pretzels, looked for something good on the radio, despaired and turned it off, honked a little to express his protest, and eventually leaned back in his seat, resigned, and began ruminating.

"We screwed him over good, huh, Ciotka?" he finally said.

C.

"Do you have any idea what time it is?! What took you so long?"

When she walked in, Shraga surreptitiously folded the newspaper—he'd spent the last twenty minutes immersed in a puzzle in the leisure section—and tossed it under the counter. Behind his head a small fan rotated, each time hitting the side of the closet where it vibrated stubbornly for a long moment until finally accepting the verdict and turning back with a moan. The air conditioner wasn't working—since it broke in late October they kept putting off fixing it, trying to save the money and convincing themselves that summer would come late this year. A measure of chill was maintained only thanks to the eternal gloom of the store.

"What do you think we did, go out for ice cream?" Dvora put the sacks down. "We've been working hard, closing a deal with Tzippi's manufacturer—he isn't an easy man, but wait till you hear the fantastic terms we got. Then we had to check the *goods* one by one (there's no denying she enjoyed flaunting her new jargon), and to top it all off, we got stuck in a heck of a traffic jam on Jabotinsky Street. There's your 'What took you so long!'"

"You could have stopped at the pay phone and called to say you'd be late. You know what was going on here?"

"What, clients?" A glimmer of hope.

"What clients are you talking about?" Shraga furrowed his brow and waved his hand as if swatting a fly. "Bina got into trouble again. I'm warning you, Dvora, I'm getting tired of this—with all due respect, I married you, not your sister. There's a limit to what you can ask me to endure. I'll remind you that I'm an insurance agent, not a social worker. If it goes on this way I'll just put her in an asylum, no question about it."

"What a hero, practically Samson . . ." his wife muttered. "Where is she now?"

It turned out that at some point during the day, Bina had gotten fed up with watching Educational Television and asked for permission to go "do some work." She said Hachimian from the stationery store promised to let her arrange the pens by color, and since his store was, as we know, only three doors down from the perfumery, Shraga saw no reason to object. He thought she'd stay there for an hour or two, flip through the European magazines she liked, maybe even get a free notepad or pencil case, a gift from the owner. How could he have known that as she sat there, sorting through the pens, Bina sold the guy a sob story—that she was hungry, that she wasn't being fed at home, that no one heeded her begging? At any rate, she managed to kindle the pity of Uri Hachimian—who could never bear the sight of tears, especially on someone like Bina—and he ordered her a pecan pie from Café Alexander. Obviously, he had no idea what he was doing; within thirty minutes her pain began and grew worse with each moment, until finally Bina ran home, scared, waving her arms; the entire street watched. Now she was sitting in her room, refusing to calm down, screaming that her stomach was burning and calling Dvora's name over and over.

"Did she get the *sratchke*, too?"

"Believe me, that's the last thing I wanted to check."

Even in the stairwell, dragging the sacks of clothing upstairs, she thought she could smell the sickening, familiar odor, and tried to push away the image of the pale excrement that was always associated with the smell. She opened the door. The tortured sobs turned into bitter weeping. Bina fell into her arms, trembling; there was no one dearer to her than her eldest sister, and as much as she was relieved to see her, she was also plagued with regret for having disobeyed her. Thank God, Dvora thought as she held her close, promising that no one was mad at her, no need to wash the clothes, she hadn't had an accident. They hugged for a while longer. Dvora rubbed her sister's head and mumbled soft words into her ears. The effect was truly wondrous, as if she absorbed the shock of Bina's large, ungainly body: the well of tears dried, the quick breathing slowly settled, a little smile appeared on those lips. Dvora pushed back the hair that clung to her sister's forehead. "Wait a minute," she said and dragged in one of the sacks. "Choose a shirt. A gift!"

There was a pot of goulash in the fridge, but the cosmetician preferred to chop some vegetables and make a cold, light meal; she wasn't hungry for anything more. In the meantime, Shraga closed the store and came upstairs for his afternoon rest. He went out to the service balcony and looked outside, his sunken chest bare and his scarecrow legs poking out of his wide tennis pants. The sky that was revealed to him was yellowish, stifling, as if the exhausted city had been covered by a heavy old blanket. Hints of the awaiting outbreak were already in the air. "You'd better take down the laundry, there's going to be a downpour," he recommended. After he glanced over at the neighbors beyond the back yard, he came back inside and got a drink.

"Come on, Shraga, how many times do I have to tell you not to open the fridge barefoot!"

"What are you worried about? Insurance, we've got. Worst case scenario, you'll be a wealthy widow." He chuckled and pinched her behind. "A knockout like you won't be alone for long."

"Oh, the nonsense you talk." Dvora pulled away and the knife flew out of her hand and landed at his feet. "You'll really make a widow out of me if you keep pulling these stunts while I work."

"Hey, don't we have any soda?"

"How should I know, look for yourself. Maybe Bina finished it. Have some water."

"I have horrible heartburn, I'm dying for some soda." Shraga sighed and wore a mask of grievance, pressing below his diaphragm with three fingers.

"What do you want from me? Have some milk."

"That doesn't help."

"Okay, go rest with your book until the food's ready."

Shraga added another moan, as an encore, and padded over to the dining table. He'd always been considered a "wasted mind" among his family members; his assessments, especially in political matters, were heeded with attention. He gained this status thanks to his great fondness for thick historical texts. Now he pulled out a volume of Churchill's war journals and delved in. Lunch was quickly set before him: salad, rolls, yogurt, herring with onions and a runny omelet, as was the custom at the Saltzmans'. The soft-boiled egg placed in front of Bina's seat was left untouched. The patient had fallen asleep in her room.

"Surprise!" Shraga announced as his wife sat down to the table. "A letter from Tuvia!"

"Why didn't you say anything! Let me read it!"

But Shraga preferred to read it out loud, with pomp. The sender, as was his habit, wrote in moderation: the letter was moderately practical, moderately heartfelt, moderately demanding; far from providing all the details Dvora was yearning to know, it did not leave its recipients in the dark, either. Dvora listened the way a hungry person collected cake crumbs with a moist finger, making sure not to miss even the tiniest bit. She sighed unintentionally; her longing for her son made her physically ache. There was a photo in the envelope as well. She took off her glasses, tilted her head, as usual, and brought it closer to her face. "That blue looks nice on him, doesn't it?"

Since he tended not to care for such things, Shraga made do with a small chirp, neither a confirmation nor a dismissal. He'd just stuffed his mouth with an oversized piece of bread and had to ball it industriously inside the pocket of his skinny cheek. Dvora put the photo back in the envelope and carefully folded in the tab.

"Don't you want to know how things went in Kiryat Arye?"

"Bah-ha whaaat?" her husband mumbled.

From time to time the events of our lives are revealed most clearly only in retrospect, after the evasive liquid of action has been poured into the clear glass bottles of language. As she laid out the events of that morning to her husband, all of Dvora's doubts slowly evaporated. The business she entered with a doubtful heart suddenly appeared as full of wonderful promise, and she, who was wise enough to recognize the opportunity, would know how to make the most of it. Turned out she knew a thing or two about business and was unhesitant to take on all sorts of characters, fighting them with their own weapons and coming out ahead. She got up, opened one of the sacks and, blushing with pride, presented Shraga with a few pairs of surfing pants.

"*Nu*, and you think we're going to get something out of this garbage?"

If he at least had yelled, she could have raised her voice too, combative, persuasive; but the words just dropped out of his mouth with incidental, awful weakness.

"It's very nice merchandise for five shekels, isn't it?" Dvora's face fell.

"How much did we pay for this, total?"

"Three hundred, and it'll make us at least four times that much." With all her might she fought to drown the twitching of her hesitation, to choke it down before it rose back to the surface.

"Three hundred," Shraga repeated slowly. He lowered his head like an attorney who had just come across conclusive evidence. "She takes good money and she throws it away. Here, right on this table"—he pointed with his fork—"is a letter from her son, and she takes good money and throws it straight to hell."

"Fat Tuvia says we'll sell it all next week, there's a fashion sale at the Last Chance club."

"Tell me just one thing—if your manufacturer is such a gold mine, why doesn't Tzippi keep him to herself? Maybe she's just tossing you a bone so she can later make a big fuss about it, telling the whole world what a good sister she is? I say: no, thank you. My wife's honor is worth more than that."

"But she made Tuvia a partner."

"*Nu*, another great businessman. You know what? I'll cut you some slack: let's say she has only good intentions and that the business will bring in a few bucks. Why not? There's always a chance. But half of it will go to Fat Tuvia, anyway. So I ask you: what do you need this headache for?" He lingered a little, allowing the defense time to object. "Listen to me, Dvoraleh. Tzippi's a firecracker, no argument there. And besides, she's been in this business for a while—your sister can sell people their own dirty underwear! But let me ask you—since when have *you* become such a fashion expert? That's life, each business requires talent; some people are born with it. But pushing your way in by force—that's no good. I'd rather you stayed at the perfumery. Listen to your husband for once: your big eyes will bring us nothing but trouble."

"When will you change your tune?!" Dvora cried. "Maybe, instead of sitting on your ass all day long and criticizing me, you'll make a suggestion of your own. Where do you think the money's going to come from?"

"Money, money, money, that's all you ever think about." Shraga took the deep breath of a man overflowing with suffering, stretched, cleared his throat, and sank back. "Enough with all this pressure. What can you do if the entire economy is in recession? Things work out. Pass the feta, please."

Tears rose in Dvora's eyes. She fixed her husband with a grudging look—the no-good bum, gobbling food like a pig, not even noticing the crumbs clinging to the curly hairs around his pale nipples. "If things work out for us, how come we never go abroad?"

"We went to Marseilles." Shraga smiled mercifully.

"Marseilles, Marseilles. With all due respect, Shraga, a lot of water has flowed through the Yarkon since then. I want to go to Seefeld for once, too."

"Very good. Now everything is clear—your sister's been putting ideas in your head."

"Enough about my sister!"

"The Zinmans go to Seefeld, and you say amen," he insisted.

"You're full of it."

"You're even willing to demean yourself as a *shmattes* seller," he said.

"Don't use your fingers," she said, handing him a toothpick.

"I'll bet you, Dvoraleh, that this won't work, this new business you've gotten yourself into. It's better to take the money and throw it out the window. Besides, who do you think is going to tend to the perfumery when you're running around the water park? You know I help you as much as I can, but there's no way I'll give up my own business now with all the suicide bombings and the insurance business in revival. You want a vacation? That's what you need? Be my guest!" He pulled over the newspaper from one of the chairs, spread it open and slapped it with the back of his hand. "There you go, terrific offers: half-board at the Dead Sea, the Princess Hotel in Netanya—just say where you want to go and I'll take you."

A whisper, the slightest of rustles that had been secretly wafting into their conversation for several moments, suddenly demanded their attention.

"Damn! The laundry!"

The heat wave had finally broken. The air thickened with moist; the wind ran wild. Heavy, dusty drops tapped on the tin roofs of the rear balconies. Sweating, swearing, desperate, Dvora did her best to control the fluttering sheets. The clothes pins jumped out of her hands and fell to the yard below. One towel clung to the sooty wall, smudged. She threw the underwear quickly into a large pail without separating them, saving what she could. And then, when her task was almost complete, one pillowcase caught on a peg, and when she tugged at it, it ripped along the side, a coarse, irreparable tear. The rain lashed down, a puddle formed on the floor. She buried her face in the ruined pillowcase and cried.

D.

April 26, 1989

Dear Mom and Dad,

How are you and how is everybody? I'm guessing you're already preparing for the Independence Day picnic! We've been having a legendary spring here this year. I wish you could see it. Mom—you would love it. Everything's green and there are colorful flowers everywhere, everyone's out on the streets, a real celebration. Things are going really well for me at the university—Professor Olander might hire me as a research assistant. It isn't final yet, but it's been hinted that I've been chosen (out of seven other applicants!). It's not only a great honor, but it can help me get ahead. There's a slight chance I'll get a paycheck, but since I'm already getting a scholarship I don't think it's going to be anything significant. Maybe you can transfer me an extra thousand dollars? If you don't have it right now, maybe next month? It's really important. I'm going to Chicago in late May—there's a big biochemistry conference and it's important to show my face.

The picture is from a few days ago—five of us went fishing on Greg Manheim's parents' yacht (he's the tall guy holding the fish—that's a cod that isn't even considered very big here!). We had a barbecue with lots of beer and I even made Israeli salad! In spite of everything we hear about the situation in Israel, I still miss it—Boston is wonderful, but sometimes I just feel like hanging out on Frishman Beach with a Popsicle . . .

Love,

Tuvia

4

Double Bad Luck

A.

In the early 1950s, several families of means in Tel Aviv purchased lots to the north of Pardes Hadassah, right on the banks of the Yarkon River, and built two- and three-story buildings. Most of the apartments were sold for key money to artisans, small-time retailers, clerks, and other citizens wishing to save some cash and escape the crowdedness and noise of downtown. The new neighborhood quickly flourished; Judah the Maccabee was set as the main drag, and all along it emerged small buildings in close proximity planned with simple modernity. The owners, who were not very wealthy and needed an income, rented out the ground floor to business owners, and settled in on the second floor.

These pilgrims spared themselves no luxury: they installed state-of-the-art kitchens, bought trendy furniture, hung flashy chandeliers, and planted mandarin and loquat trees in their yards. Once their task was complete, they set reclining chairs on their balconies and sat down to watch the businesses below them. Some allowed them to run according to their own standards, while others visited the shops each day, taking an interest, asking questions—for the purpose of being seen and feared. Nathan Kuttner from Bialystok, Shamai Lachover from Odessa, Riva and Yehoshua Yakirevich—these are only a handful of the famous names that held a reign of terror over an entire community of tenants and renters.

At first things ran smoothly and legally, but as time passed, as is the way of the world, all sorts of agreements best left unspoken were made between the owners and their tenants—whether due to circumstances, whimsy, or simple negligence. Here a man sold his rights to a sublet-ter, there a merchant went bankrupt, here a successor appeared, there a store was expanded illegally. Just as the miniature tree whose branches the Japanese cut off again and again until it can do nothing but twist and bend, so too did the neighborhood's properties intertwine and grow a thicket of title deeds and crumbling notes doodled in codes and documents duplicated with purple copy paper and written contracts and oral contracts—in short, the wondrous corpus we call life.

Thus the people of Judah the Maccabee found themselves divided into camps—the property owner camp, the key money senior rent-ers camp, and the unprotected renters camp. There was one man, a wealthy barber, who was simultaneously part of both the owners' and the renters' camps: since he opened a barbershop in the basement of his building, he made sure, for tax purposes, to pay himself rent. An eternal hatred lay between members of the opposing camps: one old man, over ninety years of age, who lived up the street, held on for dear life in the hope of witnessing the death of a certain renter who had been stuck like a bone in his throat ever since the Sinai War. The protected tenants, on their part, used every trick in the book: one who allegedly ran a concession stand hadn't sold a single bottle of soda in five years, and in order not to lose his rights he made sure to open his business every morning, presenting a juicer and a few rotting carrots in a jar on the counter for the sake of appearances. Just imagine the landlord's displeasure as he saw his property chucked like a commer-cial carcass while it could have paid him a few thousands a month!

There was no shortage of schemes and intrigues on Judah the Maccabee Street—the reader may recall the harassment Yosef Zinman suffered over his grilled chicken—but beyond all struggles and back-stabbing and rejoicing in each other's failure, there loomed a mon-strous giant that made all of the petty tricks pale in comparison, a giant that cast fear over renters and landlords alike. This colossus, cruel and shrewd, filled all hearts with terror; the mere mention of its name was enough to spread panic and ignite bitter words. Those considered in the know advised their neighbors, in private, regarding means of preparation; stubborn people who failed to heed warnings and innocents who belittled its power all found themselves climbing the stairs to the gallows, paying the hangman's fees on their way. Because the neighborhood's residents, one and all, were connected through a complex web of business, each tug at one corner tightened the rope around the neck of those in the opposite corner. The individual's battle was destined to fail, and no choice was left but to rise above small conflicts at times of trouble and join forces against the tyrant.

On the morning of May 14, 1989, at 10:55, in spite of his age-old resentment toward all Zinmans, the latter having taken over the best of the three shops in his possession for two generations (and counting!) of key money—Old Nathan Kuttner burst into the grocery store, his eyes wide, his withered arms shaking as if possessed, and called at the top of his lungs:

B.

"The tax agents! At Yunger the butcher's!"

C.

On May 14, 1989, at 10:55 in the morning, Yosef Zinman was sitting in his regular spot behind the cash register, feasting on a container of sour cream and reading the newspaper: one of the three right-wing ministers explained his objection to recent peace talks. Fat Tuvia was serenely polishing the fridge doors. A random customer was searching through the dried fruit section. And then, just as the grocer reached over for another poppy-seed roll, the landlord burst in, wearing a plaid shirt that was too big for him (Zinman took note that the man had been shrinking before his eyes in recent months, an interesting phenomenon that might have ramifications for his own business), his eyes wide, his withered arms shaking as if possessed, and called at the top of his lungs:

"Tax agents! At Yunger the butcher's!"

The grocer sat up at once, tossed the sour cream into the trash, wiped away crumbs from the counter with his hand, and tucked the ends of his shirt in, as if preparing for a surprise visit from the Department of Health. "Tuvia! Tuvia!" he called, "an attack!"

"Where?" the customer cried, trying to hide behind the soft drinks shelf.

"Ma'am, out!" Zinman ordered. "The raisins are on the house. Let's go!" And just to be safe, he typed a sale for the amount of 2.60 into the cash register, ripped out the receipt, and stuffed it into her hand on her way out.

"Don't ask, looks like Yunger is screwed," Old Kuttner chirped with excitement. "They found dollars in his store."

Yunger the Butcher—formally a butcher indeed—also dealt in foreign currency. In addition, he allowed Yosef Zinman to use the backroom of his butcher shop to store a stock of oil bottles, coffee cartons, and other goods the grocer bought (no receipts) from the suppliers on De Picciotto Street as scalping goods in the next wave of inflationary pricing.

"Did they look in the back?"

"No, no, they're sitting with him, looking at the cash register strips. Listen, Yosef, are our affairs in order? I don't want any surprises."

Another important piece of information: though legally, Zinman, as a protected tenant, transferred an insulting monthly fee of ninety-five shekels to Kuttner, he in fact paid him a few extra hundreds for the right to use the building's basement as storage space for cleaning supplies. Old Kuttner wasn't a fan of receipts—if he wasn't making a profit from the store, let him at least make a reasonable profit from the basement—but for the sake of propriety he agreed to doodle, as a replacement, payment confirmations in code (05/89 Z – 600 S → N.K. On Acc. Base.).

"There's tax agents over at Yunger's!" Peretz came in, having passed by the butcher's shop on his way back from a delivery.

"Yeah, yeah, we already know that," the grocer reprimanded him. "Instead of standing around like a putz, go peek out the small window, and if you see them finding our stock, come back on the double and tell me." In truth, there was no need for a guard, but Yosef preferred to send the fool away, lest he divulge some sensitive information around the investigators. The grocery store was close to the butcher's shop, and he knew his turn would come soon. And indeed, within five minutes two faded men walked into the store: one tall, big-nosed, gloomy; the other—a guy with small eyes and wooly hair, a pack of cigarettes sticking out of the pocket of his white shirt. Zinman winked at his son, who stood at attention in the inner room of the store. The excitement was immense, the concerns—enormous.

As fate would have it, the two spies sent that morning to tour Judah the Maccabee Street were among the junior, less prominent clerks of the district, a couple of miserable, ambitionless nothings that went together like two gray, tattered cotton gloves. The victims, having trouble relating such wretchedness to the authorities, interpreted it as a sign of hidden, even demonic powers. Occasionally, the spies even landed a subject whose terror and confusion caused him to confess his sins willingly. Nathan Kuttner, unable to control his curiosity, stood by the cookie shelves and pretended to examine a box of cookies. The tall investigator gave his partner a meaningful look, the look of a man who had come into treasure; there you go, colleague: an elderly, helpless—perhaps even demented—client: easy prey for fraudulent grocers and tax evaders.

"Can I help, gentlemen?" Yosef Zinman asked.

"Thank you, we're all right," the wooly one hastened to reply. As he pretended to check the dates printed on the jam jars, his small eyes cast a sidelong glance toward Kuttner. His partner (who took an alleged interest in canned sardines) also paid careful attention to the worn elderly man, full of expectation for the man's purchase. They were both certain that the grocer wouldn't go to the trouble of typing the sale into the register, and so, if they were lucky, they could catch him evading taxes and jacking up prices all at once. But the old man, sent by the devil, took his time. A stranger happening into the store at those moments might have thought he'd accidentally stumbled into a library: everyone standing silently at shelves, engrossed in the products with expressions of immense erudition.

"These filled cookies are excellent—I'd get the strawberry kind if I were you," the wooly one said after several minutes, in hopes of persuading Kuttner.

"The price is good, too," his partner added, as if sharing a secret.

"I hate strawberry," Kuttner announced with an expression he used for late-paying tenants and turned his back on them. Seeing how the hopes they had for the fake customer were extinguished, the big-nosed investigator tried a different tack. "Do you make sandwiches here?" he asked.

Here we go, Yosef Zinman thought. Now he was being tricked: they pretend to be hungry and purposely ask for something that doesn't have a price tag. In his thirty-five years as a grocer he never had a tax investigator come in and ask, say, for a bottle of wine or a bag of rice—formally packed products with fixed prices and documented histories. They'd ask for things like "a few olives," a piece of cheese, two to three pieces of herring and the like—products with no fixed price that existed on the margins of organized commerce; since their price was contingent on the grocer's discretion, they could tempt him toward criminal behavior.

"We do."

"What have you got?"

"Pastrami, salami, yellow cheese. You can get it on a roll or in a pita."

"Can I have pastrami on a sesame roll?" the big-nosed undercover agent asked, trying to outsmart him.

"Why not? Talk to my son." Zinman gestured toward Tuvia. "Tell him exactly what you want and he'll make it for you."

The station where they sliced the cheese included a rotting wooden bureau with shelves stacked with rubber bands, yahrzeit candles, wax paper—the poor relatives you have to invite to your event but prefer to seat at a side table. The bureau was topped with a marble plate, yellowing from years of service, on which stood two appliances: a hand-operated cheese cutter, another remnant of our founders' times, and a modern electric meat cutter bought in the days of the big renovation. From time to time an orange drizzle trickled out—the paprika-laden pastrami juice accumulating in the draining pocket. The cheese cutter didn't drizzle, but it sprayed cheese shavings that mashed together and stuck to it. And so, though they wiped and cleaned the equipment each morning and each night, the station was forever oily.

"You want mayonnaise, sir?"

"Sure. Let me have a pickle, too."

Fat Tuvia sliced the pickle into circles and arranged them carefully along the sliced roll. Then, as a mother tucking her babies in their crib, he gently layered the slices of pastrami on top and returned the seeded top of the roll to its place. Finally, just to put his heart into it, he pressed down lightly on the sandwich. "Enjoy!" he announced, handing the sandwich over with fanfare.

"Thanks," said Big Nose, whose stomach was grumbling. "You're a lifesaver."

"Maybe I'll take something too?" the other investigator thought out loud. "I wouldn't mind a sandwich like that—we have a long day ahead of us."

But before Big Nose had a chance to bite into his roll, Tuvia slapped his own forehead, yelped, uttered some popular curse directed at himself, and flew out in a panic.

"What's wrong with him?" Big Nose wondered, turning to the owner.

"Diarrhea," Yosef Zinman said calmly. "It's the fourth time this morning." An instinctive, paternal—and no less so, commercial—urge awoke in the grocer's heart, to make up some lie and cover for Tuvia, though he had no clue why he'd run out like that. Big Nose glanced sadly at his meal and asked if Yosef could pack it for him for later, and the wooly guy, who'd lost his appetite but not his desire, consoled himself with a blueberry Popsicle he found in the freezer.

"How much is it, boss?" the first investigator asked, pulling out a wallet that was no less tattered than himself. To his disappointment, Zinman reached for the cash register. "We don't need a receipt," the wooly man hastened to add with a purple mouth.

"Good sir," Zinman began, taking a deep breath and stretching himself to full capacity, "you and your friend are new customers here—I don't know you and I don't know what kind of people you are. It's certainly possible that *you* don't need a receipt, but that doesn't matter to *me*. As far as I'm concerned you can throw it out or frame it and hang it on the wall—that's none of my business. Just let me print it out. *I'll* do my part, and you can call me a sucker for all I care. Go ahead, it makes no difference to me. Shall I tell you why, gentlemen? Because I was born in this country, and it's dear to me! How are we supposed to finance the army? How can we pave the roads? How will we pay for our children's education? What will we use to support those less fortunate (he pointed discreetly at Peretz, who stood by the salt and sugar shelves, picking his nose)? Here is your answer: with this little receipt that I'm about to print. Four thirty for the sandwich, two for the Popsicle." He swirled his finger through the air and landed the receipt on the register's keys with fanfare.

But the moment the drawer popped open, the patriot paled and shrank: a small note peeked out from one of the compartments. The note was always there, presenting only one number—the total of under-the-counter proceeds last counted. The number had nothing to do, of course, with the sum appearing on the receipt strip, and might have raised some serious questions. How could he have forgotten?

On the other side of the counter, another person of interest pretended to wait his turn—Nathan Kuttner, who'd disguised himself as a cookie enthusiast, was now proceeding toward the counter, holding a tower of cookie boxes of all shapes and colors. The old landlord realized the severity of the situation immediately. He couldn't have known, of course, what the grocer found in the drawer that scared him so, but his self-involvement made him feel positive that it was one of those questionable notes—Z – 600 S → N.K.—etc. There was no time to think—this was the time to act.

"Help! My heart!" he cried, dropping the cookie boxes all around him loudly and patting his chest with a trembling hand. The two investigators rushed to his aid. At that very moment, Zinman grabbed the incriminating note, stuffed it in his mouth and swallowed. By the time they seated Kuttner on a stool and gathered the boxes that were rolling around on the floor, he'd managed to drink some water and sounded a horrific belch. The assessment clerks, whose mission was now hopeless, revealed their identity, and to retain a fragment of the authorities' honor, demanded to review the supply certificates. The counter was soon covered with dozens of pages: order logs from dairy farms and bakeries, payment postponement approvals, credit for defective goods and what not, all numbered and accounted for and clear and legally signed. After thirty minutes of examination, they concluded that they would find no salvation here; they thanked the assessee for his cooperation and the tasty sandwich, pleaded with Kuttner to take care of himself, and headed to the stationery store across the street.

D.

The whole thing would be over in an hour and a half, two hours tops. No matter. In a few minutes she'd order steaming hot coffee, just the way she likes it, and a little something sweet on the side. No reason to make a big deal, even though this wasn't how it was supposed to go, even though they promised her—and that was the only reason she agreed to even get herself in this mess!—that she wouldn't be left alone. Promises, promises. And indeed, in a way you could say she'd been abandoned—though not out of malice, of course, just bad luck. These things happened—how could you blame Fat Tuvia? He only meant well. The moment he remembered what he hadn't considered before, the moment he realized the sizeable danger, he bolted out of the grocery store—miraculously without getting run over as he crossed Judah the Maccabee—and ran for dear life to the perfumery, burst in and shouted, "Hide the goods!" then stumbled and crashed to the floor. A twisted ankle, they found out later. And to think, it was all for nothing—the sacks of clothes were hidden upstairs in her apartment! That's all she needed, to be stashing black market merchandise in the perfumery. And now what? *He* was lying at home, his ankle swaddled in ice-water compresses, everyone lauding his heroism, while *she* was at the club, among these crass peddlers, her heart quivering.

She did her best to make her stall look appealing: she folded the shirts neatly, just like at a store, and piled the pants by color. She was excited at first, having created a pattern in the chaos. But just then, folded and smoothed, her goods were revealed to her again in all their

non-glory: the sloppy sewing, the cheap fabric, the blurry prints . . .
she was plagued with shame. How had she let herself get dragged into
this? She only hoped she wouldn't run into anyone she knew . . .

Tzippi had saved her a central spot from which she could see the
entire arena. There, for example, was the stall belonging to the old lady
with the cataract—it had neither pomp nor circumstances; though the
club's doors had only opened twenty minutes ago, it was already in dis-
array. Her watches—plastic or cheap metal—were presented in crumpled cardboard boxes with misleading names such as *Sacio* and *Switch*.
Other watches didn't even warrant a package, and they were attached
with wire to a perforated piece of cardboard. The table was covered
with fake snakeskin cigarette holders, heavy gasoline lighters, and other
kitschy accessories. This meagerness awoke a sympathy, even a kind of
motherly compassion in Dvora Saltzman's heart. In spite of herself, she
began feeling resentment and suspicion toward other, more industrious
peddlers. She was especially deterred by the Pekinese-looking jeweler
who smoked incessantly and told disgusting jokes.

"Are you new here?" A short man with unkempt curly hair, already
known to our readers, addressed her.

"I'm Dvora, Tzippi Zinman's sister."

"Nice to meet you! What do the kids say these days? It's an
honor!" The man was excited. "I'm Nachliel Zarfaty from Paloma
Bianca. You've been here before, right?"

"I was here four months ago, I came to help my sister with
the models. Actually, I own a business uptown." Normally, Dvora
Saltzman wouldn't dream of having a conversation with a man like
him, but now she felt an urge to impress him, to make friends—and
simultaneously to distinguish herself, to set her position several tiers
above him, to make it clear that, though he was destined to an eternity
of peddling, she was only passing through.

"In the T-shirt industry?"

"God forbid!" His question was—obvious even, considering the
goods on her table—but still slightly insulting. "The beauty industry."

"You didn't have to tell me," he complimented her. "I could tell.
So what, you've decided to check out our business, or are you selling

on behalf of your sister? Excuse my curiosity." He came closer to her stall, pulled a pair of surfing pants from one of the piles, stretched the waistline and examined the lining as if he were an animal skinner. Then he fingered one of the shirts and read the label. "Mandy Line." He jutted out his lower jaw and nodded, clearly impressed. "Never heard of it."

"The guy is very strong with a younger clientele." In a way, this wasn't a lie, considering the hundreds of school uniforms she saw on the shelves of the factory in Kiryat Arye. She added that the stall was actually run by her nephew, an up-and-coming entrepreneur representing different surfing and youth fashion manufacturers. She was only the investor, she explained, and had her nephew not sprained his ankle, Zarfaty would have met him today. Her words seemed to have satisfied the little peddler; once he realized this stall posed no threat to his own, he found it in his heart to dispense some advice. "Can I tell you something?" he asked rhetorically. "No offense, but this merchandise isn't exactly Yves Saint Laurent; you don't have to make such a neat table. On the contrary—you need a bit of mess, so the customers don't get scared off, you know what I mean? To give them an appetite." He grabbed some of the shirts that had been so carefully folded, and with a flourish, as if he were some French marquise, flipped them through the air and allowed them to land in a heap on the table, to the cosmetician's chagrin. "How much are you selling each item for? Twenty—twenty-five?" He fluffed the heap up, then pedantically pulled out a few sleeves. "I want you to charge an extra five shekels for each item. You couldn't do it before, but now people will pay."

"How is that possible?" Dvora wondered aloud.

"Before, it looked expensive and now it looks cheap. Like we always say, it's life experience."

And indeed, like God-sent proof, a woman of about thirty-five walked over to the stall, rummaged through the heap of rags, and pulled out two pairs of surfing pants—one with green, white, and blue horizontal stripes—the other with a wave print across the left thigh. "Sixty," Zarfaty said indifferently. The customer handed over three bills like it was nothing, and he sweetly ordered Dvora to give her a bag. Sixty shekels! For goods that cost ten! This was, then, the fashion world, Dvora Saltzman thought. Her quick mind already calculated the sums and added the difference. Her new friend seemed like a secret sage, a great expert of the commercial mind, and her gratitude made her compliment his ear off and offer to buy him a cup of coffee. Zarfaty vehemently refused the gesture—where would we be if we didn't help each other, he reprimanded her. As they spoke, another customer appeared. Zarfaty discreetly retired to his stall and winked to her behind the customer's back. Her heart filled with hope.

E.

The first pigeon is the most daring of them all. Her friends are still wandering lazily back and forth, but her small eyes have already noticed something happening in the corner, something unusual, and since in her life she's already had a chance to learn the most vital commercial principle—first come, first served—she heads to that corner and flutters to the ground. There awaits her a treasure trove: a stooped, elderly woman scattering bread crumbs from a paper bag, more and more, a cornucopia. Thus, the first pigeon has a privilege—the pick of the litter. She pecks around, pulling and releasing, grabbing and dropping, searching for a crumb meant just for her, a beautiful, round piece of bread. What pleasure! But her happiness is short-lived: two or three friends who've noticed her absence land next to her. They poke their heads back and forth suspiciously, their eyes widening: What's on the menu? What are we having? And you, my dear, what are you gorging yourself on, if we may ask? Oh, indeed. Bon appétit. Now, if you don't mind, we'll divide this treasure before the entire flock attacks. With each passing moment more and more pigeons gather, pouncing on the loot, skinny and fat, feathery and plucked. The crowdedness ignites their passion: claws are drawn, wings flap. Once in a while a cloud of feathers blooms—a war on some flake or the suffocating twitches of a pigeon crumpled under her friends' bodies. The ground is covered with a lively gray carpet of birds mad with greed; take over, swallow, grab anything you can, just get it before the others. More and more and more and more, until no crumb is left uneaten.

F.

The shoppers raided the stalls: trying on and snatching, trying on and snatching; some just snatched, without even trying on. Paloma Bianca ran out of their gypsy lace skirts. Mama Frumkin opened a new box of watches hidden under the table. Even Estee Creations was pleased thanks to one lady who bought a gigantic golden bracelet—one of the only pieces of jewelry in her box that had real value. The towel manufacturer sweated, a fat peddler of fish-scale belts almost collapsed. And only at Dvora Saltzman's stall—nothing.

"So? How's it going?"

"Lousy. Maybe 180 shekels."

"I can't believe it! You mean to tell me people weren't interested?"

Tzippi finally deigned to show her face; where the hell had she been all night? Yes, she was slaving over the fashion show: models, soundtrack, pantyhose rolling around on the ground behind the screen . . . Could she not find one free minute to even pass by the stall and give her sister a kind word? *Now* she wonders, *now* she's sorry. Another woman would have already stated unequivocally that Tzippi was playing dumb, that she'd convinced her to get into this questionable business just so she could humiliate her. "Barely. And those who came over to look didn't buy anything."

"So what? So that's why you're sitting here with a face like you're going to a funeral? This isn't like you, Dvoraleh, this mess. Tidy the clothes up a little. If they didn't buy before, they'll buy later. Don't worry: it always starts up again after the sing-along, all the cheapskates have second thoughts at the last minute and come back."

She had to admit she was a bit old-fashioned, her sister; the times of Mother Hinde's old methods had come and gone—scowling behind the counter, viewing the customer as the enemy, parting with the goods resentfully, as if some shortage was expected and the merchandise had to be distributed with care. We're on the brink of a new era. You have to keep your finger on the pulse; let the stall tempt them, let the face smile—we have, God willing, a lot to learn from the Americans. Someone had to explain all of this to Dvora.

"When do you think we'll be done here?"

"We can pack up in forty-five minutes. You feel like getting blintzes on Yirmiyahu Street afterwards?"

"No, I'm not in the mood today. I want to go home."

The crowd did return to the sales hall after the sing-along, but still avoided her stall. The poor cosmetician sat idly, her heart sour; she knew very well she mustn't, at all costs, disclose her distress, but she couldn't help it. She looked desperately at every shopper who crossed her path and sent a miserable, defeatist smile to anyone who looked back. Nachliel Zarfaty, half of his racks already swinging naked on their rails, sent her signals from afar, meant, probably, to cheer her up, but succeeding only in angering her. The old Frumkins packed up first, as usual. They took out sandwiches wrapped in moist paper napkins and sat down to dine. They kindly offered her bleached slices of a peeled apple, forcing her to smile politely. Then a woman walked by with her husband and bought two pairs of pants; another man rummaged and turned the whole pile over, finally buying a black tank top. Those forty-five minutes were unbearable. The last of the partygoers gathered at the doorway to exchange jovial words of parting; it was time to retire. Dvora Saltzman was filled with pep: she stuffed the items into their sacks, all tangled up, folded her chair, returned the empty mug to the bar—in short, did her best to leave no trace of her presence.

Who knows when the theft would have been revealed had Tzippi not asked her to break a 100 shekel bill. At first—surprise. They must have put the bag somewhere when they moved the chairs. She'd better retrace her steps. Then panic, running around, investigating and questioning her colleagues. Now everyone looked for the bag—a black leather bag with a logo of the letters L and C intertwined. The servers joined the search. Mama Frumkin recalled a similar event that had happened not long ago and ended well. They turned over the entire place, but for naught. And then: a misguided happiness. Good old Nachliel Zarfaty appeared with the lost item, found tossed behind a large plant. After that, the rummaging, the searching, the clanking

of buckles, the desperate zipping and unzipping, the insult, the insult
. . . the wallet, the checkbook, the keys. They even took the little silver
amulet. All Dvora had left, a mockery, was the three 100 shekel bills,
what little proceeds she had put in her pants pocket. The peddlers
were all shocked, asking what kind of world this was and what was
going to become of us, sighing, consoling, saying the most important
thing was health but thanking the lord silently for their good fortune—they'd gotten off scot-free. A whiff of camaraderie and shared
fate passed through them, then evaporated. The hour grew late, there
was nothing left to do, and they each went their separate ways.

G.

The way from the Arlozorov Train Station to Judah the Maccabee
isn't long, as we know, and can easily be made at night within six
to seven minutes. The blue Ibiza was almost alone on the road. The
spots of light shining from street lamps danced along the dashboard
and flew over the driver's thighs to the whispers of tires. The windows were partially open. Outside—a pleasant spring wind. Inside—a
thick, stifling gloom. Each movement, no matter how small, would
now be interpreted in the worst way possible. Any word out of her
mouth could create angry ripples. It was best to say nothing, though
it was hard not to glance to the right, at her sister. Curiosity is strong,
it's hard to withstand the urge to pick at the wound. On the side of
Haifa Road a chubby soldier raised his hand for a ride. Tzippi signaled
twice with her finger—a local ride. The gesture poked through the
thick soup separating the sisters, but the holes quickly filled again.

Dvora sat, clenched, staring at the moving lights. She felt like
slamming a door or shattering a vase. But she had neither door nor
vase, only this car she was trapped in. She glanced at her sister and
immediately turned away. The gaudy necklaces and the breasts stuffed
into a too-small bra enraged her. *I return home empty-handed and her
pockets are bursting.* Bits of images floated up insistently, not letting
go: Tzippi whispering with the Pekinese-nosed jeweler and laughing
loudly; the women pushing in line to reach Zarfaty's stall as if she
herself didn't exist—one being pushed back and overturning the juice

bottle on her counter; pink drops forming at the corner of old Frum-kin's mouth; the contents of her purse splayed on the table for all to see; the shame, the humiliation . . . as much as she was disgusted, she couldn't help but sink her head in the sewer again and again, diving in and then opening her eyes. With each dive she was repelled again by the futility, the deadening futility, sucking her in like a whirlpool. With great effort she managed to shake herself free, get some air, and pray she could scrub her memory clean, expunging this filth.

In the meantime, Tzippi's mind was filled with shiny cinch chairs, a server crossing the room in fast-forward, holding firecrackers wedged into champagne bottles in both hands, a drunk guest dancing the *kozachok*. Her face brightened when she remembered her great suc-cess: the club owner was extremely pleased with her, the stall renters paid their commissions without haggling, and not only that, but no one noticed that she'd cut some corners and hadn't bothered getting even one famous model. After deducting her expenses she was left with three hundred dollars, if not more; maybe she'd offer to split the loss with Dvora? No, she'd be offended. Three hundred dollars an evening—and that was nothing compared to the jackpot that was awaiting her at the water park! She remembered how she grabbed that franchise under Anita Shagrir's nose and smiled in spite of herself. Rumor had it Anita was furious; she could get mad all she wanted for all Tzippi cared. But she shouldn't endanger her good fortune—she'd pull no punches at the water park. Each day the most famous knock-outs would walk her catwalk. A chill ran through her: maybe she'd even be able to afford Tami Ben-Ami! Merchants would be waiting in line, paying whatever she asked for—who could pass up such a gold mine, four thousand people a day? It was time they paid. People said: the great Tzippi Zinman. People spit blood before they get a chance to hear such words! Hard work wasn't enough. One needed patience, too, kindness, alertness, the ability to grab an opportunity when it came your way. Not everything was served to you, warm on a plate, like some people liked to think.

She turned onto the winding road that twists beneath the Yarkon Bridge. She was in a rush, hoping Yosef hadn't forgotten to tape that night's episode of *Dynasty*. Pleased with the thought of her future profits, she pressed down on the pedal and enjoyed the speed.

Dvora's face became even darker and begrudging, her mouth still tightly shut. Here was the Adventure Park, with its slide and swings poking through the night like the skeletons of giant lizards; there were the thin, crooked pines, planted in earth so arid it seemed petrified; there was the surface of the putrid river, sparkling and still; and there was the small dock from which amateur fishermen tossed poisoned fish back into the water. She'd be home in three minutes. In three minutes she'd say goodbye to her sister—Tzippi could have offered to split the losses, just to be polite—and she'd soon be in the dark stairwell. She'd turn on the light, wipe her shoes on the tattered welcome mat, drag her sacks up three floors (she'd stop for a breather on the second floor), stand at the door, open her bag—then she'd remember her keys had been stolen as well and would have to ring the bell, wait for her husband to wake up, tell him what had happened, suffer as he swelled his bird-like chest and preached, "What did I tell you?" "What have you learned from this?" and, after he fell asleep, keep tossing and turning until three in the morning, praying Bina wouldn't wake up early the next day.

"We might not go to Seefeld with you after all," Dvora suddenly said, to her sister's utter surprise.

PART TWO

The Water Park

5

A Summer Day

A.

Five in the morning. The July sun lingers in the east. A last breeze rises from the sea, carrying over the sandstone cliffs and through the peaceful fields, at this early hour still retaining some of the chill of night. The dry plots are separated by bougainvillea in vivid purples, whites, oranges that glow with beauty as they move in the breeze. In the distance, the kibbutz homes are visible, along with a small, deserted soccer field bordered by a cluster of massive eucalyptuses shedding crackling scabs off their trunks. The vegetal scent mixes with the smell carried from the nearby cowshed—the earthy, not unpleasant smell of cow dung. The ground at the foot of the trees—death's door. Straw stalks, filthy bits of paper, a field mouse carcass, dry leaves reminiscent of the shells of dead fish. Here and there are beer bottle caps, left by snickering boys one night last summer. The few plants that were able to strike sorry, weak roots, are destined to a thirst whose outcome is known well in advance.

But lo, even here in the wilderness, life occurs in small scale: once in a while, one might notice a hushed rustle—an evasive motion ruffling the carpet of leaves. Chunky beetles, glistening dully, faltering on their short legs. A wandering wasp searching for something to do; downtrodden ants walking in a row, who knows from where and where to, carrying all sorts of finds on their backs. The thicket is small, the earth anguished, the livelihood scarce—but we manage. None of the ants, whose perception is limited, as we know, could guess that only a few feet away, behind the chain-linked fence blocked with sheets of blue raffia, lies another world, a man-made heaven: a fertile, flourishing land in which sugar crumbs roll aplenty and all bugs are well fed and content. The name of this land of marvels is the Water Park.

Five in the morning. The eyes of the kibbutz are still webbed with sleep. A light is switched on here; there, someone puts the kettle on or brushes his teeth. Three or four Kibbutz members trudge over to the dining hall. At this hour, one can still enjoy the lovely sounds of the countryside uninterrupted: small, sooty-faced bulbuls chirp enthusiastically, insects welcome the heat of day with industrious clicks, water sprinklers hum. The hum of an engine sounds in the distance—a tractor, or maybe a forklift, riding on a dirt path. From one of the small, modest houses in the center of the kibbutz emerges a not-so-young woman, heavyset, limping slightly. Sonya Yaakov wears an old shirt, wide gabardine pants zipped above the belly button, and black sneakers. She lights a cigarette, sways slowly until she reaches the little supermarket, where a large plastic bag awaits her, full of braided rolls. This arrangement has been the custom since the days when the pool served only the residents of Shfayim and neighboring kibbutzim and the guests of the kibbutz's small hotel. She bends down to pick up the bag, sighs and walks on.

The water park's entry gates are hidden within an architectural heap: the cashier's booth, the first aid hut, the bathroom shack, and other paltry structures. The woman enters the main snack bar through the back door. She scowls and hastens to open the window. The stench that had formed in the kitchen, along with the heat discharged from the fridges through the night, is unbearable. And then—the radio; morning chatter fills the space, creating all at once an atmosphere of hopeful bustle. Dirty bowls roll around in the sink. The sticky mess clinging to them—hummus or perhaps baba ghanoush—had grown hard and yellow. Sonya Yaakov clicks her tongue angrily, but the pleasant scent of the dish soap appeases her and she washes the dishes, collects rotting bits of food from the sink, polishes the stainless steel table—in short, establishes her motherly reign. It's almost six; in another ninety minutes, the bus of teenagers picking up trash with long pokers—nicknamed "ninjas" by the kibbutz—will arrive.

Later, she'll make them black coffee, but for now, she sits down at the table to peel cucumbers, open food cans, and separate slices of yellow cheese. She reaches into the bag and pulls out a chubby roll—her hand shaking lightly, for a moment the roll seemed to flop like a fish—and disemboweled it with a sharp knife. The soft white meat is revealed beneath the golden skin. One by one, she stuffs them full of yellow or Bulgarian cheese or tuna salad, dresses them with a slice of tomato or a stem of green onion, and wraps each roll with cling wrap. They seem like the most mundane of sandwiches, but like any other dish or stew she produces, they contain an extra flavor. The kibbutz experimented once: two substitutes were appointed to fill in for her and Sonya was asked to teach them her method. But the official taste test was a failure; in spite of her careful supervision, the ingredients failed to come together and form a delicacy, and in order not to hurt sales, the cook agreed to forego her summer vacation. Her sandwiches quickly became famous, and were snatched up by the hundreds even before the waterpark was erected. When a delegation of Soviet diplomats visited the kibbutz, Sonya Yaakov was appointed to supervise the refreshments served to them at the end of their ideological tour of the cowshed. Since they rushed off to a meeting in the city, the guests couldn't linger and dine, but the delegation's chairman, one Bogdanov, an emotional type who sensed her hurt, managed to snatch up a hard-boiled-egg sandwich. They heard later that he couldn't stop complimenting the taste all the way to Tel Aviv, and even insisted on stuffing a bite into the mouth of the national kibbutz secretary with his own fingers, so that he might enjoy it as well.

It's no wonder then that even back then, some saw the cook as an industry in and of herself. Sonya found herself unintentionally leading the innovators' movement—those wishing to "march the kibbutz into the new millennium." Things went like this: one of the members, a professor, having returned from a long stay in America, proposed an idea—building tall, American-style water slides. Many objected, claiming the risk was too big, the time wasn't right, the public was laden with the casualties in the Lebanon war, the crowds would trample the serene lawns, the camaraderie would be ruined.

Even the term *water park* didn't sit well with some of the founders. But the enthusiasts had the upper hand. They fenced in a piece of land, made a budget, called contractors. Each step, of course, involved ideological arguments and complex procedures, but eventually the bulldozers roared in.

Things were settled on the day of christening of the first pair of slides. The bean department coordinator, A. A. Gurke, who was the head of the opposing party, was persuaded to climb up first to the top of the slide wearing nothing but a bathing suit. All the kibbutz members gathered, nervous and tense around the tiny fiberglass wading pool at the end of the slide. When the signal was given, Gurke went on his way. A few moments later he landed safely, rejoicing, and asked for another go, right away.

The fates had spoken. One after the other, haphazardly, the large rides were installed. The original slides—with moderate inclines and no curves—were followed by the famous wave pool and the twisting kamikaze slides. The immense success softened even the loudest naysayers. They quickly grew accustomed to the park and the profit it yielded, and gladly fulfilled the endless duties its operation entailed.

Unfamiliar cars quickly started filling the small parking lot. From them emerged employee committee representatives, demanding to schedule exclusive fun days for their groups. The kibbutz office welcomed them with generous discounts. Contracts were signed, leaflets printed, tickets sold. The park gates remained closed to "regular citizens" for most of the summer. Each morning, three, four, and sometimes even five thousand bathers arrived in loud, organized, cheerful groups, seeking fun, games, and sandwiches. The kibbutz discovered that even if Sonya Yaakov moved into the snack bar she still wouldn't have time to feed the masses. Outside caterers, rough business types, joined her during high season, erecting nine snack bars painted the national colors of blue and white and nicknamed "posts," in military lingo. Mid-level company workers were served light refreshments—no more than a pastry and a can of sweetened juice—but visitors representing large unions received a banquet: a cardboard box containing oily, sweaty sausages; a piece of schnitzel; fried pasta; salad; and a piece of sponge cake for dessert. And yet, some people still needed Sonya's sandwiches, and though the three bags of rolls once awaiting her in the supermarket were now reduced to one, she continued to contribute her talents to the kibbutz economy.

Sandwiches are piling up. It's time to arrange them on large steel platters and turn to the pièce de résistance: the omelet sandwiches. Those are made at the very last minute, so that they lose as little of their freshness as possible. But first—coffee and a cigarette. Sunshine washes over the lawns, sneaking into the kitchen through the shutters. Two young kibbutz members on duty come in and greet Sonya with kisses, open the shutters, and wash the dishes used by Sonya. One of them changes the radio station; the whispering of the DJ is replaced with upbeat music. Though the cook isn't pleased with this change, she chooses not to protest. The large pan is already hot and bubbling. One by one, the omelets are fried, their aroma spreading through the garden. The lifeguards arrive. With bare chests they circle the pools, using long-handle nets to pick up the previous night's floating victims—fallen leaves, deceased dragonflies. New sounds fill the air. The mechanic operating the giant turbines hidden below the wave pool descends into the burning inferno. The air is filled with drumming—the Brazilian band is doing one last rehearsal before the gates open. The ninja boys sit in the shade of one of the sheds, inspecting the dancers preoccupied with buttoning their costumes and chatting with the heart-wrenching excitement of virgins. Here and there the dancers shoot them forgiving smiles of contempt, raising their excitement higher. The cashier, a potbellied old-time kibbutznik, leans his bicycle against the fence, exchanges a joke with the girl on first-aid duty, and pops over to the kitchen to get a cup of Turkish coffee. Good spirits prevail, everyone enjoys the beauty of the morning and prepares for the day that is about to begin.

B.

The season, the season!

One by one, the tin whales raced down the asphalt road encircling the kibbutz. Once in a while they faltered over a bump and tilted to the side for a moment, to the protests sounded by the passengers trapped in their bowels. The sun was beating down, patience was running out. Finally, the parking lot appeared; a journey full of hardship originating from pickup points all around the country finally came to an end. The buses aligned, side by side, vomiting up swarms of vacationers consolidating into a steaming, terrifying human river. The chairman of the National Employees' Committee and his regional subordinates, all with beepers buckled to their belts, ran around trying to give orders that no one would obey. More and more buses arrived and continued to spit out a rabble—receptionists surrounded by terribly raucous children, condescending regional engineers, Public Works Department retirees along with their bundles, authoritative mechanics with their heavily made-up wives, clumsy high schoolers. All sweating, quarreling, fighting to get to the head of the line and gain possession of what awaited behind the blue raffia fence. All were yearning for salvation, some peace of mind, longing for the land promised to them in the leaflets handed out at the factory, the garage, the office, all those places in which they executed their days.

Suddenly, as they gathered and assembled before the gates, a mighty noise rose from the other side—the samba drummers, twelve in all, beating their drums with all their might and ripping eardrums with their whistles. The main beat split into subbeats, like Cerberus whose heads twist and fight against each other—the resounding base drum, repinique drums hanging on their sides, bells, tambourines . . .

The players swirled, moving right and left as one, back and forth; the dancers went wild, shaking hips and colorful noisemakers. Their skirts were short, their corsets alluring; minds heated and legs bounced of their own volition. Once inside, a paunchy vice president deserted his backpack and joined the dancing, to the laughter of his colleagues. A head accountant, a mother of soldiers, could not contain herself and burst out in ululations. An entire department of secretaries and receptionists followed suit and lost all control. The lawn grew crowded, the people in line pushed, shoved, prodded, pulled toward the festivities. Who didn't want a taste of the fun. . . . Please don't block the entrance, please don't form a crowd, the crowd is requested to proceed.

The vacationers split into groups, trying to find a piece of land on which to set camp, their jaws tight and their eyes squinting; there was no time to waste, first come first served. Some preferred to settle below one of the more distant poinciana trees. Others made do with a sun umbrella, as long as they didn't have to take more than four steps to reach the pool. Some came in tribes—grandparents, toddlers, neighbors, and friends in tow; they conceded all sorts of advantages for the sake of securing a territory large enough to seat all of their loved ones. From the moment the settlers took hold of the land—spreading their blankets and setting down their coolers—no person had any right to it, as if it were their legacy. The chosen corner, until recently nothing more than a forgettable piece of trampled dirt, became their private estate, dear to heart; to confirm its status, they rearranged the plastic chairs according to personal taste. From that moment on, it was dubbed *Our Corner* and everything else was assessed by its proximity to it. They quickly found secret advantages, known only to its owners, such as a hidden tap or a shortcut to the slalom slide. Minuses were treated with a blind eye. While pouring the first cup of coffee from the thermos, they enjoyed the qualities of their occupied estate—lauding its climate, the vegetation, and other amenities; in short, they attached themselves fondly to it, nurturing their patriotic tendencies. Because their hearts turned sour for the minuscule size of their crowded patch of land, they tried to invade the territories of neighboring clans behind their backs, on occasion even robbing a reclining chair when the neighbors went for a dip. And should a strange boy wander over and fix longing eyes on a bag of chips, one of the family's own boys would stand up and shoo him away. The parents would deliver a weak scolding to fulfill their obligation, simultaneously smiling furtively with satisfaction.

Impatient infants twisted below hands anointing their bodies with sunscreen, yearning to reach the water. Mothers, wide scarves tied below their breasts to conceal layers of fat, reprimanded, grew angry, and finally gave up. The children rushed to the pools like tiny demons, screaming with waving arms and jumping in fearlessly, out of a complete, wonderful faith in their immortality. The lifeguards launched ceaseless noisy orders through their loudspeakers: the kid with the red bathing suit, I repeat, the kid with the red bathing suit . . . but no one heeded their warnings. More and more bathers rushed in; the main pool quickly turned into a boiling pot, steaming with chlorine, dotted with hundreds of heads and colorful rubber tubes. The children's cheerfulness infected their parents. Everyone splashed water, diving down to pull on unfamiliar bathing suits and engaging in countless other shenanigans. Fearful women dipped in the shallow end, trickling droplets of water over themselves. Long lines already formed by the large slides. One by one, the vacationers careened down the pipes and were shot out into the pool at the end of their journey. The air quivered with the cackle of the loudspeakers. Screams of gaiety mixed with a deafening soundtrack of upbeat songs and the blast of shooting water. The water park, that giant of pleasures, roaring and thundering with infinite volume—the sounds of heaven, or perhaps the sounds of hell on earth.

Sonya Yaakov recalled sorrowfully the days when the visitors were doctors from Kfar Shmaryahu, levelheaded beings who made sure to swim in their lanes. From her station by the stove she twisted her face at the cashiers whenever some loudmouth cut in line or spoke crudely. It wasn't yet ten in the morning, and the vacationers, trying to embody the vague idea of "fun," were already stuffing themselves senseless. All were in a hurry, all were pushing, as if their lives depended on a glass of nauseatingly sweet juice. They fought with all available means, waving bills, reaching to tap the shoulder of the concession-stand worker, screaming with a sore throat. The self-righteous among them told off the others, while they themselves pushed and shoved; the weak ones demanded justice meekly. Those lucky enough to get a hold of a sticky piece of chocolate cake pushed their way out of the masses, and only miraculously were there no casualties. The demand for ice cream grew strong. Each time a Popsicle was taken out of the freezer, bits of ice sprayed all around, and pools quickly formed. Sonya grabbed a mop—she couldn't really clean in this chaos, but she had to soak up the water, so that no one slipped, God forbid. She grew tired and decided it was time to call it a day. She hung her apron on a nail, tied a last garbage bag, and left through the back door, no goodbyes. Outside she was attacked by a blinding light, but also a cool breeze that evaporated her sweat.

It was already eleven. She had earned the right to go home, take a shower, and maybe even have a quick nap. But before she retraced the line separating her from that foreign world, she was tempted to glance at the far end of the park. After all, she was only human. There, beneath the colorful sun umbrellas, the new peddlers had already started spreading out their wares. *I wonder what they're selling there today*, she thought, and slowly wobbled southward.

C.

"I'm going crazy. Where is she? That's all I need now, for that Romanian to screw me over, and on the first day of the season."

Many tend to blush at a time of emotional turmoil, but our speaker tends to grow pale instead; now, however, her face shone with a moist glow that alarmed her listeners.

"Tuvia! Get your mother a glass of water," Dvora ordered.

"Have some water," said Fat Tuvia and pulled out a square, beaten Styrofoam container hidden under the stall. "Don't worry. She said she'll be here—so she'll be here."

"I wouldn't be surprised if it turned out Anita Shagrir bribed her to trip me up," Tzippi Zinman complained. "Don't be naïve—that villain is capable of anything."

"The Romanian or Anita?" asked Dvora.

"Both."

"Then why do you work with her?"

"People are crazy about her stuff," the stylist said. "And at the end of the day you have to have some quality."

"No two ways about it," Tuvia agreed. "That's business. Can I offer you a glass of water, too, Ciotka?"

"Look at her," Dvora muttered, gesturing with a slight turn of the head at the creature approaching them. "How embarrassing . . ."

Mama Frumkin, who'd finished laying out her merchandise— for summer, she enhanced her watches by adding cheap sunglasses presented on a rotating device—left her denture-grating high school sweetheart to run the business alone, and with her arms folded around her back, ventured out to walk among the stalls. The spirit of vacation hadn't passed her by; over her floral bathing suit she wore a skirt that barely covered her doughy thighs. A sombrero rested atop her head, and a little plastic nose cover was attached to her sunglasses. When she saw that people were whispering over at the Saltzmans' stall, she settled for a faraway nod and peacefully floated over to the other peddlers. Those who had already finished preparing were gathered under the poinciana, sipping black coffee and making educated guesses on that day's forecasted revenues. Tzippi Zinman, wishing to increase her profits, rented out more than ten stalls this time, and since she allotted those closest to the stage to the sellers who were her favorites, whispers of restrained grudge were heard here and there. The stalls were abandoned—the vacationers weren't interested in the goods yet—they were drawn, for the time being, to other attractions. Nachliel Zarfaty, who, of course, won one of the more prestigious stalls, leaned against its counter, satisfied, following the aerobics instructor bouncing on the stage with desperate longing. And-one-and-two-and-that's-enough, he mumbled diligently. When the class was over he sighed, straightened his back, smoothed back his rebellious curls, a sign that he'd landed back on Earth, and went over to ask Zinman where Sara Consignment had disappeared to. On the one hand, he hoped some mishap had occurred to leave him alone on the pedestal of high fashion. On the other hand, he prayed for her arrival, because he didn't like the idea of remaining alone on that pedestal, surrounded by nothing but derelicts of the worst kind.

Getting Sara Consignment to agree to participate in her fairs was, to Tzippi Zinman, one of her greatest coups. She didn't miss any chance to boast—and, to be honest, practically to gloat—over the privilege given to her. The glorious name appeared on every list of manufacturers she put together in preparation for Shfayim. No ensemble was complete without her, and in spite of her shortcomings, there was no fashion merchant that came close. In a way, she could be seen as a wondrous figure—a uniquely irreplaceable person.

The early days of Sara Burko (for that was her official name) are veiled in fog. It seems she'd always been in the rag trade. We know that during a certain period she was part of Anita Shagrir's entourage, but even Shagrir herself was unable to determine when and where she came from. In short, Tzippi met Sara Consignment during the days when she herself acted as apprentice to Anita Shagrir, queen of the fashion shows. Things were different back then, of course. At that time, the Zinman girl was like a satellite circling that hot, awe-inspiring sun whose light dimmed the glow of many bigger and better than herself. Back then, Sara Burko saw Tzippi—in an uncommon error of judgment for such an astute woman—as a marginal wardrobe attendant whose entire job was to collect the clothes tossed to the floor by models and to sell tickets to benefit balls. But Zinman didn't stand still. With unending patience she learned the ropes, etched important names into memory, took notes and made contacts, until her time came to leap and detach herself at once from the magnetizing force of the great light.

Anita Shagrir chuckled derisively; Anita Shagrir followed the developments with utter amazement; Anita Shagrir shook with rage, slandered, threatened manufacturers and club owners, but all for naught—the name "Tzippi Zinman," until then attached to the spendthrift wife of a shopkeeper from Judah the Maccabee Street, now signified the name of a competing business. When she looked around she found herself suddenly surrounded by more and more ambitious usurpers. Rather than waste her time on futile wars, Anita Shagrir decided to pounce, too, and rise straight to the top tier, where superior beings called "designers" hovered about. Those who, unlike manufacturers of the old generation who boasted names such as "Lady Jane," were simply and nobly called "Jerry Melitz" or "Gideon Oberson." From now on no one spoke of "suppliers" or "goods" anymore, but only of "fashion houses" and "creations."

Sara Consignment—a discerning woman, as we've already mentioned—found that she had no grasp of the updated jargon. And if that wasn't enough, some good soul whispered in her ear that the water-park contract had dropped into Tzippi Zinman's lap, and she remembered how she had foolishly turned down Zinman's courtship with derision. Secret agents were sent, understandings were reached, agreements were made, and when the time was right, the crafty merchant defected from the Anita Shagrir Camp over to the Zinman Camp, which was perceived as a public slap in the face. In fact, Sara Consignment rescued her own reputation at the very last moment, since her dismissal was already being discussed by the powers that be. Because the scheme was made in secret and had not reached Zinman's ears, Tzippi saw Sara Burko joining her forces as an impressive achievement. This way, both parties benefited, while Anita Shagrir snorted with contempt from the heights of her penthouse in the Bavli neighborhood, wishing the two health and prosperity with a sneer.

"The guys say Sara Consignment must have changed her mind at the last minute," Zarfaty said bravely, contorting his face with worry. For a moment he thought of using this chance, announcing that if the Romanian was out, so was he, if only to strengthen his position and extort some special benefit, but since he was a small man and the agent, a roaring lion, he settled for complaining silently to himself.

"Do me a favor, Zarfaty. Don't buy into every nonsense people tell you, and go back to your stall. She's on her way, there's traffic."

She also dismissed the other peddlers with similar claims and hurried to the management office. She dialed the number again and again, waited a few minutes and dialed once more, but got no answer. All that was left was to pray that the merchant was indeed stuck on some clogged road. There were still fifty minutes left before the fashion show. Albert Ben Arroya now took the place of the aerobics instructor, with his eternal photographer's vest, and hosted entertaining games. The crowd gathered. A tall clown, frying inside a synthetic satin suit, sweating trickles of white face-paint, walked among the visitors, persuading them to buy bingo tickets. *And I am a material girl!!!* the loudspeakers screeched; *three tickets for ten shekels!!!* Ben Arroya roared at the top of his lungs, *the price is low and morale is high!!!* He winked at Tzippi as she walked past on her way backstage. Everything was ready to go—the makeshift makeup station, the fans, the models who chatted over a pitcher of iced coffee sent over from the snack bar.

Here, on the moving steel frame, Sara Consignment's dresses were supposed to hang, meant to close the first show of the season magnificently. What would she send the girls on stage in? Mandy Line's surfing pants?! How was she supposed to keep her sanity, she asked herself, and perhaps that was the worst part—that she couldn't lose her cool, that she had to find a solution while smiling at the sellers, smiling at the girls, smiling at Albert Ben Arroya who appeared backstage, allegedly to look for some lost item, but in fact to sneak a peek at the half-naked models.

"Mom, Mom." A large silhouette appeared on the other side of the blue raffia screen that concealed the dressing room. "We need you."

It turned out one of the dealers, a character who pushed himself in anywhere he could, never hesitating to abuse others' misfortune for his own benefit, insisted on annexing Sara Consignment's orphaned stall, which had the best position, and in spite of Fat Tuvia's protests, trying as best he could to prevent the disaster, began moving over his goods—towels and sequined baseball caps. When Tzippi arrived the man began a loud haggling that drew the crowd's attention, and who knows how things would have progressed if a deafening sound hadn't been heard, suddenly, beyond the fence—the explosion of an old exhaust pipe, accompanied by the appalling screeching of a gearbox. All heads were turned.

"She's here!" called Dvora Saltzman.

"She's here!" chirped Nachliel Zarfaty.

"She's here!" cheered Tzippi Zinman.

There, between the emaciated hills and the refined bougainvillea bushes, on the dirt road leading to the back of the waterpark, as if emerging from the depths of the earth, a white, beaten-down station wagon suddenly appeared, overflowing with garments, rising and falling and breaking and wobbling and faltering and gasping as if threatening to expire, driven by, who else, who else but Sara Consignment.

D.

They were familiar with the place—a charmless popular eatery at the back of one of the gas stations on the Coastal Highway. Since they hadn't eaten a crumb since that morning—that's, at least, what Tzippi, who wouldn't take no for an answer right now, claimed—they parked the blue Ibiza and sat down at a corner table by the window. They could have chosen a more central spot, of course, since the restaurant was empty at that hour, but Zinman, breaking her habit, gave up the spotlight for once in favor of a discreet corner. Until the chicken skewers were scorched, the bored cook sent out more and more appetizers: fried eggplant, mushrooms in tahini, cracked and bitter olives, toasted pitas bearing the brown fat marks of the grill, and anything else he could think of.

And lo, Fat Tuvia—normally quite lively at such banquets—nibbled distractedly. Each time he forked a piece of food, his thoughts wandered back to Shfayim, and each time he shook off his reveries he stared at the plate as if it were some foreign object. More than he was preoccupied by the events of that morning—what had happened, really?—he was preoccupied by his own preoccupation. In fact, things had gone more or less according to his expectations, and since another of his many forecasts had come true, he should have been happy and content. The thickness of the stack of bills stuffed in his pants pocket also implied that sales had been good. Mandy Line's clothes were favored by the employees of the Public Works Department, and the special prices—they eventually decided to sell each item for ten shekels—won their hearts as well. And still, Tuvia felt a stubborn tickle inside of him, which hadn't relented ever since that curly-haired girl approached the stall. Not only curly-haired, but fair-haired, too. Not only fair-haired, but tan as a peach. Her legs chiseled, her breasts welcoming as breasts should be, and glistening with freshness all over. She wore a white T-shirt, too big, that covered her hot pants almost entirely, and a whistle hung down her chest. She rummaged through the goods a bit, pulled out a pair of surfing pants and examined them with extended arms, tossed them back in the pile and chose another pair, all the while keeping her eyes on him. For a moment, Tuvia suspected she was an undercover tax agent. He drew some attention to his receipt book and even filled one in for forty shekels, just in case, but then recalled the signs his father recognized in the tax investigators and dismissed the thought. What was she looking for then, and why did she linger so long without buying anything?

"Aren't you going to eat those fries?" Tzippi asked. She looked at her son affectionately. As handsome as his father had been in his youth—the wide forehead, the shapely nose. She was only a bit sorry about his round paunch.

Fries, Tuvia wondered for a moment. Oh, fries; it's what's on his plate. "Go ahead," he said and pushed away his plate. "I'm not hungry."

"Tuvia, I want you to see a doctor," his mother said, nibbling on his leftovers. "You might have caught a bug."

She said her name was Maya, and that they'd probably see a lot of each other in the near future. Then she grew silent and gave him a strange, ambiguous look, creating the need to say something, and so he offered her five shekels off if she bought two pairs. Another customer who stood by jumped at the opportunity and he was forced to sell her four items with a discount he hadn't planned on giving. By the time he counted and wrapped the sale, Maya disappeared as if swallowed by the earth. He was relieved at the moment, but now regretted not being more assertive and allowing himself to undermine the most important commercial principle—equanimity. When his Aunt Dvora returned from the snack bar he told her he sold sixty shekels worth of clothes, but didn't mention the discount. A few minutes later, the outburst began—within thirty minutes they sold over twenty-five items—and the entire affair was pushed aside.

Tzippi finally laid her fork down in an angle signifying an acceptance of the body's limitations. The puddles the meat had oozed were already coagulating, and even the flies that had buzzed around them flew away in search of greener pastures. The server cleared the table and returned with a copper tray: a little teapot, three clay cups, and Turkish pastries dripping with oil and sugary water. The sight of the delicacies pulled Fat Tuvia back from the realms of contemplation and into the world of action. He took a pistachio-filled cone. The waiter and his busboy began setting the tables for dinner.

"Hey, did you happen to notice if the Romanian sold a lot?" the stylist asked as she lit a cigarette.

"I didn't really pay attention," Dvora confessed. "But from what I saw, at least six or seven dresses and one miniskirt suit."

"And that's only what you saw—just imagine what she sold when you weren't looking." Tzippi Zinman sighed. "What can I say, she's outstanding. They should teach her methods at the university, I swear."

And indeed, anyone who saw Sara Consignment that day couldn't have helped but reach the same conclusion—that she was outstanding, that she was magnificent, that she had a great, rare gift. This genius of the retail world read her customers like an open book. As she helped them with the clothes—a collapsible screen was set for this purpose in Shfayim—she responded exactly to what she read in that book, tightening here and loosening there, granting their most hidden wishes. If need be, she made an ambiguous comment that offended them so much they simply had to buy her merchandise, if only to retrieve some of their honor. She didn't let go until she saw a pen raised over a check. The more resistant the customers were, the more pleasure she derived. She had a myriad of methods and means. A considerable part of them stemmed from her unique talent, but she also learned quite a bit from years of ambitious, passionate observation and study. Methods that were perceived as blunt and even obnoxious when utilized by her competition were improved and—some might even say refined— in her hands, until they formed a *style*.

"In Bucharest she'd have been a head of faculty," Fat Tuvia agreed.

"I'm dying to know, just for reference, how much she made today."

"She told me she was disappointed with the sales, that it was a weak day."

"There's no such thing as a 'weak day' for Sara Burko," Tzippi Zinman said, dismissing the comment with an exhale. "But she knows how to whine with the best of them. I barely got the commission out of her—she wanted a discount because she only began selling at 11:30, as if it were my fault she was late. What can I say, that woman knows how to scrape your soul on a grater. Did you see how she screamed about that jacket?"

A model who hastily zipped up a cotton jacket tore the sleeve—not an irreparable disaster, but a tear that caught Sara Burko's eyes when the items were returned to her stall. A scandal ensued. The merchant cried out as if butchered, mourned the jacket, and announced that it was an appliqued item consigned to her and therefore she should be lawfully compensated—for example, by exempting her from the stall's rental fees for a week. Zinman claimed it was a natural risk that any professional should take into account, which boiled the merchant's blood. She yelled that there were risks and then there were cynics, and that any situation could be solved with the right combination, and who knows how the whole thing would have ended if not for a pure soul, an angel with cataracts, Mama Frumkin, who offered to buy the item for a nice discount. Her daughter-in-law, she said, needed that kind of jacket, and since she was an expert seamstress, the small tear was not an issue.

"We did pretty well, too," Dvora said. "At this rate we'll have to go to Kiryat Arye again soon."

"You don't say! How much, how much?"

"Tuvia's got the money."

This was the moment Tzippi was waiting for. Fat Tuvia sucked the sugar off his thumb with aplomb, wiped the moisture with a napkin, and removed the bundle of bills from his pocket. Some like to count by flipping the bills, but he was of the school that preferred to pass them from one hand to the other. First he arranged the bills by color: the purple ones, which he looked at with awe—they bore the portrait of one of our greatest writers, lost in thought. Then, the gray ones—necessary bills that didn't move the heart. Then, the golden ones, to which he felt a special affinity: the late prime minister whose portrait was printed on them reminded him of his Grandma Hinde. Finally, shameful, eight blue five-shekel bills with Levi Eshkol's picture brought up the rear. He treated those with the charity reserved for the less fortunate. He counted the bills once, lingered a bit, counted again from front to back and back to front, then smoothed the stack and tapped both its sides, aligning its edges.

"So?" Tzippi asked.

"I want Ciotka Dvora to count it herself," Tuvia asked and handed the bills to his aunt.

"Five hundred and twenty," the cosmetician (who, by the way, belonged to the bill-flipping camp) announced.

"You don't say!" Tzippi exclaimed halfheartedly. "Look at that—520 shekels! I work my ass off like a dog and you clean up!"

On the one hand, she was filled with pride for the achievement—after all, whose idea was it in the first place, opening a *shmatte* stall?—and on the other hand envy pinched her heart. Truth be told, she herself made eight hundred that day, not counting her promised $200 fee from the water park's office. But in light of her sister's great success, she was filled with compassion for herself for having been shortchanged, and, requiring compensation, decided to punish the vacationers and determined that, starting tomorrow, she'd decrease her expenses, settling for only one big-name model for each show.

"Well, I'm splitting it with Tuvia, it doesn't add up to that much," Dvora demurred.

"What are you talking about?" Zinman cried. Her passion for revenue made her forget her son's part in this collaboration, and now she feared she'd be accused of having schemed to bite into her sister's profits. "At this rate you'll have two flight tickets to Seefeld by the end of the month!"

"How much is a ticket, anyway?"

"Depends on the season; if we go during Sukkot it would be a little more expensive, but I heard there's a chance they'll cancel the travel tax by then. You know what I think, Dvoraleh? This water park business is going to keep us so busy that the holidays will be here in no time. Why don't you and Shraga come by sometime this week and we can discuss the trip? Yosef's told me about a million times that he wants to show you the slides. Does Wednesday work for you?"

■ ■ ■

The hour grew late. The sun, a raging grand dame that had appeared that very morning, young and innocent from behind the eucalyptus trees, gathered its strength for a last show of violence before it dropped, defeated, into the sea. Its rays penetrated the brown windows, overpowering air conditioners and spreading sunspots over the walls. Golden squares dotted with tiny shadows of dust appeared on the corner of the table, over the ashtray, across Fat Tuvia's forehead. Exhaustion, delayed on account of hunger, now attacked with all its might, gathering strength from full bellies. The three of them sank into a peaceful, sleepy silence found only in the presence of family. Someone burped. An Elton John song played on the radio. The check was presented.

6

On Stage

A.

On an evening in early July, two figures walked down Rabbi Fried-man Alley in Tel Aviv: an ageless, skinny, and flaccid man, trailing the scent of aftershave, alongside a good-looking woman in her late forties with a juicy rear end. The air hung moist, viscous, and lifeless over Tel Aviv, and the couple, though they had just left their home on nearby Judah the Maccabee Street, was already sweating. The cacophony of television sets broadcasting a party assembly rose from the open windows. The prime minister, a stubborn dwarf, was wrangling with three of his ministers who demanded the immediate cancelation of a measly peace offering made toward the Palestinians, which cast, they believed, a heavy threat over the future of the State of Israel. On its way, the couple waved at the kind Mrs. Biron, one of the neighborhood's longtime residents, who was sipping iced tea on her balcony, observing her surroundings like a retired beat cop. On both sides of the alley were skinned low-rise projects, delineated by crooked fences. Dvora Saltzman made some comment regarding the neglect that had taken over the neighborhood. On the eastern end lived renters side by side with the elderly longtime residents. No one bothered to water the dying lawns. To the west, on the other hand, there still lived some powerful homeowners. Those tended small flower gardens and tiny orchards—two or three pomegranate trees, vines, and citrus trees, their fruit frequently robbed by students from the nearby high school. At the end of the alley a couple of two-story houses built about twenty

years earlier stood out—pretty, elegant, whitewashed; erected, unlike
the neighboring buildings, on thin pillars, and featuring an electronic
door and intercom buzzers. The marble floor tiles of the lobby were
polished once a week and philodendrons grew in decorative clay pots.
This was where the privileged residents of the alley lived: an architect
who enjoyed a certain fame in the early '80s, an attorney or two and
even a member of Knesset, a conservative and cordial yes-man. And
here, in a spacious apartment that faced the street, the Zinmans had
established their home and haven.

A freezing chill welcomed the Saltzmans. Their hosts had recently
purchased an air conditioner that cost a fortune, and Yosef wanted
everyone to know . . .

In the living room, they found the man of the house and Aunt
Masha in the midst of a medical procedure. Miss Lifschitz sat up
straight and breathed slowly. Yosef Zinman, glasses on the tip of his
nose affording him a scientific appearance, pumped into a small bel-
lows attached by a tube to a cloth sleeve which was wrapped around
her arm. An excited political correspondent was on the television,
behind him a loud crowd—the party meeting was, it seemed, on the
verge of total chaos.

"How high?" Shraga asked.

"Shh!" Yosef reproached him without taking his eyes off the blood
pressure gauge in his hand. When he released the valve the needle was
on its way. It lingered over the scale for a moment, wavered and finally
stopped.

"One-twenty over eighty!" Yosef announced in a voice not devoid
of envy. "Like an eighteen-year-old."

About a year earlier, the shopkeeper (who was taken with any
sort of invention and improvement) asked an acquaintance visiting
the United States to bring back a blood pressure gauge. Since then,
any familial gathering at the Zinman residence began with a checkup.
"People should know how to cure themselves," Yosef preached whenever he had the chance. Now, when the old woman's tremendous
health was revealed, he checked himself too, to compare. He wrapped
the plastic sleeve around his arm, pumped it up as far as he could, and

then devoted his full attention to the scale. His eyes almost bugged when he saw the result.

"One-sixty-one over one-hundred-and-four," he whispered.

"Is it any wonder?" Aunt Masha said with imperial calm from her pedestal of health. "I could have told you that without the gadget. Look at you, what a belly you've grown."

"Nonsense." Yosef grew angry. "It's because of the politics. Turn off that television and we'll check it again."

His orders were followed and the same result was attained, which led to a deluge of pity and worry pouring over his head. Shraga Saltzman jumped at the chance to give his brother-in-law scholarly advice and, yearning to set an example, demanded an immediate test and stretched out his skinny arm. Zinman pushed up his glasses, wrinkled his nose as if sipping steaming soup, and looked at the gauge. He looked and looked and said nothing.

"Well?" Shraga urged him. "What does it say?"

Rather than answer, Yosef loosened the Velcro strap, wrapped it again and pumped air into it once more. He tapped the glass with his finger, tilted the gauge here and there and fixed his patient with a worried look.

"Well? *Nu?*"

"Zero over zero," Yosef announced. "According to my indication—the blood pressure of a carcass."

"The Lord giveth and the Lord taketh away," Miss Lifschitz said in a gloomy voice.

Tzippi Zinman, stepping out of the kitchen with a tray crammed full of goodies, insisted that they "stop playing with that stupid gadget already," and Shraga (who'd grown dizzy) demanded that someone make him some strong black coffee right away.

The sisters set the table with a pie, radishes, salad (which was the family's shorthand for egg salad) and pink slices of salted herring prepared by the host. They sat down to eat without waiting for Avrum, and the moment Tzippi reached her hand to the breadbasket, the doorbell rang.

"*A gast in shtetl!*" Zinman called out.

Throughout the years, the family members had accepted Avrum's tardiness and stopped expecting an apology or an explanation. Avrum never just came over or visited or arrived; Avrum Shlossman entered— even places that didn't have a door. His entrances awoke a special trembling in those present, a sort of festive expectation; for what, no one could say.

He bore his fifty-one years of age with grace—tall, elegant, his hair moistened with a cream that allotted it an eternal freshness, over-flowing with charm and double entendre. Every word he said, each wave of the hand or tilting of the head in acceptance of a kiss ema-nated ceremoniousness and burned with that theatrical, childish flame that prevented people from getting angry at him, just as they were prevented from taking him seriously.

From the moment he entered, the party grew cheerful. People talked louder, ate faster, and competed to see who could tell the wit-tier anecdote, until, as was their custom, they arrived at the tale of Yosef Zinman and the Italian nun—the story of "The Portofino Fart"—performed that night as a duet by the host and hostess. Since they remembered Portofino, they remembered Europe; and since they remembered Europe, they remembered their planned trip to Seefeld, and the Zinmans got up to prepare the living room for the slide show.

B.

A constant struggle between two opposing forces granted the Zin-man home its unique style: on the one hand there was Tzippi's affinity for the contemporary (to her, "pretty" and "new" were synonymous), and on the other was her heart's desire for the past, not necessarily her own, but a past that could have been hers had she lived in a different time and place, a past entirely made up of a reflection forever fro-zen in china pots and silver sugar dishes. This category also included the pictures on the wall—some northern landscapes, others still life; cabins, a European beach, and fishing boats. The armchair and the sofa, on the other hand, were completely modern: square outlines and gray- and pink-checkered upholstery, the most fashionable colors. At the center of the living room a low and wide glass table leaned against shiny nickel legs. Ashtrays were scattered in every corner, but the living room was clean of tobacco stench and smelled pleasantly of recently scrubbed floors. Tzippi Zinman was no less of an extremist than her older sister when it came to household cleanliness; her pedantry, however, stemmed not from refined taste, but mainly from her passion toward the spotless, the burnished, the free of any and all scars that cried out: "Now!" Sometimes, on a quiet evening, Tzippi might sit comfortably and examine her surroundings with a gloomy face, not finding inner peace until she located a corner to leach onto—say, the balcony. "Time to freshen up," she'd tell her husband then. The next evening she'd already be enjoying the four new stools adorning the balcony. They'd be equal to their predecessors in all measures but their newness, a fact that instilled them with a charm that filled her with happiness.

"Get the big picture off the wall," Fat Tuvia ordered as he entered, carrying the slide projector. Three or four volumes of the encyclopedia were already waiting on the dining table, a makeshift platform to raise the projector up higher. While he played with the knobs and pressed the buttons, his mother emerged from the kitchen for the umpteenth time.

"Voilà!" Avrum raised his pointing finger and furrowed his brow like a town crier. "The cake!"

"It's from Hans Bertele's bakery, he just opened it on Ibn Gvirol Street. You should have seen the line," Tzippi said. Speaking of which, she was also enthusiastic about new food.

"Oh, come on, who needs this?" Aunt Masha complained, nevertheless handing over her plate. "Who needs this, I ask you?! Certainly not Yosef, with his high blood pressure."

"Let me enjoy life!" Yosef Zinman grumbled, and for defiance's sake, added a few butter cookies to his plate as well.

"Criminal!" Miss Lifschitz said, her eyes bulging. "You'll do anything in your power to turn your wife into a widow! And what about you, Tzippke? Gorging on all this fatty food instead of getting a hold of yourself. You two should be ashamed!"

"I'm not about to kill myself just to be healthy," Tzippi announced proudly.

"Shraga didn't get a piece of cake yet . . ."

"Who wants coffee? Who wants tea?"

"Can we turn the air conditioning up a bit?"

The room was finally darkened. A white square flickered over their heads, bounced up to the ceiling and then sharpened and steadied in the middle of the wall. A ticking was heard, and suddenly a somewhat faded photo appeared, showing two spots of intense color—the Zinmans in yolk-colored rain jackets, holding umbrellas over their heads, smiling, behind them a few wooden houses with planters and an empty restaurant terrace.

"Seefeld," Fat Tuvia exclaimed. "Mom and Dad on the first day, going to eat butter-fried knaidlach."

Beneath the veil of darkness, Zinman grabbed another cookie.

"Oy, the knaidlach!" Tzippi sighed.

The slide changed; enthusiastic calls all around.

"Grimml Waterfalls," Tuvia said.

"Krimml," his father corrected. "An hour and a half from Seefeld, considered some of the most beautiful in the world. Look at how they pour into each other in the middle of the forest: you walk and walk and it never ends. By the way, it's recommended to do the route from top to bottom, not the other way around. What can I tell you? I wouldn't mind going again, so you can enjoy it, too. What do you say, Tzip?"

"Oh, Krimml."

A few other waterfall pictures, and then—a lovely photo from one of the towns: blue sky, rolling meadows, a church with two steeples and a greening copper roof. In front, a carriage harnessed to a horse decorated with tassels and fringe. By its side—Tzippi Zinman, hugging a coachman with an enormous chin in a green hat, his thighs stuffed into tight breeches.

"The *kaka-meister*," Fat Tuvia explained. "It was a nice day and they felt like taking a carriage ride in the area, great fun. The guy takes them to see the pedestrian mall, the church, they leave town toward the lake to catch some sun . . . but what happens? Hardly five minutes go by and they stop. The horse, pardon my French, wants to take a crap; he's only human, after all. The coachman waits for him to finish, then takes a brush and a dustpan from under his seat and gets off to collect the product! Okay. He dumps it all in a bucket that hangs off the back and returns to his seat. They keep going—and oops! Again with the brush and the dustpan. The horse must have had a hell of a meal; every ten minutes they had to stop. Eventually Mom started calling him *herr kaka-meister*, and that idiot smiles and says, *jawohl, jawohl.*"

"What a putz! Unbelievable." Tzippi chuckled.

"On the way to Mad Ludwig's castle, with Dolly and Danny Shem-Tov," Fat Tuvia said, explaining the next slide. "Is this the thing with the bee?"

"Uh-huh," confirmed his mother.

"First thing in the morning, Dad asks the innkeeper to buy some extra rolls, goes into the kitchen and makes some sandwiches for a picnic. The owner—Mrs. Bubinger, if I'm not mistaken, a nice woman, she's known them for years—lends them a thermos for coffee and puts a few hardboiled eggs in the picnic basket, just in case. Long story short, we're on our way. After an hour or two we're in the mood for something sweet. We stop at a snack bar. Dolly and Danny go in to look for chocolate and Mom steps outside for a cigarette. The weather's great, and Mom's wearing a pair of those wide pants with an elastic waist. Anyway, the two come back from the snack bar and we're free to move on. Mom gets in the car, and suddenly she feels a tickle on her butt . . ."

"A tickle?" Tzippi interrupted. "You call that a tickle?"

"Maybe a sting," her son admitted. "At any rate—something's moving around inside her pants. She begins screaming, jumping around like a crazy person . . ."

"So embarrassing . . ." Tzippi put her face in her hands and bit her lower lip to stop herself from laughing before the punch line and spoiling the story for her guests.

"And Dad," Tuvia continued. "Dad is yelling, 'What are you dancing around for, what are you dancing around for . . . ?'"

"I knew right away it was a bee," Yosef Zinman said.

"Dad knew right away she had a bee in her pants and told her to
calm down if she didn't want to get stung, and that he was going to
set it loose."

"Oh!" Tzippi moaned with laughter.

"So he bends down and shakes her pants, but the bee won't come
out and he keeps pulling and pulling and then he pulled her pants all
the way down!"

"In front of everybody!" Yosef cheered. "You should have seen
Danny Shem-Tov's face!"

"Oh," his wife yowled, crying tears of pleasure. "I can't take it
anymore!"

"What, you rented a Mercedes?" Shraga Saltzman awoke from his
fake snooze, its entire purpose signaling to his brother-in-law that he
was nobody's fool.

"We got an upgrade," Yosef boasted.

"Do you have a picture of that inn?" Dvora asked.

Tuvia changed the slides quickly until he reached a photo of a
three-story inn set in the midst of a blooming garden. The walls were
painted pink, the shutters white, the wooden balconies stretched
along the front were covered with striped awnings. A few recliners
stood on the sides of the path leading to the front door, above which
the name *Bubinger* appeared, in surprisingly simple lettering. Dvora
was impressed with the beauty of the place and Yosef explained that
there was no "not pretty" in Seefeld.

"Is it clean?"

"Come on, what do you think Dvoraleh, that I'd take you to a
filthy place?" Tzippi rumbled. "You can eat off the floor there, period,
exclamation mark."

Dvora looked at—no, practically ate up—the inn, and imagined
herself stepping inside, carefully pacing the soft carpets padding the
hallways, and, after trying out and considering her options, chose the
balcony on the right corner of the second floor, where she would sit

with Shraga as they beheld the snowy peaks. The owner walks briskly in—a chubby, smiling woman whose braid is wrapped around the top of her head like a crown—and serves hot cocoa and homemade cookies. In the garden, under the sun umbrella, she finds her sister, surrounded by a blinding abundance of petunias, buttercups, tulips, and whatnot as she flips through some journal. Avrum, whom she places in the adjacent room, smiles and waves from his balcony. His face is tan, just like in the photos from his boyhood days in Frankfurt, and his hair is fuller. Not far away, she hears the sweet voice of Julie Andrews. And then, suddenly, that despicable, gnawing, stifling worry drips into the lucid dream—a black drop that spreads and spreads until it muddies the entire vision. Though she knew if she spoke the words she didn't want to say, the loveliness would evaporate in a blink, she had no choice but to extract the question from her mouth.

"Is it expensive?"

"Pfff." Yosef Zinman shrugged. "Pennies. Maybe forty dollars a night."

"Per person?"

"Are you crazy? Per couple!"

"And she has enough room for all of us?"

"Of course!" Tzippi answered in her husband's place. "It isn't a large inn, but she'll always have room for us. It's good that you mentioned it; let's do the math, so we know how many rooms to book."

And since there was never a bigger expert at counting and accounting than Yosef Zinman, he opened his left hand and used his right thumb to bend his fingers back one by one: one room for the Zinmans, a second for the Saltzmans, a third for Avrum, Aunt Masha . . .

"Who said I was even coming?" the old lady said, frowning. "Maybe I will and maybe I won't. Who knows if I'll even be alive."

"Oh, Masha, come on," Zinman roared. "Today yes, tomorrow no . . . what do you think this is, a game? It's July! If we want to go on Sukkot, we have to start making arrangements."

"What about you kids?" Dvora turned to Fat Tuvia.

"I'm definitely in, but I wouldn't count on Shirley," he answered. "Will Yellow Tuvia come from America? We can share a room."

"Of course not, he won't even miss a day of school, especially now that he's doing so well. You know that big professor from Boston just added him to his research team. There were eight applicants, but with his grades there was no question about it."

"You don't say . . ." Tzippi said.

"And what about Bina?" Tuvia insisted.

The slide disappeared; as the discussion carried on, Tuvia turned off the projector. In spite of the darkness, Dvora could still feel Shraga's alert look.

"I'm willing to take her, but only if I'm not the only one who looks after her. We each do our part."

"Of course we'll help you! She's our sister too!" Avrum jumped up, then immediately retreated back to his armchair; even he, who was the strongest believer in his own fabrications, realized exaggerated promises should not be made with so many witnesses around.

"She can share a room with Aunt Masha, we'll pay," Zinman offered, not without malice, and got up to turn on the light. The truth was, Miss Lifschitz had already made up her mind to stay in Israel—she spent most of her days avoiding the sort of gratuitous intimacy that is forced upon travel companions, and the older she got, the more she enjoyed being alone within her own space and within her own habits. More than anything, she was revolted by any sort of change, and one could suppose that the resentment she felt toward the idea of her own death originated from nothing else than the fact that it involved a certain change. But now she didn't want to seem egotistical, refusing to share a room with Bina, and as she thanked Yosef warmly for his generous offer, began calculating the appropriate date on which to tell her family about a certain medical examination that could not be postponed—a feminine issue, say—that would take place, unfortunately, exactly during Sukkot.

"What about passports?" Zinman asked.

"We've got them," said Dvora. "We went to Marseilles."

"Marseilles, Marseilles." The man of the house chuckled from his position as tourism expert. "With all due respect, Dvoraleh, that was back in the days of the Ottoman Empire. Do me a favor and don't forget to renew your passports, we don't want any surprises. Today it's not a problem, you know, you don't have to go all the way downtown and wait in line for hours anymore. You have a station right here, by the Kastel, a Ministry of Interior office, they do it on the spot."

"How would I know," the cosmetician said, taking offense.

He sighed and went to get a passport from the sideboard drawer to demonstrate. They all gathered around to watch his demonstration—here was the expiration date, the border control stamps from each and every year, and there was one from the Milan airport, the Munich airport, and another and another . . . They were especially impressed by the French visa pasted onto one of the pages, imbuing the passport with a noble air. Then they teased Yosske, who'd lost quite a bit of his hair and gained quite a bit of weight since the passport photo had been taken. Dvora's head was spinning with terms—*duty free, turbulence, customs*—terms she had only a vague understanding of, and which were now piled up to create a threatening mountain. She was especially scared about the matter of overweight luggage.

"We'll send a fax to Frau Bubinger," said Yosef. "And what about dollars? We only buy $100 or $200 at the bank, the rest we buy on the black market."

"Then we'll do the same—we'll give you the money and you'll buy them for us," Shraga quickly declared. As a sworn bum, he was not impervious to the advantages hidden in appointing his brother-in-law with the role of trip leader. "You have someone good? I don't want them to stick us with fake notes, God forbid."

Though the regulation obligating those traveling abroad to get their passports stamped at the bank as proof of having legally purchased foreign currency had recently been cancelled, Zinman still believed the government had its own ways of tracking his actions, and in order not to raise the authority's suspicions he made sure, before any trip, to buy a modest sum officially. To maintain good neighborly relations, he also bought some marks from Yunger the butcher. Most of it, though, he bought from an old pimp on Lilienblum Street, an acquaintance of his parents from back in Poland, who made a nice living from the gap between the dollar's market exchange rate and the rate of that exaggerated hybrid the bank called "travel dollars." Since he attested that the money changer never cheated him, nor his father, Berl Zinman, may he rest in peace, the Saltzmans authorized Yosef to act on their behalf in this matter as well. Tzippi, who was tired of the small print that had taken over the evening, wanted to return to the headline, and hinted to her son that he should turn on the projector again. But just then the phone rang. Impatiently, she walked over to the little nook, designed in an antiquated style, with a little phone table and a fake Tiffany lamp, and picked up.

"Dvora," she called. "It's for you!"

And thus the evening was sentenced to an early end.

C.

When Bina Shlossman was born, thirty-four years ago, her older sister Dvora—who was at the time a fourteen-year-old girl with wise eyes and an inward expression—could not contain her happiness. From the very first moment she had a positive influence on the baby. The little one rested her head on Dvora's shoulder for hours as Dvora spun around in a slow waltz and whispered sweet nothings into her tiny ear. Later, when Bina's special condition was revealed, Dvora's love did not diminish in the slightest. On the contrary, it grew. While the parents lamented their bad luck, Dvora refused to despair. Thanks to her, the girl learned how to read and write, and made friends with other less fortunates whom the young woman also took under her wing. Everyone was impressed by her patience. In winter she knitted doll shoes and in summer the two stood barefoot in the kitchen to make fruit salad, singing some pop hit at the tops of their lungs and cracking up over a flying loquat pit. Their visits to the Tel Aviv Zoo pleased both of them equally; after Binchi rode for the first time on the back of one of the enormous, ancient turtles that served as entertainment for children at the time, Dvora was so happy she couldn't fall asleep that night. Once in a while, she organized a residential fair called "the Surprise Market," in which Bina sold plastic necklaces, used toys, and other knickknacks to relatives and friends. The merchandise was presented on the Shlossmans' large dining table, which was decorated with a floral tablecloth. Guests enjoyed pretzels and fruit and made exaggerated sounds of excitements in light of the treasures. After the fair, Bina counted her profits again and again with heartbreaking patience, and the next day went out with Dvora to buy new socks or a picture book.

In the first years of their marriage, the Saltzmans rented a two-bedroom apartment on Weizmann Street, a five-minute walk from the perfumery. This way, Dvora was able to continue to spend many hours with her little sister. No one was happier than Bina when she was invited to spend the night at her sister's new home. On those nights, they drank extra-sweet fruit soda, which sprayed out of the seltzer bottle with a cheerful sound, and played simple card games. The apartment was small; the expectations—great. Shraga, still employed at the tax department of the National Health Fund, planned to advance and promote himself, and the couple began carefully considering having a child of their own. And thus, on a fine April day in 1965, a sweet, fair-haired creature came into this world. The family was concerned that Bina might be neglected now, due to the new circumstances. This was not the case. It seemed the deep affection between the sisters only grew upon the birth of Yellow Tuvia. Dvora's heart, wondrously, contained room enough for both children, and no one was more delighted than Bina when she was asked to stir the child's porridge or fold his cloth diapers.

In those days, Bina began suffering from terrible pain. The family doctor and two experts who followed uttered the word *celiac* and provided a special menu that Bina would be forced to follow for the rest of her life. In a way, the family was relieved, having foreseen a much worse disaster. An illness solved by a healthy diet seemed simple at first. "Ce-li-ac," Tzippi Zinman rolled the consonants on her tongue with something close to pleasure—here was a respectable disease with a scientific name, garnering compassion, not pity. She made sure to wave the explicit name in public, while rarely considering the excruciating everyday burden it entailed for those who lived with Bina. Hinde, the elderly mother, bent with hard work and sorrow, could not withstand the new challenge. Once more, Dvora reported for duty with devotion. She participated in family meetings and examined the possibilities. She found an agency in London that exported small bags of special flour and learned how to make all kinds of pastries whose preparation took long hours (and which, to be frank, mostly had quite a sticky and repulsive texture). Each meal now entailed three or four pots. Since the patient herself could not fathom the sudden decrees, she often broke the doctor's rules. Being a glutton by nature, she couldn't resist the sight of a freshly baked pretzel slung over a wooden stick or a cinnamon roll just out of the oven. It didn't take long for the pain to arrive—sometimes it took two hours and other times it took twenty-four—but when it was accompanied by that watery discharge, the patient was left exhausted. The crying and the screaming tore Dvora's heart. When the crisis was over, Bina made solemn oaths and promises she couldn't keep. Though she was already an adolescent, her childhood lingered on, as we know, forever, and she seemed never truly to perceive the relation between cause and illness. Therefore, she required constant care, and Dvora was forced to spend longer hours in the apartment above the perfumery. When Shraga was fired, there was no more point to, or means for, keeping two households. Shortly before Hinde's death, the Saltzmans moved into her home, and after she passed away they were appointed as the official trustees of her inheritance.

And so, from that time on, for thirteen years, Dvora never spent more than two days in a row away from her younger sister.

D.

"Duvia, Duvia, can you break a hundred?" Sara Consignment called over to Fat Tuvia, waving a bill over the heads of customers threatening to bring down her stall.

"Don't give it to her," Nachliel Zarfaty muttered hatefully from the nearby stall. He hadn't sold one item that morning; a wandering customer stopped by here and there, touched the merchandise a little, and continued over to the competition's stall.

"Don't take it to heart," Dvora consoled him. "People will buy from you too, just wait. It's only 10:30. What's going on in Jerusalem?"

A few days earlier, a Palestinian passenger had attacked a bus driver on the way from Tel Aviv to Jerusalem, took hold of the wheel, and drove the bus into the abyss. A few terrified passengers fell out when the bus went down. Others were trapped in the flames. The bus finally stopped in a thorn field that caught fire. Many were killed—innocent people, including two Canadian tourists, a newly arrived immigrant, a little girl. The entire country had been roiling since. A group of bullies, reinforced by a divine decree, took the chance to pour oil onto the flame. They went wild during one of the funerals and stoned the cars of Arab residents in Jerusalem. People were stabbed in Yavne, shot in Gaza; death beat down arbitrarily in all directions. Nachliel Zarfaty, who, deep inside, was embarrassed to be selling in times like these, self-righteously placed a small radio at the corner of his table, listened to reports and updated the others on new developments once in a while.

"Turn it down a little," Fat Tuvia suggested. "It's depressing the clients." He himself wore his famous umbrella hat, a trick he had come up with to draw the attention of vacationers.

Sara Burko, who had despaired with waving, walked over briskly. "Duvia, honey, didn't you hear my yelling? Maybe you can break a hundred?"

"Let's see," Tuvia said leisurely, pulling out some wrinkled bills and glancing over at Zarfaty. "Twenty, thirty, fifty . . . no. Sorry."

"Nachliel, do me a favor," the peddler begged. "I'm about to lose the client."

"Hmm!" Zarfaty huffed. Here was his chance to teach that crook a lesson. She had no shame or solidarity, and while the entire country was burning—the radio just mentioned a coalition crisis!—she had only one thing on her mind. Beneath his black curls, hard words ran amok: how would he begin? How would he scold her? How could one even express such discontent? It was hard to choose. On the other hand, was it his place? What if she talked back? What if a fight ensued, just when customers arrived? It was best to save his rebuke for a more appropriate time, as he pulled a stack of twenties from his pocket.

The work of the righteous is done by others: the loudspeakers announced that the bingo game would take place in fifteen minutes, and many of the women, seduced by the new bait, deserted Sara Consignment's stall one by one. Those who remained scattered among the other stalls, and even Zarfaty finally had some work. A few barefoot, wet kids, Popsicles in hand and diving goggles around their necks, were attracted to Tuvia's whimsical hat. Since they came over, he convinced them to buy surfing pants and even granted them a "youth discount."

"We're finally having some fun," he said, patting his pocket. Dvora smiled distractedly; her mind was on Bina, who sat, limp and staring by the stall, her fat legs spread in heart-wrenching crookedness, her mouth open. She gathered her hair into a short ponytail on account of the heat, and Dvora suddenly noticed a few white hairs glistening in the sun.

"Are you thirsty?"

"Yes."

"Then why didn't you say so?" Dvora sighed and pulled out the Styrofoam water cooler. It was all Shraga's fault. He forgot to lock the bread drawer before they left the house the other night. She wasn't too happy to leave Bina unattended in the first place, but he convinced her—it wasn't like they were going out of town, they were only popping over to watch some slides at Tzippi and Yosef's, five minutes away. Bina, who knew all the relatives' phone numbers by heart, could be trusted. Bina did call, of course; crying, scared, crazed with pain after gorging on all the treasures of the drawer—toasted crackers, a sesame roll, a bag of Bissli, everything she was strictly forbidden to eat. From the moment Dvora was called over to the phone nook, things took their usual course—the run home, the regret, the remorse, the urge to compensate, to console, to distract from the suffering with some sparkling treat. And so, with an insouciance that would later be interpreted as gross irresponsibility, Dvora found herself sitting on Bina's bed, telling her about Seefeld. The exhausted Bina covered herself in a light comforter, rested her head in her sister's lap, and listened. As she smoothed her hair, the cosmetician described everything she remembered from the slide show: the snowy peaks, the steeples of King Ludwig's castle, the carriage drawn by a decorated horse. Without noticing, the Bubingers, the innkeepers (whom she'd never seen), also made their way into her stories, jolly and wearing feathered caps; behind them wobbled a small dachshund. As she exaggerated in her tales, a fear rose in her—a vague, yet certain, sense of imminent regret—but still she couldn't stop the flow of words. And Bina? Bina, who had never been out of the country—certainly not with all her relatives—drank up every last drop. The tormented face softened, the eyes twinkled behind tear-stained lids. She wanted to hear more and more about Seefeld and would not relax until her sister promised to bring her a brochure with photographs. Eventually, exhaustion won over her aching body.

After she turned out the lights and wiped away a tear, Dvora went to the kitchen to make a cup of tea and announced defiantly to Shraga that on the following Monday she would be taking Bina to the water park with her. Her husband, who could not tell where this spitefulness had come from, shrugged with wonder and said if she felt like it, who was he to stop her.

"You have to drink lots of water in summer," Bina proclaimed. "Tuvia, you have some water, too."

"Thank you," Tuvia said and took a sip, though he wasn't thirsty.

"Turn up the radio," Bina said. "The prime minister is speaking!" She'd always felt a personal affinity to the nation's leaders.

"Nachliel, do me a favor, lend me your radio for a few minutes," Fat Tuvia said. Zarfaty, who'd been sneaking looks of curiosity mixed with fear at Bina, obliged at once.

"There you goooo!" he said with the overeager cheerfulness of a schoolteacher.

Bina, who finally found a source of entertainment, put her ear to the device and listened with a worried face. Zarfaty, anxious about the fate of the radio, moved his plastic chair closer to the family's stall. The radio cackled some tune, a few flies buzzed around, the other merchants leisurely arranged the goods for the next wave of customers.

Dvora pulled out a plastic container filled with large, warm, sweet grapes and offered them around.

"The prime minister is taking care of our country," said Bina.

"So they say," Zarfaty confirmed.

"Are *you* selling those shirts over there?" Bina asked. "They're so pretty."

"Thank you very much," said Zarfaty.

"They're going to buy me a Popsicle later," she said. "Oh, look, look—a clown!"

Indeed, our old acquaintance, the very same tall-statured clown, appeared behind Dvora, a duffle bag printed with colorful circles slung over his shoulder. When he removed his powder-blue beret with the wooly pom-pom at the top, everybody could suddenly see that the guy was balding. Fat Tuvia poured him a glass of cold water, and the clown pulled a filthy handkerchief from his pocket and dabbed at the sweat that ran down his neck in two wet streams. Since he viewed Tuvia as his ally, he voiced his bitter complaints to him. He was dying to go home and peel off that terrible satin suit that kept clinging to his balls, he ranted, and next week he had a makeup exam, and of course he hadn't had a chance to study yet, but he was sentenced to wait until the end of bingo, he sighed, because he'd been ordered to go up on stage at the beginning of the fashion show, just for laughs, and walk among the models.

"How did ticket sales go?" Dvora asked.

"Very well," the clown answered.

"How much do they go for?" Dvora wanted to know. The clown said he sold one for five and three for ten. "Are there any left?" she asked.

"Of course, of course." He was about to go off on a last round of sales, he had orders from the boss to milk the audience for all it's worth.

Ten shekels, she thought; Bina would definitely enjoy it. If she was lucky, she'd win something, and if she didn't, Dvora could always console her with a piece of candy or a colorful plastic visor, anything to get her away from the stall, so she didn't disrupt sales; still, people were watching. Fat Tuvia would be fine on his own.

"Give me three." She pulled a bill from her purse and stood up. "Come on, Binchi, let's go play bingo."

E.

"Ladieeees and gentlemeeeen, employee committee members and all the wonderful families, welcome to this groovy day of fun fun fun and one big blast! Last chance to get your tickets, ladieeees and gentlemeeeen, the price is low and morale is high! Hey, you snob, have you gotten your bingo ticket yet?? In exactly one minute, yes, just one more minute, our bingo game will begin and the prrrrrizes are out of this worrrrrld: an elegant travel bag for domestic and international travel! A folding picnic set—a table and four chairs! And the grand prize—a BMX bike for kids! And many more prizes are waiting for you today, just come and get them!"

Our friend Albert Ben Arroya was on stage, wearing his old and peeling leather photographer's vest. His throat—sore; his forehead—scorched and sweaty; his eyes—bobbling from here to there, assessing, calculating. The lawn at his feet was swarming with people, but it was not enough for him. "Our charming clown is walking among you," he announced again and again, "and anyone who doesn't have a ticket yet—now's the time! One ticket for five shekels, three for ten. Three for ten, dear audience, now's the time, the time is now! Who doesn't have tickets yet, who doesn't have tickets yet, what a terrific game we're about to have, don't miss out . . . here we go!"

"Here we go!" Bina chirped. Her excitement knew no boundaries.

"And the first number, the first number is twenty-three! I repeat, twenty-three. What a beautiful number, twenty-thrrrrrree! Ladieeees and gentlemeeeen, our machine operates, as you can see, with no human intervention. No forgeries, no cheating, only luck counts—seventeen!!! Seventeen, seventeen, seventeeeeen!!! At this point, please be advised, we're going for a vertical row. The first one to complete a row—not horizontal, vertical—and yell 'bingo' will get a gorgeous prize from me, on the spot. What a day, what a day, this is insanity. The next number: tennnn! What a perfect number, ten! Sir, very nice of you to take your mother-in-law for a fun day at the park, you're a saint. Oh, that isn't your mother-in-law, it's your wife? My condolences. Four, the next number is fourrrr!"

"I've got four!" Bina cheered. "Look, Dvora, four!"

"Good, poke a hole in it."

"Thirty-six, ladieeees and gentlemeeeen, what a great day we've got ahead of us, a bathing suit fashion show with the biggest models in the country—Natalie Pepper, Miss Universe Runner-Up, the hot new talent Gali Habousha, and many more surprises. You're drooling already, huh? There's reason to live, gentlemennn, there's definitely reason to live! Let's see what the machine tells us—we'll just get the ball out of there, and . . . forty-sixxxxx!"

"And the next number—sixty-three!"

"Bingo!!!" a shout rose from the crowd. "I can't believe it! Bingo!"

Amplifiers sounded the opening notes of a famous radio sports show. The sea of people parted and the winner, a matron of about sixty, wearing a floral bathing suit and a turban headdress, passed through. When she reached the stairs that led up to the stage, she stumbled and fell on her face. Her gigantic buttocks stuck up in the air, to the joy of the other vacationers.

"What's your name, kiddo?" Albert Ben Arroya asked, sending a chivalrous arm to her aid.

"Rina Babayof," the winner answered with a gummy grin as she climbed onto the stage.

"You got something stuck to you back there." Pretending to worry about her well-being, he slapped her behind. "Oh, sorry, it's attached."

"I want that floor fan," Mrs. Babayof announced, placing her hands on her hips.

"You want, you want. Herzl wanted a country, and look what happened there," he chuckled. "Take a pair of beach paddles and go in peace."

"I don't want beach paddles," Mrs. Babayof insisted, inspiring bursts of laughter from the audience. "What do I need beach paddles for? Come on, give me that fan."

"Life isn't a request show," Ben Arroya scolded her. "But I'm willing to meet you halfway. Mrs. Babayof, may I call you Rina? Rina—is your husband here?"

"Sure," she confirmed. "His name is Nissim Babayof, he's over there, by the tree."

"Buddy!" Albert Ben Arroya screamed. The wattle below his chin reddened more deeply. "Come here, Mister Nissim, come help your wife get a floor fan out of me."

The audience soon had the pleasure of making the acquaintance of Mr. Babayof, a middle-aged man sporting a giant paunch ornamented with gray fuzz, above which rested slightly swollen man breasts. These qualities, in addition to his squinted eyes and the look of satisfaction on his face, gave him the appearance of a bathing Buddha.

"What a gentleman, what a gentleman!" Albert praised him. The host had a special gift: the more he carried on with compliments and honorary titles, the more humiliated his conversation partner felt. When he said, "with all due respect," a freezing chill of contempt blew between his lips; when he said, "sir," you heard "stupid"; and when he wanted to strike with all his might he'd treat his recipient with a "doctor," or, worse yet, "professor." After he demonstrated uninterested interest in his guest's life story—it turned out Nissim was a union member from Rehovot whose second granddaughter had recently been born—he pulled slim-fitting cotton pants from a box that was set up on stage and ordered Nissim to put them on. Mr. Babayof embarked on a strange dance—bending, breathing, straightening, and hopping until he succeeded, with effort, to wrap the piece of clothing around his rolls of fat (though he skipped the last button).

"How many children did you say you have?"

"A son who's an officer in the army and two daughters," Babayof answered importantly.

"Very good." Ben Arroya wrinkled his potholed face with a loathsome smile. "Because the way you just squished your Jozelito, I'm not sure you'll make ziggi-ziggi ever again."

Everyone laughed. Everyone but Bina, who asked Dvora with a whisper, "Why did he say that?"

"Tell me something, Rina—are you good with your hands?" Ben Arroya asked.

"My wife is very talented with her hands," Babayof answered too quickly and regretted it immediately, since Ben Arroya, only waiting for the opportunity to pounce on his prey, twisted his face, winked and gestured until he finally managed to raise bellowing laughter from the audience.

"What a fool, my God! I thought I was in Shfayim, but I guess I'm at the zoo. Rina, now listen to me. I'm giving you a needle and some thread, and this patch. You have two minutes, Rina, two minutes, to sew this patch onto Nissim's butt. If you can do it, you get to take that floor fan home. If not, you'll have to make do with the paddles. *Capisce?*" He moved a ratty curtain and revealed a large hourglass hanging from scaffolding. "Don't think twice—pay the price!" he screamed. "Ready, set, go!"

The host (who was a classical music enthusiast) liked to accompany the patch game with *Flight of the Bumblebee*—a piece of music to which he attributed great psychological effect. And indeed, the contestant kneeled down and began patching vigorously. Though he tried to contain himself, Union Member Babayof couldn't control his natural urges. He quickly began jumping and prancing around. His small nipples swayed this way and that as his wife soldiered on with a drawn needle, reproaching him to the pleasure of the viewers. Albert Ben Arroya made all kinds of bizarre exclamations into the microphone, such as "Lam-ba-da!" or "chaka-chaka-chaka!" which rallied the crowd, though no one understood their meaning. The audience went wild. This time Bina laughed, a laugh of pure, sweet, light-as-a-feather pleasure, as if she had unzipped herself and stepped out of the ungainly suit of her body. Even Dvora, who had always stayed away from party games, was intoxicated by the gaiety that overtook her sister and found herself tearing with laughter.

Suddenly, a loud buzzer sounded.

"Time's up!"

The Babayofs, only human, after all, stood at the front of the stage and took a bow.

"Let's hear it for Rina and Nissim!" called Albert Ben Arroya, pushing himself between the two, holding their hands and lifting them into the air victoriously. "You were cool, no doubt about it. Here's your prize, enjoy. We give—you get. You'll settle the score between the two of you at home."

Rina Babayof, beaming like a bride, hugged the fan with one hand and waved to the audience with the other. As she walked off stage, a gathering formed; her friends—and other curious bystanders—wanted to congratulate her, to touch her winnings, to reminisce about what had just happened. Nissim Babayof even pulled down his bathing suit a bit and presented them with a piece of skin dotted like a sieve. But their moments of fame were not prolonged. By the time Ben Arroya returned to his bingo machine, the happy winners were already lost in the crowd from which they had hailed invisible.

One by one, prizes were handed out, to Dvora's discontent. She wanted so badly for Bina to win something, and was so worried that she might not, that she pulled one of the tickets from her hand (with unnecessary aggressiveness, one might add), the one that had been mostly poked through, in order to play it for her. But Bina got angry and Dvora had to let go, muttering words of reproach she immediately regretted. At any rate, the game ended without them winning a thing. Surprisingly, Bina was not saddened a bit. She smoothed out her three tickets, placed her precious mementos in the fanny pack tied like a belt around her waist, and said, "Now a Popsicle." The two women linked arms and walked to the snack bar. Dvora, who still wanted to compensate Bina for the disappointment that never was, promised to buy her a cap with the logo of the waterpark as well. As they made their way through the masses, they recalled Albert Ben Arroya's shenanigans and giggled. Then they took their time near the wave pool, watching bathers. Over the tumult, they heard some familiar tunes, and Bina broke into song. "Every day is a holiday, a holiday every day, every day is a holiday—"

"Hallelujah!" Dvora joined in.

F.

"You Buy—You're Happy!" announces a sign outside one of the stores on Sheinkin Street. This statement, unfortunately, has nothing to do with the clothing business, since there is never a garment purchase that is not accompanied by heartache. Let us pull the curtain aside and emerge from the dressing room wearing a piece of clothing we are considering buying. A familiar, even beloved, creature looks at us from the mirror. But, being mummified in the new outfit, something strange, hypnotizing, even terrifying comes over this creature. The person in the mirror is an ambassador of a kingdom to which we are led against our will—it is not we ourselves who are reflected in this vision, but the people we might become. We are facing the future, the pattern that would fit the changes to our age and stature: a softer cut, a moderate shade. That very moment, we are plagued by the sorrow of parting from our old garment, which is tightly knit into our very being; with it, we also shed the days we spent inside of it. This was the shirt we wore on that wonderful spring outing with our loved one! And in these very pants we spent that one New Year's Eve, when we were crowned the life of the party! That same outfit we wrapped around ourselves with vanity, with conceit, with thoughtless comfort, is now tossed into the corner of the dressing room like a broken shell, wretched, faded from washing. The character that has just stepped out of the room is partially who it was in the past and partially who it is to become, but it has no being of its own—just a gust of steam painted on the glass, evaporating in a flash.

Sara Consignment's success stemmed from her wondrous ability to capture that slippery "now," born and departed almost in the same instant. This alchemist was able to convince her customers that they could burn the candle of time at both ends—the decisiveness, the heatedness, the foreign accent and the flow of European words, all positioned her as the ultimate authority, beyond boundaries of place and time. Her unique position allowed her to observe the fashion world from a certain distance and determine the true nature of changing moods. This, for example, was how she was able to foresee the unprecedented success that shoulder pads would enjoy at that time, and the massive impression that intentionally mangled jeans with lace peeking out of their holes would make in the following winter season. One should not conclude that each passing trend won her approval—on the contrary; she knew intuitively to ignore the incidental and adhere the contemporary. It's hard to say what principle guided her in assembling her goods, a mélange of garments and accessories she called "the collection." The labels could bear celebrated names, or sometimes a completely anonymous logo. One thing that must be said in her favor was that Sara Burko paid attention to details, large and small, and never placed low-quality clothing on her hangers. The items in "the collection" excited the heart and succeeded in hiding the wearer's shortcomings, and her customers showed their gratitude with cash. She herself dressed in a manner that was neither fashionable nor unfashionable, and hadn't bothered to change her hairstyle in over a decade; thus, she removed herself even farther from customary behavior. The mane of red curls partially concealing her dark eyes, the owlish nose, the average figure—all these did nothing to attest to her greatness.

"Duvia, your hat is a hit," Sara Consignment said. The bingo game dragged on and the heat-stricken merchants, welcoming the time of rest decreed upon them, gathered near the Paloma Bianca stall and enjoyed the shade of the poinciana tree and the light breeze blowing among its branches.

"These days, gimmicks are customary," Nachliel Zarfaty said, adding a scientific air to Sara Consignment's diagnosis. "Humor catches the customers' attention and relaxes them."

"So did it help you catch clients today?" she asked.

"It got what it got," Tuvia blurted with the same retail indifference he had observed and revered in his father. "Take it from me, I'm not worried—those who didn't buy earlier will buy later. No pressure.

The customer is like a carp—you have to let it swim around a little before you hit it over the head."

"The clientele has been very problematic so far," Sara Burko sighed. "The entire collection is still hanging on my stand. Everyone wants special consideration. If I were a private firm—all right, but everything I have is by consignment. I have to give 50–60 percent of every sale to the manufacturer!"

"Pfff." Nachliel Zarfaty poked Tuvia in the ribs. "She doesn't pay more than 30 percent, or I'm a monkey's uncle."

"They say today all the visitors are families of Dan Bus Company members," she continued. "They should be ashamed of themselves: they make a bundle but they don't spend a shekel, on principle. Wait and see how I'll shove it down their throats after the fashion show, straight down their throats, no shame. How is it going for you?"

"Lousy," Zarfaty lamented. "Everybody's looking for a bargain. There was a woman here earlier, she tried on a tunic made of Cool Wool—I don't have to explain it to you: made in Italy, the color won't come off even after a thousand washes. I sell it for 120, but for the *siftach*, like the kids say, I agreed to give it to her for 95 . . ."

"A freebee! A freebee!" Sara Consignment railed. "At this rate you'll go bank-robbed!"

"And she tells me—60 or I'll walk away. What could I have done, I ask you."

"Uneggceptable!" She shook her head. "Who are we trying so hard for? These degenerates? If people want cheap they should go to Nachalat Binyamin, they'll get what they deserve. What do you think, that I did any better? The meshuggaas made a phenomenal mess and hardly bought a thing. Maybe, *maybe*, I got 140 shekels so far."

"Scoundrels," Zarfaty hissed. Suffice it to say, he didn't believe a word she said, just as she didn't believe a word out of his mouth, but when there is time to be passed, it is nice to gather under the shadowy roof of complaint. The truth was, they had each managed to accumulate nice bundles of money, but Tuvia Zinman's presence fanned the flames: both wanted a discount in rental fees from his mother and were trying to create popular public opinion for their issues. Sara Burko schemed to drag Papa Frumkin into the cause, and perhaps even the bedding and towel merchant—but the attention of those two was now fully devoted to the stage, where, to the audience's glee, a plump lady was chasing her husband with a gigantic needle in hand. For now, the merchant sat near Zarfaty's stall (a spot from which she could easily watch over her goods), fished a cheese sandwich from her bag, and peeled an egg that smelled particularly sulfurous. The little man, who was being beckoned by the call of nature, asked her to keep an eye on his stall for a few moments and went off. As she devoured her meal with small, mousy bites, a myriad of words ran around inside her brain, ideas and crumbs of ideas she had not had the chance to put into words that morning. Some of them she planned to voice as comments to Tuvia, but being of developed musical sensibilities, she debated the appropriate tone: should she open with a melancholic commercial requiem, or rather go for a direct attack, accompanied by doomsday trumpets? But by the time she had her instruments in tune, Tuvia's mind was already on something else—the same matter that had been pecking at his soul for the past week, sending strange chills through his body.

"Hey, how are you?"

The blond curls had been pulled back and held with a band at the back of her neck. The round forehead was exposed in all its glory, the lips full of sweetness as she smiled. One could not help but sneak a peek at the pretty breasts, contained in a black bikini top, at the freckle-dotted shoulders or the curvy hips bursting out of shorts that had been cut by an amateur hand. Around her eyes were small wrinkles, uncommon for someone so young. They contained a very special gaze, assertive yet alert and restless.

"Terrific," Fat Tuvia said. "You?"

"Nothing. You know, the usual. Your hat is cool."

In spite of the compliment, he suddenly felt embarrassed about the umbrella atop his head, and took it off at once.

"Are you alone today?"

"No, my partner is here too, but she's walking around, probably went to the snack bar."

"I thought she was your mother."

"No, she's my aunt. My mother is Tzippi Zinman, who runs the fashion show and the stalls."

"So," Maya said, "you're stuck here until your aunt gets back?"

She shot her questions like small boats headed toward an iceberg, but Tuvia allowed them to drop anchor safely at his feet. "That's the job," he said and shrugged.

"What a bummer, standing like this in the heat all day—don't you feel like going in the water?"

"I don't mind it." (This was the truth, but also a lie; in all his days spent at the water park it had never even occurred to him, but now that she had spoken those words, he wanted to answer differently.)

"You don't come here every day, do you?"

"No, only on days when there's a closed event. That's our contract. Why, are you here every day?"

In fact, she was born in Shfayim; not just she, but her mother, too. Her father, she added (a cloud passed over her pretty face) had been living in a kibbutz down south with his second wife for years. She herself lived in a studio apartment allocated to her in what was called "immigrant housing" and was meant for single kibbutz members. It was a temporary arrangement, just until she went to South America, and since she had not yet accumulated enough travel points from the kibbutz, she worked as a lifeguard at the water park in the meantime. Her words annoyed Fat Tuvia. He roiled over all those kibbutzniks who simply got up and went to the jungles, and he felt like telling her that he was planning a trip, too—to Seefeld, no less!—but he doubted that the peaceful Tyrolean town could put up a fight against Rio de Janeiro or the temples of Machu Picchu.

"Is it hard work?" he asked.

"Beats bean picking. I had to take a course, but it was really easy—a little first aid, mouth-to-mouth, that kind of stuff. For real, I didn't get to save anyone yet. It isn't always so crowded like today—most of the time I just hang out. What about you? Where do you live?"

"Tel Aviv."

"He's hip! He's hip!" Sara Consignment called from her corner, eavesdropping and considering it her duty to improve Tuvia's stance with the young lady.

"Is she your aunt too?" Maya asked.

Tuvia Zinman was appalled to his core. "That's all I need. She's just some Romanian who sells here and likes to butt in. A real headache."

A shrill beep sounded, growing louder and immediately dying down. Afterwards an announcement was repeated several times through the amplifiers, that in five minutes the wave pool would be starting up.

"Damn, I have to go. Hey, when are you working again this week?"

"Tomorrow and Wednesday, then on Sunday again, at the police union event."

"I can let you in for night swimming if you feel like it. I'm off duty on Thursday and I was going to come just for fun. It's completely different here at night. There'll probably be tons of cool kids here, they might even make burgers. You should come—I'll wait for you by the gate at 9:30. Bye."

A racket came from the stage: bingo was over. The grand prize, a state-of-the-art bicycle, was won by the son of one of the ticket sellers, a skinny kid of about fifteen, his face covered in pimples, who shook Albert Ben Arroya's hand with immense excitement. The disappointed ones who had not won turned to seek consolation. The moment our heroes had been waiting for ever since that morning had finally arrived. Sara Consignment returned to her stall to lurk for prey. The towel merchant spread out some tropical models. Mama Frumkin pushed her table a little forward, and Fat Tuvia cleared the cups and put his umbrella cap back on.

G.

In truth, Tzippi cannot be blamed for what happened next. Many occurrences have reason, it seems, but they do not always have a plan behind them. Her intention, without a doubt, was to be helpful and thoughtful—granted, an area she had never excelled in, but had she not suggested what she did, that shameful comedy would never have been staged—a vision that pleased anyone who watched it, just as it had the one who participated in it, but ripped Dvora's heart to shreds. Some would say she was justified in her anger at her sister, who tended to scatter big promises without a thought to consequence. But this was neither negligence nor hypocrisy; in spite of the tendency—attributed to her in the family—to shirk responsibility, Tzippi Zinman respected the principles of morality no less than others. The promises she made stemmed from a deep, noble place: the fact that no actual deed could awaken in her soul the same kind of excitement generated by the mere announcement of her intentions.

Some years earlier, Dvora had been hospitalized due to a small lump in her stomach. She underwent a successful operation, but for ten days the doctors were unable to establish an unequivocal diagnosis. The worst was discussed behind the patient's back, yet she herself unknowingly acquired a bitter smile of acceptance. In one of those days of limbo, Tzippi came to visit. She took her sister for some fresh air in the garden outside of the main building, where they sat and talked, as people are wont to do on such occasions, about all sorts of intimate matters. After she herself devoured all the *bourekas* she had brought (she had forgotten about the diet undertaken by those healing from surgery), the visitor took the patient's hands in hers and swore on all that was dear to her that if her sister "came out of it," she herself would quit smoking. Dvora acknowledged the significance of the moment, since not once in her twenty-eight years of smoking had her sister made any such declaration. The vow was made with the appropriate solemnity; tears were shed and the two emotional sisters embraced warmly. Dvora had indeed "come out of it," as became clear within a few days, while Tzippi made do with that touching moment, which indeed held more awe than any act in the real world, and continued smoking as usual. Dvora was not angry; she understood, but once again had to sadly recognize her sister's frivolous nature.

Even in her youth, when the scale of hardship that life had in store for the Shlossman family was revealed, Tzippi refused to be bridled to the family wagon. Through the years, whenever she felt she might have gilded the lily, or when she was simply in the mood, she would help bear the burden for a short while. Usually her contribution did not extend beyond all sorts of flashy gestures, making an impression while not leaving a mark, but she thought it was enough to grant her temporary amnesty. Since she had never persevered in her efforts, she could never accurately evaluate the weight of the burden. Over the years, her relatives had not always bothered to inform her whenever they had to add another crate to their load; some boxes she had never peeked into, some packages she did not feel like opening. The weight fell, almost entirely, on Dvora. With time, Tzippi Zinman got used to seeing it as a sort of dusty luggage bearing the words: "Dvora's responsibility." Her own endeavors were always newer, more exciting and urgent, and therefore more important. In order to fight off criticism, she made a name for herself as one who never has enough time. She found myriad reasons to absolve what was in truth no more than pure selfishness. She avoided arguing with Dvora about anything that had to do with their little sister. In the company of strangers she would put on an act of modesty and say she had no right to intervene, and in private she would whisper to her husband: good riddance. In her mind, she imposed more and more duties upon her sister, all of which seemed appropriate due to her sister being, in her opinion, the successful daughter—or, at the very least, the one favored by their late mother. In her youth, Tzippi did all that was in her power in order to evade the reign of that tyrant, but her heart was still filled with yearning whenever she visited the family business. At Hinde's Perfumery, and especially at the atelier in the back of the store, where the eldest daughter and her mother concocted all sorts of potions, a peaceful professional life carried on, a camaraderie in which she had no part. Though legally the perfumery could not be inherited by any other than Dvora, who was a partner in the business and a key-money resident in her own right, Tzippi saw herself as having been shortchanged.

This perception was emphasized by another affair, which was also discussed only behind Dvora's back. In the fall of 1974, after a tombstone was set on Hinde Shlossman's grave, Tzippi and Avrum hurried to sell to the Saltzmans their share of the apartment the deceased had left behind. The purchasing terms were *extremely convenient*, as we have mentioned before, and not necessarily undertaken out of pure generosity. Dvora, who viewed herself as entitled to this privilege, received the terms silently. With the years, the considerations and the mood that had led at the time to the transaction were forgotten, and their place was taken, on both sides of the family, by pedantic, greedy accounting. The Saltzmans, the failing cosmeticians of Judah the Maccabee Street, complained about their wealthy relatives who contributed nothing to Bina's upkeep, while in the Zinman household, Tzippi's views took hold: she had been forced to sell her rights to her mother's apartment at a ridiculous price. Eventually, all those involved saw themselves as victims.

However, it would be wrong to say that Tzippi was coldhearted or indifferent to the hardships of others. And as evidence, that day, as she saw her sisters returning from their tour of the water park, she walked out to greet them of her own volition and offered to keep an eye on Bina for a while and even to take her for a visit backstage. Bina was very happy, and Dvora was relieved. Rush hour was nearing, and now she would be able to devote herself wholeheartedly to the stall. She made Bina swear to obey Tzippi and not to interrupt, stuffed a fifty shekel bill into her pocket just in case, and sent her on her way with a kiss, never suspecting even a hint of what was to happen twenty minutes later, or perhaps less.

H.

The stage to which Tzippi and Bina now turned was no bigger than a large hut, made up of rusting iron pipes and sheets stretched between them. From the stage, a wooden dock stretched over stilts, serving as a catwalk. Since no one bothered to build side walls that would close the space below this dock, children crawled underneath it, peeking up through the cracks. A red curtain served as a back wall; beyond it, models emerged; behind it they were swallowed, their faces revealing none of the desperation they felt about the rude audience, the miserable outfits, the humiliating conditions. Occasionally one of them twisted an ankle on the rickety staircase leading backstage—a sort of corral roofed with a sheet of blue raffia, soaking the room with darkness. Two creaking fans stood about like storks, blowing the air around, but the feeling of suffocation still lingered, because all openings were sealed as tightly as possible as protection against curious parties. A large mirror with silver paint peeling around its corners, two or three plastic chairs, a folding table and a nickel clothing rack covered in hangers gave this ruin the title "dressing room."

In Bina's eyes, there was no end to the splendor. She sat at the table as Tzippi had ordered her to, thirstily examining the many treasures: powder puffs, eye-shadow brushes, colorful bathing suits, jackets embroidered with countless tiny silver sequins, and of course the wonderful wedding dress, carefully wrapped in plastic and saved as a surprise for the finale. But all of these were belittled by the presence of Natalie Pepper; Bina had never met a real beauty queen before! She could barely stop herself from standing up and putting her hands on the woman's golden French braid. We know the constant suffering of Bina's body, but on the outskirts of her soul, ignorant of the circumstances of her fate, that dreamy brook, the water of which we all drank from in our childhoods, still babbled. Its flow was irregular and weakened by calamities, but now its bounty was brimming. In her imagination, she pictured herself walking down Judah the Maccabee Street with Natalie Pepper like a couple of princesses. She imagined them buying shiny Indian velvet skirts like the ones she had recently seen in one of the store windows, and later sitting at Café Alexander with all the important people, eating chocolate mousse and banana cake, or better yet—ice cream. When they finished, they would go upstairs to watch TV, and who knows? Natalie might even let her try on her patent-leather shoes, and in return Bina would teach her how to make paper swans. A bottle of sweet juice was placed on the dressing room table and Bina poured herself a cup. Suddenly Natalie Pepper addressed her, asking her to turn the fan in her direction. Poor Bina turned completely red and, with a shy smile, hurried to fulfil the model's wish.

In the meantime, Tzippi returned with her hands full from a round at the stalls. She gathered the models, divided the items between them, and explained the breakdown of the show. Some twisted their faces at the sight of Mandy Line's cheap shirts and surfing pants, but the agent fearlessly subdued their uprising and demonstrated how, by tying the ends of the shirt above the belly button, "like in Mediterranean beach clubs," even these rags could look fetching. Albert Ben Arroya's head appeared from behind the curtain to rush Tzippi and sneak a peek at the half-naked girls. Normally, the models would raise a riot, but now, with the increasing bustle, they did not even notice him. They all lined up in front of the mirror for a final look-over. Lipsticks were cocked for adjustments, pantyhose were stretched. The moment was approaching—not the moment they were waiting for per se, but who could have known that?

I.

First applause resounded around the stage: five models emerged wearing Paloma Bianca summery viscose dresses. Hundreds of excited viewers gathered around the wooden dock. The vacationers that were pushed to the edge of the crowd had despaired of the possibility of seeing anything and walked off to the stalls. Some bought, some accompanied shoppers as consultants, others just posed a bother, and others still decided to forego the principle of payment for goods— Tuvia caught one fat kid with the wisps of a mustache pulling a shirt out of the pile, and grabbed him by the ear. After he kicked him away, Tuvia stood behind the stall with his umbrella cap on and tossed about loud exclamations. Dvora, who shied away from any loud and flashy displays, was in charge of the cash register. They paid their respects to the law through the use of a green iron box that rested prominently on the table, and a wide-open receipt book. Each piece of income had its own destiny, and a quick look between the partners was enough to determine the fate of each payment. When a suspicious character appeared at the stall, Dvora raised her pen and scribbled a quick receipt. If the buyer was some bespectacled high schooler, Tuvia lazily stuffed the money into his ever-filling pocket.

In spite of all the concerns and lamentations we had been privy to that morning, the shoppers overtook the stalls. Nachliel Zarfaty, the Frumkins, the towel salesmen—cash flew through all their hands.

The models strutted on the catwalk, and at the foot of the stage people sold and bought, bought and sold. Estee Creations got rid of twenty-four pairs of feathered earrings. "It seems like small business, but why mock it, it's another shekel in your pocket," Tuvia said. They could not catch their breath; by the time they refolded and rearranged the clothes, another wave of customers arrived to ruffle the goods. The stacks grew thin, the surfing pants with the palm tree prints ran out. The sales awoke an excitement in Dvora; she took pleasure in the vitality of her own movements, in the wordless coordination between her and Tuvia, in the wealth accruing in the legal register and in the secret bundle, in short—in the bright face of success. "Please welcome Gali Habousha, Tami Ben Ami's hot new successor, in the beach-girl look of the summer of '89!" she heard the words spilling out of Albert Ben Arroya's mouth. "Sexy, sexy, sexy! What a celebration with Mandy Line's surfing pants, a young look for him and her, yesterday in L.A., today in Shfayim, special prices for Dan union members!" In the heat of commerce she even started believing the lies the host was disseminating, regarding the innovative sewing, the breathable cotton, and the hot young designer named Mandy. The area around the stall grew more and more crowded. Young boys and heavyset mothers were joined by dozens of eager women demanding "outfits" like the ones they saw up on stage. Who could understand the crowd—one day the stall was as dead as a cemetery, the next it was too busy to breathe. Papa Frumkin, who was proficient in the mysteries of the consumer's soul and knew one had to strike while the iron was hot, sent his old lady over to Dvora's with plastic visors offered for a special price; those quickly sold out too. Fat Tuvia ran out to get one last bag of goods he had kept in the car just in case. As the number of items dwindled, the pressure rose. People fought over each shirt, one snatching from the other, the other snatching from the first. More and more one hundred shekel bills were broken. Dvora was lost in commercial intoxication. She seemed to believe that even the great Sara Consignment was sending envious looks her way.

Suddenly laughter was heard: monkey screeches that ignited around the stage and spread through the audience like flames through a thorn field. At first, Dvora had not noticed and continued to fold shirts. Then the voices grew louder and an ominous recognition began bubbling inside of her. She dropped the shirt from her hands and turned her head toward the stage. The laughter became an unbridled, wild bellowing. Albert Ben Arroya fed the fire with a dry throat. Here and there someone whistled encouragingly. Somebody clapped; another joined in, and another. Within seconds the applause crystallized into heavy, threatening lava that flowed from the back of the stage to the dock and over to the stalls. Though she still did not know what had gotten things so heated, her heart told her it was bad news. Somebody spat out that terrible word; and then she realized. She threw herself into the crowd and the closer she got to the dock, the more crowded it became: everyone wanted to see it for themselves. From each direction, twisted, red masks, gaping mouths, lolling tongues, people calling out, "Hey, lady!" and "Will ya stop pushing??" and she was shoved back again and again. A two-minute trip seemed to take forever. Suddenly everything stopped. Her eyes went dark for a moment, as if the world were nothing more than a gigantic slide show and the last slide had disappeared, leaving a black emptiness in its wake. The whirlwind around her froze, the sounds grew faint; she felt as if she were standing alone on the banks of time. Then a new, blinding image was revealed. Her face was aflame. Shame mixed with tears of rage. Right in front of her, on stage, wearing surfing pants and a too-tight bikini top, the flesh of her breasts squeezing out of it, Bina, poor Bina, her ludicrous younger sister, wiggled her bum. The pants that rode up wedged in between the two, fat, exposed cheeks of her buttocks. One hand supported her nude waist coquettishly, while the other waved to the audience. The crowd raged and roared on both sides of the dock. When she reached the end of the catwalk she bowed to the right, then to the left, squeezed her fists like a drummer and swung from side to side in a duck-like dance. A delicate, heartbreaking smile spread across her face. There was no end to her joy.

■ ■ ■

The sun was stuck in the middle of the sky. The blinding light enveloped all, leaving no corner free of it. It seemed that nobody would ever cast a shadow onto the earth, that everything had been devoured by heat. Even noises were all melted into a meaningless jumble—songs became distorted, calls of joy weakened and disappeared, Nachliel Zarfaty's little radio produced only crumbs of words. Everything was boiling, everything was scorching, desires softened like wax. The raffia canopies painted the vacationers blue as they sat, exhausted, in the shade, poking their plastic forks at the leftovers of their food. Even the most energetic toddlers collapsed to rest, goggles raised over their wet hair, their bodies wrapped in towels. The pools emptied, the stalls were deserted, the merchants counted their earnings.

"I don't think we'll get anything more out of this." Sara Consignment sighed. "Let's go, Nachlieli, we can call it a day."

PART THREE

A Comfortable Arrangement

7

A Change of Plans

A.

On the west bank of Ben Yehuda Street, between a Judaica store and a suitcase shop, is a small travel agency called Top Tours. Nothing distinguishes it from the other small, dusty agencies with which the street is overflowing. This one, too, has a sign in English and a drawing of planet Earth. This one's window also features a faded poster from some vacation site. Here, too, a pipe hangs from the air conditioner, secreting drops of water onto the sidewalk. The interior is narrow and long, almost a hallway. On the right wall is a huge photo—a Pan American airplane floating among clouds. A couple of busy receptionists sit behind a counter coated with yellow Formica, smoking. From morning till night they scribble notes, file documents, or let their eyes wander over lines upon lines of greenish type flickering on computer screens. Each receptionist has two phones—one earpiece is constantly tucked between a shoulder and an ear, the other rolling around on the desk. Once in a while, one of them picks up the rolling one, barks some order, and abandons it again. This business makes a huge impression on customers waiting their turn. As they pretend to peruse pamphlets written in first person plural but featuring pictures of others, they eavesdrop on the unstoppable chatter on the other side of the counter—"voucher," "Q class," "half board"—and other such phrases that send a pleasing chill through one's body.

At the time of our story, a trip abroad was a complicated affair, involving myriad complex procedures. A travel ransom was imposed on anyone wishing to leave the country; each passenger had to produce a bank document confirming that foreign currency had been legally purchased; men who could be called up for reserve duty had to also show permission from the military to leave the country; often people had to stand in line for hours on end just to get some kind of visa . . . the travel agency was therefore only a first stop, filled with smoke and self-importance, as travelers normally are. The mechanism launching them to a faraway desirable destination was revealed to them without the beautification of nickel and marble. But beyond the stained rug in the hallway, beyond the neon lights and the ruptured leatherette armchairs, awaited no less than Lake Geneva, the Colosseum, the wondrous geysers of Yellowstone Park—legendary sites, the images of which glowed brighter precisely because of the local meagerness. Travelers' heads spun from the possibilities—numbers thrown around in dollars, connections in anonymous airports, three countries in seven days or the other way around. They did not always settle for a single visit to the travel agency; most of them found excuses to breathe some more of its foreign air, each for his or her own reasons.

In the back, on an elevated plateau, was an office sealed with glass doors—management. Most of its space was taken by a wooden desk, upon which accumulated countless folders, vouchers, index cards, calendars, mugs with dried sediment, a sooty Murano glass ashtray, and an award figurine. In the corner, atop a giant steel vault, a begonia in a clay pot was slowly dying. In the heart of this rubble, curled in a comfy leather armchair like a pea in its pod, a thin cigarette in one hand and reading glasses sliding down his curvy nose, sat the agency manager and head agent—no other than our acquaintance Sammy Greenberg, nicknamed Susu, as he purred over a thick book of data tables.

"It's lucky that you came now." He wrinkled his forehead and ran his fingers down the lines on that July afternoon. "I can tell you're European. The Israelis always come at the last minute, and then they complain that tickets are expensive. Let's see . . . is it important to you to fly El-Al or can it be another airline?"

Dvora wanted to say that El-Al would be best, but her sister beat her to the punch and said anything goes.

"Lufthansa has a plane going to Munich during the holiday, if you don't mind flying on a Saturday. Give me two or three weeks; we might be able to get you V-class tickets."

Tzippi nodded and Dvora concluded that this was an opportunity. She wanted to ask about the actual price, but did not want to seem provincial.

"Let's start by opening files for you. Got your passports?"

"Here."

The Zinmans' passports: faded, battle-ridden, their pages covered with red and purple stamps. The Saltzmans' passports: encased in new leather, sounding a crispy rustle when riffled.

"Oh, our nice little Shraga!" Sammy pointed out, giggling in a way that alarmed Dvora. "He got himself a great photo. Are these all of them? Who else is going?"

"Avrum said you have all his details," said Tzippi. "My son Tuvia is also going, and we're taking our Aunt Masha."

"Good children." The midget was pleased. "And where's her passport?"

"She's a difficult woman," Tzippi said with a sigh. "I couldn't even get her passport number out of her."

"We'll open a file for her anyway," the manager determined, pulling over a form book from the mess on his desk. Silence fell as he carefully copied passenger information. Dvora followed his clerk's fingers as they left a trail of round, almost childish letters, the handwriting of an immigrant. A not unpleasant strangeness overtook her: the bizarre midget tossing about mysterious terms, the faint odor in the air, a combination of print and cologne—all of these offered an evocative excitement, bringing to mind the final hour before a birthday party.

"Where's Bina's passport?" Tzippi remembered. "Didn't you bring it?"

"We haven't gotten her one yet."

"What exactly are you waiting for?"

"You only know how to criticize," Dvora said angrily. "The day we went to the Ministry of the Interior she didn't feel well and stayed in bed. Then I had other things to worry about. What can I do? Maybe you should take her."

"How can I?" Tzippi said, lightly pushing the suggestion away. "You're her legal guardian."

"No need to fuss," Sammy said by way of appeasement. "I'll open a file for her too. We won't fill out the passport number yet. But don't dawdle until mid-August—we have to get the tickets as soon as possible. How do you spell her name in English?"

"S-h-l-o-s-s-m-a-n," Tzippi said.

"We had a Shlossman in Buenos Aires, happened to be an electrician." He wrote the name carefully with a fountain pen as he shoved the tip of his tongue between his teeth. "Don't forget to pay the travel tax for her, too."

"It's on me," Tzippi told her sister. "Let me know once she gets her passport, and I'll go to the bank myself."

Then the agent said it was late and there was nobody to talk to at Lufthansa, and promised to arrange everything the next morning. Tzippi made an arrogant comment about the payment. No one named a price. And Dvora? She no longer felt like finding out how much it would cost and how she could make a payment plan; things here were completely different from anything she had known before, and the new standards were unbelievably exciting. There she was, dipping her foot in that bath of haughtiness and self-importance her sister had been bathing in for years, and the water sure was nice.

"Can I offer you an aperitif?" Sammy asked. "I have marzipan liqueur."

"Why not," Tzippi said. "My sister doesn't drink, but you can pour me a drop."

"Actually, I feel like it," Dvora said.

"Will you need cars?" He placed three crystal glasses in front of him and poured. A sweet scent spread through the room.

"Obviously," Tzippi said, treating herself to a thin cigarette from the pack on the desk. "We'll take two cars."

"Don't forget to get international drivers' licenses," Sammy reminded them. "Who's driving? Shraga?"

"Yosef will drive one car," Tzippi said, "and my son will drive the other, or maybe I will, why not. I'm crazy about those European roads; just let me hit them at 160 kilometers per hour."

"I like to race once in a while too." Sammy giggled. "But only in reverse. Cheers!"

"Cheers!"

"Cheers!"

"You know what?" Tzippi turned to her sister. "I have a great idea; we'll put the men in one car and the girls in the other. It'll be a riot!"

"Terrific idea!" Sammy agreed. "I'd sit in the girls' car."

"You aren't going to believe what I'm dying for now, and you can make fun of me all you want—I'm dying to be in one of those gas stations on the freeway, you know."

"How should I know?"

"Oh, we're going to have fun, Dvoraleh; I'm drooling, just thinking about it. In any tiny nowhere of a place you pull over and they give you fresh Danishes, speck sandwiches, amazing soups, if you're hungry. And each gas station has a grocery store—you can get the best chocolates for the road. What can I say? The Austrians know how to live, period, exclamation mark."

"The land of gesundheit," the midget confirmed.

All at once, open spaces spread in front of Dvora's eyes: a peaceful valley, a twisting road, white stripes swallowed one by one beneath the car. In a field by the side of the road a fat horse lazily pulling a cart. An ancient castle glimpsed atop a mountain, and in the distance—snowy peaks. The windows are open, a light breeze carries that pleasant aroma of recently reaped grains. Shoes are kicked off, a bag of pretzels is passed around—maybe they even sing out loud. Tzippi would be driving, but she herself would also have a job—she could read the signs. She had learned some German in her years as a beautician. In the other car—the men. Once in a while they all stop for a bathroom break and a cup of coffee. They grab a table outside some inn, smoke, and if it's chilly they even cuddle up with their husbands, why not. Fat Tuvia reads out loud from the guidebook, Avrum cracks a joke or two . . . her soul was filled with sweet yearning for a country she had never visited.

"Will you go to Mad Ludwig's *palacio*?" the agent asked. "That's unmissable."

"You're telling *me*?" Tzippi protested. "Yosef and I have been there, many times! But we'll go again—I want Dvora to see it, too."

"Is it pretty?" Dvora asked.

"There's no 'not pretty' in Seefeld," Tzippi said.

Yes, King Ludwig's palace, and Zellersee Lake, and that iceberg, she forgot what it was called, all those things she could not possibly miss, and above all—Seefeld, with its geranium-adorned balconies and the crazy balls at the club each night . . . suddenly her face fell.

For the past week, ever since that shameful vision appeared on stage at Shfayim, Dvora had been struggling with that horrible obstacle, which required an urgent solution. There were hours when she managed to cast off all worries, and just then, when she had almost convinced herself that everything was going to work out, her dark expectations and their trusted ally—experience—attacked her with all their might, each bringing her under their wing, whispering words of desperation in her ears. Everything would have been different, of course, had she not been tempted to tell Bina about Seefeld in the first place. The very moment she felt the words escaping her mouth prematurely, she realized that she had not thoroughly considered the consequences—but she could not help herself. The next morning, before breakfast, Bina called Tzippi to tell her the exciting news. Tzippi, who had heard about the entire ordeal from Dvora, pretended to be surprised and announced that in honor of the trip, she was going to buy Bina her own suitcase—the first she would ever own. After breakfast, Bina went down to the stationery store, bought a new student's datebook, and asked Uri Hachimian to mark Sukkot with a glowing felt pen. As he did so, she told him about Seefeld and said that if he wanted, she would send him a postcard. Everything she did that happy day was accompanied by some song, the words of which she muddled but the tune of which she hummed with amazing accuracy, repeating it again and again, until Dvora almost lost her mind.

From that day on, the members of the family did not bother themselves with questions; things had been said—and that was that. Even Shraga, whose reaction Dvora feared the most, reacted with complete apathy. If she wanted to take Bina abroad and take care of her, he muttered, she was more than welcome; he only had one request—to have the Zinmans split the bill, for a change. Like that well-known children's game, our friend discovered that in the brief moment her eyes had been closed, all the other participants—including Bina—had lined up in a new order, and were now standing in front of her as if they had never moved, all smiling pleasantly. This smile made it crystal clear to her that, even in Seefeld, she would be the only one to bear the load. The poor beautician was caught in a cruel dilemma. She begged—whom?—to give her a little more time to think and find a solution, but time was running out; they had to get tickets in two to three weeks, Sammy had said.

Suddenly, one of the receptionists tapped the glass: a customer about to fly tonight to the trade fair in Milan had come by to pick up his tickets. The Milan trade fair! The news impressed Dvora immensely. There she was, debating and calculating, while behind the wall someone was picking up his tickets at the very last moment. Sammy wore an official expression and turned to open the giant vault behind him. No bills of money or bars of gold were kept in there, but rather stacks of pink flight tickets secured with rubber bands and ordered alphabetically. He breathed in, puckered his lips, and flipped through slowly, taking a good look at each voucher and note. When he was satisfied he handed the ticket to the receptionist, relocked the vault and glanced conspicuously at his watch.

"We've got to run," said Tzippi. "Can you give my sister a few brochures about Austria?"

"What for?" Dvora wondered. "I don't need them."

"Didn't you promise Bina you'd bring her pictures?"

The midget collected a pretty pile of brochures and handed it to Dvora with fanfare. He reminded the sisters to obtain the missing passport numbers and parted with a light bow.

The cosmopolitanism that had enveloped the sisters evaporated at once as they stepped out onto the street. The sanitation workers' strike had entered its eighth day; the stench of decay was in the air, and they had to make their way among ruptured trash bags swarming with cats and maggots. Tzippi suggested popping over to the Hungarian deli next to city hall to get a taste of Europe—her treat. She was surprised by Dvora's meek response. She gave her a quizzical look, but couldn't invade the fortifications behind which her sister pondered a private and very important meeting she had to attend soon, with Aunt Masha.

B.

We've weighed the Bulgarian cheese
But—(appease/never cease/disease)
From us you've bought your food and drink
Our grilled chicken was on the brink
We gave the little kids free gum
And made the parents laugh for the same sum
We were like a true family, sharing the wealth
For better or worse, in sickness and health
We knew when to give a word of advice—
Free of charge, kindness has no price
And if I raised my voice here and there
Please forgive me if I gave you a scare

The years have flown by like a rocket
Most of our customers remained, but some have closed their pockets
And now the times are changing
Everyone is at the supermarket, buying and exchanging

Such is the way of the world
But I can't be bought or sold
And even if . . .

. . . .

(Y. L. Zinman)

It was almost seven p.m., the sky over Judah the Maccabee Street was darkening, and the amount in the cash register was no more than three hundred shekels. For the past thirty-five minutes, not a soul had passed the threshold of the grocery store. Behind his counter sat Yosef-Leib Zinman—that is his full name—his forehead wrinkled over a large notebook, its pages covered in scrawls and eraser marks. "And even if . . . and even if . . . even if what?" he asked himself. "And even if what, dammit?"

In the annihilating light of the neon bulb, the grocery store looked like an aquarium whose owner had forgotten to change the water. The refrigerator's glass doors were murky with oily fingerprints accumulated throughout the day, the floor tiles were stained with dry spills: a leaking milk bag, the remnants of an egg that had been broken at 9:30 that morning, sticky drops of juice. Normally, at this hour the owner excused himself to the daily task of cleaning, but tonight he allowed himself to sink into a poetic mood. He had started writing his elegy to the grocery store several weeks earlier, during an afternoon shift no less dire than this. At first he thought he would cheer himself up by writing a comic ditty (in the family he had the reputation of a rhymer, and often prepared an amusing limerick for birthday or holiday celebrations), but instead he found himself composing a sort of lament. Try as he might to push away those gloomy lines, they were persistent, sneaking back into his pages, until he gave in to them. At any free moment—and those had recently become plentiful—he lost himself in rhymes: adding and crossing out, improving and considering, changing and changing his mind, and so on and so forth. His devotion to the phrasing of the eulogy of his life's work awoke a sweet excitement in him, often bringing tears to his eyes.

Truth be told—Yosef Zinman is himself Yosef-Leib Zinman's true life's work. Over the years, he had shed his beauty, his attractive figure, and his youthful demeanor, and from the ashes rose a large-bellied Jew in his fifty-fourth year of life radiating good health and a good nature, equally popular with others as he was with himself. There was not one gray hair in his slicked-back coiffure—the receding hairline on both sides of his forehead only added a charming ripeness to his appearance. He always spoke level-headedly, and his glasses, supported by a handsome nose, not too big and not too small, afforded him with a suitable measure of authority.

Who could ever guess, then, that distress was eating him up on the inside? How fragile is the measure of happiness available to the small-time retailer—nine loaves of challah remaining on the shelf at the end of a Friday afternoon are enough to turn a holiday into a day of mourning! He was not one to ignore signs of alarm. Changes happen slowly—and a less sensitive gauge might not have even signaled the approaching transformation—but Yosef Zinman, as we know, does not require a scale in order to determine the exact weight of a wedge of cheese. . . . In the store's glory days, Peretz the workman unloaded a dozen milk crates in his little room at the back of the store: there wasn't enough room for all of these in the fridges, but most of the milk was sold before the drops of frost even evaporated; in recent months, however, the grocer realized he was left with more and more unsold milk bags each evening. When he called the dairy producer's order department he had to ask for lower quantities, and his heart fell with them. But let us not get ahead of ourselves: the deliveries made each morning from the grocery to the penthouses of Kosowsky Street and the basement offices of Zirlson Street were still enviable. Yosef Zinman's business wasn't founded on incidental riffraff, but rather on the well-established families of the neighborhood, those who had a secure tab with him, who walked in once in a while just to ask how he was doing.

Still, life took its course: children grew up, parents grew old, households shrank. Once in a while, one of his veteran customers left the neighborhood, and sometimes, God help us, simply died. Gone were the days when Yosef sat in his fortress like a feudal lord reigning over his consumers and their consumption. The words *customer* and *shopper* were suddenly distinguishable. Stepping out to the doorway for some air and a look over the street, his eyes often caught a glimpse of former customers carrying bags with the supermarket's logo printed on them. As they passed him by they hastened their steps or became suddenly lost in thought. Others, having better manners, continued to visit his store sporadically, but seemed to be subsisting mainly on yogurt and rice. In short, all signs pointed to a new era, but it was as yet unclear what kind of position Yosef Zinman would hold in it. In his sorrow, he turned to poetry, leaning on it like a man imagining his own funeral.

"Hello."

Zinman looked up from his notebook and saw before him a tan, birdlike woman of about thirty.

"Hello, hello."

An elongated shelf unit, overflowing with goods, took up most of the store's space. Of the two aisles stretching between the shelf unit and the walls, the shopper chose the farther one and paced it, her receding chin tucked into her neck in exhibited boredom, once in a while sounding a *tsk* of disappointment from between her puckered lips. Outside, the street was bustling: a bus opened its doors in a roaring bang, a dog barked loudly, a child rang the bell of his bicycle, just because. And inside—a tomb-like silence, only exacerbated by the weak simmer of neon lights. Suddenly, the shopper reached out—Zinman followed her moves with yearning eyes, hoping she would pull out an expensive bottle of wine. He thought she had noticed his look; her arm kept wandering over the shelves, debating, and was now fluttering over the row of canned fruit salads. He began wondering if she was not getting some strange pleasure from the occasion.

"How much?" she finally asked, presenting to him a can of preserved pineapple.

"Three twenty-five."

"I saw it at the supermarket for two fifty," she said, and returned the can to the shelf.

She circled the shelf unit and was swallowed in the depth of the back room. Though he knew pressuring and persuading were no good, since any exhibition of interest in her actions would be interpreted as weakness, he could not take his eyes off her. She slid open the fridge door—Zinman was convinced she was taking her time on purpose, trying to damage the mechanism—rummaged and searched, and finally took out a container of cream cheese. On her way to the cash register she passed by the hygiene section and selected two boxes of cheap soap.

"Will that be all?"

"Hold on, I need to think."

Once more a fire was stoked in the stove of his hopes. She pressed her hands to her hips and examined the shelves again, running her tongue from side to side over her gums.

"All right," she determined. "Ring me up."

Zinman approached the register and cleared his throat.

"Hold on, hold on," she stopped him. "Say, do you happen to have onion-flavored cream cheese?"

"There's a shortage in the market."

Her face fell. "Fine," she gave up, signaling impatiently for him to proceed.

Yosef adjusted the glasses on his nose and tapped the keys: one forty plus one forty . . .

"Hold on, hold on," she said again. "I can't see the expiration date!"

The small sticker on the lid of the container was covered with a white crust, which she scratched off with a pointy red fingernail.

"What's this—the twenty-ninth?!" Her eyes brightened.

"That's in four days," the owner said in self-defense.

The shopper made do with a sigh of despair, as if in despair of trying to teach table manners to savages.

"I take products with that expiration date home myself. Want me to find you another one?"

"Never mind," she announced, wiping her hands on her pants. "Have a good day, sir!" She raised her bird head and left the store, leaving the orphaned soap bars on the counter.

The grocer silently wished a terrible bowel disease upon her, and turned to polish the fridges. He was so enraged by her that he decided to lower Peretz's salary.

This is the moment to tell about how in 1970, the Zinman Grocery Store was given a governmental appointment—the authorities included it in a list of Crisis and Emergency Economy Providers. Being a CREEP filled him with pride. And indeed, in the war that came soon after, he devoted himself to the service of his homeland, and while the other grocery stores of northern Tel Aviv were locked and barred due to fear of an aerial attack, Yosef sold oil and sugar, lentils and canned goods. The lines stretched all the way to the corner of Zirlson Street; two Zinman third cousins were summoned to serve as ushers and Yosef himself stood behind the counter for twelve hours straight each day, distributing goods calmly and without bias. Thus, he did his part in helping keep the home front calm, and has since believed that "they wouldn't let a guy like him fail." And indeed, you could not find one person on Judah the Maccabee Street who did not acknowledge Zinman's status—they were all convinced he was "of means." They all said: the great Yosef Zinman, Yosef Zinman the millionaire. He happily embraced this exaggeration and pushed away worries; he never believed a merchant of his stature could be threatened by economic calamity. Once, he heard Yunger the butcher telling Mrs. Gitlis over some plucked turkey legs: look at that, Yosef Zinman goes abroad twice a year. Now he wondered how much longer he would be able to fund his pleasant habits. While he swept the linoleum floor, he tried to calculate how much Seefeld would cost him this year, and was frightened. He calculated again and reached an even larger number, because he could not resist adding one more ostentatious tribute: he would take the entire family to a sumptuous meal at the Kaiserhof Inn, on him!

As he squeezed water out of the blackened mop, he was plagued again by the shortening income columns, his landlord's greedy eyes, the postdated checks he was forced to give his suppliers . . . these all remained his private territory—he made sure to hide them even from Tzippi; he gladly waived his right to complain in public for the benefit of his cosmetician relatives. In the theater company called "family," the roles had been assigned years ago and had never changed; without ever expressly stating so, the Saltzman distress had always been poised against the Zinman success. In his generosity, he forgave his relatives for their jealousy—since he was also pleased with himself, he was sympathetic to their plight. The trouble was, he was not exempt of jealousy's bite: his heart was pinched each time Dvora proudly read the letters Yellow Tuvia sent from Boston University; each time he had to listen once again to the list of his nephew's biochemical achievements, he imagined hearing his daughter Shirley's saw melodies. In the bedroom, to his wife, he exhibited indifference, and whenever she warned him that "one day that girl will kill us all," he waved off her words as meaningless chatter. But for a long time after she began snoring, the suffering grocer lay awake on his back, painting a gloomy picture of the future in his mind, including drug dens and unplanned pregnancies. His only consolation was Fat Tuvia, his eldest, who seemed like a contemporary embodiment—still rough, but carrying great promise—of his own fine qualities. He delighted in following his son's progress in commerce, and while the kid was taking his time with other, more personal matters (the kind that Yosef himself had excelled at in his day), he was sure Fat Tuvia could be trusted, and that those matters would be resolved sooner or later. For the time being, he waited patiently.

The moment he had been waiting for arrived two days hence, when he woke up as usual at five in the morning and went to the kitchen to boil water. The house was still dark, though faint stripes of dawn were already sneaking in through the shutters. On his way, he bumped into a large silhouette—Fat Tuvia. Had his son not greeted him with a strange official air and asked halfheartedly if he had returned that Harrison Ford movie to the video store, he would have thought nothing of it. But not only the bizarre question at dawn was surprising, so too the speed with which the asker was swallowed back into his room, not waiting for an answer. Yosef, still wrapped in the fog of sleep, groaned something and went into the kitchen. Only after fortifying himself with a cup of coffee and a slice of bread with halva, he realized what had bothered him—Tuvia had been dressed, fully dressed, even wearing sandals! Then comprehension slowly seeped in. He remembered that a few days earlier a kibbutz member was discussed, having invited Tuvia over for night swimming. The more he thought the matter over, the more he could not help but come to the same, single conclusion. As he smoked the first cigarette of the day, the picture became crystal clear. Immense excitement gripped him. He stamped out the butt, entered the bedroom quietly, and shook his wife's shoulder until he finally saw the twinkle of awareness in her eyes.

"Tzippi," he whispered. "Tzippi! The kid is screwing!"

C.

There wouldn't be enough time on Wednesday—Albert Ben Arroya said they were expecting about five thousand people from the civil servants' union. But maybe he could still disappear for an hour, before it all began, and join Ciotka Dvora later? Let her set up the stall by herself, big deal. Hope was ignited for a moment, immediately followed by disappointment—Tuvia calculated and found that by the time he left and arrived he would have less than an hour left, and that was not enough . . . for a moment he considered staying on at the kibbutz at the end of the work day and catching the last bus to Tel Aviv, but rejected the idea. It was better to conduct this privately, without drawing any attention. And on the other hand, behind Wednesday lurked Thursday—and on Thursday evening he would have time. He could come over at 9:00, he told himself, trying to assess how long after his arrival he would be lucky enough to partake in the unbelievable, and immediately moved the appointment forward to 8:30. But, actually, Friday was free, too—any time would work, he was a flexible man. He would even be willing to skip the family dinner. He could not know how girls treated Friday nights, but Maya was not like any other girl, he pointed out to himself proudly.

He was in the mood to recreate everything that had happened from the moment they left the pool—when his body winked at him meaningfully. But try as he might, he could not remember how they made it to the room, an old shack she called "immigrant housing."

When they went out the gates they took a left, then walked down the path all the way to the intersection. He remembered nothing after that. The more he tried to bring the details to mind, the worse he failed. Even her face fell apart sporadically, like a radio broadcast having trouble stabilizing on the right frequency. He turned the dial; it seemed he had been listening to meaningless static for the past ten minutes. The windshield looked like a screen onto which a movie without subtitles was being projected: the Coastal Highway illuminated in the moonlight, the endless tin fence that separated lanes slicing it at its center. The fields of the kibbutz and the electric wires were quickly replaced with the shadows of ficus trees and the tiled roofs of Herzliya Pituach. He glanced at the dashboard; he had no idea if he was galloping madly or crawling patiently. At the Sira intersection the traffic light blinked—his foot clung to the pedal and the car crossed the intersection at a red light almost of its own accord.

Until that night, he had never participated in night swimming, and the truth is, he had never been too enthusiastic about day swimming, either. That branch of human activity was foreign to him, not due to animosity, but rather as a result of indifference. Somewhere in his closet an old bathing suit was hiding, but he could not find it. With no other choice, he decided to take something from the merchandise. That fateful night, he chose surfing pants adorned with a diagonal powder blue line—but eventually he preferred to watch the swimmers from the recliner on the edge of the pool. Maya was annoyed at the lazy serenity he exhibited, and encouraged him to jump in the water, but he waved her off with a merciful smile, free of any jealousy of the well-built kibbutz boys frolicking around her in the water. When they grilled the meat on a smoking tin stove—he remembered the large bites she took of the hamburger—they called him over to join and he gladly accepted. A friendly guy with a large chin handed him a bottle of beer. First they chatted about favorite parts of beef, and then Tuvia asked about the kibbutz and duty schedules. Two other young men, also equipped with bottles of Goldstar beer, joined them and made fun of some old dairy farmer. Someone walked among them, handing out chicken skewers. After they overate, everybody sprawled out on the lawn, half-naked, and, intoxicated with youth, watched the sky. One of the hired lifeguards, a student at the nearby Wingate Institute, made out with a girl, another closed his eyes and fell asleep. The group slowly thinned. Some turned here or there, others went home, and Tuvia found himself alone with Maya in a sort of hideout provided by a large oleander bush. Somehow, they ended up on the subject of family tales. As was his manner, Tuvia described in detail scenes that had taken place before he was born as if he had been present. The complex system of lineages and sublineages amused and fascinated Maya, and she insisted on knowing each little detail: who said what to whom, and what was their connection, and who said what to whom in response. Through the darkness, her eyes shone at him. In them was reflected the desire of the pauper watching a table overflowing with riches from outside a restaurant. As she continued listening, her alertness softened, until she gave in to the Zinman power and suddenly leaned her head against his shoulder.

All he remembered of Maya's room was an Arab wicker dressing table, upon which rested some cosmetics and a few books. As she showered, he sipped the coffee she had made and allowed himself to take off his sandals. She came out of the shower wrapped with a large towel. Even after bathing, her skin still smelled lightly of chlorine, a smell that, years from now, would still awaken in him a pleasantness he would not be able to explain. She stood at his side and asked if he was one of those people who needed a kiss to start things off. Cool drops of water dripped from her curly hair onto his shoulders . . . and suddenly he found himself naked. Then she allowed him to decode all sorts of ambiguities with his fingers. He felt a burning heat that threatened to make him faint.

Needless to say, he had no point of comparison. No girl had ever crossed the threshold of his parents' luxurious apartment on Rabbi Friedman Street, he had never whispered with other guys over dirty magazines. Indeed, in his rush to climb up the path leading from childhood to middle age, Fat Tuvia had skipped over lust. When he was seven years old he had a sweetheart, Netta, and when they got the chance, they would kiss: the one being kissed sat on a stool with closed eyes, then they would switch roles. Netta had a little sister, Rina. One time, the three of them were left home alone. Though the "big kids" ordered her to stay in her corner with her stuffed animals, the little one became jealous and raised a protest, and they were forced to kiss her too. Since the days of Netta and Rina, Tuvia had not kissed anybody. There was one girl, a timid wisp of a high school student whose company nobody desired. On one school field trip they clung to each other, for lack of other options. On the second night, in a desert guesthouse on a cliff over the Zin Valley, she let him touch her pointy breasts. She would not let him kiss her, and by the time they returned to Tel Aviv she had lost her appetite.

Beyond the windshield, the buildings of Ramat Aviv now appeared. Behind them a blue dot had already begun bubbling up, slowly spreading across the black sky. Tuvia turned the air conditioning down and wondered when he would get the chance to spend an entire weekend with Maya in her little abode. They didn't have to get out of bed if they didn't want to, he thought. And if not a full weekend, then at least a Saturday; and if not in her room, then the car would work, too. An army friend once told him about abandoned sandstone hills near the Acadia Beach, where one could bring girls without being interrupted. For a moment, he considered turning back and touring the site, just in case, but it was already a quarter to five, and he still had a chance of getting home before his father woke up. He postponed the tour for another occasion. But it was a shame to go home now. The empty roads, the sealed car, the monotonous hum still preserved something of the wondrous delight he had known that night, and he knew the moment he killed the engine, he would be swallowed back into the world before Maya.

His stomach grumbled. As he waited for the elevator, he remembered half of a cauliflower quiche left in the fridge since Saturday afternoon. But an unexpected obstacle separated him from the pie— Yosef Zinman, who, unfortunately, had woken up just minutes before. When they ran into each other in the dark hallway, he greeted his father festively, as if returning from a long journey. In order to dim the bizarre impression he had made, he mumbled something about a video tape they had forgotten to return to the store and escaped to his room. He sat on his bed and listened for the redemptive slamming of the door, clearing his path to the kitchen. In the meantime, his heart held onto the hem of night's fleeting frock. He imagined rolling around with Maya here, in this very room, and maybe even on the living room sofa. Maybe he could still pop over on Wednesday morning? His thoughts wandered from the weekly to the monthly calendar. August was imminent, and even September was colored by a new light. But there, at the end of summer, among green fields and snowy peaks, was a small Austrian town, with horse-drawn wagons and church steeples.

D.

On Joshua Son of Nun Street, in a Spartan apartment that contained more space than objects, lived Miss Masha Lifschitz, a former division head assistant at the Solel Boneh civil engineering company. In the darkness behind the shutters of the large window facing the street, time has been frozen for the past twenty-eight years; fashion trends have no say here. Sienna brown, shades of gray, white—those are the colors the home owner chose to decorate her kingdom. The simply designed wooden furniture was made at the workshop of a renowned artist and cost a fortune at the time of its acquisition. A gorgeous crystal vase stood alone atop the sideboard, not for decoration but for a clear purpose. The Persian rug in the living room was spread facedown—thus preserving its pretty side for parties that would never be held. The pleasures of life were tucked in the depths of drawers, hidden behind the closed doors of walnut cupboards or hanging from disguised hangers. Should you visit, Belgian chocolates and French cognac, served in simple glasses, would appear as if from nowhere. In short, at the home of the elderly baby bird, one could find all the markings of asceticism, except for abstinence itself.

Just as she frowned upon a multiplicity of objects, Aunt Masha refrained from unnecessary conversing as well. It would be a mistake to say that she avoided human company—readers must already have noticed the affection she had for feasts served at the homes of acquaintances—but just as many others who have never been married or had children, she required a certain amount of solitude. We will never know if her zealously maintained habits of aloofness were the source of her biography, or if it was the other way around. Masha Lifschitz, older by nineteen months than her sister, Hinde the beautician, was born early in the last century in one of the poor suburbs of Lodz. The family tree produced a bounty of brothers and sisters, all murdered throughout the course of one year, without even leaving behind a stone to cry on. When the Germans invaded Poland, Masha escaped eastward, to Vilna, where she joined her relatives, the famous comedian Lydia Lifschitz and her daughter, Dora. Thanks to her connections, the actress was able to find the three of them refuge in Georgia, in the Caucasus, where they spent the war in relative comfort. After the Allies won the war, they returned to Vilna. The magnet of blood relations, which led them to stick together at a time of need, reversed its pole with the arrival of peace, urging them to part. Masha Lifschitz returned to Lodz, where she learned she had not a living soul left on Polish land. But she still had one last sister, in Tel Aviv—Hinde Shlossman. Though she had no Zionist feelings whatsoever, Masha emigrated to Tel Aviv, where she quickly landed a job as a secretary for a state-owned company.

She was already thirty-nine—war had taken with it her final years of youth. There was no way of telling whether she believed there was no chance of her having children, or if she chose, as was her nature, to draw unconventional conclusions from the events of her life; at any rate, on the threshold of middle age, well established and free of commitments, Masha Lifschitz stormed the pleasures of this world. She was considered an excellent rumba dancer; she was no stranger to lovemaking, either (and not necessarily with men older than herself). Then, all at once—right after her sixty-fourth birthday, it seemed—she tired of it all and pounced at old age as if on a treasure. She stopped working. Her considerable retirement fund allowed her to afford Persian lamb fur and extreme opinions. Even before that phase, mind you, she never shied away from voicing firm viewpoints on matters she knew nothing about. Her opposers had to handle a tongue that was equivocal as it was quick. It is no secret that she enjoyed shocking her relatives (most of all, her sister Hinde) and avoided no means of achieving this goal, from changing her position from one extreme to the other throughout a debate, to throwing around scandalous statements she would fervently denounce the next day. In order to preserve her independence, she established and broke and established and broke alliances left and right, thus creating a senior diplomatic stature among her family as an ambassador of a friendly kingdom, its capital set on Joshua Son of Nun Street.

The rule of her kingdom obligated her only by borders she had set herself. When she wanted to, she cooperated, and when she did not, she turned away; when it suited her she refrained and, when it suited her, she supported. At times, she was plagued by choleric bile with which she was unable to contend. Suddenly, for no apparent reason, terrible rage would ignite in her. It was enough for somebody to click their tongue for her to turn her affections away from them; even if the same person had thus far been considered suitable, she would send them away with fire and brimstone. Then she would wrap herself in regal insult, her face pale and her gaze sailing in the distance. Only long hours of solitude could abate the storm. These attacks terrorized all those around her, who were therefore extremely careful when it came to her honor. With years, they learned to recognize the foretelling signs and escape in time, while she enjoyed deceiving them once in a while, sending false signals, just so she would be left alone.

In the eyes of her sister Hinde's children, the subversive aunt's living room glowed as a sort of foreign land—a bountiful kingdom winking from across the guard towers erected by the severe cosmetician. And indeed, Aunt Masha did her best to corrupt the children, showering her little darlings with delicacies. Here, gifts were plentiful and selfishness—an asset. Here, you would receive an omelet made of real eggs and strawberries in cream even during the regime of austerity. Here, presents were abundant: dolls, shoes with shiny buckles, dozens of Swiss-made coloring pencils. When they grew older, Aunt Masha introduced them to the splendors of the cafés on Dizengoff Street. She often covered for seventeen-year-old Tzippi as she busied herself with shenanigans, and shamelessly lied to her worried mother when she asked where her licentious daughter had spent the past Saturday night. Of all her nieces and nephews, Aunt Masha favored Avrum, whom she saw as a sort of male embodiment of herself. She loved Bina the way you love an ugly puppy, and Dvora was always a riddle to her; for years, she tried hard to corrupt her, just a little, unsuccessfully. Though she heaped gifts upon her too, and in spite of that one secret incident a decade earlier, she was never able to pull her into her influence—until now.

E.

"I've never left her," Dvora said.

"I know."

"But I'm only human, after all," she continued.

"Certainly."

"And I deserve to have fun for once."

"I understand," Aunt Masha said with blood-curdling sympathy.

"I just have to break it to her gently."

"Gently," the old lady agreed.

"But you can't discuss it with anyone yet," Dvora begged. "I haven't even told Shraga."

"He's not a husband, he's an appendix." Aunt Masha stuck out her lower lip and poured them both more iced tea. "Always there, sometimes painful, never helping with anything."

The large shutters blocked out the rays of the setting sun. The living room was immersed in shadows, blurring contours and softening the horrid words of betrayal. For ten days, Dvora Saltzman picked up the phone and put it back down before she finally gathered sufficient courage to dial her aunt's number. During those terrible days, she delayed her visit to the passport office of the Ministry of the Interior, pushing questions away with different excuses. On the southern bank of Judah the Maccabee Street, Shraga slaved over his puzzles, expecting the problem to solve itself. On the northern bank, Tzippi Zinman wondered what was so difficult about getting a passport; she was impatient, wanting to seal the deal and free herself for other matters.

Yosef Zinman also had his say—ticket prices were rising with each passing day, he kept reminding her, displeased with the unnecessary delay. The previous Friday, as he sliced a quarter kilo of pastrami for her, he allowed himself to express wonder and asked her to hurry up. She was pressured and pushed from all directions, and only Bina continued to cut colorful landscape photos from brochures and glue them into her journal.

Truth be told, the decision had been made that very afternoon, when Dvora joined Tzippi at Top Tours, but she had not found the courage to announce the change of plans to her family. First of all she had to talk to Bina, of course: she was the one who made the promise and she was the one who would bear the bad news. Days flew by. August threatened her like a boiling cauldron into which she would have to dip before she could finally join the people of the free world, those who travel, liberated of all obligations, on the opposite bank, among blooming fields and snowy peaks.

"I just beg of you, Aunt Masha, tell me the truth: are you a hundred percent sure you don't want to go to Seefeld with us?"

"Seefeld, Seefeld," the old lady growled. "All day long—Seefeld. Who put that stuff in your head?"

"So you'll do it?"

"You know I help when I'm needed."

• • •

Nine or ten years earlier, Dvora had stood at the gates of Aunt Masha's kingdom carrying a surprising writ of surrender. The old lady would never have imagined that her long-ago efforts would yield such fantastic fruit. The subject was David Harari, an elegant, cocky man, a traveling salesmen for Max Factor Makeup who visited the perfumery with quizzical diligence. Dvora was thirty-eight at the time. For months she held out against the pull of the current, until one day she let him follow her into the atelier at the back of the perfumery. They kissed. Her blood boiled over. Until then, she had never imagined such passion, such infatuation, even existed. Excruciating expectation tortured her between visits. She resisted for three weeks until finally giving in to his pleading. The perfumery was out of the question, of course, and hotels meant for this purpose terrified her. In her distress, Dvora turned to the only person who might assist her while maintaining the appropriate secrecy.

Aunt Masha listened with wholehearted sympathy, and did not demand too detailed an explanation: she willingly offered her niece the keys to her abode, and not only left the apartment empty that afternoon, but even went to the trouble of leaving a bottle of wine and a plate of cashews and almonds on the sideboard. David Harari arrived at the appointed time and things went as they did. The sight of his naked body was etched into Dvora's memory, never losing any of its vitality in spite of passing time—the dark nipples, the small masculine stomach, and, below it, the somewhat pointy penis that grew from a thick, black flowerbed. After he left the apartment, Dvora was filled with fear. As she rinsed the wine glasses, she realized that the cliché "a one-time slip," which she had come across in journal advice columns, had somehow invaded her own resume, and would never leave her be. A secretive, tearful phone call that took place later that week put an end to the madness. The traveling salesmen never set foot on Judah the Maccabee Street again, and all that remained of the affair was the invisible thread tying her to her aunt ever since.

When Dvora called Masha Lifschitz that evening in early August and asked to meet her, to discuss "a discrete matter," the old lady immediately felt a tug at the other end of that thread. She tried, of course, to find out over the phone what it was *this time*, but even her assertiveness was not sufficient in gleaning even a crumb of information from her niece. Eventually, her affinity toward scheming won over her dislike of riddles. In other words—Aunt Masha was so taken by curiosity that she gave in to the imposition and agreed to meet without knowing the purpose of the meeting in advance. When the matter of Seefeld was raised, she was surprised. She herself, of course, had an unequivocal opinion on the trip, but, since her guest spoke in circles, she decided not to reveal her position until Dvora's intentions were made clear. The cunning elderly lady noticed Dvora's embarrassment and, to her surprise, even felt some compassion. When things were finally stated clearly, it turned out that this time the interests of the two of them were in perfect synch. Her wrinkled cheeks balled in a smile of delight when she imagined how sweet Yosef Zinman would react to their plan. She had always suspected that his fervor to have her join on their trip was a result of nothing more than a vexing wish to impose an unnecessary burden upon her in the name of family (to be on the safe side, she began acquiring a slight shaking of her hands, as evidence of her weakness, should the trip be forced upon her). And here was a golden opportunity to repay him and simultaneously indebt Dvora. Hosting Bina in her apartment for an entire week— who would dare question such a charitable act? *The arrangement*, as the two schemers began calling their conspiracy, was founded on firm foundation and served both of them in equal measures. Thus, after fifteen minutes of careful investigation on the one hand and submissiveness on the other, both selfish wishes were weaved into one fabric: Dvora would go to Seefeld free of the burden of Bina, while Aunt Masha would remain comfortably in Tel Aviv and watch over her.

"You feel like coming over for dinner on Friday night? Nothing big, just us and Avrum—he mentioned this week that he hadn't been over for dinner in a while, so I said, let's do it."

"Will you make stuffed peppers?" the old lady inquired.

"Why not."

"Tell Avrum to pick me up with the taxi."

At this point, Masha Lifschitz's patience ran out. The interview was over. She glanced at her watch and got up to turn on the television. Channel two was airing a show on Danton and Robespierre—of all periods, the aunt had a special adoration of the French Revolution. Though the customary parting words had yet to be recited, Masha stood at the doorway to the living room, waiting to see her guest out. In spite of her protests, Dvora insisted on collecting the dishes. Cups were placed in the sink, kisses were exchanged, the door was slammed.

Dvora felt like walking home. She turned onto Nordau Avenue. A pleasant afternoon wind blew among the trees, the sun setting in the sea behind her scattered spots of light over the ground. She was finally relieved—the visit with her aunt had expropriated the plan from her exclusive ownership; from now on, a chain of events leading one to the next would take place. The flaming nucleus had been wrapped in soothing bandages, the fear and the shame had lost their edge. She imagined—such naïveté!—that the hardest part was behind her. Before she left the avenue, Dvora Saltzman turned her head and sent a final look west, toward Seefeld.

8

Fun on Sheinkin Street

A.

"Hello? Anybody home?"

The place—possibly a snack bar and possibly a café—appeared deserted. Sliding doors made of murky glass separated it from the filthy sidewalks of King George Street. Formica chairs and rusty-legged tables were scattered messily. The large counter, also coated with pale Formica, was stained with congealed drops of all textures and colors. The shelves behind it were covered with large, lily-shaped glass cups, alongside a collection of small, shiny, red and green aluminum plates. A number of cigarette packs were stuffed in the cubbies of a peeling cabinet: Europa, Montana, two types of Marlboros.

"Excuse me? Is anyone here?" Dvora Saltzman asked again.

"We want some ice cream," Bina added.

A rustle came from behind the partition, accompanied by a snort, which, with certain effort, could be interpreted as "just a moment." And indeed, a moment later, a scary figure emerged: a lame, wild-looking, sinewy elderly lady with thorny hair, wearing filthy rags, a sort of hybrid between an apron and a sleeveless dress. Her wiry, exposed arms stuck out from both sides of the garment, and the skin moved around them, completely detached from the skeleton. She wiped her hands on the rag, took her place behind the counter, and fixed her customers with owl eyes.

"We want some ice cream," Bina repeated.

"Banana punch?" the old lady asked stormily.

"What brand is your ice cream?" Dvora asked. "My sister has allergies, we can't have just any brand."

"We serve Strauss."

"Is Strauss a good or bad company?" Bina asked. She could not take her eyes off the owner's right palm; three of her fingers had twisted as a result of rickets, tangling tightly into each other.

"Good," answered Dvora.

"What flavors do you have?" Bina asked happily.

"Banana punch."

"I like chocolate and vanilla."

"You want it in a cone?" the lady asked.

"No, no, in a cup, please," Dvora said. "We'll eat here."

One could imagine that the snack bar owner had come across a curiosity or two in her younger days, and still an expression of wonder spread over her face—it had been three years since the last time somebody asked to sit down at her café. She would gladly have gotten rid of these two and returned to the kitchen, where a chopped onion and two scrambled eggs she had prepared for dinner were waiting. But Dvora was in no rush. She chose a table by the glass doors, through which they could watch the street, and sat down with her sister. With no other choice, the old lady slid open the freezer door and ducked until she was swallowed in its depths. Within long seconds of rummaging, she emerged, surrounded by cold steam, and coughed. When she recovered, she dove in again. This time, she equipped herself with two red aluminum dishes and a round spoon, with which she dug large scoops of ice cream from the belly of the freezer. Then she became lost in reveries, and following a silent negotiation, decided to decorate the dishes with two sugar-coated cherries, and served them.

"What a treat, banana punch," Dvora said carefully as she glanced worriedly at Bina. "Here, have my cherry, too."

The old lady wiped her hands on her robe and turned to limp back to her lair.

"May I ask you something, ma'am?" Dvora asked, and, having interpreted the woman's hesitation as approval, she continued. "Maybe you remember my mother, Hinde Shlossman, may she rest in peace,

the cosmetician from Judah the Maccabee Street? I used to come here
with her when I was a little girl."

The owner fixed her with a long, indifferent gaze. Finally, she
answered surprisingly that yes, she did remember. Not only that, but
as it turned out, thirty-five years ago, the two of them had been chosen as members of a protected business owners' union. The union's
efforts to improve her and her colleagues' stature had failed, but she
herself, she told them, had never given up her rights. And what did
they think—that she didn't want to retire like everybody else? She
would have left a long time ago had she not sworn to torture the
property owner as much as she could. A snake on two legs, that guy,
she would teach him who to mess with. From here, she promised,
she would leave only in shrouds. She herself had three sons, none of
whom, to her great displeasure, wished to inherit the business. She
was glad to hear, then, that the late beautician's perfumery had been
inherited by her daughter, and asked what they were doing in this
neighborhood.

"We went to see *Mary Poppins*," Bina interrupted. "And then we
bought a towel with my letters, for my trip abroad. Want to see?"

In response, the old lady sounded a meaningless screech that weakened the enthusiastic Bina, who returned to focus on her ice cream.

"This is my little sister," Dvora explained.

"I remember they said she had a problematic daughter," the old
lady muttered, fixing Bina with sour, compassionless eyes. Dvora told
her they were out on a fun day at Dizengoff Center and that they
might continue from here to see that Sheinkin Street everyone was
talking about. The lady waved them off—the loose skin of her arms
swung this way and that like yellowish dough—and said that, if she
were in their shoes, she would take Bina to the Moscow Cat Circus,
which had just come to town on tour. Dvora wanted to prolong the
conversation, but the old lady was impatient. "You have your ice cream
in peace. If you need anything, just call me, I'll be in the kitchen, back
there." Then she signed off with a loud snort and retired.

A few weeks earlier, Bina had been invited to the house of a friend
from handcraft class, who showed her a treasure: a towel, on which

her initials had been embroidered in curly letters. From that moment on, Bina could not rest. There was nothing in this world she wanted more than a towel like that. First, she asked Shraga to teach her how to write the English letters B and S, and sketched countless versions in her notebooks. Then she made it her habit to sign her drawings with her initials in English rather than her full name in Hebrew. As was her manner, she persisted, never letting go. Dvora had promised more than once to take her to Dizengoff Center—that wonderland, where sewing machines embroidered monograms for anyone who wanted them. But each time there was a reason to postpone the outing. The disappointment had become so bad, that one morning, left alone at home, Bina found some thread and scissors, and in a desperate attempt to solve matters on her own, ruined a new towel. Dvora was mad but had to contain herself—even Shraga, who didn't often side with Bina, justified the actions of the "poor girl" who had been waiting for naught.

Tzippi, on her end, saw the towel incident as an excellent opportunity: she advised Dvora to take their little sister on an afternoon of fun at the Center, during which she could finally reveal to her the matter of the *comfortable arrangement*. They had to tell Bina she wasn't going to Seefeld, Tzippi said, so why not give her a little consolation prize? As was her habit, she made do with putting the idea out there, not bothering to partake in its fulfilment. In long phone conversations with Avrum, on the other hand, Tzippi voiced her harsh criticism of their sister. Dvora was inconsiderately postponing and postponing so that in the end, Tzippi said, they'd have a "big old mess to deal with." What exactly that mess entailed she did not explain, but since there was nothing Avrum hated more than discomfort, she was easily able to recruit him to her camp.

The ice cream was too sweet. A thin stench of staleness rose from it. Dvora put the spoon down and turned her head toward the street. Right in front of her, on the trunk of a giant old sycamore, were notes with a phone number on detachable stubs—someone searching for a lost dog, another for a new roommate, starting in September. Another offered private guitar lessons. A bus went by, then a motorcycle, people hurried this way and that, carrying plastic bags. Suddenly, all at once, she was consumed by the past, which would never return. There she was, and there was Tzippi, girls in pleated skirts and white socks, sitting in these very chairs, eating a piece of cheesecake or maybe a poppy-seed cake, making each other laugh till they cried. Mother told them off. Behind Mother's shoulder, Aunt Masha crossed her eyes and stuck out her tongue, and another burst of laughter washed over them. All around them was a cheerful bustle: customers drinking tea, eating, smoking. Two men played chess at a corner table. Behind the counter—a smiling, red-cheeked giant, pouring fruit sodas and beers and yelling in Polish. The owner, the same owlish lady—tried as she might, Dvora was unable to imagine her beyond the curtain of years, successful only in bleaching her apron back to a glowing white—running around with appetizing trays of food. A heap of bent bones, which is all that remained now of that vitality, along with a few Formica chairs soon be sold at the flea market; and all that is what you would call "life." Suddenly, she was struck by the recognition that behind all that abundance of "life" was something singular, one of a kind. This curdled her blood. She returned her eyes to Bina, who was busy stirring the ice cream, in order to turn it into what she called a "milshek." Why was Bina the one fated to a broken, hard, miserable lonely life? Dvora did not believe tales of reincarnation, and denied the existence of God, but still she could not understand how he was able to be so cruel to her little sister.

Incidentally, this view was not at all shared by Bina herself. In her eyes, the life she was familiar with was interesting and pleasant as any other. When she had succeeded in turning the ice cream into a sticky pink goo, she grabbed her straw and sucked the delicacy with pleasure. After that, she opened the bag that was placed on the chair next to hers and spread the gift over her fat thighs—a lilac towel embroidered with a kitschy, dark purple monogram. She caressed the towel patiently, running her finger slowly along the curly writing, whispering: "Bi-na-Sh-loss-man." The bag contained another towel, blue, embroidered with the letters T. S., Tuvia Saltzman. Standing by the sewing machine and following the diligently dancing needle with captivated eyes, she had been suddenly plagued with yearning for her nephew, Yellow Tuvia, and asked Dvora to buy a towel for him and mail it to America.

"I wish Yellow Tuvia was coming with us to Seefeld," Bina said. "Poor guy. Can I open his gift?"

"Isn't it a shame about the gift wrap?"

"We'll wrap it again. Please. I want to see his letters."

"All right, but make sure not to rip the bag."

Dvora watched Bina as she carefully peeled the tape off the shiny paper and pulled out the blue towel. She spread that over her thighs too, and ran her fingers over the initials again: "Ye-llow-Tuv-ia," she whispered. "What? Why are you laughing?" she asked, insulted. "Tell me!"

But the beautician did not answer. She realized she was about to fail at raising the knife once more. Her plan was thwarted again, and she decided to tell her sister about the *comfortable arrangement* later, after they visited that crazy bead shop that had been recently opened on Sheinkin Street.

■ ■ ■

And yet, even after they left the bead shop with overflowing bags in their hands, Dvora could not muster the courage. As they climbed the street toward the bus stop, they were surprised to run into Fat Tuvia, who emerged at that moment from one of the backyards, accompanied by his sister, Shirley, and that guy with the slurred speech, Oren Mutzafi. The unexpected meeting pleased the relatives, but also embarrassed them a little, perhaps because they were meeting outside of their natural environment, and perhaps because each one of them—except for Bina—was busy making his or her own calculations. They exchanged a few words, out of a sense of obligation, and parted ways. Some turned west, others turned east.

It was almost eight o'clock. The sun had not set yet and its rays caressed Bina and Dvora's backs with its orange light as they walked hand in hand toward Rothschild Avenue. Bina, a head taller than Dvora, gangly, never stopped talking, while her sister yearned for her to shut up already. As she swung her bags back and forth, Bina re-created the events of that afternoon with excitement: *Mary Poppins*, the towels, the ice cream, the beads, and of course the happy run-in with Shirley and Fat Tuvia. It seemed there was no one happier than she in the entire world. Her endless cheerful chatter continued at the bus stop. She asked if Seefeld had chimney sweeps, like in the movie. Dvora smiled against her will. She sat on the bench, sighed deeply, and accepted the fact that the bitter news would have to be conveyed another day.

B.

At the back of one of the buildings on Sheinkin Street, behind a heavy iron door and in a cave-like space that is dusky at all hours of the day, was a pub called the Third Ear. A hidden side path led to the place. Along the path was a stone wall covered in plain orange or green posters advertising shows and concerts. With time, a mosaic thickened over the posters, made up of political stickers, handwritten Xeroxed notes and ads for all sorts of small businesses, from special offers on secondhand fridges to ear piercing. A short hallway connected the pub to a used record store—a magnet for all sorts of radical types. Evenings, the place was kicking, and when imported rock band movies were shown, it overflowed. But when the three young people visited it—about an hour before their chance meeting with Ciotka Dvora and Bina—it was still in the midst of its afternoon lull. Other than a bespectacled waitress and a pair of young film buffs in checkered suspenders, who chain smoked and argued vehemently about Pasolini, there was not a soul in the place. The three chose a corner table and ordered some beers. Fat Tuvia (whose stomach was already grumbling) also asked for a large sesame pretzel, from which stretched strings of melted cheese.

As he ate, he looked around him curiously, imagining sitting here for a pint of Goldstar with his Maya. Ever since that night at the water park, he had changed his opinion about matters he had viewed with complete indifference until then. Among other things, he suddenly felt like becoming familiar with all sorts of establishments he had read about in newspapers but had never visited—not due to sorrow for all that he had missed, God forbid, but because he had discovered the new possibilities his future held, such as making out under the cover of darkness at a midnight show at Paris Theater. "Maybe I'll find a cool record too, why not," he told his sister, Shirley, and forced himself onto her weekly trip to Sheinkin Street with Mutzafi. When she twisted her face with surprise and reminded him that he never listened to music (other than some cantorial tape of their father's that he had somehow become taken with), he did not back away, claiming that was the exact reason he wanted her to introduce him to whatever was in vogue. Their musical tour resulted in two bags filled with new and used records that now rested on the chair at his side. Shirley and Mutzafi—two mere high school students of no personal wealth—were also taken care of. Fat Tuvia, a naturally generous man, gladly wasted everything he had earned at the water park in the past two days, and was now contemplating a pair of round, black, plastic sunglasses that caught his attention in one of the store windows.

"Go on, tell him, tell him," he heard Oren whisper.

As opposed to the elder Zinmans, who saw Oren Mutzafi as a factor inciting their youngest from the straight and narrow, Tuvia liked the guy—a boy as wiry as a noodle, his straight hair hanging down to his shoulders. At school, he was widely admired for his rebellious views, but no less for his hand-cut necklines and the baggy pants he wore with unusual grace.

"Stop it," Shirley whispered back and slapped Mutzafi's hand. "Not now."

Her older brother turned to her and fixed her with a quizzical look that left her no choice but to confess.

"I'm dying to go to Seefeld."

Another man would have choked at those words, but Tuvia calmly wrapped strings of cheese around a piece of pretzel, chewed, swallowed, wiped his mouth, scratched his head and asked, "Have you lost your marbles?"

When the family members prepared for the trip, none of them bothered to ask Shirley to join; nobody imagined she would be interested. Tzippi Zinman, versed in embittered disappointment, was convinced her daughter would say no, as usual, and did not feel like facing that expression that always looked to her like infinite contempt. However, as it turned out, in the town of Rattenberg, on the River Inn, two hours away from Seefeld, was a gentleman named Anton Lupka, one of the last remnants of the ancient Austrian folk art of saw music. It would have been appropriate to say, "one of the celebrated remnants," but, unfortunately, very few people had an appreciation for this great art, so that Lupka and his Alpengeist Orchestra remained almost unknown. On summer days they performed in the small vacation towns on the shores of the lakes, and in winter they played at Tyrolean ski resorts.

Lupka was the son of a God-fearing peasant who left her home village to get married and returned fifty years later to be buried. On his father's side, he was the descendant of a family of veteran musical clowns. One of his relatives, who moved to Paris in the beginning of the previous century, was famous as "Monsieur Lupe," and played the saw on the stage of the winter circus for twenty-one straight seasons. Among professionals, at any rate, Anton Lupka had a reputation for being a virtuoso (rumor had it he once played a duet for two saws with Marlene Dietrich). A musicologist from Graz University argued at the time in a published paper that Lupka's melodies referenced Gregorian singing, but Lupka himself dispelled the assumption completely and claimed that the art originated with ancient lumberjacks, who used to gather at night around a fire and amused themselves with the only instrument at their disposal. Either way, there was nothing Shirley Zinman wanted more than to meet the revered artist. Her expulsion from the Seefeld trip was therefore a complete mistake . . . the girl had been hurt to the depths of her soul, but simultaneously garnered a secretive enjoyment from this banishment, which confirmed her pleasurably bitter assumptions about the world (most of which were doomed to dissipate, inevitably, at the end of adolescence). And so, since her honor would not allow her to plead with their parents directly, she had no choice but to ask her brother to apply on her behalf.

Fat Tuvia listened carefully, scratched his forehead some more, sank into ruminations, awoke, cut off another little piece of pretzel, around which he also dutifully wrapped the strings of cheese, put the fork to his mouth, but then put it down on the plate and muttered, "Then go instead of me."

As he spoke he tilted his head and fixed his gaze on a point in the distance while telling them levelly of his affairs of the past weeks— about Maya, his beloved, about his dream of seeing the entire family going to Seefeld and leaving the apartment on Rabbi Friedman Street to him for an entire week.

"You're going to fuck in Mom and Dad's bed?" Shirley asked, wide-eyed.

Tuvia chose not to answer.

"When are you going to tell them you aren't going?"

Soon, it was decided, and that he had to break it to them gently, so as not to insult anybody. Shirley, who saw this as a done deal, was glad to return to her own interests. She told them everything she knew about the esteemed Anton Lupka. That very week, she said, she was going to write him and ask to be accepted to his master class in late September, though she heard he was a hard man who did not spare his students any criticism. Then she excused herself to go to the bathroom. In her absence, the two boys turned to man talk; Tuvia was happy to tell and Mutzafi was happy to listen. The waitress brought over the check.

■ ■ ■

It was almost eight o'clock when the three left the pub. The sun had not set yet, its rays washing Sheinkin Street orange. The intimacy formed earlier under the cover of dusk was now replaced with a sort of distance. The two high school students turned to go visit a friend on Brenner Street, who promised to get them into a show at one of the clubs that night. They didn't feel like inviting Fat Tuvia along, and were glad to hear he had promised Aunt Masha to drop by and fix a clogged sink in the service balcony. But first, he wanted their opinion on the sunglasses he liked. They turned west when they suddenly ran into Dvora and Bina, carrying many plastic bags. Bina showed them her new beads—large, see-through Perspex candy—but Aunt Dvora, who looked nervous, or maybe just exhausted, was eager to cut the conversation short, saying they had to get home, and the five of them parted. Bina, who was sorry to say goodbye, turned back and waved as they walked away.

"Bina will be so happy that I'm going to Seefeld too," Shirley said as she watched her relatives moving away. "We can even share a room."

9

The World of Fashion

A.

One day in August, the manufacturer Mendel Cohen sat in the afternoon heat in his office at the Mandy Line workshop, tearing off, one by one, the legs of a large cockroach that just minutes earlier had been resting luxuriously under the chipped sink. He set the legs before the cockroach, arranged by size, and wondered if he would be able to tear off the tentacles without removing the head. The office was swarming with miniature life, providing their executioner with ongoing entertainment. In his extensive research on the question of life and afterlife, he had perfected a unique method of killing for each and every species. Persian beetles, those flying coffee beans, he grabbed and crushed with three fingers. Mosquitoes, gracefully hovering on a gust of wind, he butchered with the whip of a kitchen towel. A tiny trap set in the corner of the room broke the necks of wandering field mice. And to brown cockroaches, which had yet to decide whether to fly or run around, he had an array of strange deaths to offer: the slamming of a shoe, chemical spray, drowning in the toilet. But there was no doubt that the biggest challenge was posed by houseflies clinging persistently to the back of his neck, his eyelids, his bulbous, vein-webbed nose, in short—any moist piece of skin. He lured them in with traps hanging down from the ceiling, attached to bulbs that had a known addictive effect on the victims: the poor flies, their hearts yearning for the vision of light, pushed through the electrified net. Most of them plummeted to their death silently, without as much as a whisper, but occasionally one of them was burnt at the stake with small explosions, leaving behind an aroma of grilling that pleased the owner to no end.

But now, even the limping of the amputee cockroach, much like the downfall of the Communist Party in Poland, which he had just read about in the newspaper, did nothing to brighten Mendel Cohen's mood that afternoon. His spirits were low due to an article in the Scientific Innovations section that reported a new kind of trouble, global warming, due to which the entire city of Venice might soon become submerged. Mendel Cohen was angry. He had always dreamed of traveling to the city of canals, and was now worried he might not manage to see it before it was lost forever. The castles, the steeples, the Jewish Ghetto—disappearing, all of it. . . . He lost his patience. He picked up the receipt book and squashed his study subject. Its tentacles twitched for a moment within the mush of its body, and then were still forever. Mendel looked at his handiwork and sighed. A new research question tortured his soul: would he be able to pull a tissue from the bottom of the cabinet without getting up? Then, as he stretched this way and contracted that way as best he could, sounds came from the yard: the cough of an exhaust pipe, the screeching of brakes, an engine cutting off, two doors slamming. In other words, visitors. He turned to face the factory floor and waited. Soon two familiar silhouettes appeared in the blinding light.

"Hello, boss!" Tuvia Zinman said as he entered with fanfare, followed by his partner, whose name Mendel Cohen had forgotten, but whose juicy rear end he remembered very well.

B.

As summer drew to a close, sales sped up at the water park. The vacationers, fizzling like soda bottles boiling in the sun, lunged at the stalls, snatching and buying without discernment. Boxes of goods emptied one after the other. Once in a while, Tuvia walked over to a solitary corner to conduct inventory, and upon his return blinked at his aunt with the intoxication of success.

The counting of the day's final tally had become a regular ceremony, taking place at the Saltzmans' kitchen table upon the duo's return to the city in the afternoon, over a pitcher of iced coffee and a fragrant sponge cake eaten straight out of the pan. Bina looked forward to this conference, and on days when they arrived early, Shraga joined them as well. As they counted the revenue, front to back and back to front, they regaled their listeners with tales of their morning's events. Fat Tuvia had a gift for mimicking Sara Consignment's lilting lamentations as she persuaded customers or bemoaned losses that had never occurred—"What have I even sold today, Dvorrra?!" Tuvia screeched in a nasal voice, and Bina, overjoyed, would not leave him be until he sailed from Bucharest to the shores of the Volga, doing an impression of Papa Frumkin as well. Odd customers, and those were plentiful, were also included in his repertoire. Dvora showed off the tricks she had invented—how she pushed here and convinced there, how she gave a pretend discount, actually doubling the price, and so on and so forth. Over a chilled watermelon, between bites, the two partners split their loot and fastened it with rubber bands. The cosmetician took down the income in a math notebook she kept hidden—either due to fear of the evil eye or of a tax audit, God forbid—in the medicine cabinet. Then Fat Tuvia sprawled out on the floor for a short nap. The lady of the house washed the dishes and, to freshen up for her afternoon shift at the perfumery, took a quick shower. Only then did she make herself a hot cup of black coffee, sit down on the armchair by the phone, and call her sister to let her know the score.

Success intoxicated and excited the soul. Starting in the second half of August, our protagonists had already begun viewing their petty business as grand enterprise. Their greed grew. In ten days, they knew, their water-park contract would end. Children would return to schools, employee committees would return to factories, surfing pants would make room for holiday gift certificates. An elegiac mood slowly took over the stalls of the fair. Everyone did their best to ladle a few final spoonfuls of the reducing pot of gold. One sold his items for half price, another offered a free pool ball with every purchase, a third added running headbands to his goods, an item that enjoyed, at the time, momentary fame. But at our acquaintances' pants and tank top stall, no such commercial juggling was necessary. "Commerce is like kishkes," Yosef Zinman instructed his son. "It goes in on one end and out the other, and what gets absorbed in the middle—that's what you live off." After examining the elements of this formula from top to bottom, Fat Tuvia reached the only possible conclusion. And so, on Thursday, with less than two weeks left until the end of fair season, Dvora Saltzman and her nephew drove with determination to the Mandy Line factory, at the Kiryat Arye Industrial Zone.

"How's it going?" Tuvia asked with a sigh as he sat down across from Mendel Cohen, just like an old acquaintance. "Any new patterns?"

The manufacturer snorted in lieu of an answer.

"What can I say," Tuvia went on. "People love your goods, Mendele. I've never seen anything like it. Right, Ciotka?"

"They're mad for it, mad for it," Dvora was quick to confirm. Any other manufacturer would have grown smug with satisfaction, but Mendel Cohen could care less about this information. In fact, he wondered that moment how those two always managed to show up at the least convenient hours, when he was already feeling like killing the machines and sweeping away the small fabric pieces. If he had only known that this was the very principle of young Zinman's plan . . .

"We need to restock again, believe it or not."

Whether or not Mendel believed it was impossible to tell. At any rate, he led them into the warehouse, that room bathing in a sour odor, housing a depressing mishmash of garments, boxes, and tattered cardboard patterns. He blotted his wet neck with a handkerchief, leaned on the doorpost with his arms crossed, and fixed the visitors that separated him from his shower and dinner with a look of loathing. But those two, sent by the devil, were in no rush—they picked items off the shelves and then put them back, spread items over the work desk and refolded them with endless patience.

"It's a shame you don't stop by the water park once in a while, Mendele," Fat Tuvia said as he picked through the clothes. "We can let you in for free. What's the problem, don't you like to swim?"

"This waistband is worthless," Dvora noted, stretching a pair of surfing pants. "Totally loose." She pulled another pair off the shelf, checked it and debated, and wrinkled her nose, finally tossing it onto the desk. What did Nachliel Zarfaty advise her? Exhaust the manu-facturer, burden his heart with doubt, boil him like a potato until he softens, then peel off his cut of the profit. Not with violence, God forbid—with tenderness, with tenderness. She recalled the trick of the trade he had demonstrated that morning, picked up a shirt and pulled on its weak spot. She pulled and pulled and the sleeve tore off.

"Kind sir, you have no idea what you're missing." Fat Tuvia affec-tionately patted the owner's back. "There's a wave pool, there're slides, not bad, huh? Don't you feel like having some fun at our expense?"

"No," said Mendel.

"Well, not everyone likes slides," Tuvia consoled him. "But don't tell me you don't like *girls*. You know what—just stop by once to check out our models, all unbelievable bombshells, each and every one. The biggest names . . ."

"Natalie Pepper, Hanni Ben-David," Dvora said. "Oh, another torn shirt."

"You have to keep a closer eye on your workers, Mendele. Any-way, you've never seen your clothes on asses like that. We taught them how to tie the shirts above the belly button, like in Mediterranean clubs. You have no idea what it does to the audience. After each fash-ion show, they raid our stall. Honestly, I've gotten offers from other manufacturers, but I don't play those games. I started the summer with you and I'll finish the summer with you. Just for your informa-tion, though, I could have sold for double, if I only had an interest! A man needs an incentive. I'll give you an example. Right now we're buying from you for five and selling for twelve." (Actually, it is worth noting that they sold the items for fifteen.) "That's our bottom line—anything lower than that, quite honestly, I'd rather sit at home and scratch my balls. If I could only cut a few shekels off the price for the consumer . . . let's say if you sold to us for three."

"Three??" Mendel was shocked. "Me?"

"Why not? With all due respect, you're not exactly Pierre Cardin."

Indeed, anyone who met good old Mendel Cohen would have no trouble differentiating between the two fashion moguls.

"Don't worry," Tuvia continued. "The difference won't go in my pocket—I'll pay the discount forward to the customer and lower the price to nine. We can't forget there's a recession going on, Mendel, customers are expecting us to meet them halfway. You'll sell for three, but you'll sell three times more!"

"No, no, no, no."

"And it's the end of the season."

"What are you talking about, end of the season?" Mendel yelled, pointing to the window above his head. "It's ninety-seven degrees out there!"

"I've never seen anything like this—you feed a man *gribenes* and he spits it out," Fat Tuvia said with a sigh. "Make it three-fifty, then."

"If you're going to skin me, at least use a knife!"

"Not to mention we're giving you free advertising."

"Advertising?"

"Absolutely," Tuvia confirmed proudly. "And what advertising! We have a very well-known fashion show host, Albert Ben Arroya, you may have heard of him, and he has direct orders from me to mention Mandy Line as much as possible. The slogans he comes up with—I'm telling you, the man's a genius. 'Mandy Line—Looking Fine!' Thanks to us, there isn't one person in the Dan region who doesn't know who you are; five thousand new people hear about your company every day! You know how much that gift is worth? You have any idea how much money people pay advertising firms for this? You know how far you can get?"

And here, an upsetting turn of events took place: the blood ran out of the manufacturer's face. His forehead paled, his plump cheeks suddenly contracted, and even his crimson nose lost its vitality. How far could he get? Mendel Cohen knew the answer very well: all the way to the interrogation rooms of the tax department—that's how far. Long years of keeping double books would go down the drain: "Mendel for Merchants," "M. C. Clothing," "Manitex," and once, simply "Cohen Plus Sizes"—all those names, changing daily, were intended to blur the traces of extravagant tax evasions. While he reported measly profits and immense expenses, Mendel conducted secretive commerce according to the opportunities that came his way, and there was never a shortage of such opportunities: Orthodox Jews from Bnei Brak taking care of enormous families, scouts who ordered printed shirts as mementos from summer camp, merchants from the margins of the retail world, and other customers who never asked for receipts. His unholy profits were deposited in a bank account under the name of his father-in-law—a dementia-stricken elderly man—in which he himself had exclusive power of attorney. In those days, tax clerks did not depend on computerized software; their investigations depended entirely on numerous certificates, cards, and approvals that mounted into pointless mounds of files. Thus, Mendel was able to deceive the authorities freely. From time to time, when he felt his reports were dangerously nearing implausibility, he announced a liquidation and opened an identical business under a different name. By the time investigators noticed the existence of the new company, he enjoyed two or three uninterrupted years of prosperity thanks to under-the-table revenue. It is therefore clear why he was so afraid of the spotlight. Tuvia's words created a nightmarish picture in his mind: what if some industrious tax agent happened to visit the water park and made a note of Mandy Line?

"Out!!!" the manufacturer's voice finally emerged from the depths—a thin, weak, grief- and hardship-stricken voice. "You and your aunt! Outtttt!!! If you show your faces here one more time . . ."

And here the owner waved his hands as if swatting away flies, and then exited, leaving his visitors, and us, to wonder at the end of that sentence.

■ ■ ■

The blue Ibiza waited in the shade of a large eucalyptus, and did not respond easily. It grunted unwillingly three or four times, and only started when Fat Tuvia pulled on the small ignition handle.

"He can kiss my ass," he muttered. "Who needs his rags, anyway. Don't worry, Ciotka Dvora. First thing Sunday morning we'll go to Beit Romano and fix ourselves up with a new collection."

C.

In south Tel Aviv, the sun blazes over a decrepit quarter sprawling on both sides of the road to Jaffa. Its name, exuding a somewhat foppish aroma—Florentin. Many of its residents deserted it over the years, and the fine apartments were taken over by sewing workshops, cutting workshops, and other similar businesses. The dolled-up buildings, the pride and joy of their owners, European immigrants who invested what little funds they were able to smuggle into balconies and cornices, have since lost their glory. The windows, behind which holiday meals once were eaten and cards were played, are now sealed with planks of wood and sheets of tin that hide unlicensed businesses. Nothing remains of the small, well-kept shops of the past. Once in a while a wrinkled face peeks out from one of the cracks—a wizened old man or a warty old woman who were unable to escape the neighborhood in time and have nothing left to do but wonder at their fates. Stairwells stinking of urine, their tiles worn out from the weight of incessant incoming and outgoing deliveries: shoe boxes, rolls of velvet and tricot, sacks of zippers, sheets of leather emanating strong smells—everything that supported Florentin's lively fashion industry. Sewing machines ticked endlessly, porters yelled loud reproaches, a multitude of vehicles blocked the narrow streets, filling the air with soot.

From this heap of fabrics and junk, Beit Romano has stood since the middle of the previous century. Our contemporaries would find it difficult to estimate the intensity of life that used to pulse through its wide corridors—the workshops are abandoned, the doors locked and bolted, the light bulbs made their final dying flutters ages ago. But in the 1980s, the gigantic structure still bustled with the frenzy of negotiations and sales.

The founders of Beit Romano, who had viewed commerce as a necessary but unseemly activity, instructed the architects to plan a building that would embody a proper social order, and they turned to old traditions for inspiration. The building's main wings closed around a rectangular courtyard, a sort of cul-de-sac. In the roofed porticos on both its sides, shops boasting names such as "King" and "Eternity" settled over the years, in which men's shirts, women's bathing suits, knock-off jeans, workout clothes, imported handbags, and other such items were sold, wholesale. In its glory days, the quad was reminiscent of a court in the palace of some medieval duke. Horse-drawn freight carts went in and out through the main gate. Lifts and pulleys brought goods up and down between the floors. Merchants and customers ran around, arguing loudly, comparing prices, cheating, and, in moments of respite, gathered strength with a spinach *bourekas* from the corner snack bar.

A balcony decorated with a colonnade stretches all around the first floor. This is where wealthy manufacturers stepped out for some fresh air, a cigarette, looking down into the courtyard like a feudal lord looking over his manor, gravely discussing the rise in cotton prices. In the workshops facing the colonnade, dozens of workers slaved over their craft, while in side rooms, all sorts of unique experts clung to the larger workshops that required their services—ironers, belt makers, button makers, thread sellers, there was room for everyone. Even Rebecca the seamstress—one of the most famous alteration tailors of the time, a man of about fifty, with a black mustache and toupee, who had inherited the business from his mother, may she rest in peace—had a little alcove of his own.

A wide staircase leads to the second floor, allotted to authority representatives. Here the hallways are darker and the floors cleaner. In the north wing, behind half-shut blinds, the grand inquisitor of the commerce industry—Tel Aviv Income Tax Assessor 2—made the office from which he terrorized his flock of assessees. His pale clerks slipped silently through the halls, folders in hand, like zealous priests of the days of yore, emanating formal severity. Once in a while, shouts sounded from one of the rooms, and then a door opened and from it was tossed, defeated and shaken, another shopkeeper who had been summoned for questioning. Just as tiny industry developed around the large workshops, so there grew a settlement of clerks alongside the tax offices: consultants, accountants, moneylenders, and one private investigator who made his living performing industrial espionage, who also seemed to lack a sufficient knowledge of all the depths of Beit Romano. The founders' enlightened intentions were no good, and neither were the architects' fine blueprints. Within forty years, or maybe less, the proper order had been disrupted, and its place was taken by neglect, deceit, and ugliness.

D.

Even as a child, Dvora Saltzman was disgusted by the large building on Jaffa Road. Twice a year she would be dragged over to buy everything needed for the season, cheaply. When she tried on the clothes, she had to hide behind cardboard boxes or in semi-exposed nooks. Often, the saleswoman snuck a peek into the hiding place, sending over rough palms to tighten or stretch, and made her feel terribly embarrassed. Later, in the early 1970s, she had been dragged here by her sister, Tzippi, who had subscribed to the principles of the Hippie Movement—principles limited to giant necklaces and sheepskin sashes. Dvora hadn't visited the place since that style had gone out of fashion, and now she stood at Fat Tuvia's side, amazed and helpless against the abundance and tumult.

"Can I help you?" someone asked threateningly. The man, who served as both usher and guard, had long ago taken over a corner by the gate, creating a small office for himself, furnished with a Formica desk that had been thrown out of one of the offices, and a mutilated office chair, bandaged with tape.

"No thanks," said Tuvia. "We're fine."

"Just do me a favor and don't stand in the entrance," the man scolded them before returning to the documents on his desk.

The two continued into the courtyard and looked around. No surfing pants were to be found in any of the store windows surrounding the courtyard.

"Out of the way, brother, out of the way!" someone ordered behind them. When they turned around they saw an impatient man of about thirty, his sunken cheeks covered in stubble, pedaling a freight bicycle loaded with fabric rolls. The man parked it below the staircase and went to unload it. He wore nothing but a white tank top over his horribly skinny torso. All of his movements, from kicking the kickstand to pulling the rolls, were urgent, charged with restrained tension, as if deep inside him were energy surpluses he was unable to contain, and they surreptitiously gnawed at his emaciated body. A beeper hanging off his belt like a holster beeped and beeped but he ignored it.

"Need some help?" Tuvia asked generously, as was his habit. Having received no answer, he lightly loaded two rolls—one on each side—onto his broad shoulders and followed the man up to the first floor. The sun burned. Dvora wanted to get a cold drink, but her conscience would not allow her to abandon the merchandise-laden wheelbarrow. Without a choice, she waited at its side, hoping not to run into an acquaintance, and fed her growing resentment toward her nephew, who had disappeared. Why did he have to fight with that old stubborn Mendel Cohen? And what did they blow the whole deal over? Over two more shekels per item, a moment before the season ended. . . . In the meantime, their goods were running low, and who knows whether a new supplier would sell for any less . . . Two shekels! The truth was, she could understand Mendel. Now that she knew she would never be meeting him again, she felt a sort of compassion toward him, along with a hint of nostalgic affection: the trips to Kiryat Arye on Thursday afternoon, haggling in the office over a cup of black coffee . . . within three days, the manufacturer had gone from being a terrorizing monster to a cute little souvenir.

The distance between Judah the Maccabee Street and Seefeld became shorter with each passing day. She could already afford a week at the Bubinger Inn—they said a room with a balcony would cost around $350. The Austrian schillings she bought piecemeal from Yunger the butcher smelled of mildew—perhaps because he had the habit of stuffing his hands in his pocket while they were wet—but she already had 5,400 of them—5,400!—hidden in Shraga's sock drawer. This left the airline tickets. Sammy, the stocky travel agent, called on Friday morning and said they had to pay before September, or he would not be able to reserve the flight. She was still $200 short: one more good week in Shfayim, and even the doors of Seefeld's finest restaurants would open for her. And if she was going, she might as well go like a queen. She felt like taking the Zinmans out to dinner, on her. She also had to account for gifts—countless colorful bags and packages that as of yet had no clear form in her mind—which she would bring to those staying behind in Israel. She had always received gifts from other countries—blue clay salt shakers from Amsterdam, an embroidered tablecloth from Naples—but had never had the chance (unless one counted her famous honeymoon cruise to Marseilles) to be on the giving end of the philanthropic divide. She decided to make it up to Bina—a shadow passed over her when she remembered that she had yet to inform her of the *comfortable arrangement*—with a luxurious abundance of gifts, no matter the cost and no matter what Shraga said. Other than that, in recent months she had been persuaded to see herself as a woman with a European body type; they only made clothes for women like her abroad—fine shoes, mohair sweaters, and those things required money, money . . . You only live once, as Tzippi always said, and that once, the price of which was a single exhausting summer, was accompanied in her mind by colorful packages and bags with logos in foreign languages.

Suddenly, she heard loud laughter. Dvora turned her head—two Arab boys of about fifteen, their faces speckled with whitewash, sat on the nearby stone wall, smoking and chatting wildly. Behind them, skipping lightly down the stairs, followed by that skinny, nervous guy she had already managed to forget, was Fat Tuvia, his face burning and his eyes beaming.

"Ciotka Dvora—we're all set!" he announced, wiping the sweat off his wide forehead.

■ ■ ■

Neon green, shocking orange, Popsicle yellow; blinding sheets of glowing, scandalous cotton one could not take one's eyes off, hot colors that had never been seen in the history of clothing and had, until then, been used exclusively for notebook covers and felt pens. Who would have dreamed it! Still, is this not the nature of fashion? But Dvora was deterred. Since she had no "in" with the younger generation, she could not know that these wild shades did not come out of nowhere, that these were the colors of a new era that was about to introduce a new drug, which had been garnering more and more followers. In her eyes, the shirts were simply ugly. Fat Tuvia, on the other hand, was very excited about the goods and entirely convinced of their potential success. The partners stepped aside to whisper in the corner of the workshop. Dvora, hesitant as usual, suggested buying a few trial samples before they decided, while Tuvia claimed they should take as many items as possible, and the more glowing, the better. "We'll have everyone's attention at the water park with these projectors!" he promised. She could not argue with such decisiveness. Furthermore, the nervous guy with the beeper—upon closer look she found he also had buck teeth—agreed to sell the items for three. For three! How could that be explained? Perhaps he had been immensely impressed by Tuvia's generosity as he came to his aid, and perhaps his goods were not worth any more than that. At any rate, they shook on it, and Tuvia and Dvora hurried to pile up shirts of all sizes and fill sacks with black surfing pants, riddled with psychedelic prints. They paid cash, of course, under the table, and got out of there as quickly as possible, so as to leave no opening for regret.

Thus, unknowingly, the modest beautician of Judah the Maccabee Street had participated in the Ecstasy revolution, which provided the world with happiness for the price of a pill.

10

The Final Day

A.

Rumor had it that Anita Shagrir was around.

Who had spread it? Perhaps one of the merchants, and perhaps Albert Ben Arroya, who tended to promote such news out of his own motives. Though she waved the rumor off with batted eyelashes and a sigh of denouncement, Tzippi Zinman spied for signs of the presence of the regal figure—the waving train of a caftan, a thick-thighed silhouette, or a flash of blue eyes adorned with doll-like lashes. On the one hand, her heart fluttered; on the other hand, she thought, go ahead, let her come, let her deign to descend from her Bavli penthouse and see for herself where I used to be and where I am now, how I pulled myself up by my bootstraps and single-handedly took over the water park. And Tzippi's takeover was indeed fabulous: no less than four top models receiving three hundred shekels per show—three former beauty queens, the fourth involved in some sex scandal—had been booked to walk on stage for the final day of the season. She looked over the stalls. Bina and Dvora waved at her from the family stall. The merchants—not all of them were there yet—each toiled in their corner. The Frumkins had already finished arranging the plastic watches on their stands and sat down to eat their omelet sandwiches. A kind couple, actually; she had not given them much thought before, and now she asked herself how they got to the water park each morning and whether they schlepped over on a bus with all of their goods. She had already given the order to add more stalls;

they were expecting twelve merchants today. Two of them, new ones, had just recently been added, after they had begged for more than two weeks. Moreover, representatives were sent to see her from one of the Herzliya hotels. They mentioned biweekly luxurious dinner parties, a lecture by a graphologist and, of course, a fashion show. Readers would surely be glad to learn that, by her assessment, Zinman made approximately 25,000 shekels that summer—the aerodynamic contours of a new Mitsubishi in antique rose were already forming in her imagination. Let Anita Shagrir come then, by all means, and see for herself how they celebrated the last day of the season at the water park.

Tzippi had tossed and turned the whole night through, until she finally opened her eyes at five-thirty in the morning, realizing she would not be able to stay in bed any longer. After she bathed and put on her makeup, she wrote a note for Tuvia—"I took Dad's car, meet me at Shfayim"—and went down to Judah the Maccabee Street. She felt like having her first coffee of the day with Yosef. The streets were still empty; only old Kuttner, who had risen early, was serenely tending to the flower bed at the front of his house. At the Zinman Grocery Store, moist islands glistened on the floor that had just been washed. Armies of white cheese and yogurt containers stood at attention in the fridge, and the loaves of fresh bread perfumed the air with the scent of hope. No hour was finer than this: even in the worst days of summer, the grocery store was chilly, like a fairy-tale cave whose walls were laden with oil and delicacies. Peretz was sitting in the back of the store, as usual, listening to the soft chatter of morning radio announcers. Tzippi's heart was suddenly filled with compassion, and she waved to him with jingling bracelets. The kettle whistled, and Yosef Zinman—who had been somewhat surprised by her visit—made black coffee in chipped mugs. They shared a cinnamon bun, dipping it in the steaming coffee. The grocer told her he had slept wonderfully and that he had had a fantastic bowel movement that morning. Then he sent Peretz to the warehouse on an unnecessary errand and felt his giggling Tzippi up a little. The street—the bench, an Indian rosewood tree, the sidewalk across the street—began swarming with life. Sleepy dog owners, retirees in plastic flip-flops returning from the pool, mothers fetching hot rolls for breakfast. Buses ejected maids traveling from southern neighborhoods; business owners swept the sidewalk in front of their stores. At seven o'clock, as happens each day, Yunger the butcher walked in, bought a container of sour cream and a pretzel, and told a story about a veteran customer who had died, though she had believed her entire life in the healing power of soup stock made from turkey necks. Then they smoked a cigarette and discussed the crisis in Beirut. Shraga popped over from the other side of the street to say good morning, told a piquant joke, and ordered a delivery of diet orange juice.

Who among them could have foretold then, on this graceful morning, one of many that had been and would be, the fall of the House of Zinman? How could they have guessed that in two years a war would break out in the Persian Gulf—the grocery store would be operated in the famous emergency mode and the profits would be truly unbelievable—after which nothing would ever be as it once was. Gigantic shopping forts would sprout like mushrooms all around the city, customers would desert, one by one, and those who would stick around would buy only milk and cigarettes to fulfil their obligation. The wealthy families, on which the glory of the old establishment depended, would move to trendier neighborhoods; their tabs would be replaced by those of bothersome elderly ladies and degenerates whose place would not be found in the new order. At first deliveries would be reduced to Thursdays and Fridays only, and then those would end, too. Luxury items would gradually disappear from the shelves. The selection would become so meager that sometimes Zinman will be forced to buy from the nearby supermarket, all in order to avoid speaking those shameful words, "we don't have it," to his customers, over the phone. Products would be covered in dust that no one would bother to clean, Peretz would be fired and subsist on a small social security allowance. So as not to be idle, he would volunteer at a *bourekas* bakery that would open on the ruins of the nearby butcher shop, which would also meet its maker. The eternal Nathan Kuttner, the key money owner whose death had been wished for by three generations of Zinmans, would finally, at age ninety-one, depart on the trip from which no one sends any postcards, but his daughters would inherit his assets, accompanied by self-important attorneys who would pester the grocer under all sorts of false pretenses. At the end of eight years of ongoing deterioration, Yosef Zinman would have to give in. One autumn day, contract workers would remove the old SELF-SERVICE, Y. ZINMAN & SONS sign. A local paper would send a reporter, Yosef would have his picture taken, smiling behind the old scales, and that would be the end of it. Thanks to his connections, he would manage to get a job as a head warehouse clerk in one of the grocery chains. There, in the warehouse in back, where employees wallowed morning to night in rotting vegetable and the stench of cheese water, he would reign over three shelvers, who would enthusiastically listen to stories of his glory days.

And Tzippi? Even she could not guess, on that marvelous morning, that the downfall of large employee committees and small fashion merchants was imminent; that the great Anita Shagrir, who would successfully read the warning signs, would retire from the fashion-show business, start the Ambassador Actors Agency, and write an advice column for the weekend papers. Of course, Tzippi could not guess that she herself would also retire from the fashion-show business four years later and find a part-time job at a floral shop on Pinkas Street (there, too, everybody would be sure she was the owner). That morning, all she knew was that now was the time and the time was now, and at the moment, with a large keychain swinging from two of her fingers, she paced the dewy grass toward the service entrance at the edge of the water park; in the distance, she noticed her sister Bina sitting under a sun umbrella, enjoying a cigarette she must have bummed from one of the merchants. For a moment, she thought of approaching her, but gave up the thought immediately: the guests she had invited especially for this big day were already waiting outside and she hurried to greet them.

B.

"*Hevenu sholem aleichem!*" Avrum Shlossman sang, kissing his sister on both cheeks.

"Hello, Tzippi'le," Sammy Greenberg purred with a sweet smile. The third guest made do with a nod of the head.

"Go on, go on, I don't want anyone to see me letting you in," Tzippi Zinman said as she rushed them forward.

"Where are Dvora and Tuvia? We stopped at Nordau Café and bought you some yummy croissants."

"Don't bother them now, they got here ten minutes ago and still haven't finished arranging their stall," Tzippi said. "Bina's here too."

"Why did she bring her?" Avrum wondered.

"I'll explain later."

"If I had known she was here," he said, moping, "I'd have gotten something for her, too."

"No matter. There's a snack bar here, you can buy her some jelly beans. But right now, do me a favor and disperse—the kibbutzniks don't like these tricks."

"Sneaking in!" Sammy purred excitedly. His bean-shaped bald head was covered by a baseball cap printed with the words "Don't Worry, Be Happy." A small, toned belly was hiding behind a tennis shirt with a high-end logo; hairless legs sprouted from inside white Bermuda shorts, short but surprisingly muscular, ending in white espadrilles. In one hand he carried a picnic cooler; in the other, a striped sun umbrella—in short, this was not a man entering the water park but the embodiment (no taller than 5'3") of the concept "vacation." This embodiment was accompanied by another, less desirable guest: the mustachioed thug Tzippi recalled as the head stoner from the winter concert at her brother's house. Soon, Avrum and his gang mixed with the crowd and took over a piece of land by the fence around the wave pool.

• • •

Of all of Shfayim's pleasure rides—the old slalom slide, the kamikaze slope, or the pink basin known as "Children's World"—vacationers felt a special affinity for the wave pool—a sort of giant, blue seashell that could hold hundreds of bathers. At its edge was the mosaic-covered watchtower. At the top of the tower, in the shade of a faded shed, were the lifeguards: young, tan men, almost completely nude, as was the custom, looking in all directions, like a band of noble predators. "We want to remind everybody to drink a lot!" one of them announced through a loudspeaker. "I repeat: drink a lot! I repeat . . ." At this point a teasing joke spoken by one of his friends cut him off. The two were pulled into a friendly brawl, at the end of which the announcer was defeated with a neck grip. Tzippi's three guests, all sworn bachelors, followed the action with interest, exchanging lusty smiles.

Suddenly—a commotion. Excited teenagers stormed in from all directions. More and more vacationers were attracted to the pool, kicking and spraying on their way in, not satisfied until the water covered their entire bodies. The blue seashell turned black with countless heads and shoulders. The bustle grew louder; the crowdedness was inconceivable. In the meantime, lifeguards descended from their shed and surrounded the pool like large cats, assessing the sprawl of their kingdom, their swagger indifferent yet alert. They exchanged silent signals and spread out in equal distances on the edge of the pool. All eyes were turned to the watchtower with tense expectation. The head lifeguard delivered a final warning: all children under the age of so-and-so are ordered to move to the shallow water immediately. One of his assistants pulled out a toddler who snuck into the water with the bigger children, against regulations. Ten o'clock. Ten and one minute. Here we go, here we go.

At first the change is imperceptible—a kind of light wave, no more than a quick shake. But the movement does not abate; recognition quickly sets in: the waves! Cries of joy sound from all directions. Waves rise and fall, pulling with them all bathing heads with a single thrust. Here and there a head disappears and then quickly emerges with a cough and a spit. To an outside observer—for instance, to Avrum Shlossman, leaning on the fence, overjoyed with the general happiness—the sight may be reminiscent of a massive floral blanket shaken by invisible hands. Those listening in might notice a dull groan rising from the depths. In the engine room buried below the pool, in the boiler netherworld, pistons work with all of their power to operate the giant vacuum enraging the water of the pool and making a terrifying ruckus. The air boils. The head mechanic, deafened and sweaty, turns up the intensity. The water is sucked and sprayed alternately, drops spewing wildly, waves storming, one by one, from the top of the shell to its shallow edges, where they finally wane, lapping the feet of the elderly that stand on the shore with longing eyes, their hearts pulled toward the festivities but not allowing them to participate.

"Excuse me sir, where is the smack bar?"

Avrum Shlossman turned his head and was surprised—behind him was a gigantic middle-aged matron, a swollen goiter hanging between her chin and her chest. The top of this human mountain was adorned with thinning yellow hair, pulled diagonally down to her shoulders. A white tent dress, held up by spaghetti straps, gave her the shape of a wide-base triangle. The flesh of her mighty arms swung ceaselessly, as if on its own accord; only her fingers retained a surprising measure of discrete feminine charm.

"Sir, I'm looking for a smack bar," she said, waving an advertising pamphlet against her face. Shiny pearls of sweat slowly dripped from her chin without her bothering to wipe them off. As she spoke, her crowded, crooked teeth were revealed, growing one on top of the other like stalks in an over-fertilized lawn. Her eyes were heavily made up, her thick painted lips contoured by a dark line. Even those who had never laid eyes on her before could swear they had previously met. In more than one way, Lizika Burko was an *absolute* being. The former antique salesman, who was never able to withstand the absolute, was captivated immediately.

"It just happens that I'm going there myself," he answered. "Come on, I'll take you."

He tried to make conversation on the way, but Miss Burko was not receptive to his courting. All her attention was devoted to a bottle of fizzy, colorless, frosty lemonade that had settled in her mind following some advertisement, not letting go. *Tlak-tlak, tlak-tlak*, her orthopedic slippers stuck to her heels and then dropped off. Heat, crowdedness, sweat pouring down temples, burning eyes; she tossed her makeshift fan and wiped her face with her hand. She was filled with rage at the sight of the millions—or so she later described the vision to her sister-in-law—amassed outside of the snack bar; she gathered her strength and made her way through fearlessly, as glorious as a white battleship within a fleet of colorful sailboats. Avrum took advantage of the space she left in her wake and pushed through as well. Moist limbs pressed against him from all directions—arms, thighs, breasts wrapped in tingly Lycra. One stepped on his foot, another breathed on his face, the smell revealing eggplant salad. After a short consideration, he concluded that, since he was destined to be pushed anyway, he would reach the counter as a result of pure physics. He therefore decided to give himself in to stronger powers, and soon discovered—not for the first time—that under certain conditions one could derive pleasure even from the most unpleasant of experiences.

C.

"How's your handsome guy? Didn't he feel like having some fun at the pool, too?" the midget travel agent asked. He was still wearing his tennis shirt, but the Bermuda shorts had disappeared, replaced by small buttock cheeks wrapped tightly in a Speedo.

"He's minding the shop."

"That's a shame, I haven't seen him in a while." The words were pronounced with an emphasis insinuating meetings that had taken place and a special affinity, though neither of these had ever been the case. Now, Dvora Saltzman found that these insinuations no longer alarmed her. She responded with a pseudo-ironic smile and felt bold, even a little international.

"Your flight tickets are waiting for you in my safe," he added. "But it's the end of the month already; you have to pay or you'll miss out on the special offer price. Send Shraga over, have him come tomorrow. We can't drag it out any longer."

"I'd better come by myself. I'll take the opportunity to buy a proper suitcase next door, and a toiletry kit; I need a good one. I'm embarrassed to tell you what kind of luggage I have now, from pioneer days."

"I'll make sure they give you a discount, don't worry," said Sammy. "Give me a call before you come over and I'll go in with you, make sure they don't try to sell you low-grade stuff. A good valise is a long-term asset—you need strong bones, high-quality sewing. It's all about the details. Trust me, I know these things—I was pedantic even as a child. I learned how to pack a suitcase from my mother in Argentina, but she had her method and I have mine. For example, a lot of people think you have to fold shirts like at a store, in half, but that's a big mistake! That's how they get wrinkled. You have to fold them in quarters, though it might sound absurd—that way, they stay perfectly ironed, even if you fly all the way to Buenos Aires . . ."

"You don't say!"

"Take my word for it, and you'll be happy when you land. What can I tell you—it's unbelievable what a man learns in life, all by himself, no university. Ah, if only I'd written a book! But who would have bought a book like that?"

"What time are we landing?" Tzippi joined them, in high spirits. She had just completed a round of the stalls, and in spite of the early hour, had managed to collect all the commissions from the merchants with no argument.

Tzippi Zinman suffered from chronic constipation—as we may have already alluded to—a delicate matter that would not have been brought up if not for her habit of perusing travel photos as she waited on the toilet. For this purpose, she arranged a small table upon which—next to a bowl of soap flakes and a plaster angel—were always two or three photo albums. As she flipped through the pages, her imagination roamed free: here she would lead Dvora to that charming little square where they would sip coffee on a blooming veranda, and there she would take her shopping, introducing her to the best shops. Here they would take a cable car up to a snowy peak; it would be very cold and they would go into that inn, the one with the stuffed deer heads on the walls, to warm up—after all, Dvora is only human, she deserves Seefeld for once, too! The topic had become a kind of obsession for Tzippi, who could no longer imagine going this year without Dvora. She had made her peace with Fat Tuvia's choice to stay in Tel Aviv, and would have gone on without Shirley and even without Avrum, but without Dvora—absolutely not. That was the heart of the matter, for which all efforts were being made.

She had set a silent goal: 4,000 shekels, give or take, should make this trip possible for Dvora. She followed the sales at the surfing pants stall with satisfaction. Just in case, she decided to give Dvora a nice gift for the trip—$250 in cash (to spend on herself, and not a word to Shraga). And so, on this morning of August 30, though all of this was still merely a plan, Tzippi already viewed herself as entitled to complete gratitude.

"I got you on an excellent flight," the agent said. "You'll arrive in Munich at 10:00 a.m., so you'll have all day."

"In that case, maybe before we cross the border to Austria we'll go to Mad King Ludwig's palace!" Tzippi exclaimed. "It isn't a big detour. You'll love it, Dvoraleh—it's so beautiful I can't even describe it, like in the movies, at the top of the mountain, with all that view around, and the road twisting through the forest . . ."

"See, that's why I love my job," Sammy said. "I'm always part of people's fun. What could be more beautiful?"

Bina, the headphones of her new Walkman on her ears, walked over, accompanying the song she was listening to with meaningless, made-up words. She wore a red bathing suit under a large tunic. She had just visited Nachliel Zarfaty's stall, where she was sent to break a hundred shekel bill. As was her manner, she performed her task dutifully. As she counted the small bills (twice), her face wore a formal expression, an impersonation of an expression she had seen more than once on her brother-in-law Yosef Zinman's face as he counted cash money. She furrowed her brow, stuck the edge of her tongue out, and moistened her finger every so often. The sight of her exaggerated gravity filled Zarfaty's heart with love for humanity, and he gave her two shoulder pads as a gift. A smile of pleasure spread upon her face, and she hurried to push them into place under her tunic. Now, with shoulders that were too broad, she looked even stranger than usual.

"Have you told her about the *arrangement* yet?" Tzippi whispered.

"Not yet."

"I can't believe it . . . when are you planning on telling her? When we're on the plane?"

"Not now," Dvora said, angry. "Change the subject."

"I've got change!" Bina announced proudly and hung the head-phones around her neck. "Nachliel gave me fives and tens."

"Good," said Dvora. "Thank you. It's good that you came with us today—you're a big, big help."

"Next time shave her legs before you take her to the pool," Tzippi muttered.

"Where's Tuvia?" Bina asked.

"Went to say hi to his girl."

Though most of those present had already been introduced to Maya, she had not yet earned the right to be called by her name among family, and even Dvora, who truly liked her, did not dare beat her sister to the punch on this matter. She knew Tzippi was mad—perhaps not truly mad, but certainly disappointed—that Tuvia was not joining them on their journey, and since they blamed the matter on that light-haired kibbutznik, they all felt some discomfort any time they had to mention her in conversation.

"Am I allowed to have some of his juice?" Bina asked.

"Of course you can!" Tzippi cried. "Drink as much as you want, don't be shy. Guys, I have an announcement to make—I'm out of here. I have to get some more fans for the dressing rooms before my princesses arrive. I'll see you later."

D.

Ever since our ancestors were banished from the Garden of Eden due to belts crafted out of fig leaves, people have rarely removed their clothing in public. The right to appear unclothed—which, in hospital cafete-rias, for instance, is reserved for patients only—is the exclusive right of public pool visitors; in either location, the sight is as magnificent as it is bloodcurdling. At the water park, men and women reveal their defects and distortions for all to see. Here one might come across the breath-less sight of a tanned teenager, her young rolls of fat bursting forth from a miniscule bathing suit, her belly button pointing proudly out of her plump belly. Eyes travel against one's will toward an old man, skinny and smiling, the folds of his stomach scarred from an ancient operation, his testicles swollen like oranges. The gaze wanders from an athletic type covered head to toe in matted black fur to a girl well versed in pain with a hard, rocky hump growing from between her nude shoulder blades. This rabble now congregated by the stalls, indifferent to their nudity, rummaging through the clothes with lusty fervor.

Our acquaintance Sammy Greenberg also delved into the goods, and since he had been ordered not to mention Seefeld around Bina, he chatted in all directions, as if spraying an odor neutralizer. One thing led to another, and he chose a fluorescent green shirt, size small, and announced he was going to wear it to a private dance party, the bold nature of which he alluded to with a meaningful batting of the lashes. As the group discussed the shirt's many advantages—the color, in Dvora's opinion, complimented Sammy's eyes—Avrum Shlossman approached, accompanied by a heavy, terrifying matron. In retrospect, it turned out that the lady with the goiter, Lizika Burko, one and the same, was no less than Sara Consignment's sister-in-law!

The vacation, the summer, and the abundance of exposed bodies inspired a Latin state of mind in Avrum. When he saw his sister Dvora he broke into a rendition of *"Eviva España"* and tried to drag her into a round of paso doble.

"Enough of your nonsense, you idiot," she said, a smile spreading across her face. "How are you? I was just saying I can't believe you came all the way to the water park and haven't come over to say hello. Shame on you!"

"Avrum!" Bina cheered. "Hi! Fat Tuvia's around too, you know? But he isn't here now, he went to kiss his girl."

"Shh!" Dvora said. "The whole world doesn't need to hear about this!"

"I brought you fresh croissants," Avrum said, raising the paper bag with a flourish.

"Oh, wonderful!"

"Susu picked us up at 8:30," he continued (he never bothered to get a driver's license; instead he nurtured a circle of friends who gladly drove him everywhere). "You know me—those aren't exactly my hours, my eyes were still glued shut. So I said, guys, we're only human, after all. Why don't we gather some strength before we continue? Long story short, we stopped at Café Nordau. The moment we grabbed a table I saw some dark-haired guy leave the kitchen with a tray of croissants and babka. I said—aha!"

"Exactly," Sammy-Susu confirmed. "And I said: ahaaa!"

"And what did you bring me?" Bina asked.

"Here, this is for you," her brother said, handing her a bag of M&Ms, the loot from his trip to the snack bar.

"Open it for me, I can't do it."

"There you go."

Bina sat on one of the chairs behind the stall and immersed herself in the bag. She pulled the chocolate buttons out one by one, examined them carefully and ate them according to an order, the essence of which was to leave an equal number of each color. In the meantime, Dvora poured her guests black coffee from her thermos and tore off half of a croissant.

"How's it going so far?"

"People are crazy about the phosphorous. We've already made about 280 shekels, maybe more, I'm not sure—Tuvia has the money."

"The shirts are fabulous. Here, I bought one for myself, too," Sammy said. "In green, to match my eyes. What do you think? It's for Foofy's birthday party."

"You'll glow like a spotlight—we'll just have to wait for someone to get electrocuted," Avrum said with a chuckle. Dvora chuckled, too. The head lifeguard announced the nearing round of fun at the wave pool. A Madonna hit was playing over the loudspeakers, and the travel agent shook his hips and snapped his fingers to the beat. From the nearby stage came the calls of the aerobics instructor as she thanked the audience; the workout crowd gathered around the stalls.

Fat Tuvia returned from his visit with Maya—no doubt, those glorious thirty minutes were sufficient for him to get a taste of the pleasures he had recently grown so fond of, and Maya herself was quite satisfied with certain talents discovered in him. At any rate, he returned to the stall, put on his famous umbrella hat, and began to chant his slogans. Curious parties were drawn to the table and his hands were soon full.

"Can I have a Coke?"

"Binchi, do me a favor—can't you see we're working? Remember what you promised at home. Take your chair and go sit on the side."

"There's juice in my thermos," said Fat Tuvia. "Why just one pair, ma'am? Take two, your husband will thank you, I guarantee it!"

"We give—you get!" Albert Ben Arroya screamed from stage. "Three tickets for ten!"

"These colors are the height of fashion," Sammy recommended. "I bought one for myself."

"But I don't want apple juice, I want Coke."

"Listen up, listen up, at eleven o'clock, light refreshments will be served to Tadiran employees and their families at the main lawn, by the first aid station. Please bring your vouchers!"

"Just wait quietly a little longer, then we'll go to the snack bar."

"What's the problem?" Avrum said. "Why do you have to make everything into a hassle for yourself? She's a big girl, she can go get it herself."

"I chose green, to match my eyes, but if you ask me—the orange is hot, too. Besides, what are we even talking about? Fifteen shekels a shirt! It's practically a joke! I'm a family friend, by the way. I've been begging them since the beginning of summer: guys, raise your prices a little, so you'll get something in your pockets too, but they're stubborn, what can you do."

"If I buy four shirts, can I get a discount?"

"Tuvia, do me a personal favor—give this lovely lady a discount."

"Three tickets for ten, ladies and gentlemen, three for ten! Today the first prize is a twenty-one-inch Grundig color TV!"

"You know what, fine, take them all for fifty-five."

"Where's the snack bar?" Bina asked.

"Come with us, we'll show you," said her brother.

"You don't mind?" asked Dvora.

"Ciotka Dvora, can you break this into fives?"

"Why would I mind? We're headed in that direction anyway."

"We left Avigdor by the wave pool to watch our things, we have to get back, he's probably bored to death," said Sammy Greenberg, referring to our acquaintance, the hash-loving thug, who was now sitting on the lawn, discussing muscle-building dietary supplements with one of the lifeguards.

"Tuvia!" Bina showed off. "I'm going to the snack bar by myself! Should I get something for you, too?"

"Wait a minute." Dvora rifled through her purse. "What's the rush, I haven't even given you money yet. There you go. Get me a Diet Coke, too, but really cold. And count the change, don't let them rip you off."

"Come on, you don't know my husband, he'll never wear that color. How many times have I begged him—a little, have just a little awareness. Progress is good, you don't have to dress like some *alter kaker* all the time. He's a good-looking man, after all, he's got a nice body—what's sixty-two these days? A kid! But I might as well be talking to the wall."

"Come right back here from the snack bar—there's going to be a bingo game soon, I'll buy you some tickets."

"Buddy, can I have a bag already? This is the third time I've asked you."

"Ciotka!" Fat Tuvia called. "I'm all out of bags—do me a favor, there should be more in that small box."

"One second."

"Dear audience, your attention please: the light refreshments at eleven o'clock are for Tadiran employees and their families only, I repeat, Tadiran employees and their families *only!*"

Dvora Saltzman glanced at her watch: a quarter to eleven, and below the time, in a small window: August 30. She had no idea that this date and time would become forever etched in her memory.

E.

Each morning in the three weeks that had gone by since her secret meeting with Aunt Masha, Dvora woke up determined that today she would finally tell Bina about the *comfortable arrangement*. Till evening, she found all sorts of excuses to delay the conversation; the next day she swore to herself again and postponed it again. In the meantime, the house filled up with childish posters of Austrian landscapes, cut out of journals and decorated with slogans such as "Beautiful Seefeld" and "Seefeld—Family Town" and signed with the initials B. S. It angered Dvora so much that a week earlier she broke down and yelled at a surprised Bina to stop dirtying up the house. The distress grew worse each day. More than once, she decided to just give up on the entire trip. In spite of the convoluted discussions she held with herself, she knew her plan was nothing less than contemptible. One day, Shraga showed her an ad he found in the paper with imploring eyes: a small airline offered a trip for children—a thirty-minute flight over Israel in a special observation plane. She was excited for a moment, then filled with shame.

Each night she saw Bina's face on the screen of her closed eyelids, amazed and eaten up with sorrow. No explanation would console her when she told her they were all going to Seefeld and leaving her behind with Aunt Masha. Bina loved her aunt very much—a sort of love on principle, a result of familial loyalty—but Dvora knew that the old sharp-tongued lady terrified her. How could she hope for their aunt to resist for an entire week and not insult her niece? When Dvora found out Fat Tuvia was not coming with them on the trip, she was somewhat relieved. He promised to keep an eye on the events at Joshua Son of Nun Street—but how could she trust him, she thought, with all those things he had on his mind. And perhaps she should take Bina to Austria with her after all? On a secretive phone conversation, her sister declared that, should Dvora end up deciding to bring Bina along, she would help. Help—meaning, she would agree to take her to the Seefeld boardwalk for one or two afternoons, and maybe contribute a little to the expenses. An image formed in her mind: the Zinmans shaking their hips to the sounds of the band at that nightclub they talked so much about, while she sat at the table with Bina, watching to make sure she did not steal a bun. No, she thought. For years, she had sat patiently in her corner, watching Tzippi twirling around—now she wanted to get up and go a little crazy herself.

An anonymous airline clerk put an end to her misgivings, turning a random date into a fateful one: Thursday, August 31, was pointed out in her reminder as the absolute final deadline for payment. The term *ticketing*, which she had used, was written in bold over the door that separated Bina from Seefeld. The fates had spoken: the matter would be sealed by this weekend. She felt a strong urge to compensate her younger sister immediately, as if atonement for one's sins was a currency she could use ahead of time. And so, on the morning of August 30—though she had sworn, after the ghastly vision of Bina strutting half-naked on the stage, never to bring her to the water park again—Dvora decided to take her along to the water park to have some fun. And Bina, happy, never guessing the source of such a blessing, promised fervently to behave.

Alas, she did not keep her promise this time, either.

F.

The fashion show went on and on. The sellers and manufacturers, determined to make the very best of the last day of the season and sell as much as possible, sent piles and piles of items to the models backstage. The space trapped between the tin walls and the blue raffia strips steamed with the sour smell of textile. The models stripped and tossed, grabbed and wore, stepped on the tossed garments, making their way onto the stage among ripped cellophane wrappers, stickers, plastic labels, and half-empty water bottles. The ground inside the shack became muddy, fans creaked helplessly, the makeshift mirror was covered with oily fingerprints. Suffocation intensified. Tzippi Zinman, covered in sweat, ran back and forth, lighting cigarettes and putting them out after only one or two puffs. She stretched a shirt here, puffed up a skirt there, shouted, threatened, complimented, tore a zipper in her haste. Sara Consignment, who came by to watch closely over her merchandise, cackled ceaselessly. Somebody burst into tears, who knows why. Albert Ben Arroya's screams erupted from the sound system as he threatened to burst with good spirits: that day, a children's clothing merchant appeared at the fair, accompanied by a young model, a little girl of about nine years of age, who strutted flamboyantly on stage, reaping compliments. The audience was beside itself. The congestion around the catwalk became unbearable. Vacationers, smelling of chlorine and sweat and melted ice cream, pushed, cursed, goofed off, stretching sun-scorched torsos, fighting violently for a better viewing spot. The girl finally paused on the edge of the catwalk, placed a flirtatious hand on her hips, and twisted her face in a nightmarish smile. When she decided she had gotten all she could from the audience she turned on her heels and left the stage.

Then, from within the burning inferno, their heads adorned with veils, their chests strapped into silk corsets imbedded with fake pearls, and cascades of lace and white organza pouring from their thin waists, four magnificent brides went up on stage, one after the other. Their arms were covered in pale gloves, their feet were hidden as they floated like four ruffle creampuffs. Cool and fresh, indifferent to the deadening heat, Tzippi Zinman's girls swirled in a semi-see-through dance, spreading across the catwalk, pure and long-necked like princesses of a northern kingdom, out at a ball. The smiles they sent in all directions graced sun-scorched faces and cooled burning souls. Hearts were filled with wonder and yearning for the beauty. Who does not want to be a bride, who does not want to be a groom? Even the merchants stopped their calculations, their eyes fixed on the epiphany. Blinding light glowed from the catwalk. The audience held its breath . . .

■ ■ ■

The pretend brides (two days earlier, Zinman had surreptitiously entered one of the oldest bridal salons on Ben Yehuda Street and rented four glamorous dresses) made a final round, waved goodbye, and disappeared behind the curtain. All at once, the magic evaporated, replaced by utter chaos. Human waves crashed everywhere—get, fight, grab something, at any price. The morning sales were nothing compared to what happened at the stalls now. Nachliel Zarfaty of Paloma Bianca grew hoarse from yelling "no touching!" while the Frumkins, whose "Swish" watches had run out, raised the prices of men's watches by 30 percent without batting an eyelash. But all of these paled in comparison to Sara Consignment. Within fifteen minutes, she sold no less than four suits embroidered with gigantic flowers, seven pairs of wavy cotton pants, and an unknown number of wide belts. Thick-ankled women who, that very morning, had thrown a tasteless tricot tunic over themselves, discovered, with her help, that nothing suited them better than a knee-length Charleston dress. The revered merchant was at the top of her game. There was no time to breathe. The checks piled up so quickly that one flew away and landed at the feet of Zarfaty, whose eyes bugged at the sight of the sum (for a moment, an irreverent thought even passed through his mind).

Even after the initial excitement died down, they kept selling. Now the stalls were visited by customers with time on their hands. They examined, asked, chatted with the merchants. In the meantime, the exhausted models left the water park with full pockets, and Tzippi Zinman had time to tour her kingdom. She was in good spirits—compliments for her gorgeous finale were made all around. On her way to the family rag stall, she stopped at Estee Creations and bought herself a bracelet.

"Is there anything left of Avrum's croissants? I'm starving. You know how it is—when you're working you don't think of food, but the moment the rush ends, your stomach goes like this!" She twisted a fist in front of her stomach.

"I only had half of mine," Dvora said. "Take what's left, look in that bag."

"Where?" Tzippi asked. "I can't find it."

"What do you mean? That can't be—I saved half for later. Look again."

But the bag was empty. Without a choice, Zinman consoled herself with an apple Dvora had saved for an emergency, and sat down to rest under the sun umbrella. Fat Tuvia was busy with two guys who showed an interest in the glowing shirts. The goods had almost run out, and Dvora pulled the last sack from under the table, took out surfing pants and arranged them by size.

"Where's Bina?" Tzippi asked.

"Went with Avrum to get something from the snack bar."

"Did you happen to notice how Sara Consignment did?" Tzippi asked, glancing at the woman through her enormous sunglasses.

"I swearrrr to you, may I have an infection and bad complexion if I sold anything from my collection," Fat Tuvia said, impersonating the Romanian merchant. "You could get brain damage from all her nonsense. How did she do? Her fingers are worn out, poor woman, from counting all that cash!"

"Who's that tub of lard next to her?"

"I don't know," Dvora said. "Her name is Lizika."

"They say she's her sister-in-law," Tuvia remarked, "I guess she came by to help her."

"Really?" the stylist said as she rubbed the edge of her nose. "And I think she's here to pick up some business on the side without asking me. Just you wait and see what those two witches are going to get from me." She stood up and went over to review the situation.

Indeed, her suspicions had been founded. Lizika Burko, a former secretary at a reflexology clinic, was making her first steps in the diet-pill industry. A man named Doctor Matmon, whom she had met at the clinic, offered her a job as a sales agent for imported products—wondrous pills that, so he promised, reduced appetite and promoted weight loss without the need for any physical activity. The doctor's pills (a few years later, following a lawsuit, he fled the country, never to be heard of again) were based on a mysterious Swiss formula. Patients slimmed down, but every now and then were attacked by a terrible itch and uncontrollable weeping.

The wise reader may wonder what a woman with such a developed appetite, like Lizika, had to contribute to the global dietary effort; but it was exactly her dimensions that imbued her with authority among her customers. Her methods were no different than those of her sister-in-law, Sara Consignment, but while Sara called her victims *customers*, the trainee dietician preferred the term *patients*. She made sure to add the words *fat dissolvers* to her products, a pair of words usually reserved for descriptions of sink- and toilet bowl–cleansing acids. But the low voice, the foreign accent, the manicured fingers gently uncapping the bottle, and even the soft goiter hanging from her neck—all of these enchanted customers, leading them to believe that life was not worth living without Doctor Matmon's pills. "With these pills you can put *a-ny-thing* in your mouth," Lizika explained to a plump vacationer that had just joined her gaggle of fans, stuffing a medicinal baggie into her hand. "Enjoy."

"Can I ask what's going on here?" Tzippi Zinman demanded, adjusting her sunglasses, which had slipped down her nose due to sweat.

After carefully considering all of the data, Sara Consignment had reached the false conclusion that, during the commotion expected on the final day of the season, no one would notice if she snuck her sister-in-law into the water park and allotted her a corner at the edge of her stall, where she could sell her products. Lizika was asked to play down her presence as much as possible—an impossible order to fill, of course, in light of her personality. In her defense it must be pointed out that she did her best to speak softly.

"Sorry? I couldn't hear you."

"I said I was only an assistant?"

"Really?" Zinman grabbed one of the bottles and raised it. "Then what's this supposed to be?"

"That's for my blood pressure," Lizika explained discretely.

"What are your blood pressure levels, if you don't mind me asking?"

"Oh, Tzippi, come on," Sara Consignment said, coming to her protégé's aid. "It's only my sister-in-law, not some criminal, look how sympathetic she is." (Here the sister-in-law smiled modestly.) "Here, I'll introduce you: Tzippi Zinman—Lizika Burko."

"I want to know what she's doing here, period, exclamation mark. And don't you dare try to fool me!"

"Why are you shouting? I swear, first you don't let people talk and then you jump to conclusions. Here, I'll explain everything: you should know that Lizika is the number one expert against fat. Her pills are incredible: the pounds fall off even when you don't want them to, no matter what you put in your mouth. Have you heard of Doctor Matmon? No? It's *the* biggest hit right now; all of Tel Aviv is waiting in line. Long story short, last night, maybe around eleven, I was sitting in front of the television, just to relax—they were showing Chopin's Bolognese with some famous Russian pianist; I was always considered the musical type . . . and suddenly I had an inspiration. I called her and said, 'Liziku' (that's how I call her when we're alone), 'excuse me for calling so late, but why don't you bring your pills to the water park tomorrow morning? It's an opportunity.' She said, 'what, just like that, tomorrow?' I said, 'why not? I've never heard of a law against being spontaneous. You come, then we'll work it out with the boss, I mean with you.' Those were my exact words, may the worms eat me up right now if I'm lying and bon appétit. Don't worry, Tzippileh, we'll pay whatever we need. No need to make a big ba-boom about every little thing."

"When I'm done with you, you'll need more than a ba-boom, you'll need an undertaker!" Zinman cried. "Since when do you decide who sells what in my shows? And when exactly were you thinking of letting me know about this? No, I wasn't born yesterday, lady; I've known all about your Romanian tricks for a long time!"

"Anita Shagrir never spoke to me like this," the merchant said rebelliously.

"Excuse me??? You know what? Why don't you go back to her, if you're so unhappy with me? You can crawl to her on all fours for all I care. The whole world knows what she calls you behind your back."

"You'd think she calls you any better . . ."

"Not interested, thank you!"

"Grocery Girl!" Sara called. "That's what she calls you: Grocery Girl!!!"

"That moment I felt as if a bomb dropped," Nachliel Zarfaty would say later.

Tzippi Zinman paled. Her blue eyes burned, her breasts rose, she shook her lion's mane and landed her palm on the table with full force. "Now!" she screamed. "You're going to take your *shmattes* right now and get the hell out of here, or I'll rip all of your dresses, one by one! Now!"

"Duvia!" Sara Consignment yelled, waving her arms. "Duvia! Help! Your mother wants to murder me!"

G.

"What is she fussing about, your *mameniu*?" asked Avrum, who had just arrived from the area of the old swimming pool. A large towel covered his torso like a cloak; water droplets shone on his legs.

"The Romanian cheated her again," said Fat Tuvia, who had been following the events serenely from below his umbrella hat.

"Where did you disappear to?" asked Dvora. "And where's Bina?"

"How should I know? Isn't she with you?"

"What do you mean? You took her with you to get a Coke."

"There was a line, so I left her there—she said she was going right back to the stall because you promised you'd take her to bingo. *You* let her go alone—you mean to tell me she hasn't come back yet?"

"No."

"Well, it's only been about twenty minutes."

Dvora glanced at her watch. "Forty," she said.

Silence fell.

"Say, Avrum, did you happen to eat that half croissant I left in the bag?"

"Are you crazy? I'm on a diet, look at my gut."

"I don't like this one bit." She sighed. "She probably ate that croissant behind my back. Who knows where she is—she might be writhing with pain in some corner. What a mistake, what a mistake—I'm the stupid one, I swear. What did I bring her to the water park again for? After the embarrassment she caused last time? And don't tell me 'relax, Dvora'—with all due respect, Avrum, you have no idea! You haven't seen her having an attack for years."

"Okay, don't make this into a tragedy," Avrum said. "Let's both go look for her—Tuvia can mind the stall by himself for a few minutes, the rush hour is over anyway."

"Go, go," Tuvia urged them. "I'm here, just leave the cashbox."

The afternoon drew near. The sun blazed, and the vacationers deserted the stalls and searched for respite—some in the cold water; others under the blue raffia sheds. Fat Tuvia, who was now unemployed, set a plastic chair in the shade of one of the trees, took off his umbrella cap, wiped the sweat off his forehead, and began counting the earnings. He wrote down the final number in a dog-eared pad. Since he was bored, he decided to add up the revenue for the entire period, since the beginning of summer, then deduct expenses and divide in two. To his delight, he found that the profits were higher than he had thought—he and his aunt had earned no less than 4,300 shekels each—more than $2,000!—and he assumed by the time they shut down the stall, in two or three hours, they would manage to scrounge up a little more. He looked affectionately at the pile of garments left on the table and decided to donate the items they did not sell by the end of the day to a certain charity he knew in Petah Tikva. He also planned on investing his profits in a trip, like his aunt Dvora, but he replaced the family trip to Seefeld with a vacation in Greece with Maya. In fact, he had already discussed the matter with her—they had determined to go to Santorini or one of the nearby islands at the end of September; newspapers were filled with one-inch ads offering round trips for tempting prices. He pondered the voyage, but mainly the conversation he would soon have to have with his father, in which he would announce his intention to retire from the grocery store.

Ever since he could think for himself, sometime in the early 1970s, Fat Tuvia knew that the addendum *and sons* on the grocery sign referred only to him. From his early days, he prepared for the moment when he would become an equal partner in the business. In the evening, when his father sat in the kitchen and checked the supply certificates and the accounting books, he would read them over his shoulder and memorize the procedures. As early as fifteen, he would take his father's place behind the counter from time to time, and soon strummed the keys of the cash register with a skill no less impressive than his sister Shirley's as she played her saw. When he grew up, he also became an expert in petty scalping, and formed understandings with the De Picciotto Street wholesalers downtown, where he and his father went to buy smoked mackerels and British-made soap. The grocery store was a sort of old-time synagogue—a sleepy institution in which a regular crowd convened each day, and in which he had always had a reserved seat at the gabbai's bench. But lately, Tuvia had been experiencing heretical thoughts. New horizons had been revealed to him, piquing his interest. New ideas excited his imagination. He even dared to consider higher education. Of all the sciences, his heart was drawn to sociology, but since he had not taken his matriculation exams seriously in high school (they seemed unnecessary at the time), he decided, as a first step, to improve his scores. Then he might enroll in college—now he felt like going as far as Haifa. On the afternoon of August 30, on the plastic chair at the water park, he first envisioned the silver plate that would be attached to the door of his office: "T. Zinman, Youth Probation Officer."

And then, all at once, the sprawling meadows of his future were replaced with the yellowing ground of the water park. A sort of fizzling he had not sensed until then suddenly called his attention and forced him to look up from the pad. Something had happened. The heat-stroked vacationers who had been lazily lounging around had awoken by some invisible alarm. From the random scattering of people and umbrellas, an inexplicable, yet decisive and insistent motion gradually formed—inside, to the depths of the park, toward the wave pool. One by one, like iron powder pulled toward a magnetic pen, more and more people joined the flow. A medley of indecipherable voices rose—excited calls, yells; broken, distant echoes of loudspeaker announcements. The music, which had been screaming through the sound system all morning, suddenly stopped, leaving behind a bothersome vacuum. Something had happened. A sense of alarm stood in the air, accompanied by a certain festiveness. The merchants, unable to leave their stalls, stood up and stared. Mama Frumkin sent her husband to find out what had happened. Only minutes had gone by when, from among the crowd, a group of young men stood out—some were familiar to Tuvia as staff members—running together in the opposite direction, calling to each other and making ambiguous hand signals. Behind them, like a sort of trail, hopped a row of excited boys. One of them, a lanky black-haired child, suddenly let out a cry and fell down not far from Tuvia's stall.

"Kid!" Tuvia called, "are you okay?"

The boy sat up, leaned forward and examined his foot worriedly.

Tuvia walked over. "Are you hurt? Let me see."

The boy turned his head and fixed Tuvia with suspicious eyes. Tuvia examined his ankle gently.

"Ow!"

"It's nothing," Tuvia said. "Come on, I have some ice in my cooler, we'll put some on your ankle to keep it from swelling."

He gave him a hand and supported him. The boy, who finally gave in, hopped over to the counter and sat down on one of the plastic chairs. Tuvia tore a paper towel, wrapped it around some ice cubes and placed it on the child's ankle.

"Press down on it. Does it still hurt?"

"Yes."

Tuvia took a nut wafer he had been saving for himself for later out of the cooler and gave it to the wounded boy.

"Say, kid," he asked, "what was all that mess earlier? What happened?"

"I didn't do anything, honest! I'm ten and a half, I'm allowed to go into the pool alone."

"But what happened?"

"Besides, I wasn't alone, I was with my older cousins from Jerusalem . . ." The boy quieted down for a moment and bit into the wafer. "One man blocked my view, but Kobi and Ben were there, really close, and they saw everything, they said it was really gross. Then we heard that the lifeguards went to bring a gurney. We ran after them because we wanted to see, but then I stepped on that stone."

"But why a gurney?" Tuvia asked. "Was somebody hurt?"

"What, you haven't heard?" the boy asked self-importantly. "They found a dead lady in the wave pool."

■ ■ ■

On August 31, the water park was open to the public again. The employee committee season had come to an end; the merchants and their stalls, the models, Albert Ben Arroya and his bingo machine—it was as if none of it had ever happened. At 7:30 in the morning, the ninja boys were already poking their sharp sticks through the final remnants of the combined Tadiran employees and X-ray employee union fun day. Light clouds floated over Shfayim, reflecting in the pools. The meteorologists forecasted a marked relief in the heat wave. The lifeguard on duty arrived as usual, around eight. First he went to the snack bar for a cup of black coffee and to catch up with the shift manager regarding the previous day's disaster. Then he took the bucket and the net used to collect floating filth from the pools and went to work. While he treated the wave pool, a light, plump stain caught his eye. When he brought up the net he found a sort of tiny, water-absorbed pillow. Throughout the summer, he had grown used to pulling out all sorts of unexpected objects—once he even found a ring with a precious gem, and another time a fork and spoon—but he could not figure out the nature of the object he had just caught. The young lifeguard, a loyal son of the kibbutz, had never been interested in the world beyond the water park's bougainvillea hedges. His understanding of the fashion world could be summed up with the rule "shorts in summer, pants in winter"; he was unable to guess that the sponge-like object was actually a shoulder pad—one of the pair of shoulder pads that Nachliel Zarfaty had given Bina the previous day. The lifeguard muttered something about the rudeness of vacationers, allowing themselves to pollute the pool water with garbage, and tossed the orphaned pad into the bucket with disgust, where it landed among dead dragonflies and fallen leaves.

Epilogue

Early April. The land is still surrounded with a predawn veil. A vague clarity begins marking the horizon. From within the duskiness, the sharp shades of a newborn spring rise and glow. The mountain peaks in the distance are pointy and snowy like a drawing on the wrapper of a chocolate bar. Sprawling meadows strewn with purple, yellow, and white flowers become apparent. An intoxicating, almost rotten smell is carried through the air. The ringing of bells, the mooing of cows—but the cows themselves are, as of yet, invisible. Two- and three-story rustic homes are scattered here and there, and the shacks next to them contain tall stacks of blackening logs. Chimneys stick out of sloping roofs—one already raising smoke, signaling a burning fireplace, and perhaps a homemaker frying buttery omelets. In the distance, on the road, several small spots flicker, full of will and intent—cars making their way to the center of Seefeld. The last car turns onto the dirt path leading to the inn. The branches of the tremendous chestnut tree hide the view for a moment from the eyes of the woman watching from the balcony. The car pulls up. A moment later, Ernest Bubinger emerges from it, plump and flushed, a scarf tied around his neck. The gravel groans under his feet. He makes a shell from his palms, blows into them, leans down, and brings yellow paper bags from the backseat—loaves of bread, probably. Bubinger raises his head, his face lighting up at having noticed the woman on the balcony; she waves to him, her eyes following him until he disappears under the awning. The sound of the door slamming reaches her ears. Dvora Saltzman wraps her coat tightly around her pajamas. The air is wonderful, chilly, stinging her nostrils and filling her lungs. An almost imperceptible rain—transparent needles tickling her spread palm—begins drizzling. She lingers for another moment and returns to the room, careful not to wake Shraga. A pleasant dimness welcomes her. The pillows are fluffed, the sheets starched. She takes off her coat, slips quietly under the covers, and falls asleep for another unbelievably sweet forty-five minutes.

■ ■ ■

In the basket rested slices of sour rye bread and hot, white rolls, cracking from crispness. Each of the relatives had a preferred dish: Tzippi, for instance, had become addicted in recent days to pork liver pâté, which she spread generously over the bread. Each morning there were two small dishes with different homemade jams waiting next to the Yosef's plate, since he had a sweet tooth. Each day they were served hard-boiled eggs in a woven basket shaped like a chicken, and Dvora decided she would buy one for herself before they returned to Israel. When they arrived at Seefeld, she found that Mrs. Bubinger had not changed her appearance one bit since the time of that photo her relatives had shown her at the slide show—her braid was still wrapped like a crown around her head, and she glowed with serenity and good health. As she poured orange juice, the innkeeper announced to her guests that they were in luck—the weather forecasts predicted a terrific week! By the time they drank and ate and rested for a while, then drank some more and shoved another little something in their mouths, the clouds dispersed, and since Avrum had yet to come out of his room, they decide to warm their bones and wait for him in the garden. Mr. Bubinger wiped the seats with a towel, and the family sat around the large table, all wrapped up in jackets and equipped with sunglasses. Shraga pulled out a matchbox and presented a geometric puzzle to the curious landlord.

"What do you think we should do today?" asked Tzippi.

"How should I know?" said her sister. "Whatever you decide is good for me."

"We could go to the Krimml Waterfalls," said Yosef Zinman. "It's a great day for a nature walk."

"Avrum said he feels like seeing Innsbruck," Shraga reminded them.

"That's an idea, too."

"I have to see my teacher today," Shirley announced without taking her eyes off of her journal. "He invited me to a band rehearsal at 12:30. Can you sort of plan to drive through Rattenberg?"

"In that case we'll drop you off, then go to Innsbruck," her father concluded. "It's more or less in the same direction, so why don't we let the women do some shopping."

The inn door opened. When they turned their heads they found good old Emma Bubinger carrying a pot of fragrant coffee and a plate of cookies. As she set the cups on the table, she said, "*also bitte*," and as she set the refreshments down she said, "*also bitte*," and Dvora stifled a giggle.

In the meantime, the sky turned a fabulous blue. Tzippi yawned and pulled out a cigarette. "This coffee is just what the doctor ordered! I'm telling you, we overdid it last night, period, exclamation mark. I went wild—my legs are killing me. I swear I could nap right now like it was nothing at all, if I didn't feel bad missing this beautiful day."

"I don't mind some coffee myself," Shraga announced. Last night, to his wife's utter surprise, he danced until two in the morning (after finishing off half a bottle of apple liqueur all by himself), and even led a group of Hungarian partygoers in a train dance around the hall. For three straight nights, the Zinmans and their relatives had been dining in a restaurant in central Seefeld, which served traditional meals, followed by a dance with a live band. Tzippi and Yosef were the life of these parties—on their frequent visits to Seefeld they had earned the affections of the singer, who was always happy to see them. Each time they walked into the hall he signaled to the musicians, and the band played the first bars of the "Radetzky March," just for them. This tune was now played for the Saltzmans as well, and by the time they returned home it had been nicknamed "The Family Call."

"What fantastic weather," Tzippi said and added some milk to her cup. "It's so lucky we postponed the trip to April. Frau Bubinger told me last night that it was freezing cold here in late September."

Dvora fixed her with hard eyes. Tzippi grew embarrassed and silent.

After Bina's death, it was unanimously decided to cancel the trip to Austria. "Here lies," read her tombstone, followed by brass lettering:

BINA SHLOSSMAN
Daughter of Hinde, of the house of Lifschitz, and Tuvia, RIP
1955–1989
Our Sister
Who Died Before Her Time

Bina was buried next to her parents, in a plot purchased for a considerable sum. When they returned from the cemetery, the family all went up to the Saltzmans' apartment on Judah the Maccabee Street and discussed all the details of the accident until the middle of the night. They tried turning back the wheel again and again: if she had not gone to the snack bar alone, if the lifeguards had only made sure she did not go in the pool, if she had not devoured half a croissant in hiding and suffered, most probably, of spasms while she was already in the wave pool, if she had not lost, so they guessed, her wits, if the pool had not been so crowded and rowdy that nobody noticed . . .

Mrs. Gitlis, a veteran customer of both family businesses, who came over to console, said it was a known problem—many times, the retarded suffered from all sorts of complications, and she probably would not have lived long anyway, and perhaps she had been spared greater suffering, who knows. Another person went further and suggested, halfheartedly, that perhaps it was for the best. But Dvora knew these words were empty, empty, and her heart burned with grief and yearning.

On the first days, the mourners felt that canceling the family trip was a necessary tribute to honor their sister's memory, and more so—a proper means of punishment. Which one called the travel agent? We do not know. Whatever the case, they canceled the trip. Though some of the mourners tried to persuade others otherwise, all other options were negated during the days of the shivah. But on the thirtieth day of mourning, the cancelation had become an indefinite postponement, and after four and a half months, it was decided that they would go that very year. That is the nature of things. We would all have done the same.

The Zinmans led the persuasion campaign. Tzippi said—after all, what did we work our asses off for all summer? Yosef nodded. And Dvora? Just as they saw her as the main person responsible for Bina's welfare in her lifetime, so did they see her, without ever expressly stating so, as the chief mourner. They asked Aunt Masha to convince her; Shraga, who thought a vacation would do them good, also pressured her. Dvora, who did not see the point in protesting any longer or did not have the strength to object, was finally dragged into the general mood and gave in. Passover was still far away, and it seemed that a vacation over the holiday would not be perceived as distasteful. The sisters visited Sammy Greenberg's travel agency once more. The festiveness that characterized their first visit was now replaced with correct restraint. Tickets for April were booked, and at a low price. Unbelievable, how time flies, said Avrum; at the end of the Passover Seder, which was held at the Zinman home, the keys were left with Fat Tuvia, who promised to water his aunt and uncle's plants as well, and at six in the morning they headed for the airport in two taxis.

Upon landing in Munich, Dvora felt that some of that foreign glamour she had heard so much about was now sticking to her too. She took pleasure in the dry cold and the quiet German mumbling that welcomed them at the airport. The urgency that had taken over her in the days before the flight evaporated at once, and her inner clock, timing her actions from the inside, beat at a slower, more European pace. While the husbands went to look for the Avis offices, the rest of the group sat at a coffee shop, and she tasted a real pretzel for the first time in her life. Eventually, to save some money, they rented just one car—a van with seven seats. Zinman took the driver's seat, his hands gripping the wheel over his large paunch, and beside him, by Tzippi's explicit request, sat Dvora. As soon as they left town, those green pastures she had dreamt of stretched out before her; without turning her head she knew, to her chagrin, that Tzippi was watching her watch with exaggerated attention, impatient for some exclamations of wonder.

She tried to focus on the road—junctions, forested hills, church steeples with stylish edges, a village on the shores of a lake, two gas stations, in one of which they only stopped to freshen up, and in the other they sat down to eat fried sausages and potato salad. They reached Seefeld within two or three hours. The pink walls of the inn, the sign reading *Bubinger* in simple lettering, the geraniums, the room with the creaking wooden floors, even the old-fashioned wash basin—all of these seemed simultaneously foreign and familiar. The excitement she had been expecting was late in arriving. Her sister, who noticed Dvora's confusion and interpreted it as disappointment, hastened to announce that Seefeld was not what it used to be, and that there was no comparison with last year. But Dvora was not disappointed at all. The next morning, they ascended to the top of Zugspitze. The snow filled her with quiet joy, and Shraga even bought her a miniature leather mountain climber boot with a ballpoint pen at its tip as a memento.

After four days, she stopped ambushing that sensation of spiritual uplift. She realized this was how things were in Seefeld, and how they had always been, no more, no less. The discovery calmed her: she liked knowing that Seefeld was nothing but a sort of Seefeld, overall pleasant and enjoyable. And now they all sat in the garden together, waiting for Avrum to come out so they could go to Innsbruck, and the sun was warm and the yellow daffodils were blooming in the flower beds; and in the distance, the Alps, and she was here. Birds chirped in honor of spring, and Dvora recalled for a moment an image from a nature movie she had once watched on television—a weak, blind baby hawk, abandoned in a little alcove, its beak gaping in a desperate cry for help. She looked around her: her husband, her brother-in-law, her sister, and she herself, all suddenly looked like those starved creatures, opening wide, wanting more, more. She held back tears, not because Seefeld had disappointed her, but because she was truly and honestly happy with her lot, and because she was sorry to think that someday this small share of life would be inexplicably taken away.

A handsome couple, both beautiful, left the inn with light steps, teasing each other, laughing in Italian at the tops of their lungs. All eyes followed them as they skipped down the stairs to the small parking lot. Tzippi announced that she was crazy about all Italians, and Yosef told for the who-knows-how-many time his tale of the nun in Portofino. They laughed a little, then quieted down and devoted themselves to the view. The lovers' Alfa Romeo broke the peace for a moment, until it disappeared down the road. Ringing and mooing were heard again—about a dozen cows finally emerged from the valley, lazily climbing up one of the hills. The sound of rattling dishes rose from the kitchen. The branches of the chestnut tree swayed in the wind.

"What can I tell you, folks," Yosef Zinman finally said with a sigh, "this is what I call luxury."

And he closed his eyes and let the sunlight wash over his face.

Paris, 2010

Yirmi Pinkus, born in Tel Aviv, Israel, in 1966, is a comics artist and novelist, as well as one of the founders of the independent comics group Actus.

In 2008 Pinkus's illustrated novel, *Professor Fabrikant's Historical Cabaret*, was published and awarded the Sapir Prize for Debut Literature, and later translated into Italian and French. In 2010 Pinkus was awarded the Israeli Prime Minister's Award for his achievements as an author of fiction and graphic novellas. His second novel, *Petty Business*, published in 2012, was an immediate best seller and was adapted for the stage by the Gesher Theater. Pinkus was awarded a translation grant from the Israel Institute, one of only three Israeli writers to have received this support.

In 2013, he founded, with comics artist Rutu Modan, Noah Books—an independent publishing house that publishes comics for preschoolers. His comic book *Mr. Fibber the Storyteller*, based on stories by Lea Goldberg, won the 2014 Israel Museum Award for Children's Book Illustration.

Pinkus currently lives in Tel Aviv with his partner and son, and serves as an associate professor at the Shenkar College of Arts and Design.

Evan Fallenberg is the author of the novels *Light Fell*, *When We Danced on Water*, and *The Parting Gift*, and translator of Israeli novels, plays, and libretti. He has won or been shortlisted for the American Library Association Barbara Gittings Stonewall Book Award for Literature, the Edmund White Award, and the PEN Translation Prize, among others. Evan teaches creative writing and literary translation at Bar-Ilan University and City University of Hong Kong; he has also received fellowships in the United States, Canada, Switzerland, and China. He is the artistic director of the Mishkenot Shaananim Translation Residency in Jerusalem and is the founder of Arabesque: An Arts & Residency Center in Old Akko.

Yardenne Greenspan holds an MFA in fiction and translation from Columbia University. In 2011 she received the American Literary Translators' Association Fellowship, and in 2014 she was a resident writer and translator at Ledig House's Writers Omi program. Her translation of Shemi Zarhin's *Some Day* was chosen for *World Literature Today*'s 2013 list of notable translations. Among others, Yardenne has also translated works by Alex Epstein, Yochi Brandes, and Amir Gutfreund. Yardenne blogs for *Ploughshares*, and her writing and translations have appeared in *The New Yorker*, *Haaretz*, *Guernica*, *Literary Hub*, *Asymptote*, *The Massachusetts Review*, and *Words Without Borders*, among other publications.